NOIR CARNIVAL

NOIR CARNIVAL

edited by K.A.Laity

www.foxspirit.co.uk

Cover Art by S.L.Johnson
http://sljohnsonimages.com
conversion by handebooks.co.uk

ISBN: 978-1-909348-25-7 mobi
ISBN: 978-1-909348-26-4 epub
ISBN: 978-1-909348-27-1 paperback

A Fox Spirit Original
Fox Spirit Books
www.foxspirit.co.uk
adele@foxspirit.co.uk

Contents

Contributors

Caravan: A Preamble

K. A. Laity

The carnies have their footpaths.

They slip, torturous lines of ghost-tents, of dream rides, across the blasted heaths of our lives, bearing the thrill-seekers of lost souls. Few know them, even in these technologically adept times. Some things never do get written down—and it's hard to Google Map a moving target after all.

But he had a good source and his appetite had been whetted by tales of forbidden pleasures that could be had for a connoisseur with the right bundle of bills. No mere knuckle shuffler he, but an 'explorer of the further realms of sensual experience' as he liked to call himself, having seen too many movies in his time. But it made him smile.

Sure, the show had a dodgy reputation—what carnival didn't? The story went that their only elephant had been killed in a drive-by shooting somewhere near Tupelo. The incident had left the remaining humans more wary, but also more mobile. They traveled the world now, bringing thrills to new audiences.

So they had pitched up here, where his idle musings had begun to speculate and eventually run riot into the lure of possibilities. Down at the Nun & Dragon rumors flew. Reg it was who had tipped him off that such things might be on offer, if the right amount of silver crossed the right palm.

A twenty to the carnie in question led to the emcee in his worn top hat, who hemmed and hawed then said it weren't up to him, but that he ought to have a word with Madame Marinova. Didn't say if she were the owner of them or just a relation, but they were hers: Ike and Tina. Whether by blood or by contract, she would be the one to reach and so he knocked on her caravan, the thrum of anticipation in his veins.

All he knew was that he longed to plunder their treasures ever since he first saw the pair in their fetid tent, waving at the few flies with a dissolute air that betrayed boredom but did not in the least reduce their charm.

What were they? Ten? Twelve? He didn't know, but even if some gypsy charms or sleight of hand or lighting flattered (and what in that dark tent could flatter?), they could not be above fourteen—and a young fourteen at that. The caressing gaze of the crowd did nothing for them; it was merely to be endured. He hungered to consume that innocence, their soft skin like dusky peaches.

Just beginning to bud!

A delicate treat to be sure and he hungered to savor it. So he knocked again on the door of the red caravan and called out, 'Samedi sent me!' for he had rolled off the notes until they added to a cool hundred before the emcee relented and showed the path he must take.

The door opened to reveal the aged face and white hair. She looked him in the face with a challenging gaze, but he had stared down every judge in this fine city so he did not quail before her flashing eyes. 'What do you seek?' Her patter was practiced, but he saw his prize seated at the small table in the lamp's glow, side by side on the bench as they must be through all their lives.

Ike and Tina, the eternal twins, joined hip to hip.

Four brown eyes stared at him. In the gloaming he found them unutterably beautiful. His fingers itched to defile their flesh, but he had to wait. 'A deal, he said I should speak to you.'

'A deal? You want a fortune told?' She smiled at him, though it seemed more of a smirk. The old woman was not fooled.

'You shouldn't dirty yourself with such a fantomo,' said a soft voice.

He looked to the shadows where she had been unseen. It was a young woman, perhaps nineteen (far too old to interest him), obviously a grandchild or such of the old woman. It seemed best to stay silent.

Indeed the old woman hushed her. 'Go see Florescu,' she said, laying a hand on the younger's sleeve. They exchanged an inscrutable look, the young one shrugged and left. The sounds of the carnival crept in as the door opened. He noticed the sounds had grown much more quiet already. Soon only the crickets would call.

'You seek the prize,' the old woman said, gesturing for him to sit at the table so tantalizingly near the two of them. 'You must draw for the chance.'

'I have money,' he began to explain, but she waved his words away and set a cup before him.

'Drink.'

He took up the cup and swirled it. In the bottom of the cup the leaves danced. Would she read them after? Or was it all an act? The tea was bitter and cheap. But the rituals must be performed. Patience was a virtue.

She put a pack of cards before him, cut the deck and then squared them up again. They were a battered old De La Rue set, the likes of which he hadn't seen since childhood. Chances were this woman had been grifting the carnie circuit most of her life. He resigned himself to the ritual, though doubtless the outcome would be the same.

She would quote an exorbitant amount and he, after some show of reluctance, would pay it.

'Cut,' she said nodding at the cards. He did, flipping over the portion to show the familiar old Ace of Spades with the crown. 'You know what that signifies?'

He shook his head, a vague smile on his lips because he could only think of Lemmy.

'There's a special fate awaiting you.' Her smile had a perceptible edge of cruelty to it and he wondered if she got some pleasure from pimping out these children to men like him.

He pushed that thought away. For him they must seem inno-
cents or half the pleasure would be lost.

'That's what I'm hoping.'

'Drink your tea,' she demanded again, nodding at his cup.

He grinned. 'Going to read the leaves for me?'

She returned his smile. 'I already know your fate.'

'I just hope it doesn't cost more than I think,' he said,
allowing himself a predatory look at the twins, who continued to gaze at him without curiosity. Perhaps they were
mentally deficient. There were pros and cons to that.

'I think the price will be fair.' The old woman picked up
the cards and tucked them into her pocket. She reached over
to cup the chin of the boy, who looked up at her with trust in
his eyes. His sister smiled.

It began as a kind of tingling. At first he put it down to
desire, for his anticipation had grown to a feverish pitch. But
he went to reach for the cup and found he could not move
his arm more than a small jerk. Panic made him try to rise
but he fell back to his seat, noises of alarm in his throat. Their
eyes watched him without concern, even as he fell to the floor
of the caravan.

Rolling his eyes back in his head, he saw the door opening and all manner of people coming in. He looked up as the
old woman loomed over him, shushing him with wordless
sounds as she began to unbutton his shirt. He began to laugh.
The joke was surely on him, but they wouldn't take this too
far, surely. The law yet held some sway even in the carnival.

The others gathered around him, smiles to join his gulp-
ing laughter. Despite the alarm, he found himself excited too
as the old woman continued to undress him with all their
eyes upon him, including Ike and Tina. His laughter edged
between hysteria and mirth.

Then she drew the blade across his chest, just enough to
open the skin and that's when the laughter stopped.

Family Blessings

Jan Kozlowski

The punch came out of nowhere. One minute newlywed Lizi Jedrek was leaning over the kitchen table, ladling beef stew into her husband Karl's bowl. The next, she was on the floor, jaw throbbing, chunky brown sauce spattered all around her. Karl had just announced they were leaving in the morning to move back in with his mother down in Florida. She had asked him if he was serious.

He leapt out of the chair and bent over her, fists clenched, his face red with rage. 'Don't you EVER question my decisions again, do you understand?'

She stared at him. This was not the man who had swept her off her feet with his charm and humor and sweetness. This was a stranger.

He grabbed her arm and jerked her to her feet. Wrapping one massive hand around her neck, he pushed her into the wall next to the refrigerator. 'Answer me, Lizi. Do you understand? I am the boss. I make the decisions. You are my wife. Your job is to smile and do what I tell you.'

Lizi looked into his eyes, the same eyes she had gazed into so lovingly less than two weeks ago and promised to love, honor and obey until death they did part.

'Yes,' she choked out.

'Yes, what?' Karl demanded, his grip on her throat tightening.

'Yes, I… I understand…Sir.'

'That's better,' he said dropping his hand to her breast. 'Yes, that's much better, much more respectful. It's my fault though. I've been too easy on you, but it's time for you to step up. You're not a run-around little tramp anymore, you're my wife and it's time you started acting like a proper one, don't you think?'

'Yes,' she whispered. The hand caressing her breast tightened and savagely twisted the soft flesh.

'SIR! I mean, yes, sir.'

'Good girl.' He dropped her breast and took a step back. 'Now I want you to clean up this mess and then get your ass into the bedroom. After you take care of your wifely duties, you can start packing. Mama is expecting us by suppertime tomorrow night.'

Lizi's stomach somersaulted as she watched him saunter off down the hall. She stumbled over to the kitchen sink, her head spinning, the few bites of stew she had eaten threatening to come up and join the mess on the floor.

He was expecting sex after all that? Who was this animal and what the hell was he doing in her life? Eight weeks ago she didn't even know that Karl Jedrek existed. One morning he had just appeared at the Myrtle Beach Shoney's where she worked and refused to leave until he got her phone number. He was waiting when she got off shift and they had coffee, which had led to dinner and then to breakfast. They had been together ever since.

Lizi ran some cold water in the sink and gently splashed it on her face. She had known jerks before, she had even witnessed some abusive relationships, but she could always tell those S.O.B.s a mile off. Karl had never even moved the needle on her asshole-o-meter. Or maybe she had just wanted to fall in love and believe all his bullshit about their perfect life together so badly that she had ignored the clues?

Lizi sighed. Obsessing over things she couldn't change wasn't going to do her any good now. She had married Karl and she was stuck, at least for now. She could run, but where would she go? Her hand strayed to the cell in her pocket. One phone call and she knew that half the clan would be at her front door in a matter of hours to whisk her away. But there would be a price to pay. She'd be going back home with her tail between her legs and there would be the smug I-told-you-so smirks and whispers. She had never even told them she got married. No, she had to figure this out for herself.

She couldn't have been that wrong about Karl. Reading people was part of her upbringing. Maybe it was just the stress of him not being able to find work around here? Maybe once he got back home he'd feel better. Maybe this move would be a wonderful fresh start, for both of them. And maybe he was right, maybe she wasn't being a good wife, she had never been one before and God knew, growing up the way she did, there weren't a lot of good examples. She had never known her father, and her grandmother... she had had no use for men whatsoever. Maybe Karl and his mother would be good influences, they could teach her how to be a good wife and maybe, someday, a good mother.

Feeling a little better, Lizi finished cleaning up and was just about to shut off the kitchen light when the opening bars of Tony Joe White's Conjure Woman sang out. It was her grandmother's ring tone. She fumbled for the phone, terrified Karl would hear it. Gran always said she could smell it when her own were in trouble, even if they were a million miles away. Lizi hit ignore.

'Lizi! Get your ass in here, now!' Karl bellowed. She looked at her grandmother's picture one last time, turned the phone off and headed down the hall to her husband.

They were on the road by seven a.m. Karl had only allowed her to pack one suitcase. He said he'd make arrangements with the landlord to send on the rest of her things. She had also discovered her phone was missing. She had left it on the dresser last night like always, but when she got up, it was gone. Karl watched her search for it with a smirk on his face, almost daring her to ask him if he knew where it was. Lizi was a lot of things, but a slow learner was not one of them. She kept her aching mouth shut and concentrated on stuffing as much of her life as possible into her one allowed bag.

Once they were in the car she hoped Karl would relax and maybe open up a little to her, but as they made their way inland toward I-95, he seemed to retreat deeper inside of himself. He didn't want the radio on, he didn't want to talk and even the sound of her shifting in her seat seemed to grate on his nerves.

He never even told her where in Florida they were going. Up until last night, Karl had never mentioned his family and since she had no desire to talk about hers, she hadn't brought the subject up. At the time it had been one of the many things she had found attractive about him. In the South, the first question everyone asked was about your family. Who are your people, dear? What's your family name? Oh, are you one of the Spartanburg County Rowen's?

She often wondered how people would react if she told them the truth. She could just imagine the looks on their faces when she told them that her 'people' included Pretty Patti Primate, The Missing Link; Odelia, the World's Fattest Woman; Arachness, The Spider King; Leon, The Lobster Boy, and let's not forget her direct link to royalty, her grandmother, the Legendary Ioana Tobar, The Cajun Conjure Queen.

Lizi gazed out the window as they left the surface streets and joined the stream of traffic heading south on the interstate. She had grown up on the road, her earliest memories were of being stuffed in the back of a station wagon with a blanket and her favorite toy, a stuffed devil baby from the freak show exhibit, caravanning to the next town. She closed her eyes and rested her forehead against the cool glass. She fought hard to control herself but one tear leaked out and slid down her cheek. She hurried to brush it away before Karl noticed.

'Lizi, wake up! We're stopping at the next exit for gas. If you want to use the bathroom that'll be your chance, we're not stopping again until we get to Mama's in Winter Haven.'

Karl eased her Taurus over into the exit lane and Lizi caught a flash of bright red moving in behind them. She took a look in the side view mirror and sure enough, it was a red Volkswagen convertible. She had loved red Bugs since her friend Bella had taken her for a ride in her brand new one. In fact, now that she thought about it, she'd been seeing it since they had left her apartment back in Myrtle Beach. Lizi tried to get a look at the driver as the little car zoomed past them into the parking area, but all she caught was a shock of pink hair blowing in the breeze. Bella changed her hair color more often than Karl changed his socks, so it was impossible to know if it was really her or not.

The gas pumps were all occupied, so Karl circled around the lot a couple of times before finding an opening. Lizi tried to track the Bug's pink haired driver, but she seemed to have disappeared into the restaurant part of the complex. As Karl busied himself filling the tank, Lizi took the opportunity to get out of the car and stretch her legs. She was relieved to see there were plenty of people around, as well as cameras monitoring their every move.

'Karl, I'm going to go to the bathroom. I'll be back in a few minutes.'

Karl opened his mouth to say something, but after making note of all the potential witnesses, he shot her a dark look and nodded.

She tried to walk away casually, but found her heart beating faster with every step she took away from him. It would be so easy to run right now. Find a cop or a ride or a place to hide and then... and then what? By the time she reached the glass doors the reality of her situation had set in. She had no money with her, Karl had 'borrowed' the last of her tip money to pay for the gas. Her purse was in the car with all her identification in it and she had no cell phone.

Inside the store, a large sign pointed to the restrooms in the right rear corner, so she headed off in that direction. She could feel the tears threatening to erupt again and this time she didn't think she'd be able to fight them off. She rushed for the ladies room, but as she passed the Football Frenzy snack display, an iron hand grabbed her and dragged her behind the tower of soda bottles.

'Please Karl, don't...' she whispered, closing her eyes and putting up her hands to protect her face.

'Lizi, Lizi, it's me, Bella. Sweetie, it's okay.'

'Bella?' Lizi opened her eyes and threw her arms around her friend. 'It really is you.'

'Ioana sent me. She said she knew something was wrong, so when I got to your place this morning and saw tall, dark and brooding out there packing your car and dragging you out the door, I decided to follow you and see what's going on.'

Bella held her friend at arms length and looked her up and down. She gently put her hand to Lizi's head, turned her face to the side and took note of the bruise she had tried to cover with makeup.

Lizi jerked away, embarrassed at the pity she saw in Bella's eyes.

'It's nothing, I... I... just got clumsy and walked into the bathroom door.'

'Uh-huh. And what about the road trip?'

'We're just going to visit his mother in Winter Haven.'

'Meeting the parents, huh, that's kind of a big step, you must be a little nervous.'

'Yeah, no... well, actually she's my mother–in-law. Karl and I got married two weeks ago. I had a couple of days off and he knew a judge over in Conway, so we just went and did it.'

'Without telling anyone? Without even telling your Grandmother... or me?'

'We wanted it to be small... just us. We knew the more people we told...'

'The more people would try to talk you out of it? How long have you known him?'

'About two months.'

'Oh my God, Lizi! Did he make you marry him? Did he beat you until you said yes?'

'NO! He never... until last night, he never, ever laid a hand on me. Until last night he was so sweet and kind and funny and...'

'And psychopathic.'

'You don't KNOW him, Bella!'

'Neither do you, Lizi.'

'Karl's just under a lot of stress. He lost his job just before we met and he couldn't find another one and then he was worried about his mother living all by herself down in Florida.'

'Do you even hear yourself, Lizi? You sound just like Emily Driscoll.'

'You're on crack.'

'Electric Emmy, the Most Shocking Girl in the World. Remember, all of Gibtown turned out for her wedding to that asshole Slitheran, the Snake Guy. She kept passing off the bruises and injuries as clumsiness or from working the act. Do you remember what happened to them? Do you?' Lizi looked away. 'Both of them are dead. He was stabbed to death and she ended up strangled and half eaten by his pythons. Lizi, let me get you out of here. I'll take you home and you'll never have to see this guy again.'

'He's my husband.'

'A divorce lawyer can fix that.'

'I said vows, Bella. I… love him and I'm not going back to Gran and everybody like some little kid that ran away from home.'

'He's hurting you, Lizi.'

'Well maybe that's my fault, not his.'

'Lizi, let me take you home.'

'Bella, my home is with Karl… and I need to get back to him. He's going to wonder where I am.' Lizi spun around and walked back out to the car where her husband was squee-geeing the windows.

Bella watched until they both got back in the car and pulled away from the pumps. She grabbed her phone and punched in a number.

'They're heading to Winter Haven… to his mother's.'

'I tried but she won't come with me.'

'No, she'll spot my car, better tell Wally to pick up their tail. They'll be hitting the Florida line in about ten minutes. He can't miss them. They're in her blue Taurus, same plates.'

'Yes, I've got my laptop. Sure, I can do that.'

'Okay, I'll let you know when I get to Winter Haven.'

Karl slowed the car and made the big, looping turn off Rte. 17 into his mother's long, dirt driveway. The digital clock on the dash read 6:17pm.

'Shit, we're late,' Karl mumbled as the car jounced over the pot holes and dried out mud washes. Mama was a stickler for promptness and supper was always precisely at 6pm. It didn't matter if you were coming in from the back yard or 550 miles away, late was late and there'd be the piper to pay.

Mila 'Mama' Jedrek was waiting on the sagging front porch as Karl pulled the car to a stop. Tall and dark, with cheekbones that could cut glass, she gave Lizi a cold, appraising, once over and then turned to her son.

'Karl, you're late.'

'Yes, Ma'am. I'm sorry.'

'Sorry is as sorry does. You can fool with the suitcases later. Bring... Lizi in and sit for dinner. The food's cold, but it's still good. You can get settled after you eat.'

'Yes, Ma'am.'

Lizi felt Karl's hand on the small of her back as he propelled her up the stairs and into the dining room where an old fashioned Southern feast had been laid out. With ham at one end of the table, turkey at the other and millions of calories of fat and starch in between, it looked like Karl's mother had cooked for days.

'You shouldn't have gone to so much trouble, Mrs. Jedrek. This spread is incredible,' she said as she took a seat across the table from her mother-in-law.

'A mother knows there's no trouble too great to go through for her child. But you'll learn that soon enough, won't she Karl?'

Karl made muffled sounds of agreement around the large slab of ham he was already trying to wrestle into his mouth.

'And speaking of children... you two are working on making me a grandmother, aren't you?'

Lizi, who had been trying to discreetly gulp down ice tea to ease her parched throat, almost choked on the lemon slice. 'Mrs. Jedrek, Karl and I just got married two weeks ago. We talked about having kids someday, but...'

'No buts… it's my experience that 'someday' never comes. You're young and strong, so there's no time like the present to start blessing your husband and his family with children.'

Blessing is such an odd way to put it she thought, taking another long swallow from her tea. She was so tired. It had been such a long trip, such a long, strange trip, and now she could barely keep her eyes open.

'Are you all right, Lizi? You're as pale as a ghost.'

'I..I..jus tired from triiiip, I guesssss.'

'Karl, the poor girl is dead on her feet. Take her upstairs and put her to bed. We'll have all the time in the world to get to know each other after she's feeling better.'

'Yes, Mama.'

Lizi tried to stand up but found her legs buckling underneath her. Karl caught her before she fell to the floor and half walked half carried her out of the dining room and up to the bedroom. Her head was spinning and nothing was making a lot of sense. She felt herself dropped to the mattress, but she couldn't move her arms or legs. Karl was beside her then on the bed, taking her clothes off and doing something to her. She tried to pay attention to what was happening but her vision kept blurring and going dark. The last thing she thought she saw before spinning off into complete blackness was Karl hovering above her, his features contorted into his orgasm face and his mother standing above them, telling Karl to do it again.

Sunshine was streaming through the bedroom windows when Lizi finally pried her eyes open. Her head was pounding like she'd drunk a gallon of tequila, but other than that, all seemed normal. This wasn't her bedroom, but after a moment of panic, she remembered this was her mother-in-law's house. Turning her head carefully she could see Karl snoring softly beside her. Had all that just been a bad dream? She looked down at herself. She was wearing her I'm Not a Morning Person sleep shirt like always. If Karl had taken her clothes off, maybe he was just getting her ready for bed and then maybe her mother-in-law had come up to check on her and she had gotten it all mixed up in her over-tired brain.

Lizi pulled back the covers and carefully put her feet on the floor. The one thing she was absolutely positive of right now was that she needed to pee, badly. She briefly thought of waking Karl and asking him where the bathroom was but given his mood swings it would probably be easier to just find it herself.

Standing and walking took her longer and hurt more than she could have possibly believed, but eventually she made it to the bedroom door. Opening it quietly she peeked down the hallway looking for a clue to where the bathroom was. There were four doors in total, including theirs. The narrow one at the end of the hall was obviously a closet, so that left two possible options. She figured there'd be no kitschy little signs or pictures of kitties in a bathtub in Mrs. Jedrek's world, so she was just going to have pick one and hope for the best.

She tiptoed down the hall toward the first door. She had no idea what time it was, only that the sun was up and it felt early. She put her hand on the doorknob and was just about to turn it when she heard a voice on the other side.

'I've got two bids from China for half a million. The Saudi will go as high as six-fifty, but there's a client in Melbourne whom I'm told will go to seven-fifty for a blonde, blue-eyed female.'

'Yes. It arrived a few hours ago. Healthy. Ten fingers. Ten Toes.'

'If you want to pre-empt, I'm giving you the chance because you're such a good customer. Give me seven-fifty, and have your representative here to take possession in twenty-four hours or less and I'll tell the rest of them they'll have to wait for the next delivery.'

'Nine to ten months if all goes as planned. No, there won't be anything available sooner. We had a little glitch in production that's set everything back a bit.'

'No, nothing serious. No, nothing legal. It was strictly an HR problem. Trust me, the malfunctioning agent has been replaced and the next project has already launched.'

'Done, then. Always a pleasure doing business with you.'

Lizi backed away from the door and fled down the hall. At this point she didn't care where the other door might lead, she found it and threw herself through it. She was almost surprised to see it really was a bathroom. She collapsed onto the toilet and as her tortured bladder emptied, she tried to parse out what she had just overheard. Was her mother-in-law selling a baby? No. It wasn't possible. It was just some kind of weird hangover from yesterday, some kind of auditory hallucination.

She took a deep breath and tried to concentrate. Karl's mother had said the baby had arrived a couple of hours ago. She hadn't noticed a very pregnant woman last night or heard a baby cry, but then again, she wasn't sure what she'd seen and heard since she'd gotten here. And what was that bit about expecting to have the next delivery in nine to ten months? The image of Karl pounding away on top of her and his mother's face hanging behind his head urging him on flashed into her head. Her stomach heaved. She scrambled off the seat and lunged for the bowl just as wave after wave of bile roared up out of her mouth. Sometime during the ordeal, she heard her mother-in-law's voice asking if she was all right, but that only sent her off on another round of retching. Finally, there was nothing left inside, including, she was sure, her internal organs. She lay her down on the cool tile floor and tried to pull herself together.

'Lizi, are you all right?' Karl called out.

'Yes, just a little sick to my stomach.'

'It sounds like it's more than that. Mama said you were vomiting so loud you woke her up.'

'Tell her... tell her I'm sorry. Just let me clean up and I'll be out in a minute.'

Karl and his mother were waiting for her when she stumbled out into the hallway.

'Karl, take your wife back to bed. She looks like she's going to pass out any second. And get her the bowl from under the sink, just in case she's not done yet. After she gets some more rest, I'll bring her up some tea and toast, that always settled my stomach when I had morning sickness.'

'It's not... I'm not... It's probably just a stomach bug.'

'Whatever you say, dear, but remember it's bad luck to deny nature's blessings.'

There was that word 'blessings' again, Lizi thought as Karl escorted her back to their bedroom. There was no way she could be pregnant. She and Karl had been having sex for two months now... and they had been doing it every day, sometimes more than once a day, but she was fanatical about birth control. She had been on the pill until her whole pack disappeared not long after she and Karl started seeing each other. She had meant to get a refill from her doctor but with getting married and everything, it was something that had fallen through the cracks. She had insisted that Karl wear a condom though and he had been okay with that, even bragging about the new, expensive ultra thin ones he had purchased. It'll be like we're using nothing at all, he had promised.

Fuck. She was an idiot.

She let Karl tuck her into bed and close the blinds. She watched him through her lashes as he walked to the door, grabbed the key from the inside lock and let himself out. A quick snick of metal was followed by the sound of him clumping down the stairs and then the low buzz of voices and the clank of cutlery and tableware.

She tried to focus, but her mind was spinning out of control. She had to get out of here. Pregnant or not, she had to get away from Karl and his mother. She had to get home. She tried to sit up, but waves of nausea forced her back down. She needed Gran, Bella and the clan. She fought hard to stay conscious and form a plan but the next thing she knew, Karl's mother was standing in front of her, urging her to sit up and drink some of the tea she had brought up.

'It smells like ginger.' Lizi said, sniffing the steam rising from the cup.

'Yes, it's good for settling queasy stomachs.'

'Mrs. Jedrek...'

'We're family now, call me Mama.'

'All right… Mama, before I have the tea, could you please help me back to the bathroom? I'm still a little woozy.'

'Of course.' She put the tea down on the bedside table and pulled Lizi to her feet.

Using her mother-in-law to lean on, Lizi shuffled her way down the hallway. Once she closed the door, she made a bee-line for the drawers and cabinets, searching for razors, scissors or anything sharp that she could use to help her escape. Finally, in the back corner of the vanity, she spotted a couple of old bobby pins, which she quickly slipped underneath her hair.

'Everything all right, dear? Mama called.

'I'm fine, I'll be right out.'

Once back in bed, Mama handed her the tea mug and fussed around the bedroom as she urged her to drink it. Lizi made small talk and every time Mama's back was turned she poured a little more of the tea down the crack between the mattress and the headboard. By the time the cup was half empty Lizi had sunk down into the bedding and was feigning sleep.

'That's right, just get some rest, dear. I'll send Karl back up to check on you later.'

Lizi listened as her footsteps retreated out of the room, followed by the click of the door lock. She waited until she heard Mama moving around in the kitchen before sliding out of bed. She looked around the darkened room, trying to see if Karl had brought any of her things up from the car, but there was no sign of her suitcase, purse or even of the clothes she had been wearing. It looked like she was going over the wall dressed only in a long t-shirt. She didn't even have a pair of slippers.

She moved to the window and carefully peeked out through the vinyl slats. The window faced the back yard and overlooked the old, decrepit trailer they had parked behind, the rusty four-foot chain link fence that circled the property and beyond that, the tall marsh grass and cattails that marked the edge of what any true Southern born girl would recognize as swampland.

This truly was the middle of nowhere. She hadn't seen another house, or another person for that matter, since turning off the main road. She looked longingly at her car. She had learned a lot of things growing up in the carnival, but unfortunately, Gran had forbidden anyone from teaching her how to hot wire a car.

As she was staring at the car, trying to imagine where Karl might have stashed her purse with the spare set of keys in it, she caught a movement at the trailer… someone was coming out the door. It was Karl carrying something over his shoulder like a sack of Santa's toys.

Lizi felt her stomach do another slow roll as she realized Karl was carrying a body, and it wasn't moving. She watched as he carefully made his way down the steps and headed off across the back yard. She tracked him as he made his way along the fence line to the far right corner where the swamp butted up against the property. Karl paused for a moment and then, in one smooth, practiced movement, tossed the body over the fence. Dusk was rolling in, but it wasn't dark enough to hide the splashing, roiling water and the slapping tails of a gator feeding frenzy. By the time Lizi dragged her eyes away from the spectacle, Karl was back in front of the trailer. A few seconds later, she heard the sound of the screen door slapping downstairs as Mama went out to join her boy.

Lizi knew it was now or never. She rushed to the door and turned the handle hoping the lock hadn't fully engaged. No such luck. It was an old lock though, one with nice, big tumblers. She grabbed one of the bobby pins out of her hair and went to work. Two minutes later she was rewarded with a loud snick and, as the door swung open, she bolted out of the room.

Karl and Mama were in the back, so Lizi ran for the front. She flew down the stairs, flung open the same door she had entered almost 24 hours ago and raced for the tall grass and scrub pines that lined the driveway. She never saw the three people crouched in the shadows until she careened into them.

'Lizi! Lizi! Stop! It's us!'

'Bella? Tom? Eli? Help me! We have to get out of here, now!'

'Where's Karl and his mother?'

'Out back at the trailer. We have to go before they know I'm gone!'

'All right, the car is about a quarter of a mile back, near the main road. Can you make it?'

'Yes. Yes. Hurry.'

Lizi didn't stop shaking until they had piled in the waiting SUV and were speeding down the road. As soon as they were safely away and she was sure they weren't being followed, Bella pulled out her cell and made the call.

'We got her!'

'She's safe, a little banged up, but she's going to be okay.'

'All right, we're on our way.'

'Was that Gran?' Lizi asked.

'Yes.'

'Are we going back to Gibtown?'

Bella, Tom and Eli looked at each other and laughed.

'Girl, there's no need for that - Just about all of Gibtown landed here about twelve hours ago. Ioana and the clan are camped out at the old Winter Haven Motor Court over on Reaker Highway. We'll be there in about ten minutes, if traffic cooperates.'

Bella had only been mildly exaggerating Lizi thought, as they drove underneath the big neon Motor Court sign and got a look at the assembled group. There were only about 15 bungalows on the property so Tabor's Traveling Carnival had brought their trailers and set up tents. The only things missing were the big animals and the amusement rides. Lizi was deeply embarrassed that so many people had gone to so much trouble for her... and deeply touched at the same time. It took them a while to thread their way through the crowd, but eventually Tom was able to pull in next to Gran's RV... a purple, yellow and red colored behemoth that she still insisted on driving herself.

'How mad is she?' Lizi asked Bella as they mounted the metal steps and entered Ioana's inner sanctum.

'She's not mad, she's relieved that you're safe and she's upset about what we found out about Karl and his mother.'

'Lizi!' Gran called out, hurrying toward them and sweeping her granddaughter up in a massive bear hug. 'My girl, my girl… here, let me look at you.' Ioana clucked and muttered over her bruised jaw, bare feet and thin t-shirt, now partially covered by Tom's leather jacket. 'We've got to get you cleaned up and I've brought some of your clothes. I'll make a poultice for your poor jaw and…'

'Gran… Gran… no…I have to talk to you first. I have to tell you what Karl and his mother are doing…'

'They're involved in human trafficking,' Bella piped in. Lizi whipped around and stared at her. 'How did you find out?'

'Hey, I'm not just a Kooch dancer! Remember, I've got some pretty mad computer skills, if I do say so myself.'

'Lizi, if you insist on talking now, at least come over here and sit down before you fall down,' Gran said, patting the cushion next to her.

Lizi took the seat and turned back to Bella. 'Tell me.'

'We followed your car out to your mother-in-law's place. Once we had an address, it was easy to get a name and from there it was just a matter of connecting the dots. Karl and Mila Jedrek have been tangentially involved with over ten missing persons cases over the past decade. All were young women and all dated or were involved with Karl at some point, but there was never enough evidence to charge him with anything.'

'Or enough cash was offered to make the evidence go away,' Ioana added.

'Exactly. And the girls were never found, they just disappeared into thin air. My first thought was that Karl was a serial killer and that Mama was somehow helping him dispose of the bodies… but then after contacting a very talented hacker friend who owed me a big favor, we got into their financials and found they were receiving some obscenely large payments, mostly from off shore accounts on dates that matched up pretty closely with the dates some of the girls went missing.'

'Bella, it's not about the girls… it's about the babies.'

'Babies? There was no evidence that the girls were pregnant when they disappeared.'

'They weren't. He gets them pregnant, holds them prisoner until the baby is born and then they sell it to the highest bidder. Then they start all over again with another girl. I overheard Mama making a deal this morning.'

'What happens to the girls, then?'

'Karl takes them out to the swamp… I… saw… the gators… that's when I ran.' Lizi dropped her head into her hands as the tears started to flow. Bella and Ioana put their arms around her, but Lizi shook them off.

'The baby's still there. She gave the buyer twenty-four hours to come and get it. We have to stop this.'

'Lizi, there's not a lot we can do about it… or Karl and his mother unfortunately. The cops… it doesn't look like they're an option. We got you out at least. You're back with us. We'll make sure they never get near you again.'

'Bella, we have to do more. I… I never saw Karl for what he really was. It never even crossed my mind that he was this evil. If we don't do something about them, they're just going to keep on preying on other women and babies. They're never going to stop unless we stop them.'

'Lizi, you know our beliefs. We can't take human life, no matter how justified it might seem.'

'Gran, there IS one way.'

Ioana was silent for a moment. 'No. I will not allow it.'

'Ioana, what's she talking about?'

'It's an old way, something Lizi shouldn't even know about.'

'Is it a spell? A gris gris?'

'Legba Voudou Rougarou. It's the only way.' Lizi whispered.

'Lizi…' Gran started.

'Gran, please. I got myself into this mess and now I'm the only one who can stop them. You know it's true. If I don't do this, that baby and all the other girls' and babies' blood will be on my hands until the day I die.'

'At least think it over, Lizi, take a little time to…'

'There isn't any time, Gran and I've already thought it through. If we perform the ceremony now, I can slip back onto the property and just say I panicked when I woke up alone and when I went looking for Karl, I got lost in the woods. They'll be so happy to have their investment back, they'll buy it, at least long enough for me to get back in the house.'

Gran shook her head and sighed. 'Bella, find Tom and Eli and tell them to be ready to drive Lizi back to the Jedrek's. Hurry up, girl before I come to my senses.' Bella rushed out the door as Ioana turned and wrapped her arms around Lizi again. 'You know how dangerous this is, don't you? Magic doesn't always work out the way you hope and you will have to take responsibility for the outcome, no matter what.'

'I understand, Gran.'

'All right, go into my bedroom and lay down. I'll be in as soon as I have everything ready.'

Lizi lay back on Gran's ancient patchwork duvet and listened to her rooting around in the kitchen. A few minutes later, Gran entered the room chanting words that were ancient and beautiful and sinister all at once. She had changed into her robes and in her hands she held her red incantation bowl covered by a black cloth. She walked around the bed three times, circling her hand above the bowl and over Lizi's body. With each pass of her grandmother's hands, Lizi could feel an electricity building inside of her that started at the top of her head and flowed down through her body.

Ioana stopped at the bottom of the bed and commanded Lizi to open her legs. Lizi did as she was told and Ioana placed the bowl between them on the bed and removed the covering. Chanting faster and louder, the Conjure Woman picked the writhing snake up out of the bowl, lifting it to above her head, then out for Lizi to see. Lizi stared into its sparkling ruby eyes and nodded. Her grandmother lowered the snake slowly. Lizi leaned back and closed her eyes as she felt the pressure against her vagina and then the fullness as its smooth body entered her. Waves of energy pulsed through her as her grandmother made another circle around the bed, balled up the cloth into the bowl and lit it on fire. Together, they watched the flames flare up and die out until all that was left was gray ash.

The ride back to the Jedrek property was the longest ten minutes of Lizi's life. It was hard to believe that less than two hours had gone by since she had bolted out Mama's front door. Bella had insisted on coming along and it was all Lizi could do to make her promise to stay with Tom and Eli in the car until this was over.

'Bella, I know you want to help, but this is something I can only do myself. Please don't be mad.' She hugged her friend, slipped out of the car and, after ripping some fresh tears in her t-shirt and rubbing some mud on herself, she took off up the driveway towards the house. She made it about half way before she saw the first flashlight beam bouncing through the darkness off to her right.

'Karl! Karl! Is that you?' she yelled. 'Please, I… I got lost trying to find you. Something's wrong!'

'Lizi! Lizi! Stay right there, I'm coming! Mama, I found her!'

Lizi clutched her stomach and dropped to her knees, moaning and crying as the two spots of light moved toward her.

'Karl, Mama, it hurts so much, please help me!'

'Where dear? What hurts?' Mama said kneeling down in the dirt beside her.

'I thought it was just period cramps but these are so much worse. It feels like my insides are being ripped out. Please help me, it's never been this bad before.'

'I don't see any blood, but let's get her back to the house.' Karl scooped her up and they rushed her into the house and back up to the bedroom.

'Put her down on the bed and go get me some towels and some hot water.'

'It hurts so much,' Lizi whimpered, her hands cradling her lower abdomen.

'Try to lie back and take some deep breaths. I was trained as a nurse and I'm just going to take a little look and make sure you're not hemorrhaging.'

Lizi groaned and rolled from side to side.

'Karl! Karl, get in here. I'm going to need you to hold her still for me.'

Karl hurried in with the towels and an enamel basin full of water.

'Put those down and hold her legs open for me while I check her.'

'It hurts so much.'

A wave of real contractions hit Lizi. She screamed as the blood gushed out of her and her passenger began its trip back out into the world.

'Shit, she's delivering!'

'But... it's too soon...'

'There's a baby coming out, I can see it crowning.'

Lizi gave a heroic push and her offspring launched itself out of her body and wrapped its gray, leathery body around Mama's face. Snapping and tearing, its razor sharp teeth ripped through her skin and bone while it's knife-edged tail cut through her jugular. By the time it got to Mama's gray matter, the only noise in the room was its soft, suckling sounds. When it finished, it turned to Karl who was frozen in place, still holding onto Lizi's legs. Going in low, the creature dived for the back of his legs, slashing his Achilles tendons to take him down and then settling in to feast on his tasty bits. When it finally crawled off him, what was left of Karl would fit nicely in a small sandwich bag.

Lizi had watched the whole attack from her perch on the bed. It hadn't sickened her the way she thought it would. In fact, she felt sort of... proud of the job her creation had accomplished. It sat on the floor now between its first two kills, looking up at her with its red eyes and tapping its claws against the hard wood floor. She should have been scared she guessed, but all she felt was a contentment she'd never experienced before. One of Gran's old lullabies popped into her head and she began to sing-

'Bye baby Bunting, Daddy's gone a hunting. Momma's gone a milking. Sister's gone a silking. Brother's gone to bring a skin to wrap the baby Bunting in.'

Lizi's child reacted immediately, clambering up the bed and into her arms. She held it, rocking and crooning, tucking its tail and many appendages in close to her body to keep it warm. It responded by nuzzling up against her and making soft clicking sounds. Lizi grabbed the towels from where Karl had dumped them and wrapped them around the baby.

'There, there sweetheart. Let's take a little walk around and see if we can find Mommy's things. They moved quickly from room to room, collecting her cell phone, purse and suitcase as well as Mama's laptop and Karl's tablet. She piled them all by the door ready for Bella and company to pick up, along with the baby she hoped was still safe and sound out in the trailer.

She had just dug out her flip-flops when she heard the sound of a car coming up the driveway. She went to the window and sure enough, a large, expensive sedan was rolling to a stop behind her Taurus. She smiled down at the baby and rearranged the towels to cover it up, all except for one chubby, perfect human hand.

'Come on baby, we've got one more little thing to take care of and then I promise, we can go home.'

In The Mouth Of The Beast

Li Huijia

The tent flaps were down. The air buzzed with half-formed conversations. Figures young and old, male and female filled the seats, each face beaming with anticipation. Slowly, the lights flaring upon the seats dimmed. For a moment, the tent was steeped in darkness, then the stage lit up, its brightness punctuating the audience's fading murmurs. Showtime.

On stage was the jump ring, already oiled with kerosene. Torches blazed at the sides of the stage, projecting their fiery heat into the crowd, feeding their excitement.

Somewhere to Rosalie's left, carnivalesque music blared. The ringmaster's voiceover started up, chill and quiet, growing louder as he listed her achievements, building up expectations. Soon, he would be announcing her name.

'... Rosalie! Bride of the Beast...' A fanfare sounded.

She strode on stage; whip in hand, ruby hair held in a braid. Her body was clothed in a glittering suit of silver, a delicate silver rose sat at her throat. She looked out from her place, sweeping her gaze across the audience, waiting for him to enter the stage.

'The stuff of legends... king of the beasts... Charlemagne!' The voiceover continued, heralding the end of his announcement with the blare of a trumpet.

He came onto the stage, his golden mane made brighter by the flames, each stride soft and deadly, clawed paws padding silently on the ground, almost as if he were circling prey.

His fur shimmered, brilliant, blinding in the stage-light. He approached her steadily, stopping mere inches away. He raised his gaze and met hers; regarding her dark grey eyes with his own golden ones.

She cracked her whip. He replied with a low-throated roar, as if in apology.

She heard the audience gasp, as they did every night. Her heart lurched suddenly. That was a surprise. She had not felt anything for a very long time.

'I can't.' She shook her head, halting once more at the door. 'I don't want to.'

Charles, who had reverted to his handsome form only days ago, gave her yet another crushing embrace, sealing it with a kiss.

'We have to, Rosa. There is nothing left for us now.' He gestured at the empty room, the windows looking out into nothingness, the once beautiful rose garden fading as they spoke.

'This is a curse worse than yours, this, never-ending repetition of our fate.' She clenched her fist, so hard that a scarlet crescent started to form. A drop of blood ballooned from her broken skin. She pressed her hands to the doorframe, ignoring the sting, willing the door into oblivion, wishing for another way out.

'Would you rather we stay here? In this fading room? We have no food, no furniture, no servants, no land. It is a sign for us to begin again. There is no life after the last page, Rosa. You know that.'

She sobbed then, wishing desperately for something to smash, but there was nothing left even for that. The walls were fast disappearing, the doorway was the only solid thing left in the room.

'I just don't understand,' she seethed, 'I don't understand the point of it all. Why let us go through all that -- your curse, my departure, my father's illness... why all that to finally be together, and then never let us know what comes next? Why?'

'What comes next is happily ever after. You know that.'

She shook her head, a tide of red curls swinging wildly around her. Even the ribbons holding her braid were vanishing.

'This? This is not happily ever after! This is nothing. This is a trap. And I want out.'

'You know there is no way to leave. Either we stay here until everything fades but the doorway, like we did the last time. And we'd still choose to pass through it once we start starving.'

She bit her lip, recognizing the faultlessness of his words. But the deep unwillingness to admit defeat remained, looming larger and larger within her, twisting her insides in the wish for more than her share of life. 'I know. But I wish... I wish we could find a way out of this.' She whispered.

Charles pressed his body against hers, stroking her hair gently. He was used to her hysterics, she thought. They had been through this countless times, in countless cycles. She wondered again, why the forces dictating the reprisal of their roles at the end of every read had decided upon the cruel joke of restoring their memories every time the book ended. It would have been much easier if they remembered nothing at all.

Fools. The ones who own us are fools.

And then, something different.

The doorway disappeared too.

Floodlights dyed his golden mane a platinum blonde. The audience faded away, their applause a dim noise at the edge of her concentration. Eyes still on Charles, she motioned for him to begin the series of warm-up acts that would lead to the finale.

She motioned, a single sharp gesture, he ran a loop around her. She waved, pointed, he leapt on the nearest stool. Another flourish of her hand, he leapt down, back again, up another higher stool, balanced all four limbs upon it, then stopped to regard her.

On cue, someone placed a chair at the side of the stage.

She went to it, dragged the worn wooden thing across the stage, deliberately letting its legs scrape the floor in a painful jangle. His ears peaked, his wiry whiskers twitched once. When she and the chair were at an angle directly facing the stool where he crouched, she halted, sat down, crossed her arms, and met his eyes.

They regarded each other in silence. The audience's murmurs had stopped as well, replaced by the hush of held breaths.

He raised his head, emitted a low growl from his throat.

She waited, counting to ten in her head. Then, she began reciting.

The man who appeared in the nothingness gave an extravagant bow, accentuating his movement with a sweep of his cloak. It was the most beautiful cloak she had ever seen, midnight blue velvet shadowed with stars - a universe of unfamiliar constellations spiraling in and out of existence upon the undulating fabric.

'Who are you?' Charles had moved in front of her, blocking her from the newcomer.

'Come now, I merit no such hostility.' The wiry man tipped his hat, thin lips quirking up into a wide grin beneath his slick mustache. 'You wished for me, so here I am. Your personal fairy godmother, wish granter, genie counterpart, portal to another life... Yada yada yada.' He reached for her hand.

'I wished for no such thing.' Charles knocked the stranger's hand away. He fixed his golden gaze upon the man, daring him to advance. It would have been more intimidating had he kept his beast-like form, but that spell was broken now. By her. Right now, in his handsome human guise, the only danger he offered was if he triggered a swooning fit for the ladies.

'Wait.' She stepped out from Charles' shadow, keeping a hand on his stiffened arm. 'What do you mean, 'portal to another life'?'

'Exactly what you wished for, my dear, a life that continues, beyond the doorway.' The stranger punctuated his statement with a flourish of his cloak.

'But -' Charlemagne began.

'Yes.' She said.

'Rosa, we don't know anything about this man.'

'We know everything about the doorway,' she clasped his hands fervently, hoping to get his agreement. 'And I don't want to go through that ever again. I want to remember you. I want to see what comes after this. I want the real happily ever after.'

'What is the price of our wish?' Charlemagne, unconvinced, glared at the stranger. 'And who are you?'

'You may call me The Ringmaster.' He clapped his hands, and a new doorway appeared beside him, the air beyond it dusted with constellations similar to the ones on his cloak. 'There is no cost, for this wish. But if you ever want a second wish, a price will be extracted.'

'What is on the other side?' Charles, ever the planner, was uncertain.

'The real world, of course. Where people live and die full lives, unlike the immortality you enjoy nestled among the pages. That is the price of your transition.'

'Rosa - are you sure?'

She eyed the door, felt the pull of the beckoning stars beyond. She took a final look at the nothingness around her, at the world that had disappeared a thousand times, the world that forced her to relive a plot which allowed for no deviation, no future.

'I'm sure.' She took his hand, and stepped through.

'... and the marriage was celebrated the very next day with the utmost splendor, and Beauty and the Prince lived happily ever after.'

She finished the last line of their tale, gazing into his clear gold irises. He got up from his crouch, shook his magnificent mane once, then leapt gracefully down from the high stool. Within a few steps, he was at her side. There, he sank to the ground, head bowed, allowing her to climb atop his broad, muscular back.

Applause shattered the silence.

She rode him without a saddle, feeling the rippling of muscles beneath his skin as her legs tightened and relaxed, her hands pulling cruelly upon his mane to direct him as she willed. He allowed her the audacity to do as she wished, for it was the only time she ever allowed him to touch her at all.

She sat, back straight, gaze steady. Her fingers grazed his thick fur, and she found her thumb stroking the soft down at the nape of his neck. He arched his back, emitted a soft growl akin to a purr. That woke her up. She steeled her heart, did a final loop around the stage before separating herself from him in a graceful leap.

She walked to the ring, pushed it to the center of the stage, touched a burning torch to it. Flames sprang up, hot and hungry, spreading rapidly to engulf the circumference of the ring with their dangerous orange glow.

Charles took his position, starting to run even as she drew out the infinity sign in the air with her right hand, leaping through the fiery ring with not a lick of fire on his fur.

The audience cheered.

She gestured for him to repeat his jump. He did so, several times, only stopping when the flames burnt out.

Rosalie wound her way along the deserted path, passing tent after tent of midnight blue outlined in broad strokes of silver. It was near midnight, and the Carnival had begun winding down. Lights began to flicker out one by one, restoring the brightly illuminated fairgrounds to a darker, quieter gloom. Rapunzel, looking out from her window at the Carnival's northern end, had started keeping her hair, pulling her blonde braid laboriously up the three floors of her tower, singing a wistful tune while she was at it. It wouldn't be long till she was at Jack's Pub, downing the pints with Jill and Red Riding Hood.

To her left, Mother Schlau was sweeping the porch of her candied shop house, finally free from the press of wide-eyed customers and hungry hands. She stopped when Rosalie passed, offering her a lemon drop fresh plucked from her windowsill. Rosalie took it, thanked Mother Schlau, went on her way. The animals had started trotting about the grounds, free from the scrutiny of visitors. She saw the three little pigs locking the gates of the petting zoo they managed, setting free mice, birds, ducklings and swans from their enclosures. Come morning, these creatures would return to their various stations, ready for yet another day of manhandling by over-enthusiastic children. Now, they fled their pens in a riot of squeaks and squawks, eager to stretch their limbs and wings. It still amazed her, the number of creatures The Ringmaster had collected, all living together in this haphazard arrangement of tents and trailers, only a barren field away from civilization.

She recalled the moment they had stepped out of the doorway, straight into the illuminated chaos of the Carnival. The sky that night was inky black, starless, the only light for miles coming from the Carnival itself. The unfamiliar beckoned - tall lamps that shone brighter than anything she had ever seen, flashing signs in a rainbow of colors, moving contraptions powered by cogs and wheels and not magic. They wandered amongst folks dressed in the strangest fashions, cocking their heads in wonder at the sight of ladies in skin tight pants and swarthy turbaned gentlemen. They saw stalls peddling wares of candy apple, sniffed longingly at the warm smell of buttered corn, cringed as they passed vendors selling exotic selections of barbecued snakes and pan-fried ants. They were entranced with a pool of iridescent blue, and stood entirely in awe as a mermaid surfaced from its azure depths to wave a greeting.

It was a little overwhelming. She noted the despair on Charles' face, and sought to comfort him with a squeeze of his hand.

'Is this the new world?' She asked, trailing after The Ringmaster as he gave them the grand tour of the premises.

'It is but a small part of the world at large,' he turned to face them, smiling. 'I constructed this as a haven for folks like you who have wished to leave their old lives.'

'So there's more? To the world?' She asked.

'Certainly. Feel free to wander the grounds, but you can depart anytime. The real world begins once you step outside the Carnival.'

She looked hopefully at Charles. 'Perhaps -'

'We have nothing, no coin, no shelter. How will we live?' Charles asked.

'Why, stay here then. Observe the world, make yourself useful wherever you can. You can leave anytime, but in the meantime, you are welcome, as are all folks who come through the doorway. Know however, that while time is halted within the grounds, it will continue once you leave. You will age. And you will die.'

They decided to stay a while.

The Ringmaster had shown them their trailer, a boxy contraption that contained the insides of a very small house. Charles hated it at first. Used to the space of his castle, the realities of living his life in a tiny room frustrated him greatly. She planted roses to cheer him up, and in a bid to make him feel useful, encouraged him to help with the Forgotten Knights' jousting showcase. He proved so good at it, the Knights recruited him as a permanent member. Charles' good looks packed the show full of awestruck ladies waving handkerchiefs. It was good for business.

Rosalie smiled at the thought of her husband. They were used to living here now, amongst strange folks like themselves, all hoping to start a new life elsewhere. Night after night, she observed the visitors thronging the fairgrounds. They came from everywhere, most from nearby towns, some from cities further away, a few from lands so far they had traversed sky and sea to get here. She liked mingling with these strangers, learning the way they dressed, the way they lived. In the mornings, she would wander past the gates of the resting Carnival, crossing the field to visit the nearby town. She sat in cafés, browsed in libraries, strolled in gardens. Time felt more solid once she stepped out of the fair, her decisions more impactful, her pleasures more concrete. Charles accompanied her occasionally, but he seemed content to spend most of his time within the Carnival. Eventually, she had felt familiar enough with the real world to find work there, serving up coffee at a café in the day, returning to her home in the Carnival only in the evening. It was an ideal arrangement, one that sated her curiosity about the outside world while still being able to accommodate Charles' anxiety about living elsewhere.

Charles had been unhappy about her working outside, but she had insisted. It felt good to do something, to not have to depend on a father or a husband for the means to support oneself. Working gave her access to coin, and the means to spend them on the ones she loved. Once again, Rosalie fingered the tiny box in her coat pocket. She had first seen the silver rose three months ago, its delicate petals glistening shyly in the window of the curiosity shop. It had taken her months to save up for it, but she knew Charles would love it. He was a man who cherished fragile beauty, and it would make a perfect gift for the anniversary of their crossover.

She glanced at her watch. Two minutes to midnight, to the day of their anniversary. She hurried along.

The tent she sought appeared before her, its flashing sign 'Nightly Jousts by the Order of the Forgotten Knights' looking lonesome in the fair. One of the last spots of brightness in the darkening night. One by one, the lights flickered out as she stepped out into the empty arena. The last performance had ended half an hour ago.

'Charles?' she called, right hand slipping into her pocket once again to finger the tiny box.

No answer. She wondered if Arthur, the leader of the Forgotten Knights had been mistaken when he told her that Charles was staying back to rehearse a new act.

'Charles! Are you there?'

The arena dimmed unceremoniously in reply, light fled, leaving behind an empty shell of cloth and wooden fittings. Moonlight filtered though the flapping doorway, a zigzag of silver beckoning her outside.

She went home. When he returned, she was already asleep.

The music changed. It shifted from the lively canter of the previous act to a darker, more sinister tune. She led Charles to the center of the stage, into the circle of light that flared to accommodate their figures. She cracked her whip once, the harsh snap punctuating the music like a cymbal clash.

He circled her at a distance, animal paws treading softly. Never entering the area designated by the whip's length. Never daring to encroach on her personal space.

Another crack of the whip.

He stopped.

She approached him, closing the distance between them, each step marked by the clip of her boots. When she stood only inches away from him, she paused. Their eyes locked once more, his eyes upon her, his gaze regal and beastly. Sometimes, she had no idea if it was man or beast behind those golden eyes. Slowly, she wound her long braid in her right hand, then gestured with her left.

'Open.' She commanded.

He opened his mouth with a roar. A loud, deep sound tailored to impress and frighten. Someone screamed. His mouth remained open, stretched to its fullest, revealing a row of sharp teeth surrounding a soft pink tongue.

She bowed once, with the same theatricality of The Ringmaster.

Then she put her head inside his mouth.

She had awakened with him beside her that final morning, his golden hair falling into her eyes as he kissed her groggily.

'I was looking for you last night,' she murmured.

'Sorry, Lance wanted to use some new technique in the joust... we went searching for props at his trailer. Arthur said you wanted to show me something?' His voice had tapered off at the end, and he was now snoring softly. The morning rays filtered in through the trailer's small windows, lighting his face perfectly. He looked like a sleeping angel.

'Never mind, I'll show you tonight.'

She kissed his cheek, checked that her present was still in her coat, and left for work. It would be easy to trade hours with another colleague, she thought. She resolved to get home earlier that day, before his act started. It was a special day, after all.

It was dark inside his mouth. Her exposed neck fit neatly between his jaws, she could feel the sharpness of his teeth inches away. Her braid tickled his tongue, she felt it loll slightly beneath her, damping the tips of her hair.

She closed her eyes, trying to shut out memories of how she had found him that afternoon. With the girl in their trailer, bodies pressed together in a crush of mouths and limbs, clothed in nothing but the stench of betrayal. She recalled that his same mouth had kissed her own that very morning. That mouth had told her of his love time and time again. Her hands, still in her pockets, were clenched so tight that she had crumpled the box she had so eagerly wanted to show him.

Lies.

That was what the real world had wrought. It was the price of their freedom that The Ringmaster had forgotten to mention. In a world where he was not limited to her beauty alone, in a world where he had left the guise of beast behind, he had strayed.

She had shut the door quietly, her heart cold. The image of their writhing bodies, still enmeshed, haunted her. She felt a cold fury settle within, and knew then, that she wanted to make him pay.

As if on cue, The Ringmaster had appeared before her.

'I feel a wish coming forth,' he cautioned, wagging a finger. 'Know that this one, if granted, comes at a price.'

'I know. I don't care.'

The next moment, screams emerged as the girl fled the trailer, stark naked, a lion at her heels. The lion raised its head, looked at her with baleful golden eyes.

Her heart clenched, then hardened. She felt hollow, as if something small and precious had died inside.

'What is your price?' She asked The Ringmaster.

'Why, I think the Carnival needs a new animal show, don't you? With a catchy title like... 'Beauty and the Beast'. Yes, why not? It has a nice ring to it.'

That night, they premiered a new lion taming show at the Carnival.

Pure rage fuelled her at the start. The rush of anger was what got her on stage, the need to present her disappointment what made her taunt him with her whip. It began as a contest of wills, hers against his animal instincts. The show at the beginning was a display of human domination, a lover's brawl made public. She threw furniture, set the lash upon him, taunted him with a variety of quietly murmured accusations only he could hear. He responded with snarls and roars, anger flattening his ears, ire and bewilderment in his eyes. He resorted to circling her like prey around the stage, but never managed to get within an inch of her without her permission -- The Ringmaster had wrought a spell that kept her safe from his retaliation.

This went on for a long time, until one day, she found all her fury spent, leaving her with nothing but a forlorn numbness. The show continued, but it lost its heated aspect, graduating into a show of cold civility. She varied their acts, deviating from outright challenges into acts of willpower, a display of imposing her will upon his animal instincts. He too, seemed to mellow over time, perhaps learning that all attacks against her person would be in vain. She made him run circles, made him jump rings, and finally, in a display of his absolute docility, bade him to allow her head inside his open mouth.

'When will the price be repaid? When will I be free?' She had once asked The Ringmaster.

'When something dead comes alive,' He replied.

She had stopped thinking about the end a long time ago. Feeling nothing, it was the monotony of the daily shows that marked time for her. She did not realize until today, that she actually looked forward to seeing him on stage.

Slowly, she brought her head, still attached to her neck, out of his mouth. The audience let out a breath they did not know they were holding. She turned to face them, smiling slightly, inclined her head in acknowledgment.

The applause poured forth, marking the end of their final act that night. Usually, she would crack her whip, a signal for Charles to slink off before marching off the stage herself.

This time, on a whim, she turned back to the beast beside her, rubbing his chin for a moment before placing a kiss on his cold damp nose.

His eyes widened. The audience went wild.

Her heart jerked to life all of a sudden, turning from stone back to a thumping, pumping organ. And she was surprised to find in there, the sentiment, if not of love, then at least, of forgiveness.

That night, she walked to the gates of the Carnival, gazing across the barren grounds to the tip of the town in the distance, civilization's illuminated edges sparkling in the dark sky. She fingered the silver rose at her throat, the one she had never given him, touching once again the delicate edges where the silver had turned green.

Soon. Her new heart murmured. Soon.

Idle Hands

Hannah Kate

Charlie was the first one of us as got taken. Not that anyone really noticed at first. It wasn't easy to tell with Charlie, given that he was bone idle at the best of times. So if he downed tools, there was nothing in it. After a day or so, people started to talk. But it was Charlie, so nothing came of it.

When Len didn't show to open up shop, people made more of it. There was something as wasn't right in that. Charlie's one thing, but Len hasn't missed a day since his place opened. That should be 'hadn't'. Len hadn't missed a day since his place opened. Save Sundays, of course, but that's to be expected.

So it shocked us all, truth be told, when we saw that he hadn't opened up one Monday. When there was no sign of Len in his shop, and he didn't answer the bell when we rang. After a couple of hours, people started to get a bit worried. Even I did, if I'm honest, though I was never a regular customer of his. Someone suggested going to his house, in case he'd had a fall or some other accident. Someone else tried to get in a look in at the window of the shop's backroom. 'Maybe someone's done for him,' they said. (I can't remember who it was.) 'Maybe he was counting out his money and someone just burst in on him.'

'That doesn't make a lot of sense,' someone else said (I think it was Tom – it seems like something Tom would say.) 'The shop's all locked up and the lights are off. It doesn't look as if he's been back since Saturday.'

There was a bit of disagreement on this. Some said as how the thief might have turned all the lights off and closed the curtains, to make it look like Len had never been in this morning. Others thought that a thief would be more likely to do it when he closed up for the day. Get him on Saturday when he's shutting up shop. 'Maybe that's what happened,' someone said.

'Maybe he's been in there all weekend.'

'Maybe the thief's long gone now. And poor old Len's been shouting for help.'

'Who'd have done that though? Not someone round here.'

'Well, there's strangers in town.'

'Strange is right. Could've been anyone of them.'

'I saw Len yesterday. So he can't've been in there since Saturday.'

'Yeah. I saw him too.'

'He was heading off with his fishing tackle.'

'Going down to the river.'

'Maybe the thief came back this morning then.'

'Maybe he waited for Len to unlock the door and then did for him.'

'We don't know as there was a thief.'

And it carried on this way for a while. But Len didn't come, and no one could see in the window to make out if he was lying there, shouting for help. In the end Tom said as we should just go to Len's house and knock on the door. It seemed like the most sensible plan anyone'd had, so that's what we did.

Len wasn't there.

After Len and Charlie, it was Johnny Cate from the chemist's. The next morning he didn't show up for work either. Johnny Cate's like Len, so that one were a shock too. We're only a small town, see, so word gets round when something's not right. I wouldn't have known anything about Johnny Cate, only I was in the post office when Tom came in and told us. He'd given it some thought by then, and he said it was probably some sort of sickness going around, that Charlie and Len and Johnny Cate must have taken poorly and couldn't make it in to work. We all nodded at that, but it still seemed odd that we hadn't seen anything of the three of them.

While we were standing around working it all out, some kid (I don't know his name, but it's him as does a bit of handyman work at the church) comes running in, all out of breath, and tells us that he's just seen Len and Charlie down by the river. 'They're just fishing,' he says, as though he's telling us they're glowing red and hovering in the air.

'Just fishing?' Tom says.

And the kid nods his head like a crazy person. 'Just fishing.'

'Is there anyone else there with them?' says Tom.

'Johnny Cate's there. And a couple of other guys too.'

'And they're just fishing as well?'

The kid nods again, and looks more relaxed now he's got his news out. Must've been bursting to tell someone all that, as he looks a bit deflated once it's out.

Tom takes the lead, and says as how a gang of us should go down to the river and check everything's alright. 'Someone needs to be doing something,' he says. 'We have to find out what's happened.'

'Maybe the fish are just biting today,' some comedian shouts. But Tom ignores him and asks who'll go with him. He gets a group of four or so together, and they head off to the river.

Me? No – I don't offer to go. When Tom gets a bee in his bonnet about something, I prefer to keep my distance. I got the impression he wanted an argument, and I've never much cared for falling out with people. Let Tom and the others go in with their guns blazing. Let them try and drag Charlie and Len and Johnny Cate back from their fishing and make them do a day's work. I'll hear all about it later on, I've no doubt about that. I don't need to get myself involved.

And that's what happened, of course. I went for a drink that night, and the whole place was full of talk about Tom and the others going down to the river.

'Did you hear what happened at the river?' I get asked as soon as I sit down. I shake my head and wait for the story.

'So... Tom finds the men at the river...' There's about five different people telling this story, and I can't remember who said what. I'll just give you the picture. I don't suppose it matters which of them said which bit. '... and they're just sitting fishing. Like he was expecting. At first Tom just asks them what they think they're playing at. Work to be done, he says. But they just smile and keep on with their fishing. He says that it's a Monday, that it isn't a holiday, that everyone else has dragged their backsides to work, so why can't they? But no one shifts. They just sit there, ignoring him. So Tom gets angry and starts shouting about responsibility. This just gets a smirk from Charlie and a shrug from old Len.'

I take another sip of my drink. There's many of us in here as would probably have done the same if Tom had started shouting that way at us. He doesn't half take himself seriously.

'So Tom and the others decide this isn't acceptable. They storm off back to town, leaving the men to their fishing. They head to Johnny Cate's house and bang on the door to get his wife. What's wrong with your John? Tom says. He looks like he's accusing her of something, so she gets all defensive. Nothing wrong with my John, she says. He's entitled to a holiday every now and then. And she slams the door in Tom's face.'

Like I say, many of us would do the same. But I guess that Tom didn't like it.

'Tom wouldn't like that,' I say, so they know I'm listening. I don't like to seem rude.

'He didn't. Not one bit. He starts asking if Johnny Cate's been on the booze. Has he been drinking? What's he been drinking? And you won't guess what she says to that...'

I give a sort of half shrug, because I'm sure I don't know.

'She says he's not touched a drop in years. He just fancied a holiday. And then...'

Whoever it is as is telling the story falls quiet as the door opens. It's Tom, and he's got a face like thunder. He marches up to the bar and orders a pint. He's drunk nearly half of it before speaking, and his voice is like a growl when he does.

'I think we're getting to the bottom of this now, lads. It's that blasted circus. I warned you, didn't I? You have a circus in town, and no good'll follow. Well, now we know.'

Someone asks Tom what he means, but he just turns back to his drink. He finishes it and orders another.

'Was it booze, Tom? I said it was booze, didn't I?' someone (probably Stanley) says, with a knowing smile and a pint in his hand. 'My sister lives out Damfield way, and she told me that when they had a circus on the fields near them, the whole place was flooded with some sort of homemade vodka that'd take the roof of your mouth off. She said the town was half-blind for days afterwards.'

'It's not booze,' Tom says. 'I can't quite work out what exactly it is, but it's not booze.' Another big swipe of his pint. 'All I know for sure is that all them that downed tools went to that circus a couple of days before. Charlie went the first night they were in town. And then Len went with a group of his mates. None of them's shown up for work in days either.'

'Are they fishing too, Tom?' Stanley asks. He likes to impress Tom, hang on his every word, sound clever. That'd be too much effort for me. I just like to sit quiet and listen, though sometimes that's a lot of work in itself where Tom's concerned.

'They're not all fishing. I found some of them there with their rods, but some of them are just sitting out in chairs in their gardens. A couple of them have gone down to Cooper's farm to feed carrots to the horses.'

Even Stanley can't say anything in response to that.

'It's down to this circus. I can be sure of it. But I'm still working it all out in my head.' Tom doesn't like to admit that he doesn't know something. He must've caught a glance of me getting ready to leave, because he carries on quite forthright. 'We have to do something, lads. We have to deal with this tonight. This is our town, and I'm not having it fall to ruins because of some circus leading good honest folks astray.'

'What shall we do, Tom?'

'Know your enemy, Stanley. Know your enemy.'

Stanley doesn't look like he quite follows. Neither did I, if I'm honest. But I didn't much trust the direction this was heading in.

'Has anyone in here been to see that circus yet?' Tom

raises his voice so we know he's talking to the whole pub. Most folks shake their head, and a couple of people say as how they'd got tickets for later in the week or at the weekend or something similar. 'Right,' Tom carries on, in his stride now. 'I've managed to get three tickets tonight. We're going to go down there and watch that show. Start to finish, from the sideshows to the acrobats to the clowns. And we're going to watch every bit of food, every drop of drink, every magic trick, every loop-the-blasted-loop those circus people offer us. And we'll find out what it is that's dragged Len and Charlie and Johnny Cate from the straight and narrow. Then we'll find the circus boss-man and have it out with him. So I'm looking for a couple of volunteers.'

Stanley's hand shot into the air like it'd been fired from a cannon.

I didn't see Tom and Stanley for a while, or the other man as went with them that night. None of the three of them showed up for work the next day. Eventually, that kid who does a bit of handyman work at the church told us he'd seen them at Cooper's farm, talking to the horses and feeding them carrots. He'd not said anything to them, but had just stared. He expected Tom to yell something, but he reckoned they didn't even notice him watching. Someone asked him how Tom looked. 'Just happy,' the kid says.

By now, there was even more people as had been taken by whatever sickness it was as had got the others. Half the shops in town were locked up in darkness, and there was no one at the station or the bank. By the weekend, a load of the school-teachers had stopped turning up for their teaching, and the kiddies were being bunched together in the few classrooms as actually had adults in them. The headmaster had to help out serving the dinners, as the kitchen ladies had all gone to the circus in a gang one night and had been sitting in a field making daisy chains ever since. Tom's garage was shut, and a couple of angry drivers with broken-down cars chased up to Cooper's farm to drag him back. They couldn't get him away from those horses though. And Cooper didn't mind his animals getting overfed, as he'd been up at the river fishing since he'd seen the circus on Wednesday.

The pub was still open, though, so that was something. They were down to just the landlord, his wife and one barmaid, but they kept on going. At least I still had somewhere to sit.

Did I not want to go and see what it was all about? No. Not me. I never took to the circus. All that noise and shouting, bright colours and fussing. Not for me. Curious? Not particularly – why do you ask? Not my business if others drop their work, is it? I thought it was all something and nothing, something as'd blow over as quick as it came. And there was something to be said for how nice and peaceful the town had got, even if there was no one to treat a toothache or sell you your milk and potatoes.

That doesn't mean that people weren't determined to try and get me involved somehow. That's how it always works, isn't it? The more you sit and mind your own business, the more someone wants to drag you into theirs.

By Saturday night, there was hardly anyone going about as usual. Those as had already been taken by whatever it was were loafing around on chairs in their garden or lying back in the fields watching the stars or the moon or whatever it is that's so interesting in the sky. Those as hadn't yet been taken were itching to go and see the circus. I guess they must've had a packed house that afternoon. That evening too.

So I find myself sitting in the pub. There's me and the landlord, his wife (not the barmaid, as she's been taken off to see the show by her young man), and a few others scattered about the place. I'm just taking a drink of my second pint, when the door opens and there's two strangers – a man and a woman – standing there, looking like they've been dragged all the way from Damfield behind a lorry.

'Oh, thank goodness you're open,' one of them says. Or something like that. A bit over-the-top about it, if you know what I mean. Like they were expecting the pub to be shut on a Saturday night.

'Thank goodness you're open,' the other one says, as if it was so important it needed to be said twice. 'We thought the whole town was deserted.'

The landlord just smiles and says what'll it be? He says as how the pub's always open on a Saturday night, but that it's quieter than usual on account of the circus. I swear, you've never seen a face fall faster. As soon as he says the word 'circus', it's like all the colour just drains out of their faces.

'It's not the Mann Brothers circus is it?' the man says. I'm starting to think they might be father and daughter. They've got a family look about them, but he looks to be a good bit older. 'Did they come in a big train? Parade about the town with their clown bands and acrobats and dancing girls?'

The landlord nods that that was the one.

'When did they get here?' The man's voice is high and shaky, like he's had a bit of a shock. His daughter just stands there looking… well… the only word I can think for it is distraught. 'How long have they been in town? Have many people been to see the show yet?'

'A good number have. They've been here nearly two weeks,' the landlord says, and it's like he's trying to calm the man down. When his way of talking doesn't do the trick, he offers brandy instead.

The man shakes his head, but there's a glass put out for him anyway. 'Is there somewhere we could get some food? We've been travelling all day, and we haven't had a bite to eat.'

'I'm sure my wife could fix you a cold plate of something. But we don't do anything hot. I'm not sure as there's anywhere here as does at this time.'

'Not at any time,' a voice chimes in. 'Not since the Buckleys stopped opening their café.'

The daughter gives this sort of gulp when she hears this. It sounds comical, like she's putting it on. But she looks so frightened, I'm sure it's genuine. 'They stopped opening it? Are they sick?'

'Just taking a holiday,' the landlord says, putting a glass of brandy in front of her as well.

Despite him not seeming to want it, the man knocks his

brandy back in one go. 'I'm going to guess that there's a few folks round here taking holidays?' He doesn't wait for any of us to agree. 'And that every time someone round here sees the circus show, they seem to want a bit of a holiday afterwards?'

The girl touches his arm, and I wonder for a minute if they mightn't be married. She's young for him, if that's the case. When she speaks, she's all quiet like she doesn't really want to say the words. 'Tell me this... has anyone been to see that circus and gone back to work the next day?'

'I'm not sure as how that's any of your business.' The landlord's a bit huffy about this, but he's got a point. I'm not sure that it's right to go poking your nose into other people's business like that.

'The circus came to our town. That's why we're asking,' the man says. 'We know what happens next, and we think that's happening here as well.'

Two sisters – Lucy and Sara Fletcher – have come up to the bar now. Their mum and dad are sitting quietly in a corner, ignoring the strangers. 'Excuse me,' one of the Fletcher girls says. 'I don't want to interrupt you, and I'm sure I don't know you from Adam. But you're saying something about the circus, and the problems it causes. But it's not true, whatever it is. We went to the circus on Monday, and none of us have stopped going to work.'

The man's a bit struck by this, like it wasn't what he was expecting. He asks her who she means, and she says that her and her sister and her mother and her father all went to see the show on Monday, and they've not missed any work since. She's obviously a bit annoyed by the man's suggestions, and she's quick to say that her dad hasn't missed a day of work since he was in his teens, and her mum only took time off to raise her children. 'So it's nothing to do with the circus, as we've seen it and we're all just fine.'

He's not for backing down though. And he starts questioning her as though he's a magistrate or some such. Did she see the whole show? Did she see every last bit? Did they walk out at any point? Was there anything they missed?

The Fletcher girl is pretty solid. She takes all his questions with a shrug, and doesn't let him bother her. Yes – they saw the whole show. They arrived for the sideshows, saw the displays, the bands and the dancers. They went into the big top when the big show was about to start, watched the promenade concert, the pantomime, the acrobats, the riders, the dancing horses, the snarling tigers, the comical elephants stacked up in a pyramid. The clowns, some in burnt cork, some with ghost-white faces, all with oversized shoes or mismatched clothes, and the clown band that made them laugh. The giant clown ladies waddling across the ring, the clown dogs dressed up like lions, the clumsy tumblers prancing about to smeary trombone music. The Fletcher girl remembers every last minute of it, and reels it off act-by-act to the strange man and his daughter.

They take in all that she says, but they seem to be getting impatient. She's listing off all the costumes and animals and dancing girls, and the man looks like he's going to wave her on to talk about something else. They hold their tongues though, and let her get to the end of her recital.

'And then…' the daughter (or wife) prompts. 'After that?'

'What do you mean?' The Fletcher girl's a bit annoyed that her story's not enough for them. 'After that we went home.'

The man breathes loudly. It still sounds a bit like he's putting it on for show. 'So you didn't stay for the after-show?'

'That concert at the end? No. We didn't think it was worth it, after all that. We'd heard nearly three hours of the circus band, and the sideshow bands, and the clown bands. What's the point in more of the same?'

'It's not the same,' the daughter says. 'It's a different band.'

'Same musicians though.' Now the Fletcher girl is getting bossy. She obviously doesn't like the suggestion that she doesn't know how the circus works. She starts moving her hands a bit, like she's a teacher explaining something to a stubborn child. 'It's the same players, and the same instruments as was in the big-show band. It's not the first time I've seen a circus, you know. The after-show is just a small group of the players, with cornets and trombones and that silly saxophone that the clowns all dance to. We didn't stay. Most of the others did, but three hours is enough for us.'

The man looks at his daughter. 'That's what we thought,' he says, as he's speaking for the pair of them now. 'That's what happened with us as well.'

Now the landlord and his wife (who's brought out two plates of cooked meat and cheese and bread for the strangers) and the two Fletcher girls are looking at the man and waiting for him to explain. He starts eating his cheese instead, and his daughter does too. They jump right into it as though they've not eaten anything in weeks.

Once they've finished off the cheese and some of the meat, the man starts to speak again. 'When the Mann Brothers came to us, we thought the same thing as you. Once you've seen the sideshows and the big show, there's no point in watching the after-show. Turns out most people didn't agree with us, and they stayed behind to watch.'

'Sounds like that's happened here as well,' his daughter says. 'And now everyone's left their work and started just sitting around enjoying themselves.'

The landlord laughs at this. 'Sounds alright to me. I wouldn't mind sitting around enjoying myself for once.'

The man and his daughter ignore him and start to just speak straight to the Fletcher girls, like they're the only ones as'll understand them. Maybe they are, truth be told, as I can't say I care so much about what they're talking about, and the landlord and his wife are treating them a bit like clowns themselves. 'We asked some of them, the ones as weren't working, what was in that after-show. We asked them if it was just the same players as was in the big-show band. None of them would answer. They just laughed and went back to whatever it was they were doing. Which was nothing for the most part.'

'But one of them told us about the saxophones,' the daughter says. 'One of the old women who'd gone to see the circus and then sat around on a tree trunk plucking petals off flowers and twiddling bits of grass. She told us it was the saxophones – three of them – that made the after-show band so good. She said it was different to the saxophones in the clown band.'

'One of the men – headmaster at our town's school – said that as well,' the man says. 'Straight from coming back from the show, he'd been sitting in a chair on his front garden building a little house out of mud and pebbles. Never went back to the school. We talked to him…'

'Didn't get much sense at first.'

'… and he just went on and on about the saxophones. Glistening, he said they were. Shining more than the cornets or trombones ever did. And none of the frog sounds or squawking that the clown band played on their beat-up old saxophones. More like honey, he said. More like some honey as has just got up and danced ragtime around you.'

'Saxophones?' The landlord's having a bit of a good old laugh at this now. 'You're saying it's saxophones as is to blame for all these people downing tools and shirking off their work?'

'I don't know,' the man says. And he's shaking his head like it's all too much for him. 'I can't say for sure. But I know that we didn't stay for that after-show. We didn't hear any of this music, and we're just fine. And now these good people…' he gestures to the Fletcher girls and then waves his arm to take in their parents. '… can say the same thing. How would you explain that?'

Behind him, two of the last drinkers have got their coats on and are heading to the door. The man spins round and tries to stop one of them.

'Oh no you don't, mate,' the man with his coat on laughs. 'You can't start talking about this after-show and not expect us to go and take a look for ourselves. We'll come back after the show and tell you all about it.'

'Please don't,' the daughter says. 'It's not safe to go.'

'I don't mind a bit of ragtime. Let's go and hear these saxophones.'

Two others join them, and then it's just me, the landlord, his wife, the Fletchers and the strange man and his daughter.

I want to ask for another drink, but it seems the others just want to keep talking about the circus.

'If you don't mind me asking,' one of the Fletcher girls says. 'Why are you here? Have you come following the circus?'

'We had no idea it was here,' the man says. 'We had to leave and just kept going until we came to a town. We had to walk for a while, as our car's broken down and the trains weren't stopping at our station.'

The man's chewing at a bit of bread now, as though he's waiting for more questions. Did I ask him anything? What would I have asked? I think he's spinning us a yarn, and I can tell by her face that the older Fletcher girl thinks the same. The younger one's the one who starts up with the questions.

'What happened next? When did people go back to work? What happened when the circus left town?'

The man takes his time getting round to answering, so I ask the landlord for another pint. He looks like he's glad of the distraction as well. 'No one went back to work,' the stranger finally says. 'When it came time for the circus to leave, they packed up all their tents, led all their animals onto the coaches, took down all the sideshows and signs, and moved their train off the siding and onto the tracks. The train headed off, and we thought that was goodbye. But the damned saxophone band stayed behind. Once the circus train was out of sight, they started to play again. They had a banjo player and a drummer, and the leader was dressed up in a bandsman's suit with burnt cork on his face and a smashed-up pillbox hat on his head.'

'That was the only time we saw the after-show band. But we were too far away to hear the music,' the daughter adds.

'We saw the leader lift up his hand, and everyone anywhere near him – all those as had been sat around plucking daisies or throwing stones in the river for the past two weeks – got up and started to walk towards the band.'

'The band leader was playing one of them little saxophones,' the daughter says.

'It's called an alto,' the bossy Fletcher girl says. She's not ready to stop being an expert just yet.

'It doesn't matter what it's called,' the man says. He's angry now, and he's waving the last of his bread around like a madman. 'As soon as he put the blasted thing to his lips, all them as had been sitting round started to get up and crowd around him.'

'And then it happened…'

'And then it happened,' the man echoes his daughter. 'The band started to walk off down the tracks behind where the train had just gone.'

'What did the crowd do then?' one of the Fletcher girls asks.

'They followed the band,' the daughter says. 'Every last one of them.'

I think it was three days after that when the circus finished. By then, of course, most people in the town had been to see the big show. And once word got around about the two strangers in the pub, most folks had decided to go and see the after-show too. The youngest Fletcher girl had gone to see it. Sneaked out with her friends, and didn't tell her parents or sister. The landlord and his wife went the night after the strangers arrived.

When the circus started packing up, there was only a handful of us left as wasn't sitting around feeding horses or fishing or making daisy chains. The strange man and his daughter didn't stick around. They'd stole the headmaster's car from under his nose while he was sitting on his garden chair picking flowers. They headed off away from the train tracks, though I've no idea where they thought they'd end up. Helped themselves to a pile of things from Len's shop as well. I saw them break open the door, but I was too far away to stop them. And I don't know what I'd have done if they'd put up a fight about it, as there was no one else around to see it.

The circus packed up much as they'd said it would. I watched them putting the elephants and tigers into their carriages. Never seen such placid animals, especially not ones as were supposed to be wild. The tigers went along like pet dogs. Then the clowns and dancing girls and acrobats were all aboard, all dressed up in their costumes like they were still putting on a show. I couldn't see any band though, so I guessed the man and his daughter must've been wrong about that.

But when the train started to move, I saw that they weren't wrong. A small group of players waiting around by the platform. One of them had a burnt-cork face and a smashed pillbox hat, and he was holding one of them little saxophones, all shiny and glinting in the light. There were two others with saxophones – them as are a bit bigger and make the frog sounds in the clown band (or at least that's what the Fletcher girl told me) – and one with a banjo and one with a drum. They was just standing around waiting for the train to disappear. Once it did, the band leader put his hand up and they started to play.

I was too far away to really hear anything, though I could catch the odd hit of the drum. I could see the band swaying and jumping though, like they were playing ragtime. The train platform's a distance away from the town, and even further from the river, but sure enough people started to walk towards them. And would you believe it? They were all swaying and jumping too, like they knew every last note as was being played. I saw Charlie out in the front of the crowd, with Len and Johnny Cate not far behind. The headmaster of the school was behind them, and then the younger Fletcher girl and her friends. Before long, they were all there – the landlord of the pub, his wife, the kitchen ladies, Stanley, the kid as does the handyman work at the church. Poor old Tom was one of the last to arrive – he wouldn't like that much, if I know Tom.

Once they'd got near enough the whole town around them, the band stepped out onto the train tracks. Like I say, I wasn't close enough to see everything, but it didn't look to me like they missed a beat of whatever it was they were playing. And you'll probably not believe what I say next, but once they was down on the tracks, the whole crowd of folk got down there with them. Sort of just flowing down onto the tracks like it was the most normal thing in the world.

The band started moving, walking away down the train tracks, swaying and jumping and playing their instruments, the leader a little out in front. And then the whole mass of people – Tom and Len and Johnny Cate, the headmaster, the landlord, all of them – just followed them.

So now it's just us. Me and the Fletchers and old Mrs Jones and the Reverend. We was all that was left, after the band went. Oh, we stuck it out for a bit. We had a whole town full of food and beer and money and such. The Reverend tried to keep us good for a while. He said as how we shouldn't break into any of the houses or the bank or the pub. He said as how we should keep civilized. But he soon gave up on that once he got hungry.

We tried to stick at it, make a go of it. But we had no doctors, see, and one of us was bound to get sick. And things started to break or go wrong, and we'd no way of fixing them. Most of the food as we'd got was going bad, and there was only so much we could take from Cooper's farm.

In the end we just thought we'd do what those strangers did, and take a couple of cars and drive. That's how we ended up here. We're running low on petrol and thought we'd get filled up here. Maybe have a bite to eat and a drink. Maybe stay overnight and then get back on the road tomorrow.

To be honest, we didn't know if we should bother stopping. We thought everything was closed for the night, and we didn't pass a soul on our way in. But then we saw the lights on here. Most of the houses we passed were dark. Curtains shut and everything. But then we saw your pub. Mrs Jones and the Reverend wanted to go to the church first, but that looks like it's shut up for the night as well, so they've given in and come here.

I'm surprised to see it so quiet in here tonight though. Is it always this empty on a Saturday night? No one coming in for a drink? I really did think we'd see more people around the place.

The Things We Leave Behind

Christopher L. Irvin

John smoked half his cigarettes within minutes of setting foot inside the fall carnival. Let each stick burn down until he felt ash gray his fingertips. His hands shook as he thumbed a dull gun-metal Zippo. One piece of his old uniform he took comfort in never having to polish. He'd lost his confident stride mere yards past the entrance. Found the need to sit down on an overturned crate. The Montgomery County fairgrounds were packed with onlookers, from as far south as Louisville and as west as Indy. Could hear it in the twang, or lack of in their voice. Lou-uh-ville, not Lou-ee-ville. Private Schweitzer had corrected him in basic. John supposed Dayton was close to the South but he didn't speak a lick of it. Had trouble understanding the conversation when southern folk got together in groups larger than two. Union men from the National Cash Register factories dragged their women to have their fortunes read and get a glimpse of the Strongest Man in the Midwest, or the old-timer who could swallow a twelve-inch blade. It was all tame to John, like most things since the war. Strength didn't matter when you had a gun in your hand. Blades were bayonets that came out when things got real ugly. He used to have nightmares of those times, but now the images flickered through his mind like a silent film on repeat. Anger, fear and death all just variations of gray floating in the background. Most of the time.

'Somethin's missin' from those eyes of yours, Johnny,'

his father had said. Not the first words spit from his cancer-stricken mouth when John returned home from Germany, though they might as well have been. It was true that a part of John had been left behind—the softness around his midsection and the glow of a seventeen-year-old boy who lied about his age. But those were things that every soldier lost, that heal or return after a few home-cooked meals. No, what John had left behind was at home, the one thing he couldn't take with him to the front lines. The guilt he chose to carry instead rotted his heart.

He pulled his cap low as he scanned the crowds again, flicking ash into the mud at his boots. The sun began to dip, highlighting the Ferris wheel that stood guard over the right side of the field. Dark purple tents, almost black, with bits of yellow to highlight the acts, formed a row of oddities to his left. 'The Dog-faced Man,' 'Lola, the Beautiful Tattooed Savage,' 'Boy Quicksilver.' The rest lost to John, hidden behind long lines of thrill-seekers, eager to spend a coin for a glimpse of madness.

'Carnival Courbè,' read a sign on the main tent in the center of the field. 'A Most Unusual Show, Games and Wonders.' On cue, a shirtless man spat fire into the air. Wonderment alright, he thought. How long will people fall for this charade? Like most traveling shows, the carnival had appeared overnight, announced only by a small ad in the Dayton Daily and fliers posted on Main Street.

John pulled out a copy of the ad from his pocket, wrinkled creases distorting the image. Fifth down on the bill it read, Come see the amazing boy juggler - balls, torches, pins, he does them all and more! John had no doubt in his mind who it was, the face a perfect mixture of their parents. Charlie. Still, he could barely utter his brother's name. Only seven years old when John parachuted into France. What was he now, ten? The face in the photo showed signs of a hard life, aged well beyond a teenager. John felt his insides twist, his vision gray, reliving the moment he returned home a hero.

He remembered how the dried out wood itched his fingertips as he stood on the porch and watched his father drag his heels through the dirt, back toward the house, maintaining the same worn down pace, even though John was sure they had made eye contact.

John's temper got the best of him that day and he took off, almost at a run, mud spraying over the last of his pressed pants and shined shoes. Before his father could open his mouth, John spoke the words, 'Where's Charlie?' His father told him and John near beat him to death right there on the muddy road behind their house. Carried scars on his knuckles to remind him of that day when his worst nightmare came true.

Later, when he'd cooled off, John helped his father into the house and gave him a bag of ice for his face. They sat across from each other in the dark for a long time, his father in his chair, John on the couch. When his father was ready, John listened to him tell the story.

Charlie had run off less than a month after John boarded a bus full of GIs eager to fight the good fight. Or in John's case, escape from a bitter home. Charlie often hid in the woods or outback in a tent, so their father thought little of it. But those times John had been with Charlie, had been there to protect him and bring him home safe. 'Charlie would eventually come back, just like you from the war,' he said. It was no secret that their father despised Charlie, blamed him for their mother's death. She was the love of his life and granted him the only bit of order he'd ever possessed. John could hear it in his father's voice, even after the old man had been beaten senseless: Charlie was better off gone.

John had written to Charlie every month while he was away, unaware of the circumstances at home. Letters likely stacked somewhere in the house, or burned in the fireplace. John didn't want to know. It hurt too much to think about the letters going unread. Might as well have been lost at sea.

John clenched his teeth as the fire-breather reached a crescendo with two short bursts followed by an explosion that earned a few screams and burned away the fog from John's eyes. The man's mustache and eyebrows smoldered, but he bowed and went about collecting his things as if that was how the act was supposed to end. Fans dropped change in a small bucket he had set aside. John shuddered. How it could all go wrong in a blink.

Sailors on leave from Cleveland milled about discussing which attraction to head toward next, whether one more hot dog or beer was in order before hitting the bars on Brown and turning the night up a notch. Part of the crowd dispersed toward a tent containing 'Maxime The Glass Eater,' only to turn back upon hearing renewed cheers. John jumped to his feet. The fire act was only to warm up the crowd for the main event heading their way. A feeling in his fingertips said something important was about to happen. Like in the war when he'd taken cover seconds before a shell left a crater where he had once been standing.

But nothing did happen, at least for a short time. He lost hope. Perhaps he had imagined his brother's face on the flier. Night was quickly approaching and made it difficult to see, adding to his anxiety. But then he saw them, three silver orbs, shining in the twilight as they looped high in the air and then down, disappearing into the crowd. Before he could process the scene, John's legs were moving, eyes locked on the twinkling light. He didn't hear the jeers of those in his path. Didn't feel the wetness from spilled drinks as he knocked shoulders, bumping into groups on his way. He followed the act as it moved forward at a slow pace toward the center of the field. The three orbs were soon joined by a fourth and by the time it stopped moving, there were five flying high. John pushed his way through the growing circle until he reached the clearing.

A thin boy wrapped in black, white ruffles ringing his neck and hands, tossed the five spheres, faster and faster. First in a large circle, then in loops, his hands moving this way and that. The entertainer's outfit sagged on his arms like it had been soaked in water and was two sizes too big. John rubbed his eyes upon seeing the face of the boy. It was Charlie, right? It had to be. The boy's features faded in and out of focus in the gloom. His eyes were sunken shades and rough stubble was all that was left of the boy's once wild hair. For a split second the world around John became white as snow and the boy one of the many children he'd stumbled upon roaming the burnt out villages in the French countryside. Left behind, sick and malnourished, holding hands with death. The flashback punched him in the gut and he fell to his knees, clawing at his shirt. A red-headed dwarf with black lips and a torch circled the crowd, motioning with his hat to widen the circle. John could still smell the scents of burning hair and sweat left behind from the previous act. It made him gag, and he stumbled backward when the dwarf swung the torch near him. A second dwarf, dressed in matching black and white garb, stood next to the boy, two more silver orbs in his hands. Gasps from the crowd signaled their addition to the juggler's routine, now at seven.

Satisfied with the size of the circle, the black lipped dwarf buried his torch in the ground and retrieved a rusty tambourine from a suitcase full of juggling equipment. He slapped the instrument each time Charlie caught a ball, then every other time, alternating back and forth. Charlie—yes, it was Charlie, John was sure of it now—semi-danced to the noise, bending his knees and rocking his hips, still catching each ball like it was as natural as taking a breath. His hands were quick and sure—nothing like the awkward adolescent brother John remembered from the past. The crowd began to clap along with the beat of the tambourine, whooping and hollering as the orbs flew faster and faster. And then up each soared, one last time, higher than ever before, and down they came, falling quietly into an organized pile at Charlie's feet. John joined the fray, clapping like a mad man as the crowd roared with applause. Next came heavy pins in twos and threes and fours, tossed between legs and over shoulders. Each new act one-upping the previous stunt, a sight to behold. For the finale, fire was added to the mix. Charlie balanced a pin on his chin while the matching dwarf lit torch after torch, lining them up on the ground. The two assistants took turns handing Charlie the torches mid-juggle, until there were five sticks, burning bright and spinning through the air. The

Christopher L. Irvin

black lipped dwarf returned to the tambourine, whipping the crowd into a frenzy as the show reached the climax. And in a stunning finale, Charlie let the torches fall, as he had with the orbs, landing flame-side down, extinguishing as they plunged into the earth, burying the crowd in darkness. The fairgrounds shook with applause. The torches were re-lit, illuminating Charlie as he turned and bowed around the circle. The two assistants collected money in hats from a crowd that could barely contain the excitement. It was the greatest show John had ever seen.

When the commotion had died, John sat still, knees soaking up what little moisture the ground had left as Charlie piled his equipment into a beat up suitcase. First the balls, then the pins. Each arranged to fit, unlike the fire breather's haphazard exit. That was Charlie. His toys were always organized in a row beside his bed. The thought brought the first tears to John's eyes. Too much had passed, too much time lost running away. Charlie erupted into a coughing fit after finishing the pins, so hard his back arced like a cat and he leaned on a torch to prevent himself from collapse. When it was over he spit out a wad of dark cherry taffy-like phlegm. John screamed at his legs to move, to run to his brother's aid, but his muscles wouldn't respond. He looked down and discovered his hands caked with mud. He'd dug two fist sized holes during the performance, fingers aching from the filth scraped deep under his nails. Remembered he'd done this before, dug holes like this. Except the holes were larger and his fingernails ripped against the frozen soil. He closed his eyes as his ears began to hum. Concentrated on blocking out the images. The war would always be a constant companion, a reminder of lost time.

When he opened his eyes, Charlie had moved on, dragging the bag behind him across the field toward the tents. From the look of the objects tucked inside, the suitcase shouldn't have been heavy. Charlie tangled with it like it weighed over a hundred pounds, his face flush, reedy neck stretched taut.

John rubbed the clumps of dirt from his hands, dusted off what else he could on his pants and stood. Tears continued to well in his eyes. 'Charlie,' he said, barely a whisper. He repeated the name as he jogged after the juggler, his muscles tense and full of nervous energy. By the time his voice reached anything recognizable, his hands were on Charlie's shoulders, spinning him around. John pulled his brother into a tight hug and held him close. Felt bones, ribs and sharp shoulder blades through his thin shirt. The stubble covering his head felt rough and uneven like used sandpaper. Smelled of stale sweat and sickness. John's heart starved.

'What the hell man?' said Charlie, pushing back. 'Get off me.' Though Charlie had little strength, John let go and stood back. The brothers looked each other up and down. John's tears poured from his eyes. Couldn't remember a time when he'd cried so hard. The war, family, everything spilling out at the sight of poor Charlie. He looked like he'd been living in the gutter.

'What's happened to you, Charlie? It's me, John, your brother John.' He stepped forward with arms outstretched. Charlie backed up, almost tripping, almost falling over the juggling case.

'Who the hell is this guy, Charlie?' the black lipped dwarf said. Charlie shook his head, caught in a moment between remembering and forgetting. 'Who are you pal? You some queer?' John ignored him. 'Huh?' he piped up again.

'Charlie, it's me, John. I'm back from the war. I've been back, been looking for you.' He put a hand on Charlie's shoulder. 'It's been so long. I'm so—'

John felt pressure threatening his knee. The dwarf held one of the pins in both hands. 'Beat it pal, time's up. Plenty of other sights to see.' John ignored him again, turning back to Charlie. The dwarf cracked him in the shin. John cursed, ripped the pin from his hands and kicked him in the chest, sending him rolling away. Charlie stared at his fallen friend. John gripped his shirt, pulled him close. 'Stop this, Charlie. I know you're angry and I'm sorry. I'm sorry I left you. I'm sorry for everything.' He tried to rub away the tears but they wouldn't, couldn't stop. He could barely get the words out. 'I'm sorry. I had to leave. I just had to. It was the only way.'

He grabbed Charlie's neck and hugged him again, whispering, 'You believe me right? I'm here and I'm not leaving this time. We can be a family again.'

Charlie stood limp in his arms, watching the dwarf return with muscle. 'I'm afraid you've made a mistake, John.' John backed up to look Charlie in the face. 'You've made a mistake.' John didn't have enough time to follow Charlie's eyes over his shoulder. He was still in shock when The Strongest Man in the Midwest made an encore out of his face.

The strongman carried John over his shoulder as he would a towel after a long day of setup, pounding stakes and rigging rope. John was light work, even for muscles swollen from a night of performance. He reached for the flap of the manager's tent. Swept it aside and followed Charlie into the shadows within. The tent was easily twice the size of those containing the Oddities, even the 'Goldfish Girl's' which was custom made to accommodate her tank. Between the darkness and the manager's collections it felt cramped. The strongman shrugged John off his shoulder. He hit the ground with a thud, snapping awake, hands clutching at his throbbing skull. His face stung. Hot to the touch, like shrapnel caught him before he could duck. Took a breath in through his nose and gagged on a clot that loosened coppery blood into the back of his throat. Tried to stand but the strongman grabbed the scruff of his neck and dropped a knee onto his back, crushing the air out of his lungs. John craned his neck upwards, ribs screaming at him as he struggled to breathe under the star's weight. Flailed his arms, sprawling further out, finding nothing but hard-packed earth and clumps of grass. The strongman quickly took hold of his limbs, twisting them behind John's back and re-centering his bulk.

The loss of control hurt John the most.

Lanterns hung in the corners of the tent swaying in time with the breeze outside. Cast dim light over foreign crates that took up much of the office, highlighted trinkets from travels throughout the United States and abroad. Yards of silk and jade figurines, coffee and spices from Europe and the

Middle East. It smelled foreign. It smelled like war. The room dulled to the color of mud and faint memories of automatic gunfire echoed in the distance.

The sound of Charlie's hacking snapped John to attention. Charlie slumped on an unfinished wooden chair, legs splayed under his frail form. Dusky eyes blinked in slow motion, like he was close to falling asleep but chose instead to wake each time. Charlie. John couldn't find an ounce of air to fuel his voice. He grunted, pushed everything he had left into his legs, but he couldn't budge his captor.

'Please be still, sir,' Courbè said, hands busy with scraps of paperwork behind his expansive desk. 'The police have been notified of the incident.'

Courbè's voice pitched high, carried an air about it with French accents. John couldn't tell if it was faked or diluted from time spent away from Europe. Courbè hummed a tune, strumming stubby fingers along the desk. The carnival was close to another record-breaking week.

John recognized the rhythm but couldn't place it through the buzzing in his head. Charlie interrupted the tune with another fit. Tried to wipe blood away with his sleeve, but the white ruffles around his wrist left a smear from cheek to cheek. He smacked his lips like he was hungry. John couldn't tear his eyes from the horror, struggling again in the strong-man's grip, trying to get just a single word out.

'Oh, just let the fly stand, Enzo,' Courbè said. The strong-man obeyed, yanking John back to his knees. He kept a palm on his shoulder for good measure.

John quickly realized Courbè stood, not sat, behind a desk. Maybe five foot tall at best. He wore a discolored button down shirt, rolled at the sleeves with black suspenders. A tall black hat, scuffed around the edges perched on top of his oily curls. Misshapen objects with twists and funny angles that seemed to blur, held down stacks of paper that ruffled when the wind kicked through the tent flap.

'Let me go. Charlie, this is madness.' John spat pink. 'You're coming home with me.'

'And why would Charlie do that? Who are you?' Courbè

asked. He looked bored, eyes flicking momentarily from his work.

'I'm John. Charlie's brother.'

Courbè sighed like he'd heard it before. 'I'm afraid that's not possible. All of Charlie's brothers and sisters are here,' he said motioning with his arms to the festivities outside of the tent. 'Charlie is at home.'

'That's bullshit. You've… you've brainwashed him.' Charlie began to speak but stopped to cover his mouth. 'Look at him, he's sick, he needs help.'

'We have a doctor attending to Charlie. I can assure you he is in the best of care.'

'Charlie,' John said, dripping with desperation.

Courbè cut him off with barbed French. John twitched, nerves on edge. The buzzing in his ears quit. The gray scene fractured, reformed in full color as if a curtain had been raised on the final act. The tent, ruins in a bombed out city. Crates, the charcoal remnants of a family. Charlie's family. What was Charlie doing in France? It didn't matter, he was sick, part of the resistance that had been captured by Nazi sympathizers, Courbè and Enzo. If John didn't act fast, he and Charlie would be put down. He scanned the wreckage of the house for a weapon, anything left behind. Then he saw it, the stock of a rifle that had been placed muzzle-side down in a barrel. He sprung, interrupting Courbè mid-sentence, surprising Enzo with his speed. Ripped the rifle out of the barrel, slung it high on his shoulder and leveled it at the strongman.

'Get back,' he yelled, 'Charlie, let's go.'

Courbè laughed, slapped the desk. It was all a game to them. Paid off by the Nazis. Made rich for turning on their people, their allies. Enzo closed in on John, cutting off the exit. John pulled the trigger. Rifle clicked empty.

The ugly grin on Enzo's face grew so large, John swore it swallowed half the light in the tent. Before the strongman could flex his muscles, John had the rifle spun and swinging toward his face. Put him down with a clean shot to the ear and turned to Courbè. The Frenchman paled, clutched one of his strange objects tight to his chest.

'Don't hurt him,' Charlie croaked. He stood hunched, using the chair to hold himself up. 'Stop, I'm not Charlie. I'm not your brother.' John's eyes flitted between the pair. No doubt Charlie had been brainwashed by propaganda. He'd seen more than his share.

John quick-stepped to the exit and peeled back the flap, checking for the enemy, and finding none, motioned to Charlie, 'Come on, let's move.' Charlie turned to Courbè, his expression caught somewhere between thanks and regret. John grabbed his arm and pulled. Felt tendons stretch loose around bone. Wouldn't let the dead add his brother to their number. Charlie failed to protest through the pain.

'We don't have time for this. The city is lost; we need to move.' He pulled Charlie off the chair, put an arm around him as if he was placing a warm blanket over his shoulders. Used the rifle to sweep aside the tent flap and stepped out into the night. Neither looked back.

John hugged his brother close. Circled the tent, hid in the shadows. Contemplated their next move, shushing Charlie's flak. Shades gathered less than a hundred yards away, stood in a bunched line outside of a bombed out church. No, not a church. Confusion rattled the synapses in John's brain. For a brief moment, the snow cleared and he was back, both feet firmly planted in the fairgrounds, staring up at the lights of the Ferris wheel, grip relaxing on the rifle. His face flushed, anxiety threatening every instinct.

Poomff, Poomff.

Ears pricked at the subdued thud of artillery thumping into the air. Muscles tensed for action. And when the series of explosions rocked the sky, fireworks booming white, John was gone.

'Take cover,' he shouted, running low with Charlie across the field, diving behind the cab of a rusty truck as artillery zeroed in on their position. Wailing sirens of closing police cars signaled the air raid. He should have killed Courbè when he had the chance.

'Shit, I thought we'd pushed past this town.' John leaned against the front tire of the truck, rifle gripped tight to his

Christopher L. Irvin

chest. 'Who would have thought our last jump would have been into the middle of a shit storm.' He shook with each explosion. Screams from the crowd sliced through him. Nothing he could do to save them. Sirens cut off as police entered the field.

John stood, dared a look over the truck's engine. 'I think it's over.' Three cherries blinked in the distance. Charlie gripped his chest. Sniffed back salt as tears streamed down his face.

'It's going to be okay, Charlie. I'll get us out of—'Poomff, Poomff, Poomff.

'Shit, it's still on. We've got to move.'

Charlie's hands hit the dirt. Seized as the sickness squeezed his insides. Struggled to form words.

'I can't—'

'We'll hold this position, Charlie.' John rubbed a loving hand over his brother's back. Felt the nubs of his spine. 'Hold it as long as we damn well can.' His voice calm. He placed the stock of the rifle in his gut and racked the action. Discharged a tarnished casing that disappeared into the dark. Pasted a death grin on his face. 'Ready?'

Charlie sputtered to life, pushing to his knees. He grabbed hold of John's shirt with both hands. Sprayed blood as he spoke. 'I can't go back, John. I just can't.'

'But it's the only way out.'

'No, you're mad. Listen to me, John,' he cried, 'It's me, Charlie. Your brother, Charlie.'

John pierced Charlie's almond eyes, behind the tears, deep into the depths where his pupils turned charcoal black. Could almost see a reflection of himself. Maybe a hint of what Charlie had lost. What he'd left behind.

'No. You're not.'

He stood, blinked back salt that blurred his vision. Covered up behind the cab as the blue revolvers zeroed in. Cried out as the rifle spat invisible fire, downing nightmares as rounds ricocheted off the hood into his chest. Felt the boy pounce on him when he fell, suck warmth from his body. Felt at home watching their blood swirl. Brothers of a sort. That's all he could ever ask for.

She's My Witch

Paul D. Brazill

Friday was just a dull throb. Saturday ached and nagged like a rotten tooth. But Sunday was bone crunching agony. The rest of the days and nights were soldered tightly shut until my fever finally erupted.

My burning eyes ripped open.

I was strapped to a stinking bed in the back room of Duffy's Bar, the sleaziest dive in The City - no mean feat when you're talking about that neon-soaked, blood-spattered hell-hole that I called home. The freezing cold room was lit muddy brown. The wisps of a Kip Tyler song drifted in from the bar. The dirty twang of the guitar reverberated through my bones. I started to laugh when I recalled the title but the pain, like the kick in the eye from a stiletto heel, sharply turned everything black.

Cherchez la femme fatale, of course.

Unlike most of the rest of the world I was more than somewhat pleased to face the cold, grey light of Monday morning. Not being dead was not to be sneezed at. Not that I was in the best shape. I was clammy with drying sweat and stank so much even I felt like gagging. My skin was red raw, where I'd been scratching in my delirium. And more.

A shuffling sound in the darkness. A silhouette moved towards the bed and became the shape of a man.

'The Kraken of dawn awakes,' said Duffy.

He sniffed. Switched on a twisted angle-poise lamp which gave off a thankfully dim glow.

Duffy squinted at me and didn't seem too impressed by what he saw. He scratched his acne scarred face.

'I was going to say that you look like a piece of shit but that would be an insult to pieces of shit,' he said.

He checked his reflection in a dusty spider-web cracked mirror. Took out a switchblade comb and carefully sculpted his inky black quiff. He was dressed in a sharp black suit and tie, and a pristine white shirt. His shiny black winkle picker shoes reflected light from the lamp. As of late, Duffy had been looking uncharacteristically smart. A suave fuck, in fact.

Me, I'd been looking even worse than usual. And 'usual' hadn't really been so hot for a long time. Not since I'd been savaged by a gang of werewolf bikers that had been trashing Duffy's Bar. The next full moon,a grizzled, hardboiled cop turned into a werewolf, who then had the brilliant idea of becoming a private eye.

It had been a colourful life since then, no doubt about it. Gaudy, even. Usually painted in shades of red with splashes of black. But that was just life in The City these days. Neon and blood soaked nights. Grey, rain drenched days.

The City had been my home for as long as I cared to remember. Which was far too long, to be sure. But here I stayed, picking up the odd and even odder case. Boozing at Duffy's Bar - alone or with my former partner Detective Ivan Walker. Or maybe some of the other waifs and strays that were drawn toward Duffy's like a lighthouse guiding them toward the rocks. And, despite the occasional life-or-death moment I'd been getting by.

'You want me to strap you in again tonight?' said Duffy.

He pulled a bottle of perfume out of his jacket pocket and splashed it all over. Took a little nip. Coughed.

'Naw, I think the shit's out of my system,' I said.

'That's what you get for boozing with a Gypsy Woman. Slip you a Micky Finn and rip off your wallet. They can't help it. It's the way of their people.'

'You're not the most politically correct soul, are you Duffy?'

'Depends on your politics,' he said.

It was one of those infrequent full moons when I had transformed into a werewolf but still had some semblance of control over my behaviour, my human personality to the fore. And I must admit, when I was like this, being a werewolf was a hell of a lot of fun.

I was perched on top of the Basilica suffering indigestion after feasting on a couple of Ton Ton Philippe's zombie henchmen. Philippe was a nightclub owner, pimp, drug dealer, gangster, and more. He was into as many of the various strands of voodoo as you could name, too and the potions he used to turn the suckers into the walking dead really didn't agree with my insides.

There was a thick fog threatening to smother The City that night and only sharp pin pricks of neon light pierced the mist. I punched my chest with a hairy fist and let out a litany of loud burps. I felt much better after that. A clock chimed-in the witching hour and I decided to head off and see which other dregs of society I could polish off before dawn.

I knew it was better to try and keep away from Ton Ton and his crew. He had more than a few reasons to be really pissed off with me and had surely been out for revenge for a long time. Why he hadn't struck yet was something I pushed to the back of my booze and moon-addled mind. But I knew it wouldn't be long.

Ton Ton's biggest rival in The City was Count Otto Rhino. Rhino was ostensibly a legitimate businessman whose high-rise, Rhino Towers, loomed impressively over The City. But he also had his finger in more than a few dodgy pies. Although, to be fair, we hadn't had any real run-ins, and, in fact, I'd helped out one of his coterie a couple of times. An emerald eyed torch singer known as Daria.

Otto's thug foot soldiers, The Frog Boys, had been shaking up The City a bit too much for my liking of late, though. And I hadn't munched on any Escargot for a while. The Frog Boys weren't supernatural beings, like Ton Ton's zombies, they were more the product of a warped scientific experiment gone wrong but they could do enough damage alright. They were massive, muscle-bound, near identical skinheads with a propensity for wearing military fatigues and ripping people's heads off with their bare hands when they were angry. Which was a lot. Once upon a time they had been completely out of control until Otto found a way to dominate them: Daria whose siren song calmed their rage and made them her slaves.

So, I finished pissing over the dome of the Basilica and prepared to head off to Rhino Towers when, in amongst the usual screams, howls, sirens and gunshots, I heard an insistent drumbeat. A slow but forceful, skipping rhythm. Like a funeral march.

I leapt off the Basilica and onto the roof of the Inter-Euro Hotel where I could hear the drumbeat getting louder. As I raced across The City's rooftops, I heard the sounds of chanting. And through the soupy mist, I could see a stream of lights. A motorcade of lanterns was moving through The City like an uncoiled python ready to strike. Then more sounds. More instruments. Whistling. Laughter. Singing.

I perched on the roof of a red telephone box and watched the parade slowly pass by. Men and women were dressed in black suits and black wide-brimmed hats, and wearing white masks that were more than familiar. Painfully so. The same masks adorned the black banners that they carried. A face. The face of The Missionary.

There was a time when The City's darkest denizens kept to the shadows. When they were just whispers. Rumours that caught the wind. And for years there were rumours of a vigilante known as The Missionary who assassinated the depraved and decedent. The corrupt. The legend had it that he raised his bible high and sang like an angel before dispatching his victims to a hell even worse than The City.

He also killed the weak and fallow. The losers. The dregs of The City. The drunks and the junkies. Vampires, zombies and cannibals. Werewolves. And one booze-addled night, I heard that he was ready to kill me.

So, I went undercover as a homeless man and caught him. With Duffy's help, I killed him. Or thought I had, until his body disappeared from the morgue, leaving another corpse behind him.

The Missionary had disappeared without a trace. Until now.

I watched the parade trail off into the hills outside The City and furtively followed. A large crimson tent was pitched at the top of a hill. The image of The Missionary's face adorned its sides. At the back of the tent was a semi-circle of black caravans and a handful of jeeps. The parade marched into the tent and as I grew closer I climbed into the centre of a lightning damaged tree. After a moment, I could make out what they were singing.

Jesus Blood Never Failed Me Yet.

The Missionary's execution song.

A chill sliced through me. Anger erupted inside me, my eyes grew red and I let out a howl that silenced their voices.

The area was suddenly lit up by lanterns. Multi-coloured lights flashed on and off. And a flickering neon sign outside the tent said 'Welcome To The Carnival Of Fate.'

By the look of him, Detective Ivan Walker wanted to shoot the messenger and everyone in Duffy's Bar, which was, thankfully, pretty much deserted. A heavy mid-morning downpour had cleared the streets and Duffy's only customers were me and Ivan Walker. Walker had knocked back his death-black espresso and was looking longingly at the glimmering bottles of whisky behind the bar. Walker rarely touched the booze these days and when he did it usually meant trouble.

I sipped my bottle of Becks and wandered over to the Wurlitzer Jukebox. I slammed my hand down on the top and it creaked and yawned to life. 'Oh, Happy Day.' Hardly.

I sat back down next to Walker.

'It must be him,' he said.

The Missionary had killed a close personal friend of Walker's and Ivan's cold heart had been set on vengeance ever since.

'Only one way to find out,' I suppose, said Duffy, as he shuffled around the room with a dirty mop, attempting to clean up the bloodstains from the wooden floorboards. 'Best go over there.'

'Is it a full moon tonight?' said Walker.

He stretched out a long arm and plucked a bottle of Dark Valentine from behind the bar with his bony fingers.

'Nah,' I yawned. 'I've had three nights on the prowl. It's not my time of the month now.'

'Maybe we'll go as customers?' said Duffy. 'Undercover, like.'

He poured us all a shot of DV and plucked a rolled up National Geographic from the back pocket of his ragged jeans. He leaned against the bar and flicked through, stopping at a photograph of a big breasted mermaid that was said to have been caught feasting on the bums that lived down near The City's canal.

Duffy made a harrumphing sound. 'It's like a circus every day in here,' he said, and nodded toward the door as a massive bald-headed man dressed in a black leather overcoat and riding boots stormed into the bar .

'What can I get you?' said Duffy.

The giant just grunted and handed a silver envelope to Duffy. He saluted, clicked his heels and left. Duffy opened the envelope.

'Looks like we've got an invite,' said Duffy.

I took the paper out of his hand. It said that Duffy's bar and patrons were invited to a 'special preview' of 'The Carnival Of Fate.'

'Well, there you go then,' said Walker. 'Tonight's the night.'

The evening eventually melted into night and, fortified by more than a few shots of Dark Valentine, Walker and I waited as Duffy pulled down the metal shutters and locked up the bar.

We piled into the back of Duffy's yellow taxi and listened to Mel Torme as we checked our weapons. Walker had his usual Colt Anaconda. I had a Glock. And Duffy had an AK-47 that he'd kept as a souvenir of his military days.

'Old faithful, eh,' said Walker, as he eyed the gun. Duffy nodded. He and Walker had served together during 'Operation Desert Wave.' And they shared some dark secrets.

'Let's go for it,' I said. Duffy started up the cab and we drove in silence to the outskirts of The City.

The carnival was alight with neon, lanterns, multi-coloured torches. As we approached the crimson circus tent, music blasted out of speakers attached to the trees.

Duffy parked up the taxi a short distance from the tent. We all pulled on our identical black leather trench coats – Duffy had bought them cheap as a job-lot from a one armed Polish sailor – and hid our guns beneath them.

'Into the valley,' said Walker.

'Betrothed and divine,' said Duffy.

They did that a lot. It must have been some army thing. I didn't have a clue what they were talking about, though. We slowly trudged up the hill and somehow I was sharply sober.

A Salvation Army Band stood outside the tent playing the old hymn about Angels Watching Over Me. Foreshadowing, hopefully.

The bald giant who had been in Duffy's bar earlier was in the front of the band playing a big, bass drum that was emblazoned with a cartoon image of The Missionary. A midget dressed as a ringmaster sat on the giant's shoulders, waving a baton and chanting: 'One, two, three, one, two, three.'

'Well, this place is certainly… something,' I said.

Walker made that familiar low purring sound that made me wonder which one of us was actually part-beast. I waited for a wisecrack from Duffy but heard nothing. I turned and saw that he was trailing towards a massive gold cage. On the side of the cage was a badly hand-painted wooden sign: Lulu California - Destiny Dancer.

As we got closer, we could see a spotlight pinpointing the corner of the cage.

Fireworks filled the sky. A hunchbacked accordion player limped toward us and started playing a tarantella. A dark shape in the cage's corner seemed to unfold into that of a naked woman. A beautiful woman with red lipstick and a sharp black bob hairdo. Louise Brooks, star of the silent screen. Or close enough.

All three of us were magnetically drawn towards the cage as she danced. We were almost touching the bars when she started to laugh. To shake with laughter. To shake so much that her body twisted and turned and transformed. Into The Missionary.

The laughter stopped. The music stopped. And the world was plunged into darkness.

I can't remember who it was but some old comedian once said: Never Give A Sucker An Even Break. And to say that Walker, Duffy and I were suckers was a bit of an understatement.

When the darkness washed away, I could see that we were in the middle of the circus ring. Strapped to three black totem poles.

The giant, the midget still wrapped around his neck, stood in front of us banging the drum. Snarling. A fire-eater darted around us breathing flames that singed my eyebrows. In the crowd, I could make out about forty or fifty people dressed as The Missionary.

The drummer changed the rhythm to a waltz and the crowd began to sing.

Jesus Blood Never Failed Me Yet.

Beautiful and terrifying.

I glanced at Duffy and Walker and like me they were struggling to break free but getting nowhere.

Then the crowd rose to their feet and started to pray. The giant looked above, a smirk on his face. From high, The Missionary seemed to float down, making the shape of a cross. A Luger in each hand. Until he stood directly in front of us. Black wide brimmed hat. Black suit. And a face as white as fear.

He crossed the pistols and there was silence.

'We have been waiting so long, gentlemen. So long to

send you into the oblivion that you deserve. And I have no patience to wait longer.'

And the music began again. Louder. Fiercer.

Jesus Blood Never Failed Me Yet. Never Failed Me Yet. Jesus Blood.

But then another voice seemed to rise over that of The Missionary. To swamp the sound of the crowd. Not louder just more intense. A familiar voice. A chill skewered me.

The Missionary was frozen, like a statue.

And then it was Armageddon. There were so many Frog Boys that it was impossible to count how many. Their eyes glowed bright green as they burst into the tent and tore into the crowd with batons, baseball bats. Hammers, chainsaws. Their bare hands. Ripped them to shreds. A big man with a bushy beard and a lumberjack shirt had his arms torn from his body. An old woman with a wild look in her eyes leapt onto the back of one of The Frog Boys who pulled her head clean from her torso and threw it into the air. A chubby clown was disembowelled with a chainsaw splattering all around him. I turned to look at Duffy and Walker and they were laughing.

The old woman's head was quickly used for an impromptu game of football. The midget was used for another. He screamed with every kick. Duffy had tears of laughter in his eyes but Walker had stopped laughing and was staring intently toward the entrance.

Daria seemed to float through the carnage. Long hair as black as a raven's wings, she was wearing a shimmering black gown. Green eyes sparkling. Her arms outstretched, she seemed to be increasing the pitch of her singing. And then there was silence apart from the achingly beautiful sound of Daria's voice.

As she closed on The Missionary, she winked and his whole body shattered to dust.

'Took your time, I said.

She bent over and scooped up The Missionary's powdered remains. Popped them into a green and gold shoulder bag.

'You know that I do like a dramatic entrance, Roman,' she said. She kissed me on the lips. Hugged me.

'We're quits now, okay?' she said.

'Okay. For now…'

She turned, stepped over the giant's headless corpse, and elegantly walked away, humming a familiar tune. At the entrance to the tent, she clicked her fingers and The Frog Boys, drpping with blood and entrails, dropped their weapons and trailed after her, their heads bent. Obedient, as always.

'Hey, Daria, aren't you going to set us free?' shouted Duffy.

'Now, you can't have everything boys,' she said. 'And, anyway, Roman has such sharp teeth.'

'You played that card close to your chest,' said Duffy, when she'd gone.

'Well, I wasn't exactly one hundred per cent sure she'd turn up. She's…'

'She's a witch,' hissed Walker.

'That may well be,' I said, cutting into my bonds with the knife that Daria had slipped into my hand. 'But she's my witch.'

The Mermaid Illusion

Carol Borden

I always sang. I always had, one way or another. It's how I made my living before Dr. Griffen discovered me. Dr. James Phorcius Griffen's Caravan of Splendor isn't my first memory, but everything before the Caravan seems so diffuse, a blur of shifting light and sound. There's only before and after the Caravan. Everything became solid, discrete, more real. Dr. Griffen even gave me a new name for my life in his carnival. He tried several, Galatea, Sirena, Selene, before settling on Eudora, the Fairest Daughter of King Neptune. Mixing Greek and Latin never bothered Griffen if the result were 'euphonious' and profitable. It did not bother him at all that Eudora was not my name. It seems obvious now that everything should go wrong.

Dr. Griffen preferred to speak in purple prose, but he could speak English like the rest of us if the situation required it. He was all damask, flocking, bowlers and swallowtail coats. And he was diabolically handsome with sharp eyebrows and a thin mustache. The young women who visited the carnival giggled and glanced.

He took me in, and I am grateful for that. He taught me to dress and walk like a lady. He told me to say I had come from overseas when asked, to create an air of mystery. He taught me to sound more sophisticated and 'pleasant.' He took care of my finances and invested my earnings. And he found me a place among the carnival folk, the human wonders, anomalies and oddities, but he did not encourage fraternization with them, especially when I began to be friendly with the Karl Manko, the Wolf-Boy.

'A matter of class,' he said, patting my hand as he led me from the communal mess hall to my private trailer.

'Oh, lady, be good to me...' I sang, before the opening show. Dr. Griffen shushed me.

'What is our rule, Eudora?' he asked, the picture of patience.

'No singing.' The rule was publicly posted, to add to the effect, as Dr. Griffen liked to say.

The Pavilion of Undersea Wonders was filled with stuffed curiosities and anatomical exhibits, a chart postulating my branch on the evolutionary tree, and a nautical mess of netting, rigging, navigational instruments and harpoon heads. In the center, surrounded by a crowd, I performed in a woman-sized fishbowl as The Mermaid Eudora. My performance was easy work—look fetching, flash some tail, as Dr. Griffen delivered a lecture speculating on my peculiar natural history.

Swimming around and around in my tank, I observed the distorted life around me. I watched the crowd. Most listened attentively and laughed at Dr. Griffen's practiced jokes. The smart marks, who enjoyed testing the limits of illusion, circled around and around the tank, trying to find the trick. They sniffed with derisive satisfaction at the glittering scales I molted at the bottom of the tank. But the impossibly-colored scales were not a sign of shoddy workmanship, they were mine.

Between acts, I listened to the Scopes Trial on the wireless. Dr. Griffen shared my interest. 'He would have made one hell of a talker,' he said when William Jennings Bryan, Dudley Field Malone or WGN announcer Anthony Quinn started to wind up.

When the trial was over, I read a lot of books about biology and natural science. Dr. Griffen encouraged me, though he had other plans 'for our mutual benefit,' he said. He said he had some interesting potential partners in the scientific community and that soon our investments would pay off. He would build a grand museum, The Grand Oasis of Wonder, and I would be its star. I nodded and turned back to the books.

I needed to learn, but how I wanted to sing.

I only left the carnival grounds when Dr. Griffen wanted to show me off to wealthy and influential friends he cultivated. He had already moved the show—and me, fish tank and all—to a building he rented while work was completed on his museum. Dr. Griffen introduced me to his society friends. We dined at Pierre's on the Park, the Russian Tea Room and the Plaza's Champagne Porch. He told me how soon I would have a whole tank carved from the finest Italian marble and inset with crystal viewing windows. 'A palace fit for the daughter of Neptune himself!'

No matter how chaste Dr. Griffen avowed his affections were, I knew they were not and I could not transform my feelings no matter how I tried. Gratitude is not love. He claimed that it was no matter, that helping a charming 'fish out of water' was reward in itself.

Dr. Griffen was lying, not to me, but, worse, to himself. And I could feel his resentment building, tidal rage moving, even if he did not. Desire and greed, and possibly, love, tangled together and thrashing.

He stared at my lips. I quickly turned our conversation to my performance. Even then, I think I could feel a plan moving deep inside me.

No one will believe I did it. I am, after all, just a woman to them. They will all think that I tricked Karl the Wolf-Boy, that naïve dope, with my feminine charms. But people underestimate Karl. He understood. We had both lost a lot, and the little absences inside us tugged at each other.

Sometimes I think all human beings are is loss, just collections of absences, little empty boxes piled on top of each other walking down the street, hanging from a strap on the train, smoking on stoops or making sideshow props on an old table.

With his long face, heavy jowls and sad, black-rimmed eyes, Karl looked more like a hound to me, but 'Wolf-Boy' was a better draw than, 'The Human Hound.' Karl worked hard at being as peripheral as possible and even with the soft brown fur on his face and hands, Karl was easily over-looked.. All his clothes were over a decade out of style, but neatly repaired. Karl dressed to conceal himself. His shirt was always buttoned to the top, with tufts of hair curled over the collar. Whenever he was outside, he wore his trench coat. Karl wore his loss and he would never take it off. Silently shuffling around the grounds, Karl cramped his big body into the smallest shapes he could, while Dr. Griffen indicated nec-essary repairs with a wave of an immaculate dove-gray glove.

Dr. Griffen encouraged Karl not to speak, he thought it suited 'The Creature Who Is More Beast Than Man' , but Karl talked plenty when he'd been drinking or in his sleep, whim-pering himself awake late at night. Giving up on sleep, he would work on new props and gaffs until he was exhausted. Karl made the gaffs in my tent: The narwhal skull for 'the Unicorn of the Sea'; a mummified 'Gill-Man'; Blackbeard the Pirate's death mask; the last breath of a drowned man; the tattooed chests of flayed Viking sailors. As the carnival pros-pered, the best ended up in Griffen's museum. The first night I sat with him, while he worked on a devil baby for another act.

The Caravan of Splendor had not always been so splendid, according to Karl. 'Just a few trailers and later, the trucks. We drove a circuit of broke down towns filled with broke down people. Not year round like now and never in the city, before you.'

I nodded, watching him sew tiny sutures joining leather and rubber.

Karl stubbed out his cigarette. 'She didn't like to smell it on my fur.'

He said that every time he extinguished one. He felt just as guilty when he wasn't smoking as when he did. He felt like a failure no matter what he did. Karl had returned from the Great War to discover his wife, Lucy, had died of influenza while he was in France. The black edged letter informing him of her death had missed him in the crossing. Since then Karl had been trying to catch up with death.

A few nights later, Karl was working on a new project. He was carefully pulling wire tight with small pliers, attaching something to a shark. His big hands were meticulous and displayed far more confidence than he usually did.

'What are you making?

'A two-headed shark.'

'Kinda small.'

'Just a baby. Got'em at the Fish Market. Figure Griffen will come up with a fancy story for it.'

An unused tail sat on the table next to neat piles of wire clippings, fishing line, cotton wadding, newspaper and salt. I reached into my pocket and pulled out a handful of scales I'd collected from the bottom of my tank and poured them out carefully. The slight luminosity made Karl glance up from his work.

'What for?'

'I thought you could make something.'

Karl was quiet, sewing imperceptible stitches.

'A mermaid. I'll make a mermaid,' He finally said.

'Like the Feejee Mermaid?'

He smiled., 'Looking for a new gig , huh?'

'Looks like.'

'Attagirl.'

The Oasis was nearly complete. In anticipation, the Caravan's crowds were getting bigger. And my days were getting longer as I swam and smiled, twirled and fanned my tail while Dr. Griffen lectured the crowd on my points of interest.

In the evening, I would put Dr. Griffen off, saying I was exhausted from the crowds. He humored me, though he wasn't growing any more patient. I could see it on him, as if he could feel me getting away. Greed, hooked right into him.

After closing one night, he brought a bucket of iced champagne to my tent. Behind him, one of the roustabouts carried a covered tray. 'I thought we might have a little late supper together, my dear.'

Dr. Griffen glanced at Karl and the work on the table.

'What is that remarkable creature?.'

Karl looked at me. I gave a little shrug.

'See for yourself,' Karl said as he carefully unwrapped the mermaid. Dr. Griffen examined it carefully, half monkey and half fish with wildly-colored scales that effloresced in the dim light.

'Simply magnificent, Karl. You have a gift. A gift, indeed.' He handed the gaff back to Karl, giving him a pointed look.

Karl cleared his tools off the table and disappeared. The roustabout slid the tray onto the table, lit a candle to set a romantic mood and made himself scarce, too.

'This is a very special meal for a very special occasion—the anniversary of your arrival among us.' Dr. Griffen exclaimed, removing the lid with a flourish. 'Beluga caviar, sole almondine, steamed lobster, the delights of the sea--straight from the Waldorf to you!' An aspic wobbled in the center of the dishes.

He popped the cork on the bottle of champagne and laughed as it foamed. 'How delightful! One could almost think your delicate hand had been formed from foam such as this.'

He kissed my hand before handing me a fluted glass. 'To, beauty, my dear. Amor vincit omnia!'

Here it was. Dr. Griffen's big push. He wanted to get married—it would be the Ceremony of the Century. 'The arrangements at the museum will make Burnham's White City look like a pasteboard sham! Can you imagine, The Man and His Mermaid? The tamed siren revealed and standing before all, the simple bride of man!'

'I can.'

'You mean, 'I will,' darling.' He said clasping my hands to his chest. I could feel his blood pulsing beneath my fingers.

'I can imagine it and it's just...'

'You're overwhelmed. The excitement has left you speechless.' He craned in to kiss me.

I kept my arms between us. 'No. I'm not. I don't love you.' He froze.

'I don't love you, Dr. Griffen.'

'Oh, darling, one of your kind can't be expected to know love, not right away—I will teach you.'

Dr. Griffen cajoled and pleaded. He shouted and shook me. He called me, 'hussy,' and, 'frigid.' He called me, 'temptress.' He cried, apologizing for his unseemly longings. He demanded I stop tormenting him. He called my kind, 'soulless' and 'venal.' When he finally called me 'whore' I knew I was leaving.

I agreed to marry him and endured until he left, drunkenly blowing kisses and planning the Ceremony of the Century. Then I packed my things—two dresses, a pair of silk stockings, my fox stole and my much shabbier black wool coat, a little cloche hat, and my empty pocket-book. And I lit out.

Good-bye, Caravan of Wonders. Good-bye, Dr. Griffen. And good-bye, silence.

I felt a little twinge when I set fire to my trailer and to the exhibit with my mermaid still inside. But that feeling could not bear much examination. In fact, in some ways, the fires were the easiest part, just burning old scales and bones. At least the bones weren't mine.

Karl came into the light beside me and watched the flames take hold of the exhibit, his work and his tools.

'I'm sorry.' I did not know what else to say. We stood together and watched the fire.

'Here. I know Griffen keeps your money. Wherever you're headed, you'll need this.' He handed me a wad of bills wrapped in a handkerchief with the initials 'L.M.' embroidered in the corner.

'I saved nearly a dime for Luce and me. Never figured out what to do with it.'

'Karl...' I started, but I did not know how to finish. He was right. I had no money. Griffen had invested mine in his museum.

I kissed Karl on his cheek.

'Woulda been nice to hear you sing.'

So I sang.

I booked a ticket to Chicago. Swaying to the sounds of the train, I wanted to cry when the engineer sounded the horn. I was going to sing again and nobody could stop me. I was going to sing for myself this time.

I asked a girl to bob my hair in the ladies' lounge. I changed my name to, 'Edie.' and sat in the dining car with all the other weary, excited, travelers and chatted about nothing. At dinner, a new acquaintance showed me a newspaper story about the carnival fire, and exclaimed about the tragic loss of a young woman, 'Miss Eudora Achelos, recently affianced to noted showman, Dr. James P. Griffen.'

My companion shook her head. 'Why, she might almost be your age!'

'You just never know,' I agreed.

But I wasn't dead. I had slipped the line and I was never going back.

I made my way in the speakeasies that provided entertainment to help their bathtub gin go down a little more smoothly. After Prohibition, I sang in the clubs in the Loop. I only sang love songs, because my heart was not in them. I never sang about homesickness and I never took requests. I drew enough patrons that the floor managers didn't mind. I was more than a curiosity. I was more than my nature, but I still felt a tidal tug, even here in Chicago where the tide is just a few imperceptible inches. I still felt the water, but it felt like it was running out of me.

By the summer of 1933, I had almost gotten enough money together for my own club. I planned to call it Lorelei's. A lot of my admirers assumed I was German because of my accent, so it provided some extra cover. So many Germans had emigrated to the United States, the situation in Europe being what it was. I have to say, though, I don't pay much attention to the world's troubles, I keep an eye out for my own.

I knew trouble was finally swimming right toward me one morning at breakfast when I saw Griffen's name in the society column, 'The World Famous Dr. James P. Griffen, M.D. Ph.D.' He was in Chicago. 'My business is most assuredly of a personal nature,' he was quoted as saying.

He knew. He knew I hadn't died in the fire that had destroyed so much carnival property. He knew I was responsible somehow. Worst of all, he knew that I was here. It would not take long for Griffen to find me. I felt washed up on the shore, beached.

I decided to find Griffen first. I would not let anyone take my life away from me again. According to The Tribune, he was staying at the Palmer House. Griffen always was showy.

A bellhop told me that Griffen lunched in the Empire Dining room everyday at one o'clock. I tipped the hop well-enough for him not to tip off Griffen. It was just noon and I sat down to wait in the lobby. I gazed at the Regal mural on the ceiling until Aphrodite and I had enough of one another. Then I gazed at my gloved hands in my lap and thought of coral, waving kelp, the flash of fish.

At one o'clock sharp, Griffen was at his newly-acquired usual seat, about to order his newly-acquired usual dinner. He was a man of carefully-created and lovingly-nurtured, affected routine.

'Don't bother to stand,' I said, as a waiter hurried to seat me.

Griffen stared at me, a vision of apoplexy. 'How dare you!'

'I would dare a lot. You already know that I would, Dr. Griffen. How did you find me?'

'My dear, your heart has become so rotten, I could smell it from the Algonquin Hotel, ' Griffen said.

The waiter paused just a moment, and then became selectively deaf to unpleasantness. He was good.

'I wonder, how could I have ever left?' I snapped open my bag and pulled a cigarette from a black enamel case. I leaned forward for Griffen to light it, but he pointedly did not. The waiter offered a blue enamelled lighter.

'All charm.' The waiter's chest puffed. He was going to pop a button.

'Would, Mademoiselle care for a menu?'

'No, Mademoiselle would not.' Griffen's face was so red I thought he would pop a blood vessel.

'Indeed,' I said glancing at Griffen, 'Mademoiselle would. Mademoiselle is famished.'

'Of course,' The waiter said, opening the menu and leaving it in front of me. His selective deafness was probably great for his blood pressure.

'You're coming back with me, Eudora.'

'That's not my name.'

'I know your name.'

'I'm Edie now.'

'I know your real name.'

'Aren't you clever?' I blew a smoke ring.

'As you discovered for yourself, the library is quite helpful. You're coming back with me. You will pack and we will have just enough time to book passage on the Empire Express to New York. First class, of course.'

'Of course.' I would not be going back to New York, but Griffen didn't know it.

I looked at the waiter. He raised his pencil. 'The crab cakes, please. And a stinger.'

Griffen looked disgusted. He had worked so diligently to teach me to be a lady. 'All wasted,' he muttered.

'Aren't you going to eat—or have I spoiled your appetite?'

The waiter looked to Griffen expectantly. 'A steak well-done and frites.' He frowned and added, 'And a bicarbonate of soda.'

'You're different, Eudora,' He looked me over. 'But not that different.'

I sipped my stinger. What else was there to do?

After lunch, Griffen said, 'I will walk you back to your apartment. I wouldn't want you to get lost on the way.' He smiled, enjoying his own wit. I suspected no one else did.

It was mid-afternoon, humid, hot and still. 'Let's go down to the Lake,' I said.

'No,' Griffen said, wiping his forehead with his handkerchief. He was running hot and cold sweat. He took my elbow as if he were a gentleman being solicitous of a lady, but I didn't mind. The sky was clear, the air was close and I felt fine.

The heat had driven almost everyone indoors by the time we reached my apartment. The building was on Monroe St. It was well-appointed, but not well-known. I was fond of the Art Deco gargoyles on the cornices. The lobby was carpeted and cool, with a modern wood paneled desk for the concierge. The elevator doors were polished wood and steel and the elevator attendant wore a plain black suit. He smiled and nodded, but Griffen's presence kept him silent.

Griffen offered to unlock my door, but I demurred. Griffen smiled, expansive in victory and in the coolness of the building. 'My dear lady, after you.'

I opened the door and tossed my coat, gloves and pocketbook on a table by the door. I did not offer to take Griffen's coat. Let him stew. I walked out of the foyer into the living room and across to my bedroom.

'Pack just enough for the trip, Eudora. I still have your old things in New York. You can send for anything else.' He was hovering in the doorway as close as his sense of propriety would allow.

I pulled out a small traveling suitcase and packed a dress, a pair of silk stockings, some underthings, a comb and a tube of lip rouge. Griffen took my bag from my hand and I followed him silently down to the street.

I was so close to being free.

'Let's go to the Lake,' I said. 'I'd sort of like to say good-bye.'

'We have a train to catch.'

'Let's go to the Lake, James. There's time. It's not far.' I took his hand and felt a tremor. I led him along Monroe St. till we reached the harbor.

I kicked off my shoes and felt the boardwalk cool and damp beneath my feet. The Lake sang to me through the slats. I started to hum.

'No, Eudora. Stop...' Griffen told me, dropping my suitcase and raising a small revolver. 'Don't do this. There's only one way this can end.'

I started to sing, a song without words but unimaginable longing. I felt that twinge again, as I reached toward him. Sometimes, I think that it was my conscience, but the truth is that killing did not bother me. It was nature. The big fish eats the little fish, the little fish stings and poisons the big fish. It was survival of the fittest. It was my nature. My song is an adaptation. My human appearance, protective coloration.

It was easy. It always was easy, like slipping into a perfect bath.

'I know how it feels to be in too deep,' I said. I had felt the lure myself, when I walked out of the water the first time.

His hand was shaking, but he kept the gun on me. His whole body was shaking as he walked toward me. 'No, Eudora, don't do this to me...'

'You did this to yourself, James. This is how it always ends. We do it to ourselves.'

We stood together, the Lake, calm and smooth just below us. He fired one shot, and I dragged him under.

Natural Flavoring

Rebecca Snow

Wayne Krenski leaned against the scratched strip of Formica that separated the internal operations of his booth from the rest of the park. The sun had set an hour before in a flurry of wispy pinks and yellows, but the flashing lights on the coasters gave the darkened sky an unnatural twilit glow. A group of adolescent girls giggled past his stand. Wayne dragged a palm across the back of his neck, rubbing in the grime of the day. His eyes, shaded by a pair of caterpillar eyebrows, followed the tweens until they disappeared into the din of the midway.

'Excuse me, sir,' a voice cracked in front of him. 'Can I get some cotton candy?'

Wayne turned from his reverie to see a bespectacled man sporting a greased comb over. The man's spatulate fingers splayed across the gold-flecked counter, and his gaze focused on the cracked vinyl tape Wayne had used to repair the peeling silver trim.

'What can I do ya for?' Wayne asked, his affected southern drawl oozing from his throat.

'Can I get a bag of blue, please?' the man asked. A trickle of sweat crawled from his diminishing hairline and slithered around his jaw.

Wayne reached to his left and unhooked a wad of plastic-wrapped aqua floss from a wire without taking his eyes from the traveling bead of perspiration.

'That'll be four dollars,' Wayne said when the droplet fell from the man's chin.

Lifting one of his hands from the smeared countertop, the man thrust it into his pocket as if he were mining for gold.

'I'll bet the kids will be happy to get this,' Wayne said. He gave the bag a gentle shake.

'No kids,' the man said without so much as a glance away from the haphazard repair.

The man's fist reappeared trailing a wispy white thread. Uncurling his fingers, a mound of pennies, dimes, and nickels clattered near the napkin dispenser. He used his ragged tipped nails to pick out a few stray hairs and a wad of gray and brown lint. His lips fluttered as he slid each separate coin four inches closer to Wayne. When he'd reached three dollars and ninety-two cents, he pressed his other hand into the opposite pocket and fingered the lining.

'Wow, your wife keeps them purse strings tied and double knotted, don't she?' Wayne leaned both elbows onto the twelve inch barrier island and craned his neck like a vulture.

Slapping his latest treasure onto a blackened burn mark, the man shook his head. 'No wife. Just here to see the freaks.' He used the pad of his index finger to press the last eight pennies into the small lake of brown and silver.

A smile spread across Wayne's face like an incoming tide.

'The freaks, huh?' He pulled the confection back into the confines of the booth.

The little man nodded, shifting his gaze to the blue bag of spun sugar now beyond his reach.

'Well, I've got special tickets for the show. I only give 'em to special customers.' Wayne watched the man's eyes widen beyond the rims of his glasses. 'It gets you a glimpse behind the second curtain, so to speak.' Wayne eyed the empty space surrounding his stall. 'You interested?'

The man's head bobbled like a stringed cat toy. His jaw hung loose, and a line of drool slipped from the corner of his gaping mouth. Wayne reached beneath the register and ripped a neon green ticket from a loose roll. He dropped it on the counter and plucked a drying felt tipped pen from a jar.

'All I need is your name.' Wayne stood, one hand gripping the merchandise and the other poised to write the man's name. 'So we can personalize your tour.'

'L...L...Larry,' he said. 'Larry Jones.'

'L-A-R-R-Y J-O-N-E-S.' Wayne scribbled the letters and clinked the pen back into the water-stained container. Holding the ticket and the bagged blue cloud toward Larry, Wayne leered. His golden molar gleamed. 'Just tell Paulie that Wayne sent you.'

'Step right up! See the Monkey Boy from Borneo,' Paulie Watson hawked. His battered top hat sat at an odd angle on his mass of red curls. 'He'll swing from his tail for you.'

Not many people passed through this part of the park. The ones that did wandered past the tall, crooked man without seeing him or his dented cane. An observant few would toss embarrassed glances at his fading posters and ill-fitting striped suit.

'That's right, folks.' Paulie swivelled on his dipped knees and waved his cane in a wide arc. 'Pull the bearded lady's whiskers just to hear her scream.'

'Hey,' a muffled voice shouted behind the tent flap. 'We'll have none of that.'

'Don't get your knickers bunched, Peggy,' Paulie said. 'Nobody's listening to me out here.'

The canvas parted, and a hairy face popped through the opening.

'I thought you said everyone would want to see me,' the face said.

'Get back there Wolfie,' Paulie said as he strode toward the crack in the fabric. 'If they see you now, they won't need to part with their precious tickets.' He poked the shiny black nose with his thumb. 'If we don't get their tickets, we don't get paid.'

The fuzzy head disappeared. Paulie drew the canvas folds together and secured the ribbon ties by knotting them into floppy bows. He flinched when a throat cleared behind him. Plastering on a smile, he spun on his heel and threw his arms wide. A small man stood pulling strands of blue cotton floss out of a limp plastic bag. The man's tongue twitched lizard-like as he poked the bits of fluff into his mouth.

'Welcome, welcome, welcome to the show of shows. See genetic mutations up close.'

Using a sticky, stained finger, the little man pressed his glasses up the bridge of his nose. After wiping his hand down the front of his shirt, he pulled a bent ticket from his pocket and thrust it toward the barker. Paulie turned over the bright green voucher, held it at arm's length, and squinted. His eyes flicked up to the man's round face, and a smirk rippled through his left cheek.

'Well, Mister Jones,' Paulie said, shouting loud enough to be heard by the curiosities sequestered behind the heavy curtain. 'It looks like you get the deluxe guided tour.'

A moment of heavy silence was broken by the sounds of scurrying feet and excited whispers as Paulie untied the stays. Flipping back the fabric panel, he held it open and bowed low enough to dislodge his hat.

'This way please, Mister Jones. Come see the freaks the way few people ever do.'

Larry crammed the last wad of the blue puff into his mouth and threw the empty wrapping to the ground. He licked the hints of sweetness from his fingers before stepping into the dim enclosure. Paulie rolled his eyes and retrieved the discarded garbage. After shoving the litter into a barrel, he followed the little man inside the darkness. Shutting out the electric lights of the park, the closed canvas flap plunged the tent's interior into pitch black. A quick whoosh and a click echoed as a spotlight illuminated a large bewhiskered woman sitting on a red velvet cushion. The hem of her lace-necked gown showed signs of having been a meal for moths.

'Bearded lady,' Larry whispered with a hushed reverence. His owlish eyes blinked once as they roved over Peggy's unshorn face.

Peggy smiled a gap-toothed grin and wagged her ringed fingers at the little man. The sides of Larry's mouth turned up as his jaw fell. His euphoric gaze faltered when the spotlight jerked to the next display. He shuffled sideways to get a better look at the muscle bound man. Every inch of exposed skin displayed a different inked portrait. Snakes crawled from his ears, women danced on his biceps, lizards lounged on his chest. Gold and silver hoops and studs glittered from skin flaps that Larry hadn't known existed. The man's sneer revealed teeth that had been sharpened to fine points. The painted man disappeared as the light progressed around the room, exposing conjoined twins, a sword swallower and glass eater, a cat with two faces, and a boy with the head of a wolf. To Larry, each oddity was more eccentric than the last.

The small man made his way past the exhibits to the far end of the room. When he reached a flat wall panel, he stopped and turned. Larry raised his hand to shield his eyes from the blinding light shining in his face.

'Where's the exit?' he asked.

'Ah, but this is only the beginning,' Paulie's voice boomed from his place behind the incandescent ray. 'Your special ticket entitles you to so much more. Do you want to leave now and miss the marvels to come?'

The man's doughy face tilted in confusion, and he shook his head. Strands of oiled hair slid from their careful placement across his scalp to flop and dangle over his ear.

'Are you ready to see a side of the anomalies few get the privilege of experiencing?'

Larry nodded, his eyes and toothy grin lit up like the first glimpse of a child's bicycle on Christmas morning.

'Then turn and place your fingertips on the wall before you.'

Larry whirled, unsettling his remaining combed over tresses. He wiped his sweating palms down his khaki covered thighs, and smeared his fingerprints across the dingy painted surface. The wall fell to the ground, and Larry toppled with it. Hands grabbed him from all directions and dragged him farther into the recess. The panel sprang back into place, shutting out the spotlight. Again, Larry's world was submerged in darkness. Digits wrapped around every available part of his body, squeezing.

'Stop,' Larry said. 'You're hurting me.'

One by one, each grip tightened. Even the tiny pads clutching at his earlobes pinched to bruising. Larry tried to scramble free of the binding hands, but each time one fell away another reached in to knead his wriggling flesh. He opened his mouth to scream and felt a rag fill the space between his teeth. He tried to force it out with his tongue, but tape slapped across his lips prevented the evacuation.

The floor beneath him fell away as the grasping hands raised his body into the air. The bodies bumped and shuffled as they maneuvered their charge through the murky space. As if on cue, the hands released. Larry toppled a short distance onto a cold, hard surface. Before he could catch his breath and roll away, heavy straps fastened around his ankles, pelvis, and shoulders. Larry struggled against the bindings only to succeed in making them tighter.

The frightened man stilled and took in as much air as he could manage through his nostrils. His heart throbbed under his drenched Oxford shirt. He could hear breathing near him. Lots of inhales and exhales, even a few sighs. He assumed that the respiration was human or may have been once, but in the darkness, he couldn't tell.

His world snapped from cave-like black to sand beach white, and he scrunched shut his eyes in pain. Stifled giggles filtered through the brightened space. Larry blinked, adjusting his pupils to the sudden illumination. As his vision cleared, blurred shapes formed and came into focus, jostling each other for a better view.

'Paulie?' a voice asked.

'Yes, Spencer,' Paulie said as he lifted a doll-sized man from the floor.

'Did Mister Jones really get the special ticket?' Spencer asked in a child's voice.

'Yes, he did.' Paulie lowered the miniature person onto Larry's chest. 'And you can go first.'

Spencer looked over his shoulder and simpered at Paulie. From the back pocket of his doll sized pants, he produced a shining silver needle. He lifted it over his head as if he were dealing a death blow to a dragon and thrust it down between two of Larry's ribs. Larry screamed through his gag and strained beneath the leather bands. The tiny freak clung to a row of bucking shirt buttons. Lifting Spencer from the squirming man's chest, Paulie raised an eyebrow.

'You said you wanted to see a side of the freaks that few people ever experience,' Paulie said. He lowered Spencer back onto Larry's chest. 'Now we've got to get you good and scared.' Snapping on a pair of rubber gloves, Paulie pulled a syringe from inside his jacket. 'Are you scared?'

Larry nodded, bashing the back of his head into the metal surface underneath him. A simian-faced boy leaned over the quaking man. A hairy snake-like object wrapped around his glasses and removed them, placing the frames in the boy's hands. The boy drew the metal legs over his own ears and opened his mouth. Long canine teeth flickered in the light from the single overhead bulb as the boy screeched like an angry chimpanzee. He loped into the darkness, his knuckles dragging the floor.

'So you think you're scared enough?' Paulie asked.

With eyes bulging from his skull, Larry convulsed with nods. A handless woman stepped to the table and held up her empty wrists. She bent, disappearing from Larry's view, and reappeared with a surgical saw attached to one stump. Holding the saw with her other arm, she tightened the straps with her teeth and smiled. Pressing her nose to a switch, the saw blade whirred to life.

'Do you think you could be more scared than you are now?' Paulie asked.

Larry slammed his head from left to right. Tears streamed down his face, and sweat seeped from his pores. Paulie leaned close to his prisoner and inhaled. He stilled the bound man's flailing head with a palm pressed to his forehead as if checking for fever. Sliding the tip of the syringe across Larry's neck, he found the pulsing vein and pierced the skin. Paulie pressed the plunger and slid the needle free. After a few moments, Larry's thrashing subsided. His still frightened eyes stared into the emptiness above him.

'Be quick about it Stella, before the fear drains,' Paulie said to the handless woman.

'It's only the thousandth one I've done.' Stella huffed and

drove the round blade into Larry's scalp. 'You'd think I was fresh off the circus train from the way you talk, but you're gonna have to lift his head since chimp boy ran off.'

Larry thrust two fingertips up the prone man's nostrils and tilted the head off the table. After circumnavigating Larry's head with the saw, Stella stepped away from the table. Paulie nodded his approval as he removed the soiled glove and replaced it with a fresh one. The tattooed man inched forward and took her place. He placed the tip of a chipped chisel in the gap left by Stella's saw. Tapping the wooden handle with a rubber mallet, he loosened the skullcap. The pierced man placed his fingertips on each side of the loosened bone and pulled. A wet slurping pop resonated through the room followed by a smattering of applause.

'Shh,' Paulie hissed. 'We aren't done yet.'

He used his gloved fingers to wiggle the brain free from its encasement. Flipping it over, he dropped it onto Larry's chest. Spencer pulled a tiny set of goggles over his eyes and sliced into the tissue with a scalpel he held in both hands. With the precision of a surgeon, he removed two almond-shaped masses from the middle of Larry's brain and passed them off to Paulie.

'Can we turn him into an owl man now?' Spencer asked, removing his goggles.

'Of course you can.' Paulie grinned. 'It's about time we got a new exhibit.' He tilted his head to the side and stared at the dead man on the table. 'He does look like an owl, doesn't he?'

As Paulie left the room with the small pieces of brain tucked into a glass jar, he passed the monkey boy carrying a garbage bag full of feathers and a can of rubber cement. Reaching out a hand, he ruffled the hairy child's matted head. The tailed child turned and screeched a greeting.

Wayne flipped the switch to warm the machine and set the heat range dial. He grabbed a pink carton from a shelf under the counter and a metal cocoa tin from a concealed cabinet above his head. He shook the tin near his ear and frowned.

Prying open the canister, his scowl deepened. The tin held enough flavoring for a day's worth of floss but no more. He hoped Paulie would bring a fresh batch of the special ingredient soon.

Folding open the sugar carton, he poured two cups into a small pitcher. He dipped a miniature gravy ladle in the cocoa tin and lifted out a scoop of gray powder. After pouring the spooned contents into the pitcher, he mixed it into the sweetener with a plastic straw. Wayne emptied the sugar mixture into the spinning floss head.

A knock sounded on the counter. Wayne glanced up as he peeled back a dozen plastic bags and pulled a white paper cone from a stack. He nodded at Paulie's crooked top hat as he wound the wisps of pink into football sized puffs and stuffed them into the waiting transparent sacks.

'What's up?' Wayne shouted over the whir of the machine.

'I've got a delivery for you.' Paulie slid an open cardboard box filled with small mason jars over the speckled Formica.

'Your timing's spot on' Wayne's gold tooth gleamed in his grin as he continued to wind and stuff. 'I was almost out.'

'They still need to be dried and crushed, but I figure you can take care of that easier than me.' Paulie removed his hat and got his fingers lost in his tangled curls.

The carousel whined a few last notes before the horses stopped racing for the day.

'Quality stuff?' Wayne asked as he tied off the last bag and flicked off the contraption.

Paulie nodded and spit into the dust. 'Should be, but it'll have to be tested.'

The last of the revelers scurried past as they deserted the park. Wayne rolled a fresh bag of cotton candy to his supplier.

'Have one on me,' he said.

Paulie stepped away from the stand and watched the bag drop onto the trampled dirt.

'What's wrong?' Wayne asked, a twinkle sparking in his eye. 'Don't like the taste?'

'Nope, diabetic.' Paulie tossed the dusty pink fluff back through the window. 'That stuff could kill me.'

Madam Mafoutee's Bad Glass Eye

Chloe Yates

Even with the beard, Lena was a doll. I could have spent hours just staring at her. Those cool blue eyes of hers made me weak at the knees and I would get the cold sweats just thinking about them. I felt like a kid around her. She knew it too. Didn't she just.

'Mafoutee takes the eye out as soon as she gets back to her caravan and puts it in the box. The old donah will be well into her gin by midnight and you can grab it right out from under her big ugly nose.' Lena winked at me; she knew I'd do anything for her. She only had to show a bit of leg, bat those ridiculously long eyelashes at me and I was putty in her perfectly manicured hands. I didn't care either. I should have, I should have known better – how many times have you heard that old chestnut? – but the fact was I simply didn't care.

The plan was simple. Madam Mafoutee was an old fortune teller who had been dukkering with the carnival for as long as anyone could remember. She kept herself to herself, except for Joey the Bipenis Boy, who seemed to be her personal slave. There were rumours that he was either her son or her lover, but the woman had to be eighty if she was a day and Joey was just taking puberty in his overabundant stride. Neither option fitted well. Still, they wouldn't be the weirdest couple in the joint. Who would have thought that me, Evelina Strange, Strong Woman, and Lovely Lena, the Bountiful Bearded Lady, would have had such a connection? Not me, I can tell you, but I digress...

The eye was the prize. Seems ghoulish, I know, but that eye wasn't what it seemed, at least not according to Lena. Set within its depths, she said, was a diamond bigger than the top of my not inconsiderable thumb. How her eyes had lit up the first time she'd told me. I'd never seen her so excited. She said that she'd seen it before the eye had been made – and that's the only part of her story I ever doubted. Lena had only been with the carnival for a few weeks before we started up together. I'll admit it didn't take long for me to become a smitten slave to her feminine wiles, but I'd worked this rig for just over two years and Mafoutee was here a long time before me. Still, I guess I'm not the sharpest tool in the box because I didn't question her, especially not after the look in her eye turned nasty. I might be a big girl and as strong as ten oxen, but I like neither confrontation nor nastiness. Lena amping up for a barney was a beautiful sight, but the thought of the aftermath was just too much for my nerves.

'While she's out for the night dukkering those terrible fortunes of hers – honestly, have you ever heard such horseshit? – I'll sneak into the van and slip a bit of belladonna into her gin. Not enough to kill her, just enough to knock her out.' Lena looked gleeful as she told me her plan. Everyone knew the old girl liked a bottle like a flower loves the sun, but it didn't sit quite right messing with her sauce. Sensing my hesitation, Lena slipped into my lap and put her arms around my neck, wiggling that backside of hers against my needy thighs and, like the puppet I was, my qualms vanished. There was nothing I wouldn't have done for her at that moment, nothing. Her happiness was my folly. 'Sweetling, I know you're not one for underhandedness, but needs must. We could be free of this life.' She spoke so dismissively of it, the life I'd led since I was thrown out of home at fifteen, of the people that had taken me in as one of their own, or so I thought.

'We'll run away together. Live somewhere by the sea like you've always dreamed. It will be wonderful. You do want us to be together, don't you?' Her soft little pout made my heart pound. I wanted it like I'd wanted nothing else in this world. Let me be a lesson to you, friends. Never tell anyone your dreams. They take them and twist them and use them for their own ends. I didn't know that then and hearing her talk like that made me the patsy she needed. I'll be honest; the plan made my guts quake, but not going through with it made me feel even worse. Lena would be disappointed in me, she'd cast me aside and then what would I do? I was in this for the long haul and I intended to prove it.

The night was set for the following Saturday. Lena had been watching the old woman for days and knew her routine like clockwork. The only problem was that Saturdays were my busiest time. Five performances in one day usually wiped me out, strong as I was.

'Don't worry, darling, I've got something that will pep you right up.' The white powder she gave me wasn't something I'd ever tried before. I'd had a few of those mushroom things the Hurly Burly Dwarf Company liked to brew in a tea, but this was something new. The first time I tried it I knew I was going to be hooked. I was even stronger than usual on it. I loved it. It made my muscles twitch, my heart race and a grin was etched deep into my plain old face. I had a spring in my step from the get-go – which may have been the reason for me going along with all this foolishness in the first place, or so I'd like to think now.

When the clock struck midnight on the appointed Saturday night, jacked up on Lena's powder, smiling like a fool despite my strong body being battered by the day's spots, I slipped into the old woman's caravan just like we'd planned.

I knew something was wrong … no, I didn't. Even now I'm still lying to myself. Truth is I had no idea; I was a dupe and I didn't know it until it was too late. Everything went like clockwork, or so it seemed. The caravan was creepy inside, but that wasn't anything I hadn't been expecting. Madam Mafoutee liked dolls. She had hundreds of them in storage,

Lena claimed, but kept her favourites on display where she could see them. She had all kinds of them and doted on the hokey things. It gave me the heebie-jeebies to think of a grown woman brushing their hair and choosing outfits for them. I'd never liked dolls and their too-big eyes seemed to follow me as I made my way further into the van. The old woman herself was out cold, the gin glass had rolled out of her hand onto the floor but she was past noticing. Joey was asleep in his own van and there was nothing to stop me getting to that box. It was sat in full view on the little sideboard beside the old woman. Taking it was a piece of cake.

A very obvious piece of cake.

Did my foolishness end with just grabbing the box? Of course it didn't. What made me open it? Something (or someone) made me do it, and I know that sounds stupid but truth is truth and I knew I had to open it, that nothing else mattered but seeing what was inside.

So I did.

The eye blinked at me.

No, not blinked, the damned thing winked at me. I would lay my hand upon a bible and swear it as God's honest truth. Without so much as a lid to call its own, the eye – the solid glass eye – winked at me. Disbelief made me pause; it couldn't be, surely? I looked again. It winked again. Suddenly, it was as though the box that surrounded it was grinning at me, the gaping maw the open lid made threatening enough to make me drop it. I had no choice. I thrust the vile thing from my hands, dashing it against the wooden floor of the caravan with a shout of disgust.

I woke the old woman. Or so I thought.

'Ha! Now, what can I suppose you're doing in here, Evelina Strange? And what have you done with my eye?' she asked. Her distinct lack of surprise was obvious even in my bewildered state. Her voice was not as heavy with the belladonna's somniferous effects as it should have been either, I could tell that too. She had been waiting. For me.

'Did you think the Naughty Man's Cherries was enough to knock me out, sweetling? You think the dose was bona?

D'you think your beardy palone was telling you the truth?'
She chuckled quietly to herself as she stroked the doll she was
holding in her lap like a baby. Looking at her made my head
pound. I needed to get out of there but I just stood there
staring at the old woman dumbly.

'Now Mama, it's not polite to laugh at people, no matter
how ridiculous they are.' The familiar voice from behind me
was like a blow to the gut, but it broke the spell and I spun
on my heel to confront the speaker.

Lena.

My Lena.

I should have known it was too good to be true. I'd fallen
for her patter like the fool that I was.

Joey the Bipenis Boy popped out from behind her as I
stared at my golden haired downfall. Unable to fully compre-
hend this turn of events (even as I knew it was inevitable – a
girl like Lena wasn't for the likes of me) I watched as, moving
so quickly he was practically a blur, the boy scooped up the
box, slapped the lid shut and handed it to the old woman.
For a moment, without that eye staring its malevolence into
the world, my head felt clearer than it had since I'd left my
caravan. It didn't last long. Joey stood behind Mafoutee's
chair and waited. I didn't want to know what for, but I was
sure I was going to find out.

'So, my chavi has told you of the diamond, has she?' It
registered then. Lena had called the old woman "mama".
Lena was Mafoutee's daughter! How could that be? I nodded
even as my mind whirred uselessly, my eyes flitting between
the two women. I couldn't see the resemblance, not one bit.
Lena with her glorious mane of blonde hair, matching full
beard and those cool blue eyes couldn't be related to the
curve-backed, dark-eyed hag still slouched in her armchair as
if nothing had changed. 'She's been away from me too long,
that one, and I've missed her something rotten. She's a good
girl, knows how to lure 'em in. She always done well for me
in the past and that's not changed. Has an eye for it, you
might say.' She grinned at me then, enjoying her quip, and
finally I saw the whole of her face. Her empty eye socket –

more a hole than a socket in truth – was deeper and darker than it should have been. The darkness within it swirled and flickered, tiny pulses of light seemed to reach out to me then retreat, teasing me, luring me in even more assuredly than Lena had. I couldn't look away. My mind quieted, my breath slowed. The van around me receded until there was nothing but those tiny teasing lights. I felt a glass being pressed into my hand and I brought it to my lips automatically. I took greedy gulps of the liquid therein, feeling the smooth rush of it travelling down my gullet into my stomach. A numb sensation shot outwards from my gut, first surging through my veins, then running through my muscles, before filtering through my bones and into my brain until all I felt was sweet nothingness. The rush of it was more addictive than the drugs Lena had dosed me with. I wanted more but at the same time I was calmer than I'd ever felt in my entire sorry life.

It didn't last.

From out of nowhere, a heavenly golden glow seemed to shine all around me, from me; my body was filled with it. I had been expecting something awful to happen but instead my mind cleared of any doubts, any pain. I was free and I was light, and in that moment I somehow knew with absolute certainty that I was fucked.

In the grip of my euphoria, brought on by the belladonna that should have been Mafoutee's but was always meant for me I now realise, I could hear chanting. It sounded like an insect at first but, gradually, it became more singsong, a balm to my ears. A second voice joined it, seemed to tangle with it, dance with it, elevating my senses still further. My feet lost contact with the floor and I felt how light and lithe my body had become. I was beautiful serenity. I was pounding rhythm. I yearned to join the dance, to break on the rocks of the song they sang. I was graceful for the first time in my life, no longer a thick-limbed oaf hampered by rejection and ridicule. Before was lost; now was all that mattered. Like liquid gold, I poured through the air, sleek and wanton in my need to reach out with every inch of my skin, every ounce of my being.

Lena's voice washed over me even as I felt the pull of her

mother's stronger incantations. The power of the old woman's voice would have been unmistakeable even if it hadn't been licking across my skin like luscious sun rays, firing my nerve endings and yet, in truth, lulling my senses to her bidding. As soon as I recognised my true mistress, everything changed.

The gold light folded in on itself, dropping me like a stone. My body hit the floor with a thud that shook the van. I felt a loss more acute than any I'd ever suffered. I yearned for the light, ached for its tendrils to hold me again. As I lay there in misery, the first cracking noise didn't bother me. I felt nothing, just my soul-shattering loss. I didn't realise it was me until my kneecaps splintered.

Then I screamed.

I kept screaming, or so I thought, as my body realigned itself, the bones snapping and re-knitting, the muscles tearing and then re-hemming themselves into smaller and smaller proportions. It was white-hot agony, so pure in its intensity that it teetered on the pleasurable, but still I kept screaming.

Even as my voice box collapsed and then resurrected itself in a much smaller version, I screamed. The sound existed only in my head then. I knew that, but I didn't stop.

I began to solidify. I'm a meaty woman, I'm solid, but this was something else. It was as though I was thrust into a kiln, my skin hardening from clay to bisque in its colossal heat. I glanced down at my hands, once so clumsy but now like a doll's. I looked up at my mistress, Madam Mafoutee, and she seemed as tall as a Brobdingnagian queen. My head felt impossibly heavy suddenly and I was forced to look down, my chin dropping to my chest with a thud. At last the ache of my torn and re-rendered body became too much for my senses and I felt the sweet surety of death approaching. I welcomed it. Oblivion was all I sought. My mistakes were behind me and I would be free.

Or so I thought.

Consciousness came upon me slowly. I felt as though I should ache all over, the memory of what had transpired – or what I thought had transpired – enough to make the hardest of sorts sore, but I didn't. When I raised my hand to my forehead… I didn't raise anything. It wouldn't move. Not one muscle twitched in response to my command. My head didn't turn and my legs were in no better shape. The only things I could move were my eyes. Frantic, I looked down at my body, a body that was as shiny as… brand spanking new porcelain.

Realisation hit me like a bolt gun.

I was a doll.

I was a fucking doll! The panic was swift and, if I could have moved, I would have leapt off that table and scarpered like a fox from the hunt. I would never run again.

If I could have cried I would have, but even that was beyond me now.

The leering face of Madam Mafoutee came into sight suddenly, her nose enormous now, every hair and pore colossal. The darkness in her empty eye socket had gone. It was just a puckered useless lump of flesh once more.

'Well, Evelina, you look much better than you did as a big ugly human. I've had my eye on you for a while. Now, let me brush your hair and then we'll choose a nice dress for you. Something with frills, I think.'

As she brushed my locks, fuller and thicker than they had been before, she told me what would happen to me if I fell from her favour. She told me of the dark cold place where the only sound you can hear is the flicker of a thousand tiny eyelids, behind which are five hundred furiously impotent lunatic minds. I closed my eyes and waited to be dressed.

Buffalo Brendan and the Big Top Ballot

Allan Watson

Have you ever seen anyone blow their brains out right in front of your eyes? I have. It's a real nasty business. And not just the visceral mess of blood, brains and skull fragments exploding outwards at over a thousand miles per hour. Guns make a big bang, much louder than on television. You can feel your eardrums bulge and strain towards perforation point and then everything gets muffled and all you're left with is a sickening high pitched drone which at least dampens the sound of hysterical women screaming.

Buffalo Brendan probably heard nothing at all as the bullet tore through his head and straight out the tent-wall where it hit an electrical generator and brought the Octopus Ride to a standstill. Buffalo Brendan was a crowd pleaser at Oscar Morlotti's Carnival & Circus. Each night he performed in a tented enclosure, the entrance a plywood façade proclaiming 'Buffalo Brendan – Fastest Draw in the West.'

His act consisted of dressing as a glitzy rodeo cowboy and spinning his guns in complex patterns, switching from hand to hand so fast you couldn't be sure exactly when he made the exchange. Then he'd take ten dollar bets from would-be gunslingers in the audience, a high noon shoot-out using decommissioned revolvers that fired loud-banging caps. Brendan always won of course, levelling his revolver dead-steady at his opponent's heart before the poor sap had even drawn. Then came a demonstration of his lariat skills, whirling his lasso round and round as he stepped in and out of the spinning noose like a line-dancer on speed before finally capturing one of the womenfolk at the front of the crowd and reeling her in for a chaste kiss on the cheek.

It was the last part of Brendan's act people really came to see. Deep down everyone likes an execution and that's why they flocked to watch him risk certain death for nothing more than cheap entertainment value. Brendan performed a trick where he'd perch on a stool and have me blindfold him. A lady from the crowd got to place a single live round into the chamber of a silver plated revolver and then spin the cylinder. The whirring ratchet of that spinning chunk of cast metal always made me think of the devil himself hunkered over a smoking roulette wheel in the hottest casino in hell, preparing to rake in a stack of souls scattered like gambling chips across the red baize table. Brendan claimed he could tell from the sound of that very last ratchet click if the chamber was empty or not. When I put the loaded gun into his hand, you could feel the audience suck in their breath as he laid the barrel to his temple and pulled the trigger. The loud, dry snap of the hammer falling on the empty breech chamber always elicited a huge whoop of relief, and sadly, it has to be said, a few sighs of disappointment. Sometimes Brendan would stare coldly at the gun for a few moments and then shake his head, asking the lady to spin the cylinder again. He did that to increase the tension, notch up the drama a bit more; he was a showman after all. He knew exactly what he was doing. At least until he shot himself through the head.

One of the first people on the scene was Oscar Morlotti himself. He'd been on his way to the Big Top wearing his ridiculous ringmaster costume; a red jacket with brass buttons, white breeches, a black top hat and a bull-hide whip. He also sported a large waxed moustache. You have to understand that Oscar had a thing about circuses. He was obsessed by them. He told me he wanted to be a ringmaster when other small boys were dreaming of batting for the Red Sox or flying rockets to Mars. Unfortunately, despite the carnival itself being pretty decent, Oscar's circus was a laughing stock. The Big Top, a reclaimed, much-patched canvas marquee held only fifty people at a squeeze and the acts consisted of a strong man, a clown, a gimpy acrobat, a one-armed juggler and a troupe of performing goats. Lame didn't cover it.

Pushing through the last of the crowd streaming out the tent, Oscar gawped at Buffalo Brendan lying in a pool of blood with his brains leaking out through a fist-sized hole in his head. Exit wounds are always ugly fuckers.

'He dead, Kid?'

I rolled my eyes. 'Well, if he ain't we're gonna need us some extra strong Aspirin, Boss.'

The murmuring of anxious voices made us aware a new crowd was gathering at the entrance trying to see what the commotion was all about. A few even had their phones held out in the hope of snapping a picture they could stick on Facebook or Twitter. Oscar grabbed my arm. 'Quit being a smart-ass and get a blanket to cover this poor bastard up.'

'Will do, Boss.' Oscar liked being called Boss. In fact he insisted on it. I, on the other hand, detested being called Kid. I was twenty seven for Christ's sake. They nick-named me Kid when I joined the carnival at the tender age of sixteen and it seemed they'd still be calling me Kid when I was an old fella with false teeth and whiskers down to my knees. But this was no time to quibble about names. Reaching through the back flap I grabbed a spare ground-sheet and quickly draped it over Brendan's corpse, already attracting the attention of some keen-nosed blowflies.

More and more people were rubber-necking through the entrance, a few of them even spilling inside the tent itself. Oscar cracked his whip, forcing them to shuffle back. 'The police will be here any minute,' he bellowed. 'Go on home, folks. The carnival is closing early tonight.' The crowd retreated slightly but didn't exactly disperse. Oscar tugged on his moustache and cracked his whip again to show he meant business, making the crowd inch back a little further, or maybe they just breathed in some to make it appear so. I wondered if Oscar was acting out some old childhood lion-tamer fantasy. I half expected him to pick up Brendan's stool and brandish it like a big cat trainer.

'Call the cops, Kid, and then go tell Black Samson to refund the circus ticket money. We have to close down for the night. Go spread the word.'

I hesitated. 'Boss, we really have to do something about this shit. Brendan is the third serious accident in two weeks. If this goes on we won't have a carnival worth a shit this time next month. People are already talking about moving on.'

Oscar's moustache visibly wilted and he sighed heavily. 'You think I don't know that, Kid? But what am I supposed to do?'

'Call a meeting. After the police have finished up we should have a Carny ballot in the Big Top. We all know who's to blame for this run of bad luck.'

'You don't know anything for certain, Kid.'

I shrugged. 'Maybe not, but you know how superstitious us fairground people are, that's why we need that meeting. Bring it all into the open.'

Oscar paled a little. Carny ballots were sacred rituals and only used in the most serious of circumstances. Sometimes people died depending on which way the votes were cast. 'Okay. Tell everyone to be in the Big Top at midnight. We'll talk about it.'

I ducked through the back flap to save fighting my way through the mass of people thronging around Brendan's pitch. I could already hear the Doppler whoop of a police siren in the near distance. Someone had already alerted them to the shooting, which saved me the job of doing it. I headed straight up the midway towards the Big Top, breathing in the aroma of cooked dough, diesel oil, candy-apples, electricity, burgers, grass-cuttings, sweat, cinnamon, sun-baked earth, dog-shit, fried chicken, pizza, and the eye-watering tang of sizzling onions. Dusk was falling and the coloured lights draped over every stall and fairground ride were drawing the usual collection of bugs.

At the entrance to the Big Top, Black Samson, the circus strongman, wore his customary singlet and a voodoo mask. He was a steroid junkie with oiled muscles like gleaming dark oak, which I thought perfectly matched the density of his wooden head beneath the mask.

'Hey, Kid,' he growled, 'you seen the Boss fella anywhere? Show's runnin' late and the crowd gittin' ressless.'

I peered in and saw maybe a dozen bored-looking people on the benches. 'Show's cancelled. Buffalo Brendan put a bullet through his noggin. Got to close everything down for the night. Oscar says you've to refund the ticket money and send everyone home.'

Black Samson's small eyes gleamed behind the slits in the painted mask and I could almost hear the slow moving gears of his thinking matter crunch over the possibility of just tossing everyone out and keeping those dollars for himself. He picked up an iron bar lying at his feet, twisted it into the shape of an Egyptian ankh and then straightened it out again. I guessed he was keeping the money.

'You say Buffalo Brendan is dead? For real?'

I nodded. 'Brains all over the floor. Can't get any more real than that.'

Another voice spoke up behind me. 'What's that? Old Buffalo Brendan gone to meet his maker? As they say, it's an ill wind etc. etc.'

I spun around and there was white-faced Keppie the Clown. Keppie seriously gave me the willies. Unlike most circus clowns who laugh in public and weep in private, Keppie played a miserable clown but outside the ring he was constantly grinning, the same way a shark seems to grin as it trawls through the deep oceans looking for fresh flesh to sink its teeth into. I'd heard it said he kept a picture of clown-dressing serial killer John Wayne Gacy taped up inside his trailer. He was grinning right then as he fumbled in the pocket of his loudly checked jacket to make his polka-dot bow tie spin like a propeller.

'What the fuck you mean it's an ill-wind, Keppie? You making an insinuation of sorts?'

Keppie laughed out the side of his scarlet painted mouth and his red plastic nose flashed on and off like a warning beacon. 'Seems to me, Kid, that with Buffalo Brendan planted six feet under in Boot Hill, there's gonna be an openin' for his 'prentice.'

'I was Brendan's assistant. Not his apprentice,' I snapped back at Keppie.

Black Samson slapped me on the back and almost knocked me flat on my ass. 'Not sure I see the difference, Kid. Brother Keppie here has a point. You were the one cleanin' the guns and makin' sure them ole' lassoes didn' get snarled. Once all the gee-jaw dies down I e'spect the Boss will ask you to take over the pitch. Bound to.'

What Black Samson said was quite true. I knew all Buffalo Brendan's tricks and there was no reason for me not to step into his still-warm cowboy boots. 'Maybe so,' I said, 'but I resent Keppie dropping hints I might have played a part in things.'

Keppie yanked violently at the red tufts of hair above his ears like a grieving parent at a child's funeral. His grin, however, stayed plastered to his greasy white face. 'No, Kid. You got me all wrong. Brendan blowin' out his brains wasn't nothin' to do with you. Just plain bad luck. But I think we all know fine well where that bad luck's been coming from lately. It's that witch and her Freaks.'

Carnies are even worse than sailors concerning streaks of bad luck and who or what constitutes the source of such a phenomenon. It was true there had been a spate of accidents in recent times. Bud Stanley, a mechanic who serviced the rides, lost his fuck-finger when a driveshaft flange shifted while he was aligning the bolt holes. A common enough accident I suppose, and as an experienced wrench-monkey Bud should have remembered the old adage never to stick your finger in a hole unless it has short, curly hair around it. Then Walt Howell who operated the kiddies' carousel slipped on a patch of oil and broke his leg in three places. Needed a plate put in to hold things together. And now we had Buffalo Brendan heading for the morgue. Bad luck does indeed seem to run in multiples of three.

There were other, less serious, bad luck stories going around the carnival. The performing goats came down with some weird goat disease and instead of jumping through hoops and tap-dancing in Oscar's Big Top they lay around in their pen, sluggish and lethargic, refusing to eat or drink. Two of the main generators kept blowing fuses bringing several of the rides to a halt, and there was also a bizarre and almost Biblical infestation of crickets inside the Haunted House. I suppose in any place of work there is always a run of accidents and bad luck, but carnival folk like to attribute the source to a specific person. A nominated Jonah. That way we can deal directly with the problem. Keppie was just saying aloud what everyone else was whispering about behind trailer doors.

'Oscar green-lit a midnight meet,' I told him. 'Looks like we're gonna get a Carny ballot.'

Keppie's red grin stretched almost all the way across to his ears. 'Wonderful,' he whispered.

Black Samson slipped off his voodoo mask, his bald, ebony head gleaming under the midway lights as he wrapped his iron bar around his thick trunk of a neck and twisted the metal into the shape of a noose. 'An' then mebbe we git to have us a hangin'.'

The look of dark joy on both their faces made me shiver despite the clammy evening heat and I was just glad I wasn't the one being put to the vote.

As Oscar had instructed, I made the rounds of the carnival, telling the ride operators to close things down. Everyone was genuinely upset about Buffalo Brendan, but they still seemed reluctant to shut down their machinery. Closing early meant fewer bucks in their pockets. Pancho Pete, a swarthy Mexican who ran the ghost train, spat on the ground and muttered something about careless Gringos, but he did pull the chain across the platform where college boys were waiting to take their girls into the dark tunnels filled with flashing skeletons and trailing cobwebs. One by one the coloured lights dimmed and the endless chatter of pistons and gears and crankshafts faded as the Waltzers, the Cyclone, the Rollercoaster and finally the Ferris wheel clanked to a halt.

My last stop was the Freak Show & Burlesque pitch run by a statuesque blonde called Madeline Cheezum. Madeline had two strikes against her regarding who was getting blamed for the run of bad luck. The first was that her collection of heebie-jeebie mutants had only been with us for three weeks. Unlike other carny workers, Madeline and her Freaks moved from carnival to carnival, never settling with a company for any length of time. Her assorted muties consisted of Crab-Boy, whose undeveloped hands did actually look like soft, pink lobster claws, Alligator Man (terminal psoriasis), Cyclops – a strapping black man with a growth in the middle of his forehead that eerily resembled a closed eye, and last but not least, Hettie the Bearded Lady who sported a fine set of strawberry-blonde whiskers on her face. Pancho Pete said Hettie looked like her cunt had crawled up out of her drawers for a bit of fresh air.

Ordinarily this motley group of freaks wouldn't have done much business, but Madeline herself pulled her weight by performing a vintage burlesque act once a night. I have to admit she did look spectacular doing her bump and grind routine dressed in a tight-waisted corset, seamed stockings and six inch stilettos. Keppie the Clown said Madeline had a crippled daughter she kept hidden away in her trailer. No-one had ever seen this child but Keppie swore the girl had been born without a head, nothing above her shoulders except a shrivelled stump of a neck. To keep her alive the doctors had inserted two metal tubes into this stump, one for breathing and one for feeding. This was the reason Madeline and her troupe of freaks moved around so much. Keppie also said the little headless girl carried a voice-box cut from a doll that when squeezed said, 'Mama,' over and over again. I didn't know the truth of this story but we had all seen a medical supply van deliver packages to Madeline's trailer, so maybe there was something behind the macabre tale.

The second strike against Madeline was that she actually was a witch. Not the sort that flew around on a broomstick and stirred a bubbling cauldron cackling like a mad rooster. She was one of those new-age Wiccans. A fact she had freely admitted to Bette Gleeson at the hot dog stand as if it were completely normal. Thing is, you can put a new spin on the warty-nosed witch image all you want but I reckon it still amounts to the same thing, and as the Bible itself says, 'Thou shalt not suffer a witch.' If Madeline was getting blamed for all the bad luck in our carnival it was her own doing.

I caught Madeline just as she'd finished her hoochie-coochie act. I couldn't help but notice her expansive cleavage and the bare tops of her thighs were coated in a fine layer of sweat that gleamed with a mesmerising sheen. She ran a hand through her mane of lustrous blonde hair and eyed me suspiciously. 'What you want, Kid? Hope you're not mooching around to get a private dance.'

I made a big show of not staring at her titties while I told her about Brendan and how Oscar had called a midnight meeting. She looked sad about Brendan's death but the news of the meeting caused a much darker shadow to flit across her face. 'Carny ballot? Guess maybe me and my family of freaks are going to be moving on sooner than we'd planned.'

I tried to say no-one was accusing her of anything, but the lie must have shown on my face because she stopped me in midsentence. 'Look, Kid. I know how this goes. Newcomers get blamed when things go wrong. Tell Oscar I'll be at the meeting, just don't expect me to stay long.' Then she was striding away, those long legs bound in sheer nylon climbing the steps to the trailer and her fine ass giving me one last haughty fuck-you sashay as the door closed.

When I finally got back to Brendan's pitch I had to give a formal statement to a state trooper who seemed bored with the whole thing. I guessed he already had plenty of witness statements backing up my account of things. Brendan's body was already loaded into an ambulance for transport to the morgue and I hung around while the police took measurements and photographs of the scene. It was late before I got a chance to spruce up and make my way to the Big Top. By then it was near midnight and the tiered benches were crowded with carnival folk all whispering about witchy Madeline. Oscar, still wearing his ringmaster's outfit, stood in the centre of the ring as a distant church bell tolled midnight. That's when Madeline made her entrance, the corset and stockings replaced by t-shirt and jeans. She took a seat in the front row, looking neither left nor right.

Oscar cracked his whip for silence. 'We got a situation here, folks. I have to say it gives me no pleasure to do this, but a ballot's been called for......'

Madeline stood up and interrupted Oscar. Her voice was clear and carried all the way to the back rows. 'Let me save you all a bit of trouble. I'm guessing you want to pin all this bad luck shit on me and my family, so let me make this easy for you. We've already decided to move on at first light. Okay? That keep you all happy?' When no-one so much as breathed a single word, Madeline made for the exit. She was almost there when a huge figure stepped in front of her and grabbed her by the arms. It was Black Samson. Madeline was a big woman but she was no match for the brute strength of the strongman as he dragged her cussin' and yellin' back into the middle of the circus ring.

Oscar looked embarrassed about the whole thing. 'Sorry about this, Madeline, but you know once a Carny ballot has been called we've got to see it through. It's tradition.'

Madeline's eyes were blazing mad. 'Fuck your traditions and every last one of you. Hurry up and get it over with, I've got a sick daughter to tend to,' she hissed back.

A few people had the decency to look uncomfortable, but not all. Keppie's scare stories had obviously been doing the rounds. Oscar cracked his whip and shouted, 'You all know what you're voting for, so what's it to be? Exile or death?'

I know this all sounds a tad dramatic but Carny ballots are a ritual that go all the way back to the old days. Never actually knew anyone to get the death vote, although according to rumour, some carny across state got strung-up after getting caught messing around with little girls.

I sat back expecting to hear cries of, 'Exile!' but Keppie strode forward and shouted, 'Death!' Then someone else did the same. Then another. It was like something was in the air that night, something dark with outstretched wings and sharp claws that dripped venom. Psychologists might call it mass hysteria but I thought this outpouring of hate and vengeance had a different name. And a tail. And horns.

More people screamed out the death vote, I even found myself hollering for death. Only Oscar seemed immune to the bad mojo flying around. He looked distressed and I heard him say, 'Now just wait a goddamn minute here...' But Black Samson already had a firm hold of Madeline's head in his shovel-like hands and he twisted her noggin around so hard it was facing in the wrong direction when he dropped her limp body to the floor. Then there was silence. I found myself crying a bit, this wasn't the way it was supposed to happen.

It got a bit crazy then with people hollering and scream-ing and shouting as whatever malignant force dissipated and left us with various degrees of guilt and blame. Oscar, the only person in that Big Top not to have yelled for death, was the one who got things organised. He was a pragmatist and although he probably despised each and every one of us for what we had set in motion, he knew he'd lose his precious circus if swift action wasn't taken. First he delegated a few men to bury the body. We were on the edge of town so it wouldn't be hard to find a secluded spot. Next he sent some people over to drive off the Freaks and tell them Madeline had scarpered with their wages. It sounded a plausible story, but when they got there the Freaks had already gone. That caused a little worry in case they'd seen or heard something but Oscar said the police never listen to Freaks anyway. Lastly he got some womenfolk to go check on Madeline's sick daughter but there was no trace of any child. Just a plastic doll with a ragged hole cut in its belly. Weird, huh?

It was late by the time I trudged towards the trailer I'd

shared with Brendan. On the way I took a quick detour to the pitch, now criss-crossed with police tape. I had a lot of thoughts going through my head. Guilty ones mainly. I knew I shared in the blame over Madeline getting killed, but Brendan's death was on my head alone. All that baloney about Brendan being able to tell which chamber held the live round was nothing but a crock of shit. The revolver was one of a matching pair and every night when I turned my back on the audience to hand him the gun, I simply switched it for its unloaded twin hidden inside my jacket. It was child's play. Thing was, Brendan was always talking about hanging up his gun-belt and giving the pitch to me, but as the years rolled by he'd keep trotting out the same old bull-shit without making any solid plans to stand down. So I took matters into my own hands by handing him a gun with a bullet in every chamber during the switch. Bang. The perfect murder. Naturally I made sure the unfired rounds vanished while all hell was breaking loose. I was still stuffing the last of those bullets into my pocket when Oscar appeared.

I knew the blame for yet another unfortunate accident would fall upon Madeline as the whispering was already doing the rounds, but I never planned on her getting her neck snapped the way she did. Sometimes fate works in a strange way. It was real sad but I'd get over it. To cheer myself up a little I stood there in front of the plywood façade and imagined how it would look in a day or two. Instead of Buffalo Brendan's name up there, I would repaint it so it read Billy the Kid. I had some better tricks than old Brendan anyhow. The show would go on.

From inside the tent I heard a small sound and I wondered if some local ghoul had decided to sneak back and get himself a grisly souvenir. Ducking under the tape I entered the tent and pulled on the light cord. Then I stopped dead. Sitting on Brendan's stool in the middle of the tent was a little girl of maybe three or four years old wearing a gingham dress, her bare legs swinging as if she didn't have a care in the world. That could well have been true as the girl didn't have a head, just a stump of flesh where two metal tubes poked through.

In her hand she held a little circle of plastic which she held up and squeezed.

'Mama'

The horrible, scratchy voice almost made me piss my pants and I took a quick step back but found myself held firmly by two sets of hands. Looking down I saw one was actually a set of claws, while the second pair of hands was scaly like a lizard's. Crab-Boy and Alligator Man. I tried pulling away thinking to duck out the back flap but the hulking form of Cyclops was already there along with Hairy Hettie. That queer growth in the middle of Cyclops's forehead that so resembled an eye fluttered and fully opened to reveal a bloodshot eye. Fucker really did have an extra peeper. I opened my mouth to yell for help, but before I could draw breath something solid whacked me on the back of the head and everything went dark for a while.

When I came to, I was trussed and gagged and standing upright on the stool where the headless child had been sitting. Hands (or claws) held me firmly in place so I wouldn't fall. I realised one of Brendan's lassoes had been looped around my neck and pulled tight. I could hear some sort of music, like badly played pan pipes. Then I looked down at Hettie cradling the little headless girl in her arms while softly blowing across the two metal tubes sticking out of her neck stump. Helluva way to play a lullaby.

Cyclops moved into my view, a look of real hatred on his dark face. 'This here Missy, is the bad man to blame for your mama dyin'. She told me she pulled the thought right out of his head when he was over earlier on. Used her witchy powers on him. Told us things might get ugly and to go hide until she got back.'

Up on the stool, my legs were trembling like jelly and I felt my bladder let go, soaking my jeans with warm piss. If Cyclops noticed he didn't bother mentioning it to the girl with no head.

'She said Missy, that if she didn't come back we were to have ourselves our own Carny ballot with this murderin' devil. So here's the question, Missy. Exile or death? What you say?'

The headless child said nothing of course, the stump of her neck swaying from side to side like a blind snake. Then she held up her hand holding the circle of cheap plastic and squeezed it.

'Mama,' it croaked.

Cyclops closed all three of his eyes. 'Guess there's no more to be said then.'

And that's when either Crab-Boy or Alligator Man kicked the stool away and left me swinging and twisting all the way down into hell.

Or so I thought.

Whoever tied off the rope around the main tent support hadn't reckoned on it breaking under the buckling force of my frantic flailing like a landed fish trying to breathe. I hit the ground hard, landed badly and snapped my spinal cord. Ended up paralysed from the neck down.

Now I spend my days in a state sanatorium shitting into an adult diaper and watching endless repeats of Star Trek and Oprah while learning to type by blowing down a plastic straw to a computer. I'm guessing those Freaks could still come back and finish what they started. It might even be a mercy.

Sometimes on quiet nights I swear I can hear a little scratchy voice outside the window saying the same word over and over again.

'Mama.'

'Mama.'

'Mama.'

Carne Levare

Emma Teichmann

I watch the second hand on my watch jerk towards twelve, where the minute and hour hands are already loitering. Tick. Tick. Tick...

Midnight.

I down my whiskey, wincing at the bitterness, and signal to the waiter for another. I catch a glimpse of my reflection in the bar mirror. God, I look like shit. A patchy beard and dark bags under my eyes.

A notebook lies open on the alcohol-stained table in front of me, a list of names and addresses filling the page. Each is slashed through with a thick black line, all potential avenues that have led nowhere. Nobody saw anything, apparently, when my sister was killed in a hit and run last February. The investigation run by the Rome police had been similarly fruitless. 'This happens,' Lanza said apologetically, 'It's a busy junction.' But I think the homicide detective seemed dissatisfied, tired and upset by something he didn't want to talk about.

We all flew out here – my parents, Charlie and I – when we heard the news. But when the rest of my family returned home three months ago, devastated, despairing, I stayed, desperately seeking out information. I have spoken to, begged and cursed every shop owner, waiter and resident who works or lives on or near Via del Corso. I've spoken to commuters, street artists, tramps. A couple of wayward women. But the answer is always the same. Nobody knows anything. And yet... certain people seem to be hiding something. Or hiding from something. What are they scared of? The Mafia? No, that's crazy. All my theories are crazy. I flick the notebook closed. It's time to call an end to all this searching and start looking forward again.

I settle the bill, pull on my coat and head out into the night. Damned rain, I think, dodging a puddle. A street artist dressed as Satan is loitering on the corner of Via del Corso, hopping from foot to foot. His face paint is running, and stripes of dark skin have appeared beside the red. He looks cold in his spandex jumpsuit and cape.

'Denaro, per favore?' he holds out a clawed hand.

I shake my head, pull my hood further forward. Why doesn't he just call it a night? The old town's empty, everyone holed up indoors. I'm only out because a bar's more comfortable than my apartment, which has no heating, dodgy electrics, and angry neighbours; at least it's dry, I suppose.

A couple scurry past, huddled under an umbrella. Ahead, a waiter is hauling tables and chairs inside. Rain drips from my hood onto my nose. Yuck.

'Denaro?' A figure in grey steps out from an ingress in the wall. Hunched, hidden behind a mask, a massive hooked nose and two lumps where eyes should be. How can they see? I wonder. The voice sounds vaguely feminine. Low and cracked. Probably smokes forty a day.

'Mi dispiace,' I say, turning away.

My shoulder is wrenched back, nails digging into my skin.

'Hey!' I try to shake free, but the woman is remarkably strong.

The figure leans in close, and I can smell her breath, sickly sweet, like lemon drops. 'Edict says the carnival's to go ahead,' she snarls, running her elephantine nose down my cheek. 'Watch yourself.' I frown, surprised to hear English words… And then stumble, as she pushes me forcefully away.

'What the…?' I stagger round, but the figure is gone. Crazy cow. Her accent was peculiar, not English or Italian. Sort of… old. I wrap my arms around my body, feeling cold and shaken; step off the curb to cross the road… And jump back, out of the way of a wooden cart, packed full of squealing pigs.

I blink, and the cart vanishes.

I'm finally losing it. I've spent so long searching for clues that I'm starting to make things up in my head. Why did it have to happen? I think for the millionth time, tears pricking at the corner of my eyes. I hurry back to my cold apartment, where I dig into my coat pocket to find the keys. My fingers rub against a scrap of paper and I pull it out. The paper is thick and brown, the letters gilded: Invite to the Feast of Fools. There's no address. It'll be some stupid street act, I think, stuffing the paper back into my pocket and drawing out the keys.

I sleep badly, disturbed by strange sounds. Someone outside must be having a party. The noises seem to seep into the room. They slide about the walls, scuttling into my ears and around my brain.

I wake feeling fuzzy and dry-mouthed – the hint of a hangover – and with a nagging thought: what if there was something more to that grey figure? What if she was trying to tell me something... about Stella? Come on, Tom, I scold myself. She was just some crazy peddler.

I stagger out of bed, into the living room. Something's not quite right. Somehow the room's changed. I can't put my finger on it. The sunlight on the walls seems to flicker black and white, like noise on a TV screen. I go to the window and look outside. The rain is still beating down, but the droplets... it's as though the light is being refracted through them, making each translucent drop crackle with colour. I turn back inside, kneading my temples. This better not be the start of a migraine.

There's no milk in the fridge; bread but no butter. I decide I'll go out for breakfast. I pass my angry neighbour on the stairs – he's carrying up his post – and give him a tired nod. 'Were you kept awake too?' He scowls and mutters something under his breath.

There are a few more people out and about today, braving the wet. I walk along the pavement, staring up at the sky, and collide with an old man carrying a basket of pies. 'Sorry!' I stammer, 'Mi dispiace!' A woman pushing a pram along on the opposite side of the road frowns at me, perplexed.

I avoid the Via del Corso this morning, and take side alleys south towards Piazza Navona. On a street running behind the Church of Saint Agnes there's a little café, Agone, which does some of the best coffee in the old town.

Francesco is standing in the entrance to the café, his hands on his hips, frowning at the rain. The café owner smiles when he sees me and holds out his arms, 'Buon giorno, Thomas!' He pronounces my name in that funny Italian way: tome-ass.

A group of men in masks hurry past. More street artists? 'Might be a bit busier today?' I say, nodding towards the retreating figures.

Francesco shakes his head. 'No, I don't think so. Not until this rain goes away.' Inside, he pulls back a chair for me. 'How are you doing?' I grimace. 'Café?' he suggests gently.

'Si. And toast, per favore.'

I look about the dimly lit room. Black and white photos of Rome back in the early 1900s on the walls. A newspaper rack in the corner, and Agone painted in calligraphic letters above the doorframe. There's one other customer in the café – a woman, turned away from me, her dark hair trailing down the back of the chair. Same colour as Stella's, I think sadly.

Francesco brings my breakfast, and I sip my coffee, planning my day: food shopping, plane ticket, phone call to Mum. 'I'm ready to come home,' I'll tell her. The woman gets up to leave, and as she moves towards the door I see her in profile. I baulk. She is covered in hair. Her face, her neck and arms, her torso, her legs. I don't think she's even wearing any clothes. Just... hair. It should be a funny sight, she looks like a patchy Wookie, or Cousin It, but it's... horrible. And it looks so real. She must have glued each patch of hair on separately; that would have taken hours of preparation. I can guess who she's dressed as. Poor old Saint Ag, the original miracle hair-gro. God, I hate this city right now.

'Ciao, Francesco,' I say, slipping a five euro note under my coffee cup. The spectral rain is still falling. I wonder what the fountains in Piazza Navona look like today. A crowd of people are clustering around one of the entrances to the square, dressed in old-fashioned farming clothes. If there's a farmer's market on I might as well go check it out – I need some more food for the apartment.

Piazza Navona is filled with people, but there are no market stalls. Instead, a space has been cleared in the centre of the square and a man on a horse... I double take. Yes, that's right; a man on a horse is circling about, a long stick in one hand. A wooden trellis has been set up in the clearing, about three metres high, topped by a long horizontal plank, on which sit three steel buckets. Attached to each bucket handle is a length of string, and on the lower end of each string is a metal ring, about as wide as a grapefruit.

The man on the horse is wearing a jester's patchwork costume, but his face is mean. He glowers at the mob of people and approaches the rings; pauses, his head cocked. Then he drives forward, shoving the stick through the right hand ring. The string pulls taut, the bucket tips sideways, and a stream of dirty water soaks the horse and rider. There are jeers from the crowd. The rider growls, and jumps to the ground.

This is an odd sort of street performance. There must be some meaning behind it all, something I'm not getting. I turn to the person standing next to me, an ugly woman with a wart in the crease between her nose and cheek, but her focus is on the clearing, where another man is now straddling the horse. This man's face is hidden behind a mask, a grotesque green visage, severely sagging on one side. The man bows to the crowds, and spurs the horse forward, lowering the point just in time to thrust it into the middle ring. The bucket tips... and a torrent of blood and bile slops out.

The crowds go wild. Hands reach up to the rider and tear him from his horse, the mob panting and spitting, slashing at his clothing, clawing at his mask. He disappears beneath the writhing bodies. 'Should have chosen the left one,' says someone nearby. 'The gold's always in the left one.'

'Until it ain't, that is.'

'Hey,' I shout, trying to shoulder my way in, 'stop!' But I am thrown backwards, out of the crowd.

I spot a man walking along the edge of the piazza, dressed in conspicuously normal jeans and a mackintosh, and run towards him. 'Did you see that? Those people? They just tore a man from his horse... They'll kill him. Look!' The man frowns, and looks across to where I'm pointing. His expression turns to one of vexation. He doesn't understand, I think. I point to my eyes, then across at the crowd, heaped on top of the hooded rider. I put my hands round my neck as though strangling myself. The man shakes his head angrily, and continues walking.

He can't see them! I lean against a wall, pressing my knuckles to my forehead. What is going on? Am I going mad? But the people look too real to be made up. Somehow I can see into another world. A secret world, long past, but, unfathomably, present. And the realisation brings with it the rest of the secret. Something in this world was the cause of Stella's death. The taste of it, the heaviness of the air. Somehow I know... My eyes seem to spin round and round in my head, the black and white dots filling my head, now, whirling, whirling... And this strange, new old Rome crashes down on top of me.

I feel like Dorothy. Except that this isn't Oz.

There is a shriek of glee, and the crowd, which has swollen to a hundred or more, surges forward, pushing and pulling me along with it, like a great tidal wave, across the piazza, down a side street... Banners fly overhead, and I can hear the beating of drums. The smell of hot buns mixed with the stench of sweat, piss and vomit.

'There!' cries someone.

Ahead, a woman on stilts, dressed in a long feathered cape and wearing a parrot mask, waves a whip in the air. 'Pieces of silver,' she screeches, and coins are shoved into her hands. 'Pieces of silver to see the little men run.'

A cackle ripples among the crowd. Fingers wriggle in delight. 'Little men! Bring out the little men!'

The parrot woman cracks her whip, and four dwarfs spill out from between her stilts. Their arms are raised defensively above their heads, or out in front of them, as though to ward off the crowd. The whip shudders through the air again. There is a yelp, and the dwarves race away, chased by the parrot woman and, in close pursuit, the peasant crowd.

'Little men! Little men, we're coming to get you…'

A cart pulls out suddenly from a side street, cutting off half the throng. Furious shouts are answered by the squeal of pigs, over half a dozen, squashed inside. A few of the men beat impatiently on the back of the cart with sticks. 'Move! Move!' The cart trundles slowly away, but the crowd has lost momentum. Masked peasants jostle each other. An old man grabs a woman's ample breasts and gives them a hard squeeze. A twig of a woman lifts up her skirt and flashes her pubic hair, dyed all the colours of the rainbow.

And then I spot her. The grey figure from the Via del Corso, still wearing the mask with the elephantine nose. She is limping away, weaving a path through the hordes. 'Stop!' I shout. She knows what happened to Stella. She brought me here for a reason, made me see… I try to push my way through the crowds after her, but get caught in a tangle of arms and legs. I reach into my pocket and pull out the scrap of paper. 'Stop!' I shout again, waving the paper in the air. 'Please stop!' But it's no good. She's disappeared.

'Is that an invitation to the Feast of Fools?' A grubby boy is standing in front of me, eyeing the paper in my hand. A dark nebula bruise covers half his face, and his right eye is red with blood. God, what happened? 'Well, is it?' the boy presses.

'I… yes, I guess. A woman in grey gave it to me…' Nearby, a chubby girl kicks a crippled man in the backside and the man flies forward into a puddle. 'I need to find her. I think she knows what happened to my sister.'

'I have a sister…' The boy points to the chubby girl who is now trying to surreptitiously snatch a pie from out of a woman's basket. 'Where's yours?'

'Mine's… dead.'

'Then you know what's happened to your sister,' says the boy, unperturbed.

'But I don't know how it happened.'

The boy scratches his nose thoughtfully. 'You should speak

to the Lord of Misrule. Bet he knows about it. He'll be host-
ing the Feast, so you might as well go…'

'But I don't know where that is. There's no address.'

'Oh, but it's always held in Peter's Place,' says the boy. A
dwarf stumbles out of a side alley, glancing anxiously about,
trying to spot a hiding place before… 'Little man!' yells the
boy. The dwarf sprints away.

'Little man!' bellows the crowd. I cower against a wall as
the crowd rushes past. The crippled man is still sprawled in
the puddle, eating a pie.

I stay there for a while, leaning against the wall, shaking, feeling sick. Peter's Place… Where the hell is that? I need help,
but who's going to believe me? Detective Lanza? I swear he
knew more than he was letting on. Was this world it? I stagger through the carnival crowds towards the police station,
ignoring the disapproving looks of ordinary passers-by who
mistake me for a drunk.

The inside of the police station seems extraordinary in its
ordinariness. There are no masked figures. No banners, or
bile, or bright sparks of rain. I could hide in here forever…
But no, I have to get to the bottom of this. I have to know
what happened to Stella.

I ask to see Detective Lanza and take a seat in the waiting
room. My head is pounding. I glance about the room. There's
nothing strange to be seen… Maybe I am just losing the plot?
But it was all so real… And then there's the invitation. I pull
the piece of paper out of my pocket and re-read the words
written on it: 'Invite to the Feast of Fools.' Will Lanza think
I'm a fool?

'Thomas,' Detective Lanza is striding towards me, dressed
in a smart blue-grey suit, his bald head shiny with sweat.
'How are you?' I must look terrible, because he frowns when
he sees my face, and says, 'Shall we find a room…?'

I nod mutely and follow him down the stark corridor, to
a cramped, dimly lit interview room, with a table and two
chairs. Lanza shuts the door behind us, and takes a seat opposite me. 'What happened?'

I try and explain what I've experienced, horribly conscious of how ludicrous I sound. But my suspicion about Lanza must be right because the old detective doesn't laugh at me or call me mad. He listens in grim silence, nodding occasionally, his expression one of apprehension rather than disbelief. When I show him the invitation, he scrutinises it with the same care one would take over a crucial piece of evidence found at the scene of the murder.

'You don't think I'm crazy, then?' I ask him when I've finished.

'No. I think I believe you. This city is very old and full of secrets…'

He's still not telling me everything. 'Do you know something about Stella's death?' I say quietly, 'I think you do.'

Lanza sighs deeply, and hands me back the invitation, 'I don't know any more than I told you. But I suspected it wasn't just a hit and run. You see,' he takes off his glasses and rubs his eyes, 'there have been quite a few deaths on that road over the years. Four in the last decade. The last one was two years ago. A little girl was knocked down. I decided to make some more thorough enquiries. I thought it might be somehow gang-related, even though there was no obvious pattern to the victims. But some of the things I found seemed to defy explanation. You know people have been mysteriously dying on Via del Corso for more than a hundred years? The locals won't talk about it. They think it's a ghost…'

'The people in that world are, in a way,' I say. 'They're invisible to everyone else.'

Danza shakes his head. 'But the locals had a particular ghost in mind. A little boy who got trampled to death during the Barbary Races, back in the 1850s.'

'What's that?'

'A horse race down Via del Corso. No riders. It was one of the major events during the Rome carnival, back when Rome had a carnival.'

'The carnival?' I remember the grey figure's words. 'Then they are linked…'

Danza nods slowly. 'Yes, I think they are. But how? What's really doing this?'

'We need to speak to the Lord of Misrule.' I say, 'It sounds like he's the king of this realm; he should know what his subjects are up to.'

'What if he's the killer?'

But I'm determined, 'We have to try.'

Danza is staring off into space. 'You said the boy mentioned Peter's Place... Thomas, I think I know where the Feast is being held.'

We walk together to the Tiber. Behind us, the old town is revelling in sex and gore. The statues leer at me as I cross Ponte Sant'Angelo, sniggering behind their bent wings, 'Terror this way lies...' Danza can't see any of it, of course, but he keeps glancing at me, his expression full of concern. We turn onto Via della Conciliazione, and now I can see the Basilica, jutting up into the effervescent sky. Peter's Place.

A queue snakes round Saint Peter's vast square. There must be nearly a thousand bodies, all waiting to be let in. Everyone appears to be wearing masks. Grand Venetian masks, black and white mime masks, grotesque clown faces... A lot of people are dressed as pigs. 'There's so many,' I say hoarsely.

'Come on,' says Lanza, placing a hand on my elbow. We walk past them all, right up to the basilica steps.

'Oi!' A man emerges from the atrium, dressed in red and black livery. He is carrying a long pike, which he holds out to the side, blocking our path, 'You'll have to get in line.'

'I need to speak to the Lord of Misrule,' I say. 'I have an invite...'

The man's eyes narrow, 'Let me see.' I hold out the invitation. The gold letters seem to squirm across the paper. 'My apologies,' the man's mouth twists into a smile, 'Please... this way.' I start up the steps after him, Lanza beside me, but the man spins back around and growls, 'Not him', the spiky head of his pike mere inches from Lanza's protruding tummy.

'Detective,' I grab Lanza's arm, 'you need to stay here.' My eyes are fixed on the spike near his stomach.

Lanza looks at me and then down at the space in front of him. He frowns, confused, but nods slowly, 'Okay.'

I follow the guard into the shadows. We pass through a huge iron door, into the great hall...

This is not the basilica I know.

The walls are a mass of screaming gargoyles, agonised faces illuminated by a moat of fire that skirts the edges of the room. The ceiling is a squall of black smoke, and the floor is carpeted with splintered bones. In the centre of the hall stands a colossal banqueting table. Places are set, candles lit. I count six chairs on either side. At the head is a throne of thorns.

There is turmoil behind me, the multitudes of people pushing to get in through one of the side doors. They form a ragged ring around the banquet table, no-one daring to get too close to what is, I realise, the stage for the forthcoming event. The Feast of Fools... You're such a fool, Tom, to come here!

A bell chimes, thirteen times. Twelve hooded figures file in and take their places behind the chairs. Another man in red and black livery steps forward, holding out a scroll. He jerks it open, 'Announcing... the Lord of Misrule.'

A gargoyle growls.

Tendrils of black smoke reach down from the ceiling, spinning into a ball. The smoke stretches out, squid-like, then curls inwards, becoming thicker, blacker. It oozes, thins, bends and straightens. Slowly, a human form materialises, solidifies. A bearded man, broad-shouldered, proud. The shadows playing on his face seem like dancing tattoos, ever shifting, changing – now a beetle, now a scythe, now a gaping skull.

This is hell.

I want to leave. I want to cry, to scream, to tremble in a corner with my eyes shut tight, willing it all away. But I need to find out what happened to Stella.

The Lord of Misrule lifts his arms. 'Welcome. Please,' he bows, 'be seated.' The twelve figures take their seats at the banqueting table. Speak, Thomas! Speak up, and get it over with. I clear my throat to speak, and the Lord of Misrule's head jerks up. He fixes his eyes on me, 'And who have we here?'

'Please,' I choke, 'I have this invite. I... think you might be able to help me.'

There are excited whispers from the masked spectators.

'Help you?' the Lord's voice seems to permeate through my skin. 'How?'

'My sister died last year, knocked down on the Via del Corso. I think someone – something – from your world did it.'

'My world? As opposed to...'

'The real one.'

The Lord of Misrule opens his jaw and laughs.

'This world is entirely real, Thomas. You of all people should know that.' I flinch at the sound of my name. This was a mistake, you fool. A mistake! He picks up a fork, examines its teeth, 'But, yes, I can help you. I know exactly what happened to Stella, after all.'

My heart is beating in my throat. 'Please...'

The Lord of Misrule presses the fork hard against his fingertips, drawing blood, and sucks the droplets from his fingers, as though they are the sticky remains of an orange. 'Won't you come forward?' he calls into the crowd, and there is movement as the sea of spectators parts to let someone through... It is the grey figure, limping towards the banqueting table, and the Lord of Misrule is grinning wickedly at her. 'Why don't you show our guest?' he says.

The grey figure bows and reaches for her mask. She levers it open like you would a door, and I realise that one side of the mask appears attached, the plastic fused with her very skin. And then I see the face beneath...

My dead sister looks back at me with glassy eyes. Her skin is green-grey and mottled. Her lips are black, melting into the cavity that is her mouth, and they tremble, forming words, 'Carne levare...'

What have they done to her? What is she, now? Bile

is welling up into my mouth. I gasp for air, I feel like I'm suffocating.

'Carne levare,' whispers the crowd. 'Carne levare.'

The Lord of Misrule returns the fork to the table and seizes a meat knife. He stands and repeats the words, slowly, with relish, 'Carne levare. To remove the flesh. That's what carnival's about, after all...' The Lord of Misrule moves along the table. 'This is a time to flay our sins. Strip them away, so to speak...'

Stella looks hungrily at me. 'Carne levare.'

'Carne levare! Carne levare!'

I turn and run. Hands reach out for me, but I wrench free, throw my weight at the doors, fall through, out, out into the night. The masked hordes swarm out through a side entrance, screeching. 'Little man! Little man!'

Lanza is sprawled over the basilica steps, his face purple. Dead.

I sprint across Saint Peter's square, the thump of my feet mixed with the pounding of my heart and the beating of far-off drums. I cross a bridge, onto the main thoroughfare. There is a procession further ahead. I race towards it, into the throng of candle-bearers, pushing through the packed rows, past countless figures dressed in white robes, each wearing a ghostly wax mask. They are chanting some ancient tune. I dare a glance back. The peasant horde is nowhere in sight. I begin to cry, whether from terror or relief I can't say.

We have come to a crossroads. To our left is Via del Corso. To our right, one of Rome's many piazzas. Piazza Venetia. Fitting, somehow. The Venetian carnival is famous, even now. Let this end, I silently beg. Let things return to normal. Will things ever be normal again, now that I know?

The procession slows to a halt as the song ends. The singers bring the candles up to their faces, fire flickering across wax features... and they hold them there, as the masks begin to melt, exposing skulls beneath.

I run.

Down Via del Corso I run, screaming.

The horses charge. Eight of them, hurtling down the road towards me. Riderless, and frothing at the mouth.

Leave No Trace

AJ Sikes

The festival didn't disappear this year. Small paper bags sail across the lawn on the breeze, releasing yellowed chips of popcorn. Soda cups roll in confused arcs, unable to choose between following the zephyrs and staying still. Mickey and Delia walk in and out through naked wooden frames, the skeletal remains of arcade and carny stalls that stand along the old boardwalks by the seaside park. Every year the festival grows flesh along the rickety salt-stained posts and beams, draping them in colorful banners and batiks. The whole becomes a mandala maze of bright colors. Around each corner, down every walk hide bizarre and colorful artists and crafters showing their wares to the buying public. Jugglers and gymnasts spin and skip, entrancing and hypnotizing. And weaving through the throngs, a serpentine haze carries scents of far away lands, distant mysteries unexplored and tempting. In the middle of the park grounds, the town's Maypole still stands in its widening pool of concrete. Over the years, more concrete has been poured around the original setting to reinforce the pole, keep it upright. Every year, festival goers plant incense sticks and set flower wreaths around the pole. The town leaders call the Maypole a silent sentinel, a guardian of the park and festival grounds.

Mickey and Delia never come to the festival. They're too young, Delia's parents say, and it's just a bunch of dirty hippies smoking dope, Mickey's father says. Next year they'll go, when they're ten.

But this year they have to wait until after the festival departs, after the tents and fabrics, the scarves and flowers and incense are packed up and carted off, after the drummers and dancers and fire spinners are on their way, carrying their acrid scented bodies and breath into the night. After the last school bell, Mickey and Delia come to the seaside park and walk the maze without its walls. Their feet clap like horses' hooves on the weathered wood planks of the boardwalks, dry and cold as forgotten bones in the mid-morning sun.

Delia kicks at a cup. 'Why is there so much trash? It's never like this. They always clear it all away. Every year.'

'My dad says it was big this year, way bigger than before. Lots of people from the city came out this time.'

Delia picks up the soda cup she'd kicked. 'We should do it then. The festival always disappears the next day. And besides, it's ugly.'

Mickey bends to pick up a soda cup and two cigarette butts. 'We should have gloves, and those things you can grab trash with, but you don't have to bend down. Like a claw on the end of a stick, and you squeeze the handle, the claw opens and then you pick up the trash and put it in the bag. I saw the jail van on the highway once and all the guys had them.'

'When were you on the highway?'

'When me and my dad moved here. We drove all the way from Sacramento.'

'You're probably right. We should have gloves. This is gross.'

Mickey smiles. He always smiles when Delia agrees with something he says. They both turned nine in February, and Mickey knows it's too early to talk about things like going steady and first kisses. So Mickey waits. He keeps picking up pieces of trash and collecting them in the soda cup. Delia does the same with the cup she grabbed.

Before long they separate, following trails of trash around the park. Delia moves back along the boardwalks and Mickey meanders towards the cliffs. They aren't really cliffs, just steep slopes that stand about twenty feet above a rocky stretch of sand that rings the bay along this edge of town. But Mickey and Delia call them the cliffs because they've been warned off of playing around that edge of the park. A fence went up one year, but it washed out with heavy rains. After that parents were careful to keep their children away from the edge.

Mickey looks down the steep slope. He doesn't see any trash by the water's edge, so he turns around. That's when he notices the Maypole is falling over. It looks like that tower in Italy, like the ground tried to turn over and got stuck halfway. Something moves at the base of the pole, like a ripple in the ground. Mickey walks towards the Maypole, thinking he might be able to see what's buried beneath it, maybe see its roots.

'Mickey!'

He turns to see Delia, halfway across the park, holding up a piece of paper and waving it like crazy. He runs over and sees she holds a poster. It has funny pink and orange and green colors, like the flavors of fruit gum Mickey likes best. He thinks the poster would taste of lime-mango-raspberry-punch if he chewed on it.

A black man plays a guitar in the middle of the picture. His lime pants and mango shirt stand out like caterpillars on the background. Raspberry worms sketch in his facial features against the black, too. His fuzzy afro, outlined in a squiggly pink line of punch, sticks out around a lime-mango scarf he wears as a headband. Above the guitar man, fat yellow letters say Jimi Hendrix and his Band of Gypsies will play at the festival. Voluptuous yellow numbers tempt Mickey and Delia to go back in time almost fifty years, to 1967.

'Let's show my dad,' Mickey says. The old man loves black musicians. He'll probably flip when he sees the poster.

When they get to Mickey's house, his dad comes down the drive carrying plastic garbage bags in both hands.

'What's going on, son?'

'We were just at the festival, Pop. It's all messy. Like they didn't clean up this year.'

'Yeah? Well I'm cleaning up here. You could stick around and help, hey?'

Mickey's dad tosses the sacks into the garbage can on the

curb and walks back up the drive to get two more waiting by the house.

'What're you throwing away?'

'Old stuff,' the old man calls over his shoulder. 'Some of your toys. Clothes don't fit.'

'My toys?' Mickey asks, a tear creeping into the edge of his voice, lingering there and drying up just in time to avoid triggering his dad's temper. He remembers the poster.

'We found this, Pop. At the park. There's all this trash, but they always clean up.'

'Always, huh? Hippies probably got too much smoke in their eyes this year.' Mickey's dad looks at the poster and slowly sets the garbage bags down. He takes the poster in both hands and peers into the swirling color sea on its surface. 'I didn't know Hendrix played here in sixty-seven. Summer of Love…'

'Summer of Love?' Delia asks. 'What's that mean?'

Mickey's dad doesn't answer. He turns the poster over in his hands, rubs the paper between his fingers and brings it up to his face to sniff at it.

'Where'd you find this, Mickey?'

'At the park by the seaside. There's lots of trash everywhere. Like popcorn bags and soda cups. I bet there's more of those posters, too. C'mon Delia!'

But Delia keeps her eyes on the poster. 'What're you going to do with it, Mr. Downs?'

'I don't know. Why don't you go look for more? You find some; you can have one of them.'

Delia sniffs and turns around, then steps away down the drive with her arms crossed. Mr. Downs nudges his chin at the garbage bags at his feet. Mickey looks after Delia for a moment and then struggles to lug the sacks, one at a time, to the garbage can by the street. He pretends not to see the outline of the button nose on his favorite stuffed panda. And he doesn't mention it when his mother calls to tell him she loves him and to wish him a good night's sleep.

The next day, after the last school bell, Mickey and Delia

walk side by side all the way to the park. 'Why'd you leave like that, Delia? He didn't do nothing.'

'He took my poster is what he did.'

'Well there's probably more of them. Right? I bet we find all kinds of posters. Maybe even from 1867!'

Delia keeps her eyes straight ahead and walks on towards the park. Mickey worries he's lost his best girl before he even had her, even though he doesn't know what it's like to have a best girl. Maybe she's his best girl because she always walks with him after the last school bell. That sounds good, Mickey tells himself. He decides that's the truth, even though his stomach tells him he might be sick soon. When they get to the boardwalks, Mickey's stomach settles from the rolling, twisting fear into a slow burble of worry. He promises himself not to show his dad anything they find this time.

Delia picks up more soda cups and popcorn bags, snatching them from the breeze like a falcon latching onto topsy-turvy gulls. Mickey tries to duplicate her grabs, snaking his arm out, fingers extended, ready to strike at the flapping bits of paper. But he moves too fast or too slow, or just too clumsy, and he always misses. Delia doesn't seem to notice. Together they go around the park, collecting bits of garbage and stowing them inside larger plastic bags they find blowing around the site. They take the bags to the trash cans at the edge of the park and stuff them inside. It takes the whole afternoon, and they only clean a small area along the boardwalk. It'll take the whole week to make it look like the festival has disappeared again.

They sit on the cliffs after they finish, looking down at the rocky beach below and the persistent waves that take more of the cliffs each year.

'The waves will eat the whole cliff away and the park and boardwalks will fall into the ocean. My mom and dad told me that,' Delia says. 'That's why we have to pick up all the trash. So more doesn't go into the ocean.'

Since yesterday, soda cups and empty boxes and bags have blown down to the beach below Mickey's feet. If they had more time, they could climb down and collect all the trash.

But the tide surges higher and higher with each breath from the sea. A few bags and cups already bob in the surf.

'I hate trashers,' Delia says.

'Me, too,' Mickey says back, hoping that means she's his best girl again and still wondering what that means even as he knows it means something good, something he never wants to lose.

They watch the sun slip down to touch the water, casting rosy fingers overhead through the puffs of late spring clouds. Mickey concentrates on one soda cup rolling along the surface of the water, just off shore. He thinks he sees a tentacle sprout from the wavy surface and wrap around the cup and pull it under, or maybe it's a tongue from some big fish. Mickey doesn't know about any fish that eat trash, but the ocean, in his mind, has always been a place of mystery and also one of fear.

The next day is Friday. Mickey meets Delia outside Mrs. Nuñez's classroom, like he always does. She smiles when she sees him, like she always does. Mickey's heart warms and he tells Delia a joke he heard on the playground. She laughs and tells him a joke while they walk to the seaside park. Mickey laughs at Delia's joke, too, and by the time they reach Main Street, they're holding hands again.

On the way to the park, they meet a young woman handing out flyers at the intersection by the drugstore. She stands next to the old telephone box, its red frame sticking up like a lump on a cartoon character's head. The girl thrusts a flyer at Mickey and Delia as they pass by the phone box.

'We're just kids,' Delia says, stepping away. The flyer girl puts her hand out. Her arm blocks Mickey's path. He notices a cord of wooden beads dangling from her wrist. Mickey takes the flyer and the girl smiles.

'Give that to your parents, okay? Lots of people need help these days. Thanks!'

And then the young woman turns to confront the next unlucky souls to cross the street, unaware they're approaching the telephone box lair of a flyer girl.

Mickey has to run to catch up to Delia. He reads the flyer as they walk. It's a pale green slip of paper, cut from a larger sheet. Uneven edges and hand-lettering give the flyer a trashy look. The printing on it says the local shelter agency wants household discards: old clothes (clean), toys, small appliances, office supplies. The items will help people looking for work or starting over in life.

'What's that mean, starting over?' Mickey says out loud, not really meaning to ask Delia for an answer. But he's still happy to hear her voice when she replies.

'It means they want your dad to give them that stuff he was throwing away the other day. He can just leave it on the sidewalk and they'll come pick it up. See,' she says, stopping to take one corner of the flyer and point at the phone number at the bottom. 'He just has to call them and they'll come take it all away.'

'Why didn't you tell him that the other day then?'

Delia looks at Mickey like he's stupid. They walk on to the seaside park in silence. When they get there, it's like they haven't picked up any trash at all. The weathered planks of the boardwalk peek out from beneath even more garbage: loose bits of popcorn, hotdog ends sticking out of stale half-eaten buns stained yellow and red, soda cups, candy wrappers. More posters fly around the site, mostly ones that are ripped in half or torn on the edges where they'd been taped to walls and posts.

'What happened?' Delia cries. She stomps her feet and makes fists to beat at the air in front of her, like she holds an Etch-a-Sketch frame around the whole scene and can make all the trash go away by shaking it.

Mickey leans down to pick up a poster blowing around at his feet. As he bends over a shadow falls on the ground. A new candy wrapper flutters down in front of Mickey, followed by a soda can that clunks on the boardwalk and splashes cola across the surface of the poster Mickey is reaching for. A malicious laugh tells Mickey they're in trouble, and he stands up quickly to avoid taking a sucker shove.

'What you doing, Mickey boy? Hanging around this white girl going to get you in trouble.'

It's Moses. His real name is Kavon Mosely, but everyone calls him Moses. He and his friends, 'Slim' Jim Reedy and Joe Dumar go to school in the city. They ride the bus every morning. On days when it rains, Mickey has to ride that bus to school instead of walking. His dad doesn't want him getting sick walking in the rain or showing up to school looking like he's gone swimming in his clothes. Even though he gets off after only a few blocks, it's still enough time for Moses and his friends to give Mickey the business.

Mickey hates the rain.

'So what you doing in the park with this white girl, Mickey boy?'

'My name is Delia.'

'Yeah, I know. I know. Ain't no secret Mickey's girlfriend's a little white girl name Delia. But I asked Mickey. Not you.'

Moses and the other big kids stare at Mickey, and his cheeks burn where their gazes touch him. He knows if he doesn't tell them what he and Delia are doing, they'll punch it out of him, and then he'll go home crying again. But if he tells them, they'll make jokes and then punch him anyway. Mickey thinks it's better to say something though, so at least when they do punch him he can tell his dad that he stood up for himself first and that it was three against one.

'We're just picking up the trash.'

'Picking up what? You picking up trash, Mickey boy? Like some nigger slave? Why you want to pick up trash? Who cares about them hippies' trash? Unless you they slave now. That what you doing out here, being this little white girl's slave? You shine her daddy's shoes, too?'

'He doesn't shine shoes, and he's not a slave!'

Moses lifts his hand like he'll slap Delia silent and Mickey feels himself explode inside. His feet push off from the boardwalk planks and propel him at Moses. Mickey has his arms outstretched and he hits the bigger boy in the middle, knocking the air out of Moses' lungs. Moses staggers backwards with Mickey still clutching onto his shirt and bringing his legs up and around the older boy's waist. Mickey claws and thrashes around until the other boys grab him off of Moses and throw him to the ground.

Moses stands with his hands on his knees, gasping. 'You going to pay for that good, Mickey boy. Time to teach you about respect.' All three of the older boys grab Mickey and slap him a few times until the tears begin to fill his eyes. They carry him bodily across the lawn. Delia follows at a distance, a dark glare pulling her face into a mask of hatred. Mickey can see her eyes through his stinging tears, see how angry she is. But he also sees her eyes pinch up like she might cry, too.

'You want to pick up trash, Mickey boy? Here you go,' Moses says. Mickey looks at where they've brought him. They're standing around a trash barrel lying on its side in the grass. Slim Jim lifts the empty barrel and puts it back into the metal frame that normally holds it. That explains the extra trash. Moses and his friends had been dumping the barrels around the park for fun. Before Mickey can think to yell at them for undoing his and Delia's hard work, Moses and his friends stuff Mickey's feet into the top of the waste barrel. They have his arms pinned so he can't hold the edges of the trash bin. They keep pushing him down, but can't get him in all the way.

'What's he doing?' Slim Jim asks. 'He got his feet on something in there. Shove harder now. C'mon.'

Mickey can feel something firm under his feet, something that supports his weight and prevents the older boys from putting him all the way into the trash can. Then he feels it move, feels it twist out from under his feet and slither around his lower legs, up to his hips. Mickey screams in terror, and Slim Jim lets go of him for a moment. Moses hollers at his friend to keep pushing and the older boy gets his arms back around Mickey just as the first tentacles sprout from the mouth of the barrel around Mickey's hips.

Mossy green tendrils and sinew snake out, whipping the air around Mickey as he struggles. Coils wrap like taffy around the older boy's necks and pull them over at the waist, headfirst towards the trash bin. Mickey feels their arms release him and he flings himself out of the garbage can. He tumbles headfirst onto the ground where he lands with a thud on his shoulders. The air goes out of him and he closes his eyes. He hears a gurgling and screaming above him and a sound like thousands of dry sticks snapping underfoot.

When Mickey opens his eyes again, Moses and his friends are gone. Delia kneels next to Mickey, looking at the trash can with blank eyes. Tears run down her cheeks in slender streams and drip off her chin.

'What happened?'

'It ate them. It ate them because they're trashers. Because they called you a slave for picking up trash.'

'How do you know?'

Delia doesn't answer him. She stays there, sitting back on her feet with her knees on the ground and crying softly. Mickey stands up and looks at the edge of the trash can, staying back from it so he can run in case the tentacles come out again. The rim of the can is smeared with blood mixed with something black and sticky, like the slimy stuff Mickey's dad makes him clean out of the sink drains.

'Let's go home, Delia. C'mon. We got to leave now.'

Delia lets Mickey help her up and holds his hand the whole way back to her house. She says goodbye at the curb and walks to the front door without looking back. Mickey waves even though she has her back to him as she goes inside. He keeps the hand she held in his pocket all the way back to his house. He doesn't want to lose any of the feeling of Delia's hand touching his, and he holds that memory in mind as he walks. It's the only way he can keep from remembering what happened in the park.

Trash still fills the park when Mickey and Delia return after school on Monday. They pick up as much as they can and throw it away in a can at the other end of the park from where Moses and his friends got eaten. The shore breeze has blown that end clean, so they don't have to go over there anyway.

'The wind's helping us,' Mickey says, motioning at the

clean area. Delia nods and murmurs an agreement, but she doesn't look at that end of the park. They keep stooping and picking up bits of food, paper plates, popcorn bags and soda cups, and more posters, some with dates from before 1940.

As they're finishing, they hear a laugh come up from below the cliffs, carried to them on the breeze. Mickey goes to see. Delia comes up behind him and looks over his shoulder as he lies on his stomach and creeps to the edge to look down. A boy and girl play in the surf. She has on a short dress and he wears pants rolled up to under his knees. Their shoes lie in a jumble with his shirt and her handbag over against the rocks at the base of the cliff.

The boy smokes a cigarette. The girl takes it from him and sucks in a mouthful of smoke that she blows in his face. He snatches the cigarette from her and takes a puff off it then flicks it away into the surf. Mickey and Delia watch the butt arc out, see it tumble in the tidal spray and get caught by a lightning fast tendril that snaps out of the surf. The boy laughs but the girl looks at the tide and has stopped playing. Mickey feels Delia backing away behind him, but he keeps watching. He watches the rope-like snares explode from the surf and grapple the boy and girl. Her screams are muffled against the green-black skin of the tentacles. The boy's head lolls on his broken neck. A thick tendril squeezes so tightly there that his head pops off and falls into the water. It's sucked down by another whipping sludge-colored snake.

Mickey watches until the bodies disappear under the waves and the tide returns to a calm ebb and flow. Then he pushes himself up and away from the cliff's edge. Delia has already reached the edge of the boardwalk. Mickey feels his face trembling with fear as he approaches Delia. He reaches out his hand to take hers, and she lets him. But he knows she wants to run away home and he knows he wants to do the same thing.

'We have to tell somebody, Mickey! We have to.'

Delia's tears fall in rivers down her face. Together they turn to leave the park and halt where they stand. Trash cans wait for them, threatening to prevent them leaving. None of the

AJ Sikes

cans have moved, but from where Mickey and Delia stand, every path out of the park takes them too close to the cans. Too close to the hungry tentacles and the memory of bones crackling like kindling under a bonfire.

Mickey looks at the Maypole. It still leans to one side. The ground beneath it ripples as Mickey watches the pole right itself a bit, not quite enough to bring it straight up. But almost. Almost there. Almost back the way it was before the festival. Mickey sees the streamers dangling from the top of the pole. Three glossy black streamers hang in the breeze like brackish kelp in the tide. As he watches, two new streamers unfurl from the top to join the other three, flicking at the air around the pole like grotesque dancing fairies.

Mickey tugs on Delia's hand and they run, dodging clumps of garbage as they go and squeezing together when they pass a trash can, even though it sits several feet off to one side, silent and still.

'It already ate. It ate that boy and girl in the water, so it's not hungry anymore.' Mickey says.

Mickey can feel Delia wanting to ask him how he knows this. He wants to ask himself, too, but at the same time he understands that he knows. He just knows. The monster under the park is awake and hungry. It eats people who trash the park. But will it eat them, too? They stop running a block away from the park and catch their breath.

'Don't you think it let us go, Delia? Because we picked up the trash?'

'I don't know. I think it's just eating trashers. Like you said. Maybe we're safe. We can still pick up the trash, or maybe not. Maybe we shouldn't come back here after school anymore.'

Mickey feels his heart pound with the thought of losing Delia. She's his best girl, even if they haven't said it or talked about it. He knows it like he knows there is a hungry monster living under the park. He figures Delia has to know it, too, the way she held his hand while they were running. But if they don't come back to the park after school, what happens? How can he be sure Delia won't go with some other guy from school, some guy who lives on her street instead of around the corner and over two blocks?

'What if it wants us to keep cleaning up the park? What if it's going to keep eating people until the whole town is gone unless we pick it up?'

Delia looks at Mickey with her eyes wide open in shock. Mickey feels his breath leave him as his heart stammers. He didn't want to scare Delia, but she recoils from his words. And he feels her stare choking him like a glare of rejection. He has to say something to get her back by his side again, back to where she's his best girl and he's her fella.

'Maybe the park monster was sleeping,' he says, feeling a rush of reassurance in his belly as he speaks. 'Maybe the festival was too big this year and all the people woke it up. So now it just needs to eat enough and then it'll go to sleep. As long as we're not trashers, it won't eat us.'

Delia shakes her head, but she uncrosses her arms and takes up one of Mickey's hands in hers as she turns to walk home. They walk side by side past the fire station, then past the drugstore and the banks. They cross the street at the corner with the old telephone box, sidestepping a stack of pale green flyers that the girl must have left sitting there. The breeze peels the top flyer off the stack and sails it down the street. As the wind kicks up, more flyers skim away from the stack, tumbling and buoying on the wind towards the ocean. Mickey sees a string of wooden beads next to a storm drain as they step off the sidewalk. Delia doesn't notice it, and Mickey doesn't point it out to her.

They keep walking home and pretend not to notice the trash cans that overflow around Main Street. They pretend not to notice the flyers with Moses' picture on them tacked up on the telephone poles. At the last block, on the edge of the downtown streets, three of the town bums sit and joke around a jug of wine. They sit on the curb with their feet in front of a storm drain, kicking popcorn bags and soda cups down the drain. A stream of trash rolls down the street towards the bums, spilling from an unseen source.

One bum takes the last swallow from the jug and throws it

over his shoulder and into an empty lot behind them. Mickey and Delia run when the tentacles shoot out from the drain and snap the bums' legs off at the knees. Mickey looks over his shoulder as they run. The bums roll in the street, howling until more of the mossy black whips shoot out of the drain and pull them down. Gone, vanished.

Mickey and Delia don't say anything until they get to the main intersection at the edge of their neighborhood.

'So are we going to go back tomorrow?'

'I don't know, Mickey. I'm afraid of it. I think we're safe, like you said, because we're picking up trash. But I'm still afraid. I'm afraid of what you said. About it being asleep all this time and now it's awake. What if it doesn't go back to sleep? I'm scared.'

'Me, too,' Mickey says. He hates himself for saying it as soon as the words leave his mouth. His best girl needs him to be strong for her, protect her. But he just told her he was weak.

Delia surprises him when she puts a hand on his shoulder and looks him in the eye, her face set in a grim mask.

'It's okay, Mickey. It only eats trashers. We're not trashers.'

Mickey walks Delia to her house and they say goodbye on the sidewalk, like they always do. Delia walks up the drive but Mickey calls to her.

'What is it?'

'I was thinking maybe, like, we should be together. You know? Like I'll be your guy and you be my girl.'

'Like partners?'

Mickey thinks about this for a second. It sounds right, even if it doesn't sound like what he was thinking when he suggested they be together.

'Yeah, like partners.'

Delia smiles and comes down the driveway.

'Next year, when we go to the festival, we'll make sure the monster stays asleep. We'll make sure the trashers pick stuff up.'

They shake hands to seal the deal.

When Delia is safely inside her house, Mickey turns

around and walks three blocks back down to the main inter-section and then another two over to his street. His dad is cleaning out the garage again when Mickey gets home.

'Mickey. You been hanging around that little white girl again?'

'. . . name's Delia,' Mickey mumbles.

'I know her name, son. You want to put that attitude back in your pocket now and help with this.'

Mickey's dad hoists a box in both hands and kicks at a smaller one beside him, motioning with a tilt of his head for Mickey to pick it up. The boxes end up next to the garbage can. It's already stuffed full.

'What're you throwing out now, dad?'

'Your mom's old clothes she left here.'

'Why'd mom leave?'

'Already told you, son. She didn't want to live in a small town like this. Didn't want to come to no backwater, she called it. Wanted to live in the city where the money is. Forgot you got to work to get that money.'

'But you work, dad.'

'Yeah, I do. But I work for myself. Get my own money. In the city, getting money means working for the man instead of being your own man. Ain't nobody owns me but me. Same as for you someday.'

'Yeah.'

Mickey stands by and listens to his father, like he always does. He helps carry boxes of his mother's old clothing to the curb and resists the urge to cry. Mickey's dad doesn't like it when his son cries. At least he won't have to cry when it rains anymore, Mickey thinks to himself. The bus ride won't be so bad now that Moses and his friends are gone. This makes Mickey think about what happened to Moses, and he has to work twice as hard to hold in the tears.

'Hey, dammit, I'm talking to you. Damn, son, wake up.'

'I'm awake, dad. Just thinking.'

'Yeah, you thinking. Always thinking, Mickey. Never lis-tening. You know, Mickey, that poster you brought home. That was the real McCoy. Must've been some hippy's prize possession. Too much smoke, like I always say. Makes them forget things.'

'What'd you do with the poster?'

'Sold it down at the shop. Guy came in to buy a guitar for his boy, saw the poster on the wall and said he'd give me five hundred dollars for it. You find some more of them, you be sure to bring them back. You hearing me, son?'

Mickey has his back turned to his father. He's watching a few popcorn bags and soda cups blow down the street to gather in front of the driveway.

'Yeah, dad. 'M hearing you.'

Mickey's father grunts behind him and then pulls the garage door closed. It settles against the concrete of the drive-way with a thud that makes Mickey jump. The popcorn bags are swirling around the garbage cans and boxes of clothing now.

'C'mon in, son. Dinner time soon.'

'Hey, dad,' Mickey says, turning around. 'Maybe we can go down to the park and look for posters tomorrow.'

'Ain't you wanting to save that kissing spot for your little white girl?'

Mickey feels the anger rising in him, but he pushes it down. He needs his father to go to the park with him tomorrow.

'She didn't want the poster, dad. Not for money. She just wants to have one for looking at. But you said we could sell them, so I figure that's better. Right?'

'Glad you got some kind of sense in you, son. Alright, then. Little father-son time. Do us good. Now c'mon in for dinner.'

Mickey pushes his hands into his pockets, feeling the wadded mass of the shelter agency flyer with his fingertips. He looks at the boxes, and at the popcorn bags that have set-tled into the spaces between the boxes. He shivers and follows his father inside.

Mickey sits beside his dad in the little red pickup truck they drove from Sacramento three years earlier. It still clanks and rattles at start up and coughs out a cloud of smoke as they back down the driveway.

'Huh. Looks like somebody came and took them boxes,' Mickey's dad says as they pull into the street. The garbage can is still full, but the popcorn bags are gone. So are the boxes, picked up by the shelter agency Mickey called after his father went to sleep the night before.

They drive through the neighborhood, the truck belching smoke when Mickey's dad shifts gears. The smoke used to be a light gray color, but over the years since they moved here, it got darker. Now it's nearly charcoal black and follows them like a swirling swarm of ghostly insects.

Mickey's dad pulls into a drive-thru at a burger joint and buys two breakfast sandwiches. Mickey eats his with ketchup, like he always does. Mickey's dad tosses the garbage through the window in the back of the cab, like he always does. The garbage blows around the truck bed, some of it catching on the wind and sailing away behind them. Like it always does.

At the park, the trash is mostly gone. Stray pieces of popcorn bags still flutter around in the breeze, and lots of posters. Most of the soda cups and hot dog papers are gone. The candy wrappers, cigarette butts, and ice cream sundae cups. Almost gone, all of them. Mickey stays away from the trash bins and pretends not to look at the Maypole. There are a lot of streamers hanging from it now. A lot more than the five that were there yesterday when he and Delia ran out of the park. The pole is upright again. Back to normal. Except Mickey knows the monster isn't asleep yet. He can feel it under the grass and soil beneath his feet.

Mickey's dad wanders around, stooping to pick up posters. Sometimes he hoots out loud and holds up a clean poster with no tears or missing corners. At other times, he grumbles when he picks up a torn or dirty poster.

'Some of these are real old, Mickey. Real old. There got to be some angry hippies somewhere right now.'

Mickey doesn't say anything. He just watches his father stumble around the park, drunk on the dreams of money in his head, clutching greedily to the posters in his hands. Mickey keeps watching as the tentacles slither from a nearby trash can, aiming across the stretch of lawn towards his father's ankles. The old man leans down and scoops up pieces of a popcorn bag that cover a poster. The tentacles stop moving and retreat back into the trash can until Mr. Downs tosses the scraps of trash aside and collects the poster they'd covered.

The tentacles sprout anew and move faster across the grass. They're almost there. Almost close enough to catch the last trasher so the monster can sleep again.

'Dad!'

'What? You look like you seen the Devil himself, son. What is it?'

'Just pick it up, dad. Please. Pick up the trash you dropped.' Mickey feels tears spilling down his cheeks. The tentacles are only a few feet away from his father's ankles now. The old man leans down and snaps up two pieces of the popcorn bag, leaving a collection of scraps still eddying around the lawn in the breeze.

'This? You want me to pick up this trash, son? Some hippy's leftovers?'

'Yes.' Mickey's voice shakes around the word, expressing every bit of trembling horror he feels in his chest. His father stoops to collect the rest of the scraps around his feet. The tentacles disappear into the trash can again.

'Okay. I'll do this for you. But I ain't spending my morning playing janitor to them hippies. Damn, what's got into you, son?'

Mickey's father tosses two handfuls of filth into the trash can. He peels one sticky piece of tissue off the palm of his hand, uses it to smear the old ketchup off his skin, and then adds that last scrap to the collection in the waste barrel. Shaking his hands, he steps away and picks up the poster he had his eye on.

Back in the red pickup truck, Mickey's dad shows him the posters he's picked up.

'These are real old, son. Wonder how they came to be out here anyway.'

'Maybe the hippies just threw them away or something.'

'Be something if they did. Treating a piece of history like garbage. Ain't that just like them hippies. Throwing things away that somebody could use just because they don't want to carry it around.'

'You mean like mom's old clothes and my toys?'

Mickey's dad stares at him through narrowed eyes, his lips pinched together like he's holding back a curse. Then he shakes with laughter and claps a hand on Mickey's head.

'You all right, son. Look at you teaching your old man something and you ain't even ten years old.'

Mickey's dad looks at the Maypole for the first time since they arrived.

'Look at them streamers, Mickey. Somebody ought to clean them off of there. Sure looks ugly, that pole all dirty and rotten like that.'

They drive out of the parking lot, smoke whispering shame behind them.

'About time I fixed this truck, don't you think? Get it running better so you have something to drive someday.'

'That's all right, Pop. That's all right.'

Fair

Robin Wyatt Dunn

'Hey, pick a willow dream, boy!' I say, looking down, my painted lips bright and cheerful.

The child reaches for my arm, where I hold the balloons. Our tradition is to save the children who remember, to send them away. Saving people is funny, it's like sowing. A few spilt seeds more for some time we know we'll need.

The boy laughs when he draws down the blue balloon and it wreathes around his head, squeaking and making his hair stand up.

'How much for the dream?' asks the boy's father, smiling. My smile in return is fake but well rehearsed and I say, 'Whatever's fair, sir, whatever's fair.'

Fair, fair. A fair, you see. And how can you know what it means, a fair, if you have never undergone one? This simple English word we have carried so many centuries now is this burden I carry next to my heart, not my heart but my second, blacker carny heart, the heart that beats for your destruction.

'Try the cotton candy!' I call after them.

First fair, from the Latin, feria, holiday.

Second, fair, from the Teutonic, fagro. Beautiful.

Third, from the same root, equitable. But beautiful and pleasing and equitable are the same Teutonic word, you see, so let's start there. The scales of justice have no place in this four letter word, fair, because to be fair, you see, right there in this goddamned word, is to be beautiful, and thus fairness in dealing is no different in principle from fairness in a woman's face, from the pleasure you get from getting more than your share.

And so we skew, and so we rue: forever promising one another these lies that while away the centuries.

You're at a fair, child, the holiday pleasure, the holy day pleasure, the whole-day pleasure, keep yourself whole and hale, healthy and intact and this is yours, your own, your day, your spot on the Earth, before it's all taken away.

'Ratchet them down, Sandy, we've got seventeen little fairgo-ers left over in the East and our third container has shrunk a bit from our Afghani importage now hasn't it, yes run that elevator please, run it well,' I shout, or announce, feeling the rhythm of the descending night.

Ever seen a town disappear? That is, all the people in it?

What is entertainment? I ask myself that.

'I'm asking you boy, what is it to laugh?'

He's bawling, the brat.

'I'll hit you, boy. Now stop that.'

He stops pretty quick.

'That's a good boy. Tell me, what is it to laugh, eh? What words have we told so long we've blinded ourselves to it all, I ask you!'

He starts to cry again.

'Sandy!' I shout.

'Yes?' She stands at the door to my office, a glorified closet. She's so svelte, almost a boy I think her at times.

'Sandy, how many this time?'

'Forty-seven.'

'We'll have to give them a good final show, eh?'

She watches me. She doesn't know the pressure of manage-ment, not yet.

But think of it: why is a fair designed to be fair? Why is this holiday whole and hale? Only a rest from the labors of the summer and the autumn? Only a feast before the great winter? Surely that, yes, this promise of the year that will follow but seems so far away, but I'd say its promise is even more urgent in the near term, the next minute, hour, day.

When fair is fair, you can pretend your whole life was a

memory. You can pretend that this stage we tread for you, you our souls, this stage we tread is holy, that it will deliver us from our sins, our so many mistakes in this life, that it will deliver us from you, our audience, our captors, our hates and loves who hound us down the centuries, whether we be Gypsy, Jew, Frank, Frisian, Finn or Fardancer (those so recently arrived from else), whatever we call ourselves you hound us, you make us cast the spell.

We wind the pole. We oil the locks and set the metal teacups spinning. We set the bottles standing straight and place the three rings where you can try your hand.

Can you see them spin, child?

'Sandy!'

'Yes sir.'

'Bring me below.'

She opens the trapdoor to the container vessels we've secreted below the fairground and I follow her down our ladder. Many of them will die down here. The secret is the digging. Make it look like nothing was ever dug. You have to be archaeological about it, but thieves are good at that: we know where people like to look for loot. Try to put it in plain sight.

I am dressed, as is my custom, in red and black with white circles of pain round my eyes. A merry chap.

Our audience is roped and gagged and waiting in the lamplight. They are moaning but they quiet at my entrance, as though they know that making the wrong sound could set me off, could earn them a swifter, less uncertain death.

'Welcome to the World Beneath the World, my brothers and sisters. My neighbors from above. Tonight my assistant will be Utnapishtim and I will be the Ocean and we will blow a breeze for you, a breeze just for you, NEIGHBORS!'

They tremble and I begin, making the sounds of the ocean and rolling on the corrugated metal floor in lamplight, shhh-hhh, rumble, shhhhh, I am seawater under the moon.

And beautiful svelte Sandy sends out her doves to no avail, to no avail, awaiting doom midst her animals and all their excrement floating in her little boat.

But she escapes to land, someone always escapes. I let the boy go.

It's a beautiful thing, how little we believe children. The boy can shout anything he likes to anyone he can find, in an hour or two. Most likely he'll find us again, and join the circus.

I decide this one should be a burning, because this is a holy day, a holy smoke, and that phrase has been with us a good 15 centuries at least, folks, the holy smoke of a whole burning.

Our vehicles are taut and tied and fueled and the town is buried beneath. They wanted a smaller government: yet another irony. Their borders are their own and no one to forget or remember them.

I the carny sing a song at night, and it is the song of revenge. I know my next life will be poor, perhaps I will be tortured. But this one is sweet, though it carries the burden of teaching.

Tonight Sandy will wear her cape, and nothing else. And I will play Rachmaninoff, as we ride.

Things Happen Here After Dark

Sheri White

Jeff and Lisa were bored, looking for something interesting and fun to do. There wasn't much going on in their small town, especially on a chilly Friday night in autumn. They weren't supposed to be out, but they had skipped school all day and didn't want to go home just yet. Jeff had thought about stealing one of the farmer's tractors for a joyride, but then something better came to mind.

'Hey, I know what we can do.'

Lisa blew a few strands of blue-tinged hair out of her eyes. 'What is it? It better be something good. This night's been a crapfest so far.' She hated living out here in the country. She used to live in a town that had a lot more to do, then her parents divorced and her mom moved them to this stupid town she grew up in back in the 60s.

Jeff smiled, a cigarette dangling from his lip. He took it from his mouth so he could talk. 'Let's go climb to the top of the Ferris wheel.' Lisa folded her arms and shook her head. 'I'm serious. I know the carnival is closed for the night, but it's not like there's a fence around it to keep us out. And it's only here for one more night.'

'What if we're caught? My mom will kill me if I get into trouble again. I'm not even supposed to be out with you after the last time we got caught skipping school.'

'Who's going to catch us? The place is pretty much deserted right now. Come on—I thought you wanted something cool to do.' Jeff wasn't worried; he knew Lisa would go along with the idea. She always wanted to please him and hated it when he got mad at her. And it would be a great story to brag about to his friends at school on Monday, if he decided to go. His dad wouldn't care as long as Jeff stayed out of his booze.

'All right. What's the worst that could happen?' Lisa shrugged. 'I'll just get grounded again, big deal.'

'Great. Let's go.' He gave Lisa a gentle pat on the butt and they ran toward the empty carnival grounds.

The moonlight cast an eerie glow over the dark carnival. The Ferris wheel loomed over the other rides, like the T-Rex skeleton in a dinosaur museum.

'I don't know about this,' Lisa said. 'It looks really spooky. And how are we supposed to get to the top, anyway? It's a lot higher than I remember.'

'We're gonna climb up the frame. I mean, the carnival workers do it when they put it together, so it can't be that hard. Seriously—it'll be fun. Come on. I heard you were good climbing the rope in gym class; this is no different.'

Lisa looked up at the ride, which seemed so much higher than it did when she was here the other night. She pictured herself slipping and falling to her death. 'Oh, screw this—I'm going home.' Lisa started to walk away, but Jeff pulled on her jacket.

'C'mon, Lisa, don't be lame. It'll be fun, I promise. And after we start climbing, if you still want to stop, we'll go home.'

Lisa sighed. She knew she'd do it; Jeff was a Junior and she was only a Freshman. They had known each other since Lisa had moved to town a few years ago. They lived on the same block, but only recently started going out. He was so cool and sure of himself, he could go out with any girl he wanted. She was always a little nervous that he'd break up with her, so she rarely said no to him. 'Okay. Might as well.'

They made their way through the carnival, passing the mini rollercoaster, a few kiddie rides, and the giant slide.

Hints of cotton candy and popcorn wafted through the air. A few deflating balloons gently bounced along the ground. As they walked by a large blue tent with green stripes, they heard yells and raucous laughter.

'Must be a tent for the carnival workers,' Jeff whispered.

'Oh, great. What if they hear us? Will they have us arrested? I think we should just go home.' Lisa didn't really care if her mother grounded her; she was usually able to sneak out anyway, but she knew she'd be in for a lot worse if the police brought her home again.

'It's fine, come on!' Jeff knew he sounded irritated, but he was tired of Lisa's hesitation. Sometimes she was such a baby. He thought she was a lot cooler when he had to spend detention with her. Now she looked like he had hurt her feelings. 'Sorry. I didn't mean to snap, but I really want to do this, and I thought you did too.'

'Okay, but I don't want to stay too long. We can make out for a little bit when we get to the top, though.'

Jeff smiled and put his arm around her. Maybe she was cool after all.

'Hey, wait. Let's listen to the workers for a minute. Maybe we'll hear something interesting.'

Surprised at Lisa's sudden bravery, he knelt down with her to eavesdrop.

'Get anything good tonight, Charlie?' a voice boomed from the tent, making Lisa jump.

'Only about a hundred bucks; tonight was pretty slow. Not as many people as usual for some reason.'

'Probably the cold weather. I don't know why the boss insists on traveling in the fall.'

'He must be a pickpocket or something,' Jeff whispered. 'I've heard that a lot of carnival workers are thieves.'

'Really? They were nice to me a few nights ago when I came here with my sister.' Lisa was young for her age and tended to see the good in most people, even though she tried to act tough.

Jeff, amused, just shook his head.

'Whatever,' Lisa said. 'Let's get to the Ferris wheel; I'm getting cold.'

They quietly tiptoed past the tent, not wanting to attract the men's attention. As they walked through the moonlit carnival, Lisa again grew nervous. She knew she could climb at least part way up the Ferris wheel; she sometimes went rock climbing with her dad when he was in town. That wasn't what was scaring her. But unable to put a finger on her unease, she let Jeff lead her to the towering ride.

Lisa looked up at the Ferris wheel. 'Oh yeah, it's definitely a lot higher than I thought,' she said. 'I'm pretty sure I won't make it all the way up to the top.'

Jeff wasn't sure he would either, but he wasn't about to admit it to Lisa. 'Come on, we'll be fine. Just don't look down.' He grabbed one of the colorful metal bars that made up the ride's frame and began to ascend.

'Oh, God. I'm an idiot.' Lisa took a deep breath and followed Jeff up the ride.

About halfway up Jeff admitted to himself he couldn't make it to the top. His hands were getting sweaty, making him nervous about slipping. 'How about we stop here and get in this car?' He gestured at the car closest to them. 'I don't want to make you climb anymore,' Jeff said to save face.

Lisa sighed with relief. 'Sounds good to me. It's still an adventure, right?'

'Right.' Jeff swung his legs into the car and then gingerly climbed in. He helped Lisa in once he was secure. The car rocked back and forth a bit but stopped once they were both seated.

Although they weren't all the way at the top, they could see the whole carnival in the bright light of the moon. The smell of hot dogs and pizza lingered in the air; here and there mice grabbed morsels of food that had been dropped on the ground.

'It looks creepy, doesn't it? So different when there aren't any bright lights or music playing or people walking around,' Lisa said.

Jeff looked around. 'Yeah, it's weird. But still kinda cool.' He took Lisa's face in his hands. 'You're so beautiful in the moonlight,' he whispered. Then he laughed. 'Romantic, huh?'

She rolled her eyes. 'No, ridiculous. Who are you supposed to be, Romeo?'

'Who?'

'Geez, no wonder you're failing your Literature class. Come on; kiss me since we have to get out of here soon. I'd rather not miss my curfew again.'

They were really into it when Lisa felt a tickling on her leg. She broke away from Jeff and saw a spider climbing up her thigh. With a squeal, she smacked it off, launching it into the air. 'Let's go, Jeff! It's getting colder and there are bugs around. Why would a spider be way up here anyway?'

'Yeah, all right.' He grabbed the metal bar to pull himself out of the car when there was a loud metal clang. They looked down to see a man hit the ride with a baseball bat, repeating the loud noise.

'Hey, you kids! What the hell are you doing on my Ferris wheel? Git yer asses down here right now!'

Before they could move, he threw a switch and the ride jerked and rocked, bringing the kids down slowly. By the time their car reached the bottom, Lisa was crying.

'This ain't no place for a couple of stupid kids right now. Don't you know all kinds of things can happen after dark in a place like this? Now go home before you regret you didn't.'

Lisa sniffled and wiped her nose on her jacket. 'Sorry, mister.'

'Yeah, sorry,' Jeff mumbled. 'Come on, Lisa. We don't want to piss off any spooks that might be around.' He waved his arms in the air and made a scary face. Lisa smiled through her tears. Jeff was so cool.

'Don't say I didn't warn you. Just git yourselves home and everything will be fine.' The man glared at them and then walked back to the tent, shaking his head and muttering under his breath.

Jeff watched him go. 'Stupid old man. Trying to scare us.' Jeff had been startled when the man banged on the ride, but didn't show it. Now he was more irritated than scared. 'Let's go look around a little bit. That jerk can't tell us what to do.'

'Are you crazy?' Lisa looked at Jeff in disbelief. 'I'm going home before that guy calls the cops or something.'

'He's not gonna call the cops, especially if the workers have been stealing from people. He's just trying to scare us into leaving. This place seems really cool at night—remember how it looked from the Ferris wheel? I want to explore a little. We'll just stay away from that tent.'

Lisa desperately wanted to leave, but she didn't want Jeff to think she was a baby. She'd been wanting to go out with him for a long time, and she was finally with him. Her mom thought he was a bad influence, and maybe her mom was right, but nothing was going to stop her from hanging out with him.

'Okay,' she said. 'But only for a little while. If I get home after curfew again, I'll be worse than grounded.'

Jeff pulled on Lisa's arm. 'Come on, I'll get you a stuffed animal.'

'But that's stealing, Jeff! Let's just go look at the other rides or something.' Lisa knew Jeff had gotten caught shoplifting once, and didn't want him to get arrested for taking something as lame as a stuffed animal.

'Shh! Just come on.'

They walked quietly through the grounds. The carnival had a different feel when there were no people around; it was eerie, too silent. The animals on the carousel seemed alive, as if ready to break free. Even the kiddie rides were different; the cheerful little bug cars that were charming when the carnival was lit up became menacing under the moonlight.

'I really don't like this place, Jeff. I feel like we're being watched or something. What if that guy is following us?'

'I know, it feels kind of creepy to me too. Let's get out of here. But I don't want to go back the way we came just in case that guy's following us. He might actually call the cops if he sees we're still here. I don't need that hassle again. We'll head out past the Tilt-a-Whirl.'

They walked for a few minutes, passing by the bumper

cars and the funhouse, as well as the cotton candy stand. Jeff stopped and looked around uncertainly.

'I could've sworn the Tilt-a-Whirl was around here. I rode it a few days ago with my little brother. I remember it was right next to the funhouse.'

'It's somewhere else then, but I don't remember where. The carnival isn't that big; it's got to be nearby. We just took a wrong turn or something.'

They headed back and turned past the haunted house. The fronts of the game booths were covered with tarps but loosely draped.

'Oh, wait a minute,' he said, his uncertainty momentarily forgotten. 'I wanted to grab a stuffed animal for you. There's the dart game booth; they always have good prizes for that one.'

'Oh, God. Can we just go, please?' Lisa had finally had enough and didn't care if Jeff got mad at her. 'I don't care about a stupid stuffed animal.'

Jeff ignored her, and moved the tarp aside. He spied a bunch of stuffed animals hanging on a wall in the dark booth and stretched his arm to grab a teddy bear. Suddenly he snatched his hand back.

'Damn, I think I scratched my hand on a nail or something.' He looked at his palm. There was a long scratch on it, with little beads of blood popping to the surface. It stung, making him forget about the teddy bear. He looked through the tarp, but didn't see any nails poking out. He was trying figure out what had scratched him when Lisa grabbed his arm, hurting him.

'Jeff!'

'Ow! Damn it! What is wrong with you?'

'I saw someone peeking around the fried Oreo stand over there. It might've been that creepy jerk. I knew he was following us!'

'Oh, what the hell?' This night wasn't turning out at all the way Jeff had hoped.

'Hey!' he yelled. 'We said we're leaving; just give us the chance to get out!'

Jeff then saw the face Lisa had seen. It wasn't the old man, it was one of the clowns that roamed the carnival, bugging people and giving away balloons. Little kids thought the clowns were great; Jeff hated them. They creeped him out. The clown stepped out from behind the cookie booth, giving Jeff a better look at him. Why was the clown out this time of night, and why was he still in costume? And his costume was all dirty--the white suit had dark stains all over it that almost looked like blood. In fact, Jeff thought he could actually smell blood—a rank, coppery smell that caught in his throat and almost made him gag.

The clown caught Jeff's eye and waved at him with a shriveled hand. The fingernails looked like claws, thin, long and black. Then the clown grinned—and all Jeff could see were teeth. Big teeth, yellow and sharp, that looked like needles.

'Oh, God… we really need to go right now, Lisa. There's something wrong with that clown.'

Lisa looked again toward the fried Oreo booth. Her eyes widened with horror. 'Run!'

They took off running, racing back toward the Ferris wheel, hoping to get out the way they came in.

'Where's the damn Ferris wheel?' Lisa was crying again, and she didn't care about Jeff thinking she was a baby. She was terrified.

They saw it looming ominously in the distance above the other rides but couldn't find where it was grounded. They couldn't get any closer to it no matter how far they ran.

'This is crazy!' Jeff was scared and frustrated and just wanted to go home. He regretted not stealing the farmer's tractor in the first place. He didn't feel like such a badass right now.

As Jeff was silently cursing himself, the clown jumped out from behind the candy apple stand right in front of them. Jeff stumbled against Lisa, making her fall on the rough dirt surface. She lifted her head in time to see the clown roll a bright red ball toward them. It landed in front of her and exploded into hundreds of tiny spiders.

Lisa tried to get up, but before she could, spiders scuttled up her arms and into her hair. She stood up, frantically raking her fingers through her hair.

'Get them off, get them off!' she screamed.

'Get what off?'

'Spiders! They're all over me!'

Jeff looked at her, but he didn't see any spiders. And now the clown was gone, as if he hadn't even been there. 'There's nothing on you! Shit, where'd the clown go?'

'I don't know and I don't care—I just want to go home! This place is scary and there's something wrong here. I know those spiders were climbing on me.'

Jeff gently smoothed Lisa's hair. 'We'll find our way out, don't worry. I know it's weird around here, but I bet the carnival workers are just trying to scare us for trespassing.'

'But the spiders—'

'You imagined them. Maybe the clown played a trick on you. But whatever, they aren't there now. Come on, let's go.'

Lisa closed her eyes and inhaled deeply. 'I didn't imagine them, but fine, I'm ready.'

She grabbed Jeff's hand and tried to walk on, but he didn't move. She looked over to prod him on but saw it wasn't Jeff's hand she had taken.

It was the clown's.

She screamed and dropped the clown's hand, his nails scraping her wrist, drawing blood. She ran through the carnival, his laughter following her.

Lisa ducked into the first tent she came to. She hadn't seen it when she and Jeff were walking around trying to find their way out. It smelled odd, somewhat musty. The tent was empty except for cobwebs covering the walls. She put her hands on her knees and bent over, trying to catch her breath. She wanted to leave the tent and try to find her way home, but she was scared the clown was waiting outside for her. She didn't feel safe in the tent, either; the cobwebs frightened her and gave her the creeps the way they were fluttering without any wind. Suddenly she heard the clown's laughter; this time it was all around her. She looked around but didn't see him.

'Please leave me alone!' she sobbed. 'I'm sorry we messed around with your carnival! I'll never do it again. Please just let me go home!'

She felt a tap on her shoulder and knew the clown was behind her. She closed her eyes and clenched her fists, hoping he'd disappear. She whispered a prayer, knowing it wouldn't be heard. She felt herself being turned around; she was helpless to stop. The clown now stood in front of her, baring his teeth. Then he opened his mouth wide and roared, exhaling hundreds of spiders. They hit Lisa's face, climbing into her mouth when she opened it to scream. They slid down her throat, choking her. She fell to her knees, clawing at her neck, trying to cough them out.

Darkness overtook her and she mercifully knew no more.

Jeff couldn't understand how he'd gotten separated from Lisa. He'd seen that damned clown again, and it had caught him off-guard. He'd nearly fallen and realized Lisa had. But when he went to pull her up, his hand had taken that of the clown's instead, and he ran as fast as he could to get away, all thoughts of Lisa gone.

Now he felt like a coward, leaving her behind. You're such an asshole, he thought. He walked back to find Lisa but heard the clown's laughter all around him. He froze in place and looked around. Jeff took a few cautious steps forward and then heard a noise behind him.

He whipped around, but nothing was there. He turned back to search for Lisa and found himself face to face with the clown.

The clown put his face right up to Jeff's, held Jeff's chin in his hand and ran his slimy tongue along the side of Jeff's face. Jeff wet his pants, but he didn't care. He tried to turn and run, but the clown grabbed him by the throat and lifted him off the ground, holding him in the air. The clown tilted his head left, then right, as he stared into Jeff's eyes. He threw Jeff to the ground and dragged him by his shirt through the carnival, Jeff pulling at the clown's hands on his collar all the while. Then the clown pulled him inside a run-down tent and threw Jeff to the ground.

Jeff saw Lisa lying motionless on the ground, her face frozen in a silent scream, with only the whites of her eyes showing. A spider crawled out of her mouth while Jeff looked on, horrified.

'You're next,' the clown whispered in his ear, running a fingernail down the side of Jeff's face.

Lisa's body suddenly began to shake, then violently erupted with hundreds of spiders. They swarmed as they ate their way through her flesh, trailing blood and tissue. They skittered toward Jeff, who lay helpless as they bit him and tore at his flesh, while the clown laughed and clapped his hands.

The carnies played poker and threw back whiskey shots in their tent, laughing at each other's raunchy jokes.

The Ferris wheel carnie shushed them. 'Did you hear that? I thought I heard a scream.' He stood up and listened. Yes, there it was again. Definitely a scream; someone was in trouble or hurt. He worried it was one of the kids he had chased off earlier. He'd given them a chance to get away from the carnival, but maybe they didn't take it.

'We told you before to let it go, Stan.'

'But that's the third time this month it's happened. What can we do?' Stanley had only joined up with the carnival a few months before and still didn't understand the way of things.

'Trust me—we don't get involved. Bad things happen. Just drink your whiskey. It'll be quiet again soon.'

Stan reluctantly sat back down, trying not to hear the terrified screams echoing in the night, and pretending he hadn't seen a sharp-toothed clown peeking at him from around tents.

Mister Know It All

Richard Godwin

Eddy had another blister on his hand. It made him feel no better than a manual labourer. The sky looked bloodshot that morning, the sun oozing through the clouds that hovered in the distance. Eddy stared down at his hands, spat on them and rubbed them dry on his torn jeans as Mandy walked up to him.

'Been fixing the carousel, nuts loose again,' he said, swinging the wrench between his two fingers like a pendulum.

'Your hands are sore. Well, Eddy, you'll just have to let me rub some of that cream into them,' Mandy said, laughing.

Hank was watching them from the window of his trailer, laughing. Hank ran the carnival.

'Her voice always makes me think she's going to bust a window,' he said to his wife, Sandra, who yawned at the newspaper in front of her. She was sitting there in furry pink slippers and an egg stained nightie.

'Another town for our carnival,' she said, 'I love it each time we enter a new place and watch the locals gather for our entertainments.

'This nowhere place between States gets you excited?'

Sandra opened her nightie and laughed as Hank drew the curtains.

As he explored the warmth of Sandra's flesh, Eddy and Mandy returned to their trailer. He was six feet tall, heavily built, with a long gray ponytail. He wore a few days' stubble and had thick heavy hands. Mandy was small and thin, with the face of a rodent, and sharp yellow teeth. She had several

175

piercings in her ears and her voice was as strident as a scream. She would sometimes raise it so she drowned out Eddy.

'Been fixing nuts all my life,' Eddy said, throwing the wrench onto the bed.

'I kno-ow,' Mandy said.

'I even invented a wrench, better'n that one.'

'What happened to it?'

'I got ripped off. Company bought it and buried it, since it would've put a lot of people out of business, including them, you know how it is.'

'You should be wealthy with all the things you've done Eddy.'

'I was. The wife took all the money, you know that Mandy.'

'Is there nothing you haven't done?'

'Pretty much not, used to run a huge company, had over a hundred employees.'

'You're too good for a carny.'

'Don't I know it? Still we'll move on from this, I'm owed a lot for some diamonds I sold.'

'Let's lie down for a while before they start queuing up.'

'I need to borrow some cash.'

'Want to lick my nipple ring?' Mandy said, pulling her T-shirt over her head.

They lay down on the cramped bed beside the tiny kitchen area that smelt of grease and burnt oil and Mandy put her head on Eddy's chest as he stared at the ceiling. Light was flooding in through the windows as he said, 'Might as well get up.'

Mandy slid over and got on top of him. She began unbuttoning his shirt, dragging her nails through his thick chest hair.

'We got time Eddy.'

He fumbled with her jeans, unzipping them and putting his hand inside. Mandy began to pant, slid out of her jeans, wiggling her arse as Eddy slid inside her, looking out at the sky, listening to her gasps.

He couldn't suppress the chuckle that rose from his chest

and made his shoulders shake as Mandy's voice broke across the carnival ground and the still hot morning.

'Oo-oh Eddy, oo-ooooh! You is so go-od!'

She pounded him like a piston and as Eddy looked at her haunches rise and fall on his hard cock, and felt her wet thighs against him, he thought of all the well-oiled machines he used to fix in another town. To Eddy she looked grotesque as she grimaced and spent her brief moment of pleasure, her back arched, her nipples erect like pierced bullets. Then she fell silent and Eddy rolled over and got everything ready for their first day in the new town. He was standing outside their trailer putting up the sign for the Bearded Lady when Mandy came out and put her hand down his jeans.

'Hot dawg,' she said, 'You fill me up real good, satisfy my ever twitching pussy with your hard rod.'

'Just like an engine, huh?'

'Come back inside, we got time till it opens.'

'Inside? Now what opening might you be talking about?' Eddy winked.

As Mandy chuckled, the sound of Stevie Wonder's voice filled the air.

'I don't know why he always plays that,' he said, peering through the chink in the curtains on Hank's trailer.

Inside Sandra was climbing out of bed naked.

'Why do you always play that?' she said to Hank.

'Because it's him, sums him up perfectly.'

'What's him?'

'"He's Misstra Know-It-All", it's Eddy.'

And he began singing along, 'He's a man with a plan, got a counterfeit dollar in his hand, He's Misstra Know-It-All.'

'Yeah he is Mister Know It All,' Sandra said, putting her bra on.

'There's another song I like better though,' Hank said as he watched her full breasts fill the cups, her nipples visible beneath the lace.

'N what's that?' Sandra said, standing there, hands on her hips as Hank's eyes wandered down to the blur of her pubes nestled above the inviting opening that would ease his morning.

'"Do that to me one more time."'

'Captain and Tennille?'

Hank nodded. Soon Stevie Wonder's voice stopped and only Sandra's low and contented groans could be made out in the sleeping carnival.

No one stirred, from the Tattooed Lady, to the Albino. The only movement was inside Eddy and Mandy's trailer as he went through her purse. He found only small change and looked down at his partner with discontent, at her sleeping face and pierced metal body. He felt there was something abhorrently innocent about her, in her naïve vulgarity and simple sexual pleasure in a man who clearly deceived her at every turn. But Mandy was a romantic, and her need to believe in someone was the only thing that kept her from falling apart.

Eddy looked down at her and at the faded scars on her body. She'd left some earrings on a shelf above the bed and he reached across her and put them in his pocket. Then he went outside, left the carnival and walked into town. He sat in the early sunshine outside the pawn shop, waiting for it to open. He sold Mandy's earrings and returned as she was stirring.

'Where you been Eddy?' she said, stretching her arms.

'I heard someone outside, caught a young guy running away.'

'A thief?' she said, covering her breasts.

'I guess so.'

'I hope he didn't steal anything.'

'Well it's too late now if he did.'

Mandy got out of bed and Eddy looked away as she put her G-string on. She came over and began making coffee.

'If you caught up with him,' she said, wagging a finger at Eddy.

'I'd hurt him real bad. You know what these hands can do?'

'I know what they do to me,' Mandy said, taking them and placing one on each breast.

'He's lucky I didn't catch up with him.'

'What was it you did again?'

'The lot. Karate mainly, I fought professionally for years, I used to teach the top guys in the world, I was famous.'

'What made you give it up?'

'I invented a new form of automobile and sold the patent.'

'And here's you working in a carnival.'

'Yeah, well, we're going to be moving on soon, I got some plans.'

'Tell me them plans Eddy.'

She sat down and stared up at him with the anticipation of a child who is about to listen to a fairy tale. Eddy leaned into the sink and spat some yellow phlegm into it.

'I wish you wouldn't do that,' she said.

'Why? My spit's not good enough for you?'

'It's not hygienic.'

'You like my other bodily juices. When I fill you up and pump my gasoline inside you like it, don't you?'

'Why do you have to talk like that? Sometimes I think sex disgusts you.'

She began making breakfast. 'Chocolate pancakes, eggs, bacon, hash browns' she said. 'You need to keep your strength up, it's gonna be a busy day.'

'Sure.'

'Why am I the Invisible Girl? Of all the things I have to be in this carnival I have to be that, I've been invisible all my life.'

Mandy screeched into the trailer, but Eddy was far away, unaware of what Mandy was saying and of the smells rising from the skillet, thinking of Yellow John, the man he never wanted to see again. He heard his voice in the cramped dirty trailer. He saw his jaundiced face and the scar that ran the length of his cheek. He thought of how his name was a contradiction, since there was nothing yellow about him and of the time he nearly killed Eddy with his fileting knife. And John's voice echoed over and over in Eddy's head.

Eddy heard him say, 'The day you disgust yourself for what you are is the day you might get honest.'

He was aware of a hand on his shoulder and looked up at Mandy's face.

She put his plate down front of him and poured him some coffee.

'Tell me your plans,' she said, sitting down.

'I'm going to make some money and we're going to get out of here.'

'And how you gonna do that?'

'You'll see.'

Mandy placed a piece of bacon on her tongue and chewed slowly, eyeing Eddy as he bent his head and stuck his fork into his food.

He remained silent throughout breakfast and was outside when Mandy discovered her earrings were missing.

She stepped out of the trailer and stood looking at Eddy as he set up some of the rides. Her shadow fell across the torn grass almost to where he stood and she looked at him and thought about all of his stories and walked slowly over to him. Eddy was standing with a screwdriver in his hand and sweat breaking out across his back.

'Looks like the thief snuck in while we slept,' she said.

'Oh?'

'My earrings are missing.'

'Ah, they're probably in the trailer.'

Mandy shook her head.

'They're not. I put them on the shelf before I went to sleep and they're gone. He must have snuck in and reached over us. Think of that Eddy.'

'Well if I catch up with him I'll...'

Eddy carried on checking the ride.

'What will you do Eddy?'

'I'll get em back.'

'Funny how you didn't catch him. Funny how I didn't hear him. That trailer makes a noise right by the door when you come in, I always hear you when you come in late.'

'That right?'

'It is. There's a squeak and I never stir, I carry on sleeping, but I know when you get in, I know what time you get in. I can smell things on you.'

'What are you talking about?'

'I can smell what you've been drinking. Sometimes I smell other things.'

Eddy looked at Mandy and her eyes were narrowed in the morning light. There was something in her face he hadn't seen before and he tried to define it, to identify its use to him. She ran her eyes down his body, past the blur of hair on his chest to his pockets. One of them was torn and hung open, the other had a bulge in it.

'How much money do you want to borrow?' she said.

'Ten would do it.'

'That all?'

'Should be.'

'Then I'll have to see what I can do for you, Eddy,' she said, patting the pocket full of cash. 'My kind of guy, always keep a load in their pants.'

Eddy stared at her retreating back as he carried on with his work. He glanced from time to time at their trailer where Mandy was getting ready. She scraped the remains of last night's makeup from her tired eyes and gently hummed a song, whose provenance she could never recall. It brought to mind green rolling hills and some sharp pain that had been lodged in her for as long as she could remember, but she was attached to the tune and would always hum it when she was alone and engaged in the detached contemplation of her face and the signs of age that were creeping into it day by stolen day. Mandy had felt ever since she joined Hank's carnival that her time was being washed away, and her frustration had built until Eddy wandered into her life with that glimmer in his eye and his bag full of stories. When she was finished she looked at him through the window. She realised it was the pleasure he afforded her that made him valuable and dangerous. She thought of the way he touched her. And she thought of all she did to him and wanted to do, eventually snapping her purse shut sharply as unwanted images that did not belong to her swam into her mind.

When she left, Eddy watched her walk away and went inside, coming back out a few minutes later.

At 9 am they flooded in, the families with children hungry for excitement, the young couples already bored of the weekend in the idle city that existed like a scar at the edge of larger industrial towns that offered only the hope of work, like a promissory note with no funds. Eddy eyed them, knowing he was witnessing the disillusioned and the gullible, and he cracked open his first Miller as he watched a pretty young girl being kissed behind the Albino's trailer.

Eddy looked away and walked past the crowd waiting to get on the carousel and the fat man clutching candy floss in one hand and in the other the sticky fingers of his son. He walked past the Bearded Lady who yawned at him and followed the young girl to the ladies toilets behind the carnival. He'd set it up there, right away from where the crowds flocked.

He waited long enough, drinking his beer, face to the sun, a shine on his face that wasn't there when he got up, and then he lifted up his shirt. The mask was tucked into his jeans and he put it on and went inside. What the girl saw would never make sense to her. She was about sixteen, blonde, attractive, and she began to scream when Eddy touched her. He laid one hand across her mouth while he fumbled with her blouse, thinking of the father with the candy floss and the small boy waiting for the ride. The girl put up a fight, kicking Eddy in the crotch, but he closed his knees over her foot and pushed her up against the stained wall, as he ripped her bra off and began his compulsive humiliation of another young thing, as he thought of them. She stared into the white face and the small black eyes, not seeing the piece of card that Eddy had made up for his fun, but wondering what carnival freak was inflicting this punishment on her.

Eddy didn't see her face either as entered her there in the isolated toilet, the smell of sewage filling the air. He was looking at a dark eyed girl from long ago, who had found out about him and informed the police. He was staring into her eyes as he took the only thing she had held onto, the single item she considered of any value as she went about the business of getting married in a world of poverty and destitution. He recalled the high he got those many years ago before he took the bus out of Arkansas and began his life on the road.

Now he pulled out and wiped himself on her blouse as she fell to the floor. Then he turned his back and removed the mask, tucking it back into his jeans, and he left with a piece of her heart and a piece of her sanity in his clenched fist as he stepped outside into the bright sunshine, where her boyfriend was walking towards the small building.

'What you think you're doing, following girls into the john?'

Eddy could see the Albino walking towards them. He held out his hand and said, 'Earrings.'

'What did you say?'

'I know you took them.'

No one could have heard the brief conversation between them, or detected the conflict between fear and mendacity, but those men and women who were approaching the scene of the commotion would have seen Eddy punch the young man in the mouth, kick him across the grass and drag him screaming to Hank's office, where a crowd had gathered, among them Mandy.

Hank heard the boy yelling to be let loose and came out.

'What is going on?' he said in irritation, staring at the boy with the broken nose.

'This is the thief.'

'What thief?'

'Last night someone stole into our trailer and took Mandy's earrings.'

'How do you know it was him?' Mandy said.

'Because his girl was wearing them.'

'And where is she now?' Hank said.

'She ran off, and he threw them over the fence into the field at the back.'

'He was in the john,' the boy said. 'He came right out and punched me, I don't know nothing about no earrings.'

'Tell it to the Sheriff,' Eddy said.

He had his fist clenched in the boy's denim jacket and held him while Hank went into his office to make the call. Mandy looked around at the crowd feeling an old bad memory begin to trouble her mind. She saw a man with a horribly scarred face among them. He was grinning at her. The sun was in her eyes and she turned away to look at Eddy. Somewhere in the carnival Thin Lizzy's "Don't Believe a Word" was playing and the words floated across the hot air towards her. She looked back into the crowd and the man had disappeared like a shadow. Standing in his place was the Albino, and he was shaking his head.

Eddy stood stock still eyeing Mandy as Phil Lynott sang, and the tired world looked just a little bit more blurred to her than usual. The words drifted across the hot air as she tried to focus on Eddy's snarling face:

'Don't believe me if I tell you

That I wrote this song for you

There just might be some other silly pretty girl

I'm singing it to

Don't believe a word

For words are so easily spoken

And your heart is just like that promise

Made to be broken.'

Suddenly everything looked sharp, too sharp. She could hear crying and turned to see a plump woman with her arm round the shoulders of a girl who was shaking. Her clothes were torn and the boy tried to dart away from Eddy, but he yanked him back and said, 'Stay there.'

'She says she's been assaulted,' the woman said.

'Cover up by a couple of thieves,' Eddy said. 'She was wearing Mandy's earrings.

'I was not.'

'Where are your earrings then, how come you ain't wearing none?'

The girl put her hands to her ears and felt the two missing pieces of jewellery that lay in Eddy's pocket next to the cash. Mandy followed the movement of his hand as he instinctively dropped it to his pocket. He rested a thumb there as he shoved the boy towards Hank's office.

'Wait in there until the Sheriff arrives.'

There was something about the way Eddy was standing in the middle of the thinning crowd that made Mandy think of her old home town and the time she ran away and sat crying in the fields. She looked at the crowd and a boy eating ice cream caught her eye. It was dripping from his fat chin, and Mandy shuddered and walked away in disgust.

A small group of men and women hunted for the earrings in the field at the back but found nothing. They stopped their search when the Sheriff arrived.

He went into Hank's office, asked a few questions, and took the boy and girl away, returning a few hours later. What he had to say he said to Hank alone.

'I don't think they're thieves. I've known young Angelica most of my life, and Tom's a good boy. She says she was assaulted, her father is mad as hell and wants the carnival shut down. She says a man with a white face did it. They wouldn't make something like this up.'

'Well, Eddy swears they stole Mandy's earrings.'

'Does he?'

'We're running a carnival here, we want people to come, we don't want to drive them away.'

'How well do you know your employees?'

'Pretty well.'

'Does the girl's description mean anything to you?'

Just then the Albino walked past the office. Hank looked at his pale skin, his pin point eyes as he glanced at Hank and shuffled off, swinging his arms in the simian manner Hank had never taken to. He thought of how he considered him a necessary attraction, but a man he could never trust.

'That description makes no sense to me,' Hank said.

'I'll have to come back and speak to your employees. I want to talk to Angelica and Tom again first.'

Hank watched as the Sheriff drove away and then went straight to the Albino's trailer.

The Albino was counting some cash when Hank walked in.

'Where did you get that?' Hank said.

'I been saving up.'

'What for?'

'I have a life beyond the carnival.'

'Is that a life that includes raping young girls?'

'Now hold on.'

'I want you out of here.'

'Why?'

'I'll never prove that time it was you when the money went missing. You laid the blame on Eddy but I don't think it was him.'

'I ain't a rapist.'

'Are you a thief?'

'No, I'm an albino, I'm someone people don't want to see.'

'I'm giving you till the morning.'

Eddy was standing outside as Hank left the Albino's trailer and went back to his own. The Albino saw him through the open door and came out.

'I know it was you,' he said.

'What was?' Eddy said.

'Raped that young girl, I saw you leaving the john.'

'Did you?'

'How'd you make it look like me?'

'I know you stole that money,' Eddy said.

'You want me to keep my mouth shut, I want cash.'

'Why would I give you any cash?'

'I'm giving you until the morning.'

Eddy looked at the Albino in the dark. His face looked like a sheet of paper, and an idea came to him.

He went back into his trailer where Mandy was drying herself with a towel.

He looked at her body and opened a beer and sat drinking with his back to her.

'Do I disgust you?' she said.

Eddy didn't say anything.

She came over and stood in front of him.

'Do you like sticking your prick in me and lying to me?'

Eddy slammed his beer down. He looked at the foam spilling out over the can and said, 'I know what you want.'

'Yes you do, Eddy.'

He lifted her up and threw her on the bed and entered her without ceremony as she turned her head away and began to cry.

Afterwards he said, 'Isn't that what you wanted?'

'Why can't you love me Eddy?'

'What's to say I don't?'

'Sometimes I think you're wearing a mask and behind it is all this hatred.'

He was about to hit her when he turned away and sat drinking until she went to bed.

It wasn't long before she fell asleep and dreamed of the time the man with the scarred face chased her in her home town. He chased her all the way into the field where he lay on top of her singing until she stopped screaming and lay there sobbing. She woke to find her face wet and she got up and looked at the empty trailer. Then she went through Eddy's pants and found the cash and the earrings she had never seen before.

And the song she hummed entered her mind and she knew then what it was. John Brim's "The Ice Cream Man" had haunted her for years and she began to wonder why. She looked out of the window and saw the light on in the Albino's trailer.

Eddy was inside and the Albino said to him, 'You got the cash?'

'I got something else for you.'

He took hold of the Albino's throat and began to choke him. The Albino tried to fight but Eddy was too strong for him. He squeezed until the Albino lay back on his bed. Then Eddy stained his face with ink and broke his neck.

He wrote 'That'll teach you to mess with young girls' on a piece of paper he left beside him and walked back out into the moonless night.

He climbed into bed and slept for a few hours as Mandy watched him.

When he got up she was dressed.

'Where did you go to last night?' she said.

'I went to get some air.'

'Is that all?'

'I'm going into town.'

'Do you think that's wise?'

'Why wouldn't it be?'

Eddy walked into town where he studied the buses that would take him out of there. He was unaware of a tall man wearing a hat low over his eyes watching him. When he left the man followed him at a distance. When Eddy stopped at the top of a hill he heard the man stop some feet away. Eddy turned.

'I knew I'd catch up with you,' the man said.

Eddy looked around. The scene was deserted.

'What do you want John?'

John walked up to him and took off his hat. His yellow face looked illuminated by some wild passion.

'Revenge for my daughter.'

'I told you it wasn't me, it was your brother.'

'My brother was crazy but he wasn't no rapist.'

'You knew him did you?'

'I know you.'

'You don't know nothing.'

'I've hunted you from state to state since you killed her.'

'Killed?'

'She took her life after what you did. What is it about young girls? You have to defile them? You feel so dirty inside? I bet you're still doing it, that's why I have to make an end of you.'

Yellow John reached behind him to where his gun was tucked into his belt. But Eddy moved too fast, he struck him across the jaw, knocking him to the ground, and pulled the gun from him. He pressed the muzzle deep into John's face and looked at him, thinking of the fear he saw in his daughter's face all those years ago.

Then he blew John's head off and walked away.

Back at the trailer he began packing. Mandy came in as he was walking over to the wall by the bed.

'What are you running from Eddy?' she said.

'I'm not running from anything, I'm done with this carnival.'

'You taking me with you?'

'Sure I am Mandy.'

'You won't get sick of me?'

'I'm gonna set up a business.'

'Doing what?'

'What you got there?'

Mandy had her hand clenched and she opened it and showed Eddy the earrings she'd found.

'This the young girl's earrings, Eddy?'

'I never seen em before.'

'How did they get into your jeans?'

'The Albino must have planted them there.'

'Well he's dead, and the Sheriff's coming.'

'Na, I saw him last night.'

'I know you did.'

'What are you saying?'

'Someone painted his face.'

'Sounds to me like someone from the town.'

'Or round here.'

'We know he wasn't no good.'

'Are you?'

'Am I what?'

'Good.'

'Someone rapes a girl someone kills The Albino, it ain't me Mandy.'

'Let me tell you something. A long time ago a man chased a girl through some fields. He took something from her and she held onto herself believing in one thing. It was the thing that kept her alive, that made sense of life after that. You know what it was she believed in?'

'Money?'

'Love, Eddy.'

'What's this got to do with anything?'

'You lie to me.'

'When?'

'You lie to me with your body, I've just been too dumb to see it.'

'You ain't making no sense.'

'You raped her didn't you just like the man with the scarred face raped me all those years ago.'

Eddy began to walk past her but Mandy grabbed him and pulled him back. They were standing in the kitchen when Eddy struck her across the face. He had his fist clenched and was swinging it at her when she reached behind her and picked up the knife that was lying on the counter. Then she watched Eddy stagger across the trailer, and collapse.

He fell and lay there staring up at Mandy.

She was crying as she said, 'I found the mask Eddy, stuffed into the false panel in the wall by the bed. All I wanted to do was believe you loved me and I found the mask.'

She sat there in the trailer thinking of all the things Eddy claimed he was. She was still crying as the Sheriff led her away, with "The Ice Cream Man" running through her head.

Trapped

Joan De La Haye

Hey you!

Yes, I'm talking to you. Don't pretend you don't see me. There is no way you could possibly miss a woman locked in a box in the middle of a field. You're not completely blind are you?

Please don't just walk away. I need your help. Come a little closer. I won't hurt you. Can't you see I'm trapped in here?

Okay, I can see from your expression that you think this is some sort of hoax. There are no hidden cameras. No one's going to jump out from behind a bush and scream "surprise". Have a look around; it's just you and me. Yes, I feel it too. It feels like we're being watched, but I'm sure it's nothing. Please just get me out of this thing. Sorry! I shouldn't have yelled at you. I'm a little frustrated. Being locked in a box for a night and all day will do that to a girl. They've all gone. Packed up and left in the middle of the night like something was chasing them. Hopefully whatever was chasing them isn't here. Don't worry. I'm sure it's not.

Those freaks from Dark's Carnival left in such a hurry they left this field scarred by their caravan wheels. It'll take the earth a while to recover from their destruction. And that god awful smell, in case you're wondering, is elephant and horse shit. It'll be dark soon and if I don't get out of here before then something terrible is going to happen to me. Don't pull that face. This is no joke. I'm being serious. Look, I'm still not sure how it happened or why she did this to me. I didn't insult her, or at least I don't think I did. Did I?

Okay, so I might have told her that her tarot reading was

the biggest load of crap. And maybe I did freak out a little, but if she'd told you the things she told me, you would also have freaked out. Anybody would. I'm not some homicidal demon stuck in human form. The woman is clearly off her rocker. Tarot readings are supposed to be fun. They're not supposed to be all gloom and doom, are they? I'd never had one before. Have you?

Anyway, Madam Zinzi and the rest of her tribe of unwashed carnie folk left me here, stuck in this bloody box stage magicians use to saw people in half, with only my head, hands, and feet sticking out. They wrapped that chain around the top and the bottom and the padlocks are out of reach. They also didn't leave me a key to unlock them. I don't suppose you have any tools in your car? I'm not an escape artist for fuck's sake. It doesn't matter how hard I bang around in here, I can't get out. And now thanks to the constant rain my head is also soaking wet. I just know I'm going to get a cold. Those bastards told me I had until sundown then he would come for me. You're not him, are you? It's not an unreasonable question. You are a he, aren't you? And it's almost sundown, and you're here in this field. So it's not completely beyond the realms of possibility that you're him. So… are you him? No. You sure? Okay. I believe you.

Sorry. I'm rambling. I've gotten a little ahead of myself and forgotten my manners. Let me take a breath and a virtual step back so I can tell you the story as calmly as possible. I'm Josephine. If you take a step over this way, I can shake your hand. It's a pleasure to meet you. I don't suppose you can move your umbrella to cover my head as well as yours. I'd really appreciate it. Thanks.

So… This mess started last night when my friends decided that a trip to Dark's Carnival would be a good laugh. Boy were they wrong. It certainly started off as a fun night out. Who doesn't enjoy candy floss, toffee apples, and carousels? I know I certainly do. We even met a few attractive guys from town who bought us a couple of drinks at the beer tent. Some of the men from the carnival were also rather cute, although there were a few freaks as well. The elephant man scared the crap out of me. Don't get me started on what some of the women looked like. If I had a face like some of them I don't think I'd have a mirror anywhere in my house. Were you here last night? Did you see what the bearded lady looked like? Talk about being hit by the ugly stick. Sorry! I'm digressing. I tend to do that when I'm freaking out.

It was shaping up to be such a promising night. Jeff, I think his name was Jeff, asked me if I'd have dinner with him next week. I even gave him my number. I don't normally do that but it's been such a long time since I went on a proper date. I was actually feeling a little giddy. I haven't felt like that since I was a teenager. Jeff took me up on the Ferris wheel. I hadn't done that in years. I couldn't bring myself to tell him that I'm afraid of heights, but I think he guessed that I was scared and held my hand the whole time. We kissed right at the top and, for a few moments, I forgot all about my fears. For that moment in time I was just a girl enjoying her first kiss with a boy. It was all so very romantic.

The hall of mirrors was a little creepy. A sign of things to come. I always thought that those mirrors were only supposed to make your body look a bit funny, but this one was different. Jeff said it was just trick lighting, but I'm not so sure. I kept seeing a shadowy figure just at the edge of the reflection, but when I turned around to see if anybody was behind me, there was nothing there. When I turned back to look at the mirror, my reflection was different. My eyes seemed to change. It was slight, almost imperceptible. My eyes went from brown to red then back to brown. I would probably have thought it was a pretty cool trick if it hadn't been for that shadow giving me the creeps.

I was already feeling a little on edge when Jodi came up with that hare-brained scheme. Stupid bloody woman. She decided that we all had to go have our fortunes read. Madam Zinzi was at the edge of their encampment. The bright red caravan stood out of the dark like a beacon in the night. Mist from the river swirled around our feet, giving the whole place an otherworldly feel. Although she may also have had one of those fog machines they use in night clubs. I wouldn't put it past that bitch. We all took turns to have our fortunes told. Jodi went first and came out in tears. Apparently Madam Zinzi had seen death in Jodi's near future. I mean, everybody dies at some point or another. Nobody gets out alive. Why death was such a shock to her system was beyond me. But then the rest of the gang had similar experiences. Which was a little strange, I grant you. They all came running out one by one, with these horrified expressions then they all gawked at me as though I'd killed their dogs. From the looks they gave me, one could have sworn that I was pointing a gun at them and threatening to pull the trigger then and there. It was completely nuts.

Madame Zinzi's voice came from inside her blood red camper, calling my name. I must admit the sound of her voice gave me a shiver up my spine. One of my so-called friends must have told her my name. There's no other explanation for it, is there? She couldn't have known it by herself. She couldn't have plucked it out of the ether, could she?

My heart was thumping up a storm as I walked up those steps to her caravan. Candles were burning all over the place. A real fire hazard if you ask me. She sat in the corner behind a small makeshift camping table which looked like it would buckle under the weight of her ample breasts. They had to be a double D at the very least. After I recovered from my cleavage envy and got my heart to stop racing I managed to observe more. A crystal ball rested on the counter. I was mesmerized by the smoke churning inside. The smoke formed into a huge eye and as I watched, I felt as though I was being pulled towards it. The eye was staring at me, into me, and examining my soul. Judging by what happened next, I think my soul came up wanting.

The candle flames flickered in the breeze, but I couldn't figure out where the air was coming from, the door and windows were all closed. Madame Zinzi's eyes went pitch black. My throat tightened and my palms got sweaty. The hair on my nape stood on end. I've always heard that expression but never actually experienced it until last night, and I hope never to experience it again. My heart still hasn't recovered. My ears itched and felt blocked. You know how your ears get blocked up when the cabin pressure changes in an aeroplane? Like that. I didn't think things could get stranger, but I was wrong.

Madame Zinzi shuffled her deck of cards and grinned at me. Her teeth were skewed and yellowing from smoking too many cigarettes. A cigarette smouldered in a dirty ashtray that was already filled with butts. The smoke mingled with that from the candles; the small space filled up with smoke quickly and I struggled to breathe. I've never suffered from claustrophobia, but last night I did. I wanted to run. I needed to get out of that tiny, smoke-filled caravan, but the door was locked. I know I didn't lock it when I went in. I know I didn't. No matter how hard I tried, the damn door wouldn't open. I even tried kicking it, but it wouldn't budge.

'Calm yourself.' Her voice was sharp and heavily accented. She sounded Russian. I couldn't help but do as she commanded. I was transfixed. I had to obey her. 'Come. Sit.' The cards flew through her fingers as she shuffled. The Tower, Death, and The Hanged Man landed on the table in front of me.

'A sacrifice is required.'

'What is that supposed to mean?' I asked. I thought it was a perfectly acceptable question, but she didn't seem to think so. She just ignored me.

'He is coming.' She sounded like one of those cryptic oracles foretelling death and destruction.

'Who is coming?' I asked. Once again she ignored me. It took me a while, but I eventually realised that she was channelling something. Madame Zinzi had left the building. Okay the caravan. Same thing. You know what I mean. There was something else inside that camper, and I don't think it was human.

'He comes on the wind calling for Josephine. All will die who stand in his way. He searches for his mate, his other half trapped inside the human. She must be given to him. Death will follow swiftly unless he is reunited with his love.'

The next thing I knew I was in this box and everybody was gone. My friends abandoned me. I can't believe they left me here to die. How could they believe that fortune teller? Don't look at me like that. Not you too? It's ridiculous. I'm not some demoness trapped in human form. I told you the crazy bitch was off her rocker. I'm not some great evil's long lost love. I know that crap is all romantic in the movies, but when you're the one shoved in the box waiting to be sacrificed, it's not so romantic. Trust me.

What are you looking at? Do you see something?

Shit! The sun is setting. I have to get out of here. Please. Help me. What was that? Did you hear that?

No. Please don't leave me here alone. Come on. Be a man. Where's a hero when you need one. I'm sorry I didn't mean that. Please come back. Fuck! Please don't leave me here. I'll do anything. Oh! Come on. This is so not fair. And now I'm talking to myself. Great. Just when I thought things couldn't get worse, it goes pitch black.

Oh my god! What the hell is that thing?

No!

The Price of Admission

Neal F. Litherland

The world was built from the bones of the gods. Their children had slit them up and spit them out, finger painting a cosmos from their blood and brains. They'd placed their eyes in the skies, and strewn their teeth for the mountains. They made murder into magic, and said that it was good. They made man in the image of their madness, and he bred, fed and spread. Across hills and valleys, cutting, breaking, burning, children who had learned from the very best the art of creative destruction. There was still mystery in the meat, though. No matter how many forests man cut down, or how big his cities became, there would always be places where the skin peeled back and fetid secrets seeped out. Secrets like the Crone's Carnival.

It was the sort of tale told over brown bags and burn barrels, or whispered in dragon dens thick with poppy smoke. A traveling show of secrets, the Carnival called to drop-outs, burn-outs, castaways, runaways, the misplaced, the displaced, the unloved, unwanted and otherwise forgotten. A tatterdemalion of magic, myths and monsters, no one was sure what the sack cloth circus truly meant. One backwater legend whispered the Carnival held all the monsters god had made on the seventh day, and that it was ringmastered by the devil himself. The waterfront rumor mill claimed the place was a shanghai sideshow, and that today's visitors would be tomorrow's freaks after they'd been cut, carved and made into unrecognizable sculptures of scars and stitches. In the roach rooms and lower levels of higher education, the disenfranchised talked about a place where the collective unconsciousness sat, pooling like blood in a corpse. A place full of mirrors like facets of the soul where the truth of the world could be looked into like a great abyss full of the answers to life's great questions. Answers that swam in darkness like cave fish; simple, ugly and blind.

One thing that all the stories agreed on was that the Crone's Carnival chose its staking ground with the utmost forethought. Places where the topsoil had worn thin, and the flesh of the underworld showed through in piebald patches. Harper's Hollow was one such place. The town was bent and crooked, like a bone broken over and over again but never rightly healed. Buildings leaned like toothless old men looking for their missing glass eyes. Old asphalt humped and buckled, and between the cracks a red, sullen light burned like hell's boiler room. It stank with the rotten-egg smell of perdition, and the coal fires belched gray smoke into the air. The black veins of the Hollow had burned so long no one alive remembered when they hadn't. It was a town that had committed suicide, and turned itself into a burnt offering. That was why the young man came, treading on the train of a dying day.

On the surface he was nothing special; the Damned rarely were. Just a fair-haired boy with shaky hands and empty, restless eyes. He walked the secret streets and hidden highways of the world in run down boots and a dusty, black coat. A pockmarked pilgrim with needle tracks on his arms and a penny under his tongue, he was two steps from Death's doorstep. He'd sought her in unhallowed swamps with sinking tombstones, and looked for her in ghost towns swallowed by deserts. But even when he'd stropped his wrists in a warm bath, she'd done nothing more than watch him from beneath lowered lashes. This time would be different; all he had to do was find the path to the Carnival, and he'd finally be allowed his end. Or so he told himself.

He paused at the city limits, and looked at the old, twisted sign. A crow perched on the post with its shoulders hunched, glaring at the boy. The traveler cocked his head, and scattered a small handful of maize on the ground. The crow coughed. The boy nodded amiably, and passed on into the choking, holocaust haze of the coal fire town. He stroked his belly as he went, softly singing a lullaby his mother had taught him before she'd died. The one she'd used to sing his brother to sleep.

The dead town grumbled at the interloper. Floorboards creaked and dry rot beams groaned, whispering to each other about the boy. He walked on and paid no mind, peering through the smoke and looking for the Signposts. He ran his fingertips through the ash and touched them to his tongue, frowning as his guts rolled over. He leaned through broken shop windows, and studied where the manikins pointed. A broke-down rust box with four flat tires was slewed across the main road, and its smashed headlight stared down a side street. The bones of a dog sat at a crossroads like a compass, the dead rat it had choked to death on still lodged between its jaws. He walked a spiral through the town, and his footsteps cut a trail through the choking down that settled on everything. Black birds watched from perches on silent power lines, and hunkered on drooping gutters. He couldn't always see them, but he felt the birds' gazes.

At the softening mouth of an alley he found a half fan of black feathers; a child's sunrise done in gritty charcoal. The boy strode down the crumbling throat, and stepped abruptly out of town. He stood on a naked dirt path, and long reeds of witch grass reached for him. The moon had risen, a cankered eye peering over the mountains, and he saw everything. The path wound down through the stunted, sickly scrub, to a leaning foot bridge over a polluted slick of creek. And there, on a flat rise, was what the boy had been looking for.

A shadowy tent city sat on the hilltop. Lead ropes creaked and canvas flapped in the night breeze. Snatches of music slithered through the thin air; serenades from a songbird with cancer. Ragged pennants snapped and cracked above the black big top. Lights moved inside; pretty pinpricks in the mouth of the night sky. The whole thing bulged and sweated, brooding at the summit like a black dream waiting for the right sleeper. A solemn circus, a meat grinder in midnight mourning, it could swallow up cities and render them into bloody bone meal. It would have no trouble with the likes of him. The boy walked a little more quickly, and licked his cracked, bloodless lips. The Crone's Carnival waited for no one.

He trod carefully, rolling his steps heel to toe like a drunk trying to keep the world from spinning. Ragged leaves clutched at his dungarees, and they whispered warnings to him. Stay away, they said. There's nowhere for a boy like you in a place like that. He smiled a bit at that; a sharp, flick-knife smirk that twisted his face into something harsher. Something older, grown cruel and sly with years. Then it was gone, and he continued.

The boy stepped gingerly over the crippled bridge, testing each board before he shifted his weight. The black water gurgled and gagged, stinking like vomit and black tar heroin. He almost fell once, but he caught the guardrail and stumbled onto the other bank. He sat there on all fours, sour spit in his mouth and his belly burning with bile. He half expected the Carnival to be gone, vanished like faerie fire. But when he raised his gaze it was still there, real as the witching hour. He found his feet and came on, barely blinking as he scuttled up the rise. He murmured the soft, breathy song like a mantra. A charm against dark powers awakening.

The Carnival grew larger with every step. Voices chanted in dead languages, and the crack of scourges snapped like pine knots in a fire. Women wailed, and children bawled. Smoke rose in a dozen shades of darkness; lost souls perfumed with scented coals. There was no sign emblazoned above the entrance, just a thin veil that separated one world from the next. You either knew why you were there, or you had no business behind the curtain. The youth panted, and wiped dirty sweat from his face as he approached the shivering shroud.

He was reaching for the gauzy gate when a hand closed over his wrist. It was the color of marble in the moonlight, with thin, blue veins running beneath smooth skin. The knuckles were heavy, the fingers slim, and heavy calluses ground against the scars on the underside of the boy's wrists. His gaze followed the hand into a black sleeve, along an expanse of rumpled jacket, up the slope of a shoulder, and across a face that was Mooncalf pale where it stuck out of the shadows of a flat-crowned hat. Eyes glared out of the shadows, darker pits in the blackness, and they burned as hot as corpse fires. The pale man held his other hand out, palm up. He never spoke, but the boy knew the ferryman never did.

The boy's belly clenched, and his mouth went dry. He pushed two fingers into his mouth and pressed aside the limp meat of his tongue. He plucked out the coin, and put it in the man's hand. It was an unevenly milled slug of bronze, and it bore a two-faced tyrant with eyes in the back of his head. A dead man's coin from the other side of the world, it had taken the boy a long time to find. The barker closed his free hand, and for each finger that curled around the coin, one more released the boy. The youth snatched his wrist back, but the pale man paid him no mind. The ferryman parted the veil and held it open. The boy hesitated, but before the ferryman could close the door the boy threw himself into the gap.

Pandemonium waited on the other side. A parade of penitents with their heads in covered cages shambled in single file, each one lashing the man before him. Blasphemers in black marched the opposite way, sweating and straining to carry a gilded juggernaut across their backs. Women in bloodstained white wandered, blind Fates with prayers in their mouths and holes in their eyes. In between them wandered the rabble. Men, women, children, they followed the flow of the curious crowd looking with wide eyes for a shepherd to lead them out of this realm which wasn't life or death. Somewhere, anywhere, nowhere, it made no difference to the lost. They'd come there hoping to find answers, but found they only had the coins to pay the entry fee. Getting out cost something else entirely.

Tents lined the paths through the Carnival, and they were filled with gaudy miracles and freak show soothsayers. Giants with constellations burning in their bellies, horned children who spoke doomed rhymes in singsong voices, and crippled chimeras who had seen and done things neither man nor beast would or could on their own. They entreated, cajoled and offered to passersby, creating a dull roar that slapped the ears like waves on a wharf. Every wave was strange in its own way, but together they made a sea of sameness the boy found comforting. He inhaled the smells of sin and sorrow, and plunged into the crowd.

Myths and monsters were on display like common criminals. The Lord of the Flies held court in a temple of rot, preaching decay in the buzzing voice of a thousand vermin. The Mule, a tired, old hunchback that had been ridden by every demon with a name, guzzled brackish water and wheezed one confession after another from thick, fly-specked lips. Razorblade Betty, the Queen of Suicides, ran rusty red scissors through her fingers and moaned as she cut sin into her skin. They went on and on, an endless procession of the pious and depraved offering their own forms of empty salvation and tasteless damnation. The boy watched them all in passing, but he didn't see the one he was looking for. His stomach burbled, let out a drooling, acidic snore, and he bent over, gasping.

Now, now lovely, don't be getting sick on my stoop,' a soft, slippery voice said. The boy looked up, and found himself eye to eye with a dwarf. He sat on a padded pillar with his bandy legs crossed beneath him, and a cloudy pipe in his lap. His chest and round belly were bare, both of them covered in thick, coarse hair. His face was smooth and pink below the folds of a dingy turban, but the skin was sweaty around his small, piggish eyes. He gave the boy a lecher's gap-toothed grin, and set his pipe aside. 'What brings a precious thing like you to a place like this?'

'I need to find someone,' the boy said. He swallowed back bile and forced himself to stand straight. 'Can you help me?'

'Of course I can help pretty boy, but it's going to cost you,' the dwarf said. His nostrils flared, and he blew smoke dregs from his nose. A drip of viscous phlegm landed in the dirt. 'Give me your hand sweetling, and let's see just what kind of price you can pay.'

The boy hesitated, but the dwarf snatched his sleeve. The little man's thick fingers held the boy's right hand like a captured bird, stroking over the knuckles. Slowly the boy relaxed, and took a half step closer. The Oracle smiled again, and gently turned the boy's hand over. 'Soft skin, but used to hardship,' he cooed. 'Youth on the cusp of experience, yes, reaching out into the darkness and looking for something. Well, it seems you've grown lucky my boy, very lucky indeed...'

The dwarf trailed off, and a tremor went through his thumbs. He glanced down at the boy's palm, and his eyes saw what his fingers had been shrieking. The lines, so much the same from one person to another, slashed wildly across the boy's flesh like lightning scars. There were more lines than any one man should have been born with. There were fainter tracks of a fresher life, the light traces left by fate on a new soul, but they mingled with the deeper ruts of something older. Life lines that never ended, heart lines like skinning cuts, trenches of violence scabby with flakes of drying blood and crying out to be fed. His palm was a dull, angry red. As if he'd scrubbed it till it bled, but couldn't make it clean again. 'Y-you,' the palm reader stuttered.

The small man tried to let go, but the boy snatched the dwarf by the wrist. The dwarf reached behind his back, but the boy yanked the soothsayer off his pillar. He tumbled to the dirt, and a curved knife spun through the dust. It bounced against the boy's boot, and the youth retrieved it. He held the blade like an old lover he'd known many, many nights. He crouched down, a cobra holding the rat in his gaze.

'Tell me where to find her, little man,' the boy said. His

voice was soft, but something burned in his eyes. His thumb stroked along the spine of the dagger, and his nose twitched at the smell of fear sweat. In an unfamiliar place, he'd found some familiar ground. 'Just tell me, and I'll go.'

The Oracle looked up at the looming scarecrow with his straw-colored hair and stained hands. His turban had come loose, and folds drooped around his neck and shoulders. Beneath it, left of center on the fortune teller's forehead, was a third eye. A milky, cataracted pustule that never quite closed, it saw dim and dark past the here and now. Crusty tears dripped from the corners, and it opened like a blossoming sore. He whined and shivered, panted and shook. The Oracle Saw the boy, and once he had Seen him there was no way for him to unSee.

'The Gemini,' the dwarf burbled, whining the two words like a kicked puppy with a blocked bladder. 'Defiler and despoiler, stealer of innocence, matricide, father of-

'Hush now,' the boy whispered, and pressed the blade against the ridge of the dwarf's belly. 'Where is she?'

The Oracle's two eyes rolled back, and something in the third opened. An empty iris yawned, and dipped its mouth in time's stream. The dwarf's lips quivered in terror, or ecstasy. Maybe both. His teeth chattered, and foam flecked his mouth. The crowd slowed, and onlookers watched. They drew closer, trying to breathe the magic and fill the empty places inside themselves. The little man trembled, and spoke in a voice like far away thunder.

'She waits in darkness in the House of Souls. Follow the path of the dying sun as the Crow flies, and look you close for the Signs.' The dwarf's lips peeled back, showing his stained teeth and thick, phallic tongue. 'Her abhorred shears sit sharp, ready to cut.'

The Oracle went limp, and his feet twitched like a man dreaming of burning coals. The crowd moaned, a greedy lover who wanted more. The boy stood and turned, the knife still in his hand. They drew back, panting and shuddering. A host of believers finding the divine standing in their midst. They didn't know him, but they knew of him. They whispered, and invoked his legend in hushed voices. The Dark Janus. The Baby Killer. The Bloody Prophet. All of them and more, names written in the blood of the innocent with his own, stained hands. A legacy of death and destruction that turned his every step into a graveyard. They stood in awe, and their reverence called to the Thing inside him. It stirred, and murmured. Spoon cooked dreams welled, and the heroin lullaby he'd shot up ran out of his arms like needle freak stigmata. Then a crow cawed, and the whispers turned into a surprised shout. Just like that, the spell was broken.

The boy looked up. The psychopomp alighted on a pole, and rapped its beak three times. It flapped its wings, tucked its head and plucked a feather. The single pinion see-sawed back and forth, and the boy stepped forward. The crowd jumped back, and he snatched the feather. It was still warm, the nib slick with a single spot of dark blood. The crow flew, and the boy followed.

The sea of supplicants parted before him as the boy chased the croaking harbinger. The little gods and divine stains shrank back behind their playbills and held their tongues. His shadow cavorted and leaped from his heels, drinking in light and spewing it out as it passed. The bird banked West. The bright lights fell behind, as did the bells and the songs. Canvas stood empty as coffins, and soon their only companions were the wind and stars.

A broken doll lay to the right of the path, its stuffing torn out in muddy handfuls. Three rusty darts jutted out of a tent pole, their feathers festered to drooping remnants. Someone's initials had been carved into a lightning-struck tree, and the letters along with what they'd once meant had been burned away. Round stones jutted from the path like teething molars; remnants of some ancient ruin long buried down in the darkness. The place smelled like mud and graveyard flowers. Decay's first kiss lingered everywhere. The seams that held him together were coming undone, and the Other's breath hissed in his throat, but the boy ran on.

He burst onto a small square, the center ring of the bullseye that was the Carnival. The skeleton of a roller coaster reared against the night sky like the corpse of a monstrous serpent, and the carts were filled with weeds, the tracks gummy with dirt. A time-weathered haunted house sat like an old widow at the window, reminiscing about when she'd been young and beautiful. A broken down bandstand creaked in the wind, and tried to whistle a tune through its splintered, dry rot mouth. He came to the place where the springs wound down, and it was always one minute shy of midnight. His guide settled on a solitary fencepost, and ruffled its feathers. The boy came closer, breathing harshly. The crow glanced over its shoulder, then back up at the boy. He followed where the bird had looked. At first he didn't see anything. Then the moon glinted on something slick, smooth and nearly invisible.

The Glass House sat in the gloom, a forgotten monument to vanity. Streaked and grimed, diamonds still lurked in its dust. They sparked like falling stars, and promised a thousand wishes to the one that could find them in the night. The boy put his hands in his coat pockets, and cradled his stomach. It squirmed, writhed, and he sang in a low, cracking voice as he stumbled toward the third station. The crow cawed one more time, calling down doom. Or perhaps just wishing him luck. The boy couldn't be entirely sure anymore.

As he drew closer, the boy saw how the place must have once looked in his mind's eye. A pristine palace of sheen and shine, it would have seemed simple from the outside. With a sweeping veranda, and the sun stroking every surface, it would have been impossible to find the door without walking into it. Impossible to know who among the wanderers inside was real, and who was fake. Equally impossible to know if the one who came out was the one who had gone in, if the person came out at all. The years had not been kind though, and they'd wiped greasy fingers along the beautiful puzzle box until the trick of the entrance was clear for anyone to see. The boy stepped up the creaking stairs, and glanced into the yawning maw. Light wavered and bent, bounced and broke, framed in pale panels with fading edges like something out of a child's fairy story. The kind where the darkness had teeth, and the children got eaten up. The boy took a deep breath, and stepped between.

He'd barely taken three steps into the mirror maze before the outside world became an idea; a shadow cast on the wall of a cave. He held his hands out, and walked like a blind man. He shuffled his feet, and scraped his boots against mummy leaves. The scent of mildewed dust puffed up like corpse breath, and he tasted the richness of grave dirt in the back of his throat. Shapes moved in the mirrors, and pressed against the shining doors and windows. They whispered for him to come closer, and to look inside. The boy closed his eyes, and clenched his jaws tight. He wouldn't look, and there was nothing they could do to make him. They were phantoms, but in this place that didn't mean they had no power.

The boy turned left again and again, trailing his fingers along the walls. He knew if he kept turning he'd eventually find where he needed to go. But inside the Glass House time was funny. Distance and direction as well. He might have gone one step, or a thousand. It might have been moments, or years. In that darkness between worlds where ghosts told tales, there was no difference between eternity and now. He smelled fresh blood in filthy drains, along with the ripe scents of rape and madness in a hundred no-name hotels. He heard the rip of a skin blade, and the wet gurgle that always followed. The death rattle of unwilling mothers, and the cries of their half-born children rang like cracked church bells. He pressed his hands to his ears, but they couldn't keep out the memories of the things he had done. And the things his brother had done.

He ran from the recollection, arms over his head. He careened off the walls, eyes wide and staring. Witch light burned in the depths of the house, and the windows to his soul told their tales of his misdeeds. A young woman with blonde hair, her eyes empty as sea glass, and her throat cut messily from ear to ear stared sightlessly from one mirror. An older black woman with ashen skin and too much makeup slumped against another. She looked like a dead woman in a glass coffin, but there was enough light left in her eyes to stare at him through the mirror. Her lips had drawn back to reveal yellowed, snaggly teeth like an old she wolf. His mother was in another. Her dark hair was disheveled and greying, and she gibbered in terror while she clawed at the pane like she was trying to find the door handle. He stood behind her and stabbed again and again while her swollen belly squirmed and thrashed with unholy life. Life his brother had put inside her while he held her down and spoke secrets mortals shouldn't know. The boy in the mirror was younger, smaller, and his eyes held all the sick, desperate panic of an altar boy chaining up the devil.

The memories came, a frenzy of furies shrieking in his skull. The walls shivered as he bounced from one hall to another. The magnet of his internal compass spun like a broken wheel. The light pooled and puddled, then vanished altogether. The blackness grew blacker, and fingers reached out of it. They stroked his back and teased his nethers. Unknowable beings hissed in his ear, and shook the shoulder of the Thing that lived in his hollows. The Thing yawned and stretched, filling up the boy's skin and twisting his insides as it tried to shoulder him out of the way. His knees buckled. The boy shut his eyes against the pain, and the driving, empty hunger that always came when his brother woke up. The boy clutched his head and screamed. The sound reverberated, and the past laid back down in its shallow graves. The whispers ceased, and the fingers drew back. Even the sleeper on his soul seemed taken aback.

'Where are you?' the boy whispered into the blackness.

'Right behind you,' the Crone answered.

The boy opened his eyes. The Glass House had vanished, its tarnished mirrors and howling ghosts so many fun house frivolities. In its place was an abattoir. The ragged reek of spilled entrails and voided bowels mixed with the stale scent of peeled skin and hung flesh. It was an animal stink, a visceral, murderous miasma that choked him with its familiar smell. Smoke hung heavy in the air, and gutted meat swung in the gentle breeze. Too much meat to be readily counted.

The Crone sat in the silence of the slaughter, seated in a

rocking chair built of baby bones. Stooped and aged, she was wrapped in black too dark to deserve the name. Gray hair hung like a threadbare veil over her face. Her shears flashed in the half light of the fires, a bloody tool for doing bloody work. He'd found what he sought, and fear warred with relief.

'Stand up boy,' the Crone snapped, teeth clacking like a raptor's beak. 'Let me see you proper.'

He stood, and pulled at the charms he wore. The cassock of a de-frocked priest, the prayer beads of a suicide, a lucky coin smashed flat and the boots of a wrongly hung man. Layer upon layer, he stripped off the remnants of broken promises and forsaken faith, peeling back the weight of blasphemy he'd carried just to keep the secret he carried asleep in its morphine dreams. He pulled back the last of them, and revealed his brother. The Twin. The Gemini.

His brother's head and shoulders hung from his belly like over-ripe, cancerous fruit. Its stick bug arms were ropy with tendons, and it bore only a few, malformed fingers on either hand. It grasped the boy's belt and lifted itself, looking up at the Grandmother. It's mouth was slack, and full of teeth. Drool ran from the lipless slash, and dribbled in idiot rivers along the boy's stomach. Its veins bulged, and it spat out the remnants of the drugs the boy had mainlined to keep it quiet for so long. Its half-formed snout sipped the sepulchral scent of the place, and the blank, blind flesh where its eyes should have been looked at the glory his brother had brought him to see. It gurgled, a child pleased with its latest delight.

'Come closer,' the Crone said, her shears snapping. The Gemini walked closer, half in a dream as it looked all around. it looked closer, and saw that each body was one he'd put on the hook. The thing stared at the remnants of its unwilling conquests, and of the pleasures its better, mortal half tried to deny it. 'That's far enough.'

The Gemini came on, moaning like a babe hungry for the breast. It reached for her, splashing through the muck and offal of a hundred times a hundred deaths. It sent ripples through the carrion pools, and all around him the meat swung and stirred. Bulging, sightless eyes opened, and a wave of animation swept through the torn forms that had once been women. They reached for him with hands and mouths, with their guts and their bones, bearing down on him with the sheer weight of misery and madness he had sown. The thing thrashed and gnashed, pulled and hauled, but it was flesh now and subject to the rules of flesh for all its strength. It fell, and this time it did not rise again.

She looked at them as a tailor might a bolt of quality cloth with a run through the center. The issue of a pregnant woman raped by a dying god, the flaws ran whole through the pair of them. The Bloody Prophet who took women as his father had, and his brother who had cut the burgeoning children from the wombs of unwilling mothers who had lost their mind at the Gemini's horrible, whispered prophecies. A monster trying to beget other monsters, and a boy who'd tried to hang onto his mind long enough to make sure the world wasn't filled with the offspring of the dark divinity attached to his hip. If you cut one, you'd cut the other. She grunted, and frowned. The frown made the fires flare, and sent the shadows scurrying.

'Please,' the boy moaned. His eyes rolled back and forth, back and forth, a metronome lost in a waking nightmare. 'Please... kill me!'

The Crone shook her head slowly. The boy sobbed once, and the Gemini laughed a wet, viscous laugh. The Crone bared her teeth, and the Gemini went silent. The boy as well.

'No,' she said. The Crone laid her shears in her lap, and idly wrapped a long, red thread around her fingers. An unconscious gesture, as if she'd once been a girl who had played cat's cradle. Or whatever name the game had gone by, before men had risen from the settled dust of a new world. She reached up a hand, and stroked the edge of one blade across the boy's forehead. Blood welled, and dribbled down across his eyes. The lids fell, and locked the boy in complete, comforting blackness. 'Sleep now, Janus that's passed. You are no longer your brother's keeper.'

Hours went by in the dying place. A young man stumbled out of the Glass House. On the surface he was nothing special. The Damned rarely were. Just a fair-haired boy with shaky hands and blind, bloody eyes. The Gemini walked slowly, a bloody crown upon his brow, and muttered its prophecy to the winds. The King of the Crone's Carnival, a god crucified to the tree of flesh, he joined the festival of the fast, and confessed what he had done. Perhaps when he'd reached the end, Death would consent to come for him again.

Take Your Chances

Michael S. Chong

I had been away for a year and my mother greeted me as if I'd just returned from picking up a pack of smokes. She could barely remember the day it was and from her gaunt face and stick-like frame, I think she had stopped eating regularly. She probably had forgotten to eat, believing she had when she hadn't. She had had a hard life, including having me as a son, but it was difficult to pinpoint which vice or trauma had her in her present state. More likely it was an accumulation of all the shit which stuck to her and couldn't be shaken off.

The way things were, I guess I took the coward's way out and left my mom to her own vices. Sure, she loved me, and I her, but I always felt like I was in the way of her having a good time. When Scotty, my summer carny boss, offered me the gig to travel the circuit with the show, I had to take it. With no money for college and no employable skills outside of talking a rube out of his money for the chance to acquire some chintz, it was the best way for me to get away, survive and thrive.

I started being a carnival worker as a summer job between the school years. It was the best summer job I ever had and I never wanted it to end. What more could a teenage kid want? It allowed me to be a showman, stay outside, and make some money. Running a game at a carnival, you can make as much money as you can squeeze out of the marks. I made good coin for a teenager. It was only 3 weeks of work but I made

212

what most of my friends made for the whole summer. My boss, Scotty, was the nicest guy you could meet. Thin, short, with salt and pepper hair and mustache, Scotty was wiry with the gift of patter and a heart of gold. When I did really well, had them lining up like I was giving prizes away, he'd give me bonuses like a chunk of hash or the latest Stephen King novel he'd just finished.

Scotty asked me to travel during my third summer playing carny. By this time, I began to feel like an old pro, casual with all the travelers and comfortable with the ebb and flow of the midway. I had just finished my last year of high school and was unsure as to what I wanted to do next. I had gotten accepted to some of the colleges I applied for, but I had a few friends taking a year off to travel, work or both and I really didn't feel like jumping into another bout of schooling just yet. I didn't even know what I wanted to study. This time working the midway would allow me some time to figure it out. The future would be there. I didn't need to sprint towards it.

In this indecision, Scotty had offered to take me on the road with him. I could stay with his crew and share the trailer with his son, whose girlfriend had left him a couple of towns before. She had been a local picked up in some bumfuck town but it still broke his heart and put him on an irreversible bender. I liked Jimmy but he was a drunk with a bad attitude that never knew when to stop. Jimmy had a constant hangover and drank his way out of them. Scotty rarely spoke to Jimmy and when he did it was usually an order. I noticed they never made eye contact or stayed very long in the same area. It was if they both reminded each other of past misdeeds.

With my dad long gone from my life, I had Scotty as a surrogate. He treated me with respect and talked to me like a friend not a worker. My mom had taken it well. I almost felt a sense of relief from her after I told her.

Once we got out of the big towns and started doing the tour of the 'fartland' as Jimmy called it, our environment stayed the same, just the marks looked different. The fur-

Michael S. Chong

ther away from urban centres, the more the crowds seemed
stranger and more surreal. Maybe it was the city boy snob in
me but the locals looked like freaks with their extreme body
shapes, skinny from skag or fast-food fat. It was as if the long-
gone carny sideshows had died since they could no longer
compete with the real world. Looking at my fellow carnies,
which were made up of runaways, Natives and more than a
few ex-cons, they were the normal ones.

I got close to a concession girl by the name of Donna.
She had left home only a few months before pulling into my
hometown and had joined an aunt who ran a corndog shack.
Donna had freckles that spanned the bridge of her nose
which wrinkled each time she took a toke. She would always
cross her eyes looking at the tip of a joint as she lit it.

I had first met her at a get-together in the base of the
Polar Bear Express, a ride that had those rows of seats spinning backwards at quicker and quicker speeds. Franklin who
ran the ride and worked the mike saying 'do you wanna go
faster?' held the carnies beer holdings, which he doled out at
2 bucks a beer.

I first noticed Jimmy talking her up, drunk and slurring,
and thought I could get in there and save her and him the
embarrassment.

'Is this guy bothering you?'

Jimmy looked at me, focusing, then smiling and weaving
on his feet. 'You're bothering me. Fuck off.' He tried to shove
my shoulder but I stepped around it.

'Leave this poor girl alone, Jimmy. Can't you tell she's not
interested?'

Donna looked at me, smiling as she stood up. 'You got
some smoke.'

'As a matter of fact, I do.' I took her by the arm and we
walked to the back of my flat just down the midway. We
smoked a joint that night and spoke of everything we could
think of. She like me, had no idea of what she wanted to do
for the rest of her life but thought traveling with her aunt,
dipping and deep-frying corndogs was better than telemar-
keting or burger flipping in her little town. At least she'd

214

see some of the world and she always liked her aunt more than her bible-thumping parents. You see her aunt Liz was the wild one in her family of churchgoers, having run away with the carnival at about the same age as Donna was now. Childless but full of love for her niece, Liz took in Donna to help her get free of the biblical tyranny at home. Her folks had now disowned Donna and her main joy was a little stray cat she had adopted at the first lot she met her aunt at. He was a scruffy little tomcat she named Mr. Yumyum. That cat somehow found us that night as we lay together in the back of my game. He was purring at our feet when I woke up with Donna in my arms.

After that Donna and I spent all of our free time together, what little spare moments a carny can find. Starting work at 9 am when the midway opened until 2 am when you get the stock to reload for the next day, carny game runners had only late night freedom.

By the time we got down to Louisiana, Donna and I had inherited our own trailer from a retiring childless couple who had run a tiny donut concession. They went to live in a trailer park where all old carnies go to finish the show.

Scotty's great aunt lived there too. I had heard stories of her from Scotty and Jimmy, talking of their matriarch who could talk the soul out of a saint and decipher the deceit of a devil. She was the first of the family to go with the show, and the next generations followed her lead.

One night after close, Scotty asked me if I wanted to meet his great aunt and of course, after all the build up, there was no one I wanted to meet more. Scotty drove me in his pickup to the trailer park not too far from where the levee broke. Scotty asked Jimmy to come but he was too busy partying. I was happy to not see him come. Donna was always too busy to come, not wanting to spend her off time talking to an elderly woman.

Scotty walked me into her presence like I was to meet a holy figure; an audience with a deity. Kathleen was her Christian name, but she went as Kath. Even her kids called her that. I met a son in his late 60s, still young at heart with a full head of white hair. There were candles burning and some incense that didn't cover the smell of the marijuana. She had worked the circuit pre-television, as she called it, and had run a mitt camp with a madball – palm reader fortune teller with a crystal ball. She looked glowing and regal, with platinum blonde hair she wore long, smooth skin and radiant pale, cornflower blue eyes. She was one of those people that look at you like they know exactly what you're thinking.

'What do you want to do with your life?' was the first thing she said to me. I told her I didn't know. She said that was a good thing. She asked if I liked working the carny and I told her it was the best time I'd ever had. 'You're too young to know any better, and young enough to appreciate it,' she said. I didn't understand her and thought it was praise, which I rarely received, so from then on I couldn't wait to return to her. I felt she had quite a bit to teach me and I was right.

Every night I sat with her in her warm trailer and she taught me the ways to read a mark and 'reach.' The 'reach' was the leap of faith where the mark lets you read them and pull from them freely. The old tabula rasa where they would feel affinity to any fortune cookie bullshit you threw at them. You might even go beyond the bullshit, but that was just intuition and you never want to look too closely at that or question it for fear that the light of day would make it disappear. This was a money maker as Kath called it. Anyone that could do the 'reach' could make a good living and not just with the show.

Kath showed me another thing once, what I thought was a trick, which she called 'fanto.' Her grandmother taught it to her and it only worked for her once in a while. Basically pulling stuff out of a 'beyond' place to get yourself out of a tough spot. She said the older she got, the tougher it was to pull off, but in her younger days, it came easier and on quite a few occasions it helped to save her skin and the livelihood of the show she was on at the time. This wasn't a sleight of hand. It was some mystical magical bullshit, which I considered a senile delusion. If one could reach through dimensions, why weren't they rich, pulling gold from Fort Knox or diamonds from De Beers? 'You can't do that,' she said.

'Why not?' I asked.

'It doesn't work that way,' she said. What a crock, I thought. How wrong I was.

That time, she reached into her pocket and pulled out a red scarf and handed it to me. 'Take this,' she said. 'You'll need this.' I took it and thought 'so she pulled a scarf out of her pocket. Big deal.'

Later that night, I got a bloody nose walking into the tent pole, too drunk to do otherwise. Feeling the blood flow down my lip, I reached into my pocket and found the scarf there, holding it to my nose. When I pulled it away, it looked no different, the colour of the scarf being the same as my blood.

The last night I saw Kath and we were leaving the lot near her the next morning, she told me she hoped we would see each other again and that she would keep an eye out for me. I thanked her and hoped the teaching she gave me would stick. We held hands while we talked and her hands were soft and warm.

At the next few lots, I started trying to 'reach' the marks. I'd talk to them like I knew they wanted to be talked to, letting them know that I was on their side, and that we were a team to make sure they got the prize. 'Look, I'm just here to make sure we can create a spectacle to gather more players and nothing works better than me giving you a prize and you know, you were so close that last time.' They were starting to spend a lot of money and Scotty would always come by and say, 'That Kath knows her stuff…' then walk away counting money.

I started to be the carnies super seller, raking in more money than any other joint on the whole midway. My game would be tipping from open to close with crowds lining up for the chance to lose a bunch of cash for some prizes worth pennies. It was a good life, if you don't care about the marks. Sure they were spending a fortune, but they were getting a challenge, part physical, part mental, displaying their ability to chuck a ball at some aluminum milk bottles for a chance to win a prize the size of a compact car. I was just the enabler. They could impress their friends and their mate, but it would cost them a bit of money.

One lot in South Carolina brought out a rumble after one joint was found to be impossible by a local news show. A group of vigilantes came down one late night full of booze and anger wanting to point it at any outsider who'd dare rip them off. They barreled in, about a dozen of them, roughing up some carnies and scaring away locals. I found the supposed leader yelling his head off and armed with a hammer. Speaking to him close, I tried to 'reach' him but his shouting and spittle made me lose my concentration. As he swung at me with the hammer, a head strike coming right at my nose, I saw Kath's face, reached into my right pocket, felt something like a cold caress along my wrist and pulled a bat out, striking the hammer from his hand then clubbing him across the back of his neck. During the confusion, I think only Scotty noticed the 'fanto,' everyone else was grappling with their opposite.

After the leader was knocked unconscious, the rest of the vigilantes lost their spark and quickly ran off. The cops came and cleared it up and no one asked about the bat. I wouldn't have known what to say if they asked.

When I examined it later, the bat was a wooden one that looked old and worn as if it was from the 30s, hand-turned and unvarnished with no writing on it at all. It could've been a club from some prehistoric time, but it was a bat, now blood stained. It felt rough in my hand but like it was meant to be there and had been before; familiar and grooved to my palm. When Donna asked where it came from, I told her Kath had given it to me and I guess in a way she did.

For the rest of the circuit, I slept with the bat near my futon. Some nights I'd cradle it as I slept. After that, I tried the 'fanto' a few more times but knew it wouldn't and couldn't just come that way. I even started to think I dreamt it, a waking delusion where I had just grabbed a bat from beside me, someone left it there or placed it into my hand during the melee.

By the time the carnival did the return circuit back to my hometown, I considered the bat a good luck charm, something to ward all the bad things away from me. I should have taken it as an omen when I emptied my sleepover bag in my old room to find it missing from where I nestled it between my dirty jeans when I was packing.

That first night in my old bed, I dreamt of skeletal hands reaching out to me in the dark, never touching but trying to.

That morning home was the same as all the ones before I left. I had a rare day off from the lot as the big rides were being put up and my mom just sat on the couch, watching her daytime television, chain smoking and drinking her cheap bourbon. Occasionally, she would trundle off to the washroom and do whatever drug she was on right now. The phone would ring and when I went to get it, she told me to leave it alone. 'It's just friggin' bills,' she said.

The constant ringing was driving me crazy and I answered it. As I said hello into the receiver, the voice on the other end asked, 'Who is this? Where's Janie?'

'She's stepped out to get some smokes,' I said. 'Who's this?'

'This is the person Janie owes some money. Is this her son? I know about all about you, you little shit. Tell your mom I want my money and soon.' Then he hung up.

When my mom returned, she must've heard and said 'I told you not to answer that,' sat back down, lit a smoke, took a deep inhale, and as she exhaled, said, 'don't worry, he stops after a while.'

'Mom, what the hell is going on?'

'Just some guy I met when you were away.'

'Why is he saying you owe him money?'

She took a drink from her tumbler. 'He treated me like shit so I borrowed some money.'

'What'd he do to you?'

'Let's just say he was a jerk and I decided to fine him for it.'

'How much money?'

'Less than he thinks. It couldn't been more than fifty grand.'

'Fifty thousand dollars? How the fuck-'

'He's a pretty big-time dealer.'

'Shit, mom.'

'Don't worry yourself about it. I've been fine taking care of myself. Just go on back to your circus.'

'It's a carnival and a job. Some people have to make money. Where's the money? '

'I don't know. It's gone. I partied with some friends, lent some out to those in need then one day it was all gone. I'm sure they'd pay me back only I don't remember who got the bulk of it. Must've been Susie, you know Susie, she moved down to Florida to get away from her old man. Didn't leave no forwarding address, but said she'd drop me a line.'

I knew speaking to her when she was high there was no dealing rationally with her. I went through the washroom and hid all her drug stashes away. She was too stoned to protest and she probably knew I was only trying to help her.

I came back and sat down next to her. 'Mom, I got a little saved up and maybe we can work something up with this dude.'

'He's not very flexible,' she said.

I went down to our trailer by the lot and found Donna. She had been hanging out with some of the other carny girls, smoking a joint and drinking cokes. I took her aside and filled her in on my mom's situation. Lovely Donna told me she'd kick in the money she had saved up. Altogether we had about eight thousand, nowhere near the debt, but maybe enough to keep my mom safe until we could make up the rest somehow or just keep paying on a monthly instalment basis.

I would've gone to Scotty for help and advice but knew that an ex-wife of his had cleaned him out and his son Jimmy gambled away the rest. Scotty didn't need any more problems from me. I was his super seller, making him money; the model 'son' or so I hoped.

With the money gathered, I kissed Donna and made my way back to my mom's. When I got there, parked at the curb right in front was an older black Maserati. It was out of place for the neighbourhood and my mom's front door was open which was really unusual with the deadbolts locking down the doors of every other house. Inside sitting right next to my mom was her friend she owed money to in an expensive black tracksuit with golden piping down the sleeves and legs. His carefully groomed stubble made me hate him even more.

'What the fuck are you doing here?' I asked.

'This is Steve,' my high mom said.

'Your mom let me in,' he said. 'We were just talking about how she was going to pay me back.' He put his arm around my mom and she cringed a little.

'It's all right,' my mom said, 'we're working it out.' My mom looked like she'd been crying.

'Look, I was just about to try and contact you. I have eight g's which I can give you now and we'll pay you the rest later.'

'Give it to me,' he said with his hand out.

I gave it to him and he didn't even look at it, just put it into his pocket and said 'This is just the vig. You still owe me fifty large and I wanted it yesterday so sooner than later.'

'Okay, just give me a little time to gather it.'

'I'm a fair man, I understand you're doing your best to help your mom, I can appreciate that. Hell, I respect that. You got a week.'

'I need more time than that.'

'Let's say two weeks then. I think that's more than fair considering what your mom did to me, disrespected me.'

'Okay. You'll get your money. You deserve it. We owe it to you.'

'Your mom knows how to reach me,' he said, turning to kiss my trembling mom on the cheek. He got up and walked out with all the money Donna and I had.

As I heard his shitbox Maserati pull away, my mom started crying, rocking back and forth. 'Sorry... I'm sorry...'

It shocked me since I could not remember my mom ever crying, not even when my dad left her so many years ago. I went to her, held her for the first time in a long time. 'We'll figure something out, mom, don't worry.'

'You don't know what a shit, Steve is, he's a real bad ass. I know he's done some nasty shit. Stuff you wouldn't believe.

Fucking crazy shit. I really thought he'd let me slide. Fifty g's is nothing to a guy like him. I've seen him spend ten on a night out. '

'It's not good for dudes like that to let it get around people are taking money from them and suffering no consequences. Well then we better pay him or make him stop asking for money. One way or the other.'

Since I was working on points, or a percentage of my take, the next few days I hustled as hard as I could to make as much money as possible. Even when the midway crowds were thin, I went out of my joint with the stuffed animals to shake under their faces to draw in even the most hesitant. The 'reach' was working and Scotty noticed, calling me 'killer.' I told him I wanted to buy a nice gift for my mom, which isn't far from the truth.

On off hours, I joined the nightly poker game and was in the money more often than not, but by the end of that first week, I knew that at the present rate, I wouldn't have anywhere near eight thousand let alone fifty by the end of the next week.

That night, I called Steve from my mom's place. He didn't sound happy when I told him the amount I had and my forecast for how much I could get by deadline. He gave me another week and hung up.

I knew I had to do something drastic. There was no way I could get all the money in time. That morning before work, I grilled my mom for everything she knew about Steve. With enough information, I could take the game to Steve. Maybe not kill him, but find some weak point I could exploit.

My mom gave me his address, a big house in a bad part of town. She told me to be careful since Steve came and went all the time, meeting connections, showing off at his hangouts, but always coming home to replenish his stock and bring home some junkie whore to please himself more for the power than the sex.

At around 2 am that night, I cased his joint, watching from a nearby doorway of an abandoned house seized for unpaid mortgage. There was a light on in one of the top floor windows but his Maserati was not on the street. It could be parked in the garage behind, but the door was shut and there was no window. I had to assume he was out, driving around in his sports car, bragging, intimidating and getting people high. Walking up to his front door, I pressed the buzzer and after some time, knocked on the door then banged on it with my fist. If he was home, I could just give him the cash I had on me and leave. After a few minutes no one answered and I could hear nothing from inside. I took a quick look around and there was no one on the streets so I hopped the fence and went around back. There were two glass doors that opened out into the backyard. Through the partially shuttered blinds, there was just a dark living room with large screen TV, a long leather couch and a coffee table covered in drug paraphernalia.

I put my fist in the sleeve and punched the window, which resulted in nothing, but bruised knuckles. In the backyard I found a shovel and after a few swings, smashed in one of the doors. An alarm went off, a whoop-whoop noise, deep, sharp and loud. Looking around, hoping locals might just think it a car alarm triggered by a fallen branch, I saw no signs of anything, so I stepped into the living room, twilit and cool. It smelled like a gym locker room, stale sweat and cigarette smoke. After a few minutes, the alarm stopped and then I could hear some music coming from upstairs. It sounded like death metal, fast and violent.

Above the metal, all I could hear was my heart beating in my ears as my eyes adjusted to the low light provided by the moon and the streetlights just past the backyard fence. No one was coming down the stairs, the music being too loud for them to have heard the alarm. Steve lived a minimal lifestyle. Every stick of furniture had a purpose, no art, no culture, no love… Drugs were the main drive with mirrors and syringes littering the tabletop.

Walking up the stairs, the stench of body fluids and sex was overpowering. It made me a little lightheaded and I got hard. At the top of the stairs, I heard some muffled sounds under the thrash of guitars and scream singing. It didn't sound like fucking but more like punishment, a slap, a sigh, a cry, not of pain, more like satisfaction.

At the top of the stairs, the light from the crack of the partially open door shot moving shadows across the hall and wall. I peeked in and saw Steve standing naked over my nude mother bound to the bed by scarves. He was whipping her with a leather cat-o-nine-tails. I reached into my pocket, grasping for the 'fanto' and felt it slip beyond into the cold empty and then something like a leathery claw shoved my hand out until I just felt my own pocket again. My mom turned her face to the door, saw me through half-swollen eyes and whispered 'go.' Steve never noticed me, being too full of drugs and his power over my prone mom. His face glowed and he was in his own powerful world as I ran down the stairs and out of the house.

I left then in a daze, not really understanding what I saw and felt until I found myself on the street outside my mom's place. I slept that night and had more dreams of skeletal hands, now groping for my mom, scratching down her body and leaving deep brown, red grooves that welled with blood, filling my eyes then everything.

That morning, I knew the only way I could get my mom and myself out from under this creep was to pay him off. And the only way to access the kind of money I'd need was to steal it from the carnival. They were probably insured so it would be a victimless crime. My mom, my real family, despite her faults, deserved a better life and I would have to take a little from my carnival family. The most money would be taken from the final day's earning of the midway. That last day, dubbed 'Black Monday' because of the crowds of kids who would riot and steal prizes would provide a good cover and usual suspects when all the cash takings disappeared. That was also the day Steve made the payoff deadline. It would have to be quick and dirty with the heist then the meet.

I debated bringing Donna into it, knowing I could use another set of eyes and hands but knew if we did get caught, we'd be doing some hard time and I couldn't put her in danger of that just to save my mom.

The last day of the carnival in my hometown always falls on the last Monday of the summer holidays. Kids go back to school the next week so they all come down for one last blast before the fun ends. It always leads to crowds and more often than not violent runs stealing in masses all through the carnival. Even with the extra security and cops, the sheer numbers of young punks, full of soft drugs and alcohol, maintain a promise of chaos all day with their swollen numbers undulating and flowing like a self-contained organism. Occasional bursts of disorder and disturbance would draw the rest and the group would surge towards it, some pulled along in the torrent of bodies, then an uproar at another point would have the bodies billow and rise that way always constantly in motion with each agitation causing an onrush here, there finding purpose and excitement.

By mid-afternoon, I had a huge crowd, tipping the joint, and holding the tip by kicking over the milk bottles and giving away some prizes to the obvious leaders of their packs, getting them ripe and friendly for when we closed down and the money was gathered.

Scotty came around, bringing me a coke, then stood beside me as I watched the marks play the game. 'There have been a few incidents up by the food building. Some guys got hurt and all their stock was stolen. Think we'll have to shut down soon.'

He started towards the wooden padlocked box at the side of my joint where I tucked all the 20s, 50s and 100s. By my count, I had taken in nearly $5,000 today. The midway's game and ride ticket booth total take would be somewhere near $100,000 even with the shortened day. He unlocked the box and started to empty it into a rucksack he carried for such purposes. 'Someone'll let you know when we're shutting down. Hell, you'll notice. It'll probably happen quick. Watch your apron if it gets too crazy and leave your float with the cashier's trailer. We'll meet for a beer at mine when it's all over.'

I told him I would try but had to run an errand for my mom.

He looked at me, patted me on the shoulder and smiled then said, 'You're a good kid,' then walked away. Not to you, I'm not, I thought. Sorry, Scotty.

I estimated it would be another hour before all the money, or at least enough to free my mom, would reach the cashier's trailer. I spent the next bit of time taking in money and giving away prizes.

I lost track of time, getting lost in the spiels and deals, then heard all the joints closing, shutting their openings in consecutive clangs of iron bars and vinyl, slamming tight. I threw a fist of cash in the air behind the crowd amassed at my game and the crowd surged around it. Untying my apron and balling it into my arms, I shut my joint from inside and put on a hoodie, sunglasses and cap to obscure my face. Squeezing out the back to the alley behind the midway, I made my way to the cashier's trailer. The security for the cashier's trailer consisted of a Plexiglas wall and Formica counter, which could only be entered through one locked door. One fat old dude named Scatman, who we all called Fatman behind his back since he also paid us, ran it like he was better than the rest of us, barely looking up or anyone in the eye, with few words other than 'yep' and 'nope.'

I climbed on top the trailer, making sure the coast was clear first. Through the opened vent on top of the trailer, I lit and threw a smoke bomb and four large packs of M-90s I strung together. The bangs and pops with smoke flowing out of the vent had Scatman coughing and shrieking with high-pitched squeals. He flung the door open, ran out and kept running towards the main office just down the alley. I hopped off the trailer and slipped into the open door.

Behind the counter, the padlocked box, where through a slot on the other side of the counter the day's take was passed through, was still locked. I assumed it would be open and possibly it was before Scatman skedaddled and mindfully locked it before he left. I had not considered this nor had I ever been on this side of the counter. With no keys around and only minutes before someone showed up, I started to kick at the lock. Harder and harder I tried, but nothing was going to remove it, beside the key or a grinder. I locked the door from the inside and started to search around the smoky office.

I heard voices then a commotion and knew I was busted. I peeked up over the counter and saw gangs of kids smashing at the Plexiglas with iron bars torn from tents. It seemed like about a hundred of them and they started to rock the trailer. I reached into my pocket through the chill and pushed into my hand was another bat, this time even more club-like and studded with stone-like protrusions. One swing from it shattered the lock. The trailer flipped onto its side with me falling to the bottom, knocking the breath out of me and some of the bills fluttering onto my body and all around me. Some of the punks found the vent, pried it open and they started piling in. Swinging blindly with my bat through the haze, I could feel it striking, crushing bone and mashing flesh with some blood spattering my face and hands. Some screams and cries while forms would disappear back out the open vent. At a respite with more bodies going limp or out the vent than in, I started to grab handfuls of bloody money and found the 'fanto' pushing the money into the frigid void, ignoring the freezing talons trying to push it back out. I heard Scotty shouting outside then getting closer, while I feverishly shoved all the money into the back beyond my pocket where I hoped sometime soon it would save my mom.

More forms came at me and I started swinging again, one swat of my arms made the fog filter clear for a second as my stroke took Scotty straight in the head, then closed around him again as he slumped to the ground. I stopped for a second to see if he was breathing, lying on top of the other fallen, 3 young kids unconscious if not dead. He was breathing but shallowly or at least that's what I told myself when I crawled out the vent and ran from the carnival to my mom's place.

When I got there she was in her usual place on the couch in front of the television. She looked at me once then her gaze went back to the screen and asked with the ethereal voice of the stoned, 'What happened to you?'

'I got the money, mom.'

'Oh yeah, you're a good son. Where'd you get it from?'

'I just got it, mom, don't worry about where.'

Her eyes never left the screen. 'That's good son, because Steve said if you didn't have the money when he showed up today, he'd kill you and keep me as his own personal…how'd he put it again, pin-cushion fuck slave… I'm really glad you got the money. Where is it?'

'Don't worry about that. It's in a safe place.'

'Well, he's due soon…'

I went to my room and tried to conjure the 'fanto' by pushing my hands into my pockets; nothing, no cold, no void, no nothing. I kept at it, trying on different pants, a multitude of jackets and coats, lying down, jumping up and down, but nothing happened other than me poking through and breaking the stitching on all these 'fanto' empty pockets.

My mom shouted, 'He's here.'

I left my room and ran to the front door, chained it then opened it to the chain-taut crack as he walked up to it, his gun held discretely at his side down by his thigh. 'Let me in. I guess you ain't got it.'

'I have it, just not here. Give me some time to gather it.'

'You've had plenty of time. Just let me in and we'll talk about it.' Steve put his foot in the door.

'Gimme a sec,' I said, kicking his foot out and double bolting the door. Steve started to kick at it, the frame buckling but holding. 'C'mon Kath,' I whispered to myself and squeezed closed my eyes and strained to picture her, the ghostly visage I spent hours with, learning the family secrets, but all I saw was Scotty's bloody, unconscious face as I plunged my hands into my pockets, as Steve shot at the locks of the door. My hands, both of them, slipped through the 'fanto' with the rush of ice flushing all up my arms as my hands reached down, grasping for the money. Both hands found some slimy wads of bills and as I started to pull them up and out, I felt the claws pierce through my skin then flesh then start shredding and stripping my meat from my bones, the burning and pain happening so quickly and sharply, my wrists locked into place and they sheared all but the tendon and bone. Now free of the void, I held them to my face and where palm, fingers and thumbs once were, now from my nightmares were the skeletal bones of my own hands, dripping blood and empty of money and flesh.

Not to worry, I wouldn't need them when I was dead. I hoped Scotty survived and Donna would have a good life and then closed my eyes. She was there, of course, Kath staring at me in the dark. I felt her take my hands in hers then she was gone and so was I.

Mooncalf

Katie Young

Madame Dvornikov tapped her cigarette holder against the side of the ashtray and exhaled, a dry rattle following the plume out from between her puckered old lips. Adam could see red lipstick bleeding out into the deep lines around her mouth. She shuffled the tarot deck, sprinkling ash on the tablecloth between them. She turned the top card over.

'The Lovers,' she said. Her accent was thick and ambiguous. 'Perhaps you are facing temptation, or contemplating matters of the heart.'

Adam stifled a snort and looked down at the picture on the card, a man and a woman bound together by the roots of a tree.

'But they also represent secrets and truths. Yes, yes that's it. You're looking for something, or someone, no? That's why you're here? You lost someone.'

Adam glanced up at the woman and that seemed to be all she needed. Her smudgy mouth turned up in a hint of a smile. Adam listened to the barkers hollering outside the fuggy, incense and smoke-filled tent and wished he could just stand up and walk out. He suddenly really wanted to see sunlight.

Madame Dvornikov dealt another card.

'The Moon.' Her brow furrowed and Adam's pulse quickened slightly. 'She lights our way and leads us through the darkness towards the answers we seek. But we cannot know where she steers us, for it is a false light she gives out. A mere reflection of the true light of the Sun. She speaks of betrayal. Uncertainty. See the wolf and the dog, howling below her?

They are your fears. They are the savage beasts which lurk within us all. The cruelty. The Moon draws them out. Perhaps it is vengeance, you seek.'

She quirked a pencilled-in eyebrow and Adam looked down at his lap and kept silent. She laid a third card in the spread and winced when she saw the image on it: writhing, naked forms falling from a burning tower.

'Perhaps the next card will clarify -'

Madame Dvornikov made to turn over another card, but Adam stilled her hand, covering it with his own.

'Wait,' he urged. 'Tell me what it means.'

The old woman paused.

'It could mean a revelation is upon you. An epiphany. A shift in perception. Perhaps you must think differently about the question in your mind. Things may not be as they have seemed to you.'

She licked her lips and puffed on the cigarette.

'Or?' Adam asked.

She took another deep drag.

'It... it could mean the path you are set upon will end in ruination.'

Adam shuddered despite himself and crossed the old lady's palm with silver once more.

'You're right,' he said. 'I lost someone. There was a boy, way back. He'd just turned thirteen years old when he vanished. We never did find him. His mama died not knowing what happened to him. You looked different back then, but I reckon your heart was just as black.'

Madame Dvornikov held his gaze and stubbed her cigarette out.

'What do you want?' she hissed.

'Where is he?'

She paused, choked out a rough laugh and lit up again, blue curls of smoke shrouding her face, her jet black hair.

'I don't know what you're talking about.'

Her voice had regained its thick, blunt musicality. Her mask had slipped back into place but Adam had knocked it askew for a moment and he could do it again.

He grabbed the fortune-teller's frail wrist and felt the tiny bird-bones grind under his fingers. Madame Dvornikov's eyes narrowed, but she wasn't going to give him the satisfaction of crying out.

'Listen to me, old woman. His name was... is Tobias. He'd be a few weeks shy of his thirty-second birthday, and I last saw him standing in the shadow of that rickety old Ferris wheel out there nigh on twenty years ago. What'd you people do with him?'

'You're crazy. Get out of here before I scream.'

Adam rummaged in his pocket with his free hand and closed his fingers around the cool handle of his switchblade. He took it out and flicked it open, the blade glinting dully in the low light.

'Just you try screaming with your throat cut. Now start talking.'

Adam strode through the people milling about the stalls, his heels kicking up dust, his gaze flickering over each and every face in his path. The old seer had sworn blind that she knew nothing, but Adam couldn't leave yet. Someone here had answers. He felt it in his marrow. Adam scanned the barkers and the men manning the coconut shy, Hoop-La stall, and the High Striker. He stood for a while watching bodies fly down the Helter-Skelter, a brightly coloured parody of Madame Dvornikov's tarot card, until the patrons' screams and whoops became warped and portentous in his own mind and sent shivers skittering over his skin.

A gaggle of young women stood around waiting for a chance to watch their beaus ride the mechanical bull. The men were all a little young, but Adam wove his way in and out of the queue anyway, just to be sure. It smelled of stale beer and cotton candy in the midst of the crowd.

'Come on, gentlemen! Ride the bull. Could you be the next king of the rodeo?'

Adam recognised the tout from the last time the carnival was in town. His beard was grizzled, his skin more weathered and leathery, but it was definitely the same guy. It was as if an invisible thread connected that day with this one, and Adam had wound it around and around his fist until the long years in between simply vanished, and his boyhood memories came sharply into focus. Disappeared like Tobias.

It's a dry, summer morning when the carnival rolls into town, and Adam and Tobias are in high spirits. They ride the Tilt-A-Whirl until they feel queasy, taking refuge in the cool gloom of the gypsy's tent while they recover before gorging themselves on hot dogs and candy apples. They take a post-lunch rest, their backs propped up against the trunk of an old yew tree as they watch the Ferris wheel roll lazily around and around.

'We should do that next,' Adam says, pointing up at the big wheel.

He feels Tobias' shoulder jostle his own as he shrugs. A damp heat bleeds through the soft cotton of his shirt and seeps into Adam's skin.

'I don't know,' Tobias replies quietly. 'You know I ain't so good with heights.'

Adam scoffs.

'It ain't so high. Hey – you can always hold my hand if you're scared.'

Adam laughs, but Tobias' head whips around, a wounded look in his clear blue eyes, and Adam knows right away he shouldn't have joked about that. Tobias hates it when Adam calls him a pansy on account of his fears. He elbows Tobias softly in the side.

'Don't get sore. I was just kidding.'

They make their way into the Big Top and watch the acrobats spinning and flying above them. They sit as close to the front as possible. Adam likes the smell of greasepaint and fresh sweat wafting off the performers. The women glide from the trapeze as if they're weightless, slender, pale limbs almost luminous under the spotlights. Tiny waists and feet, sequins and red lips and white teeth flashing as they soar through the air only to be snatched out of it by strong hands. Adam shifts a little in his seat as he feels himself swelling, his hot blood running south, imagining what their powdered skin would feel like under his fingertips. If Adam notices that Tobias' eyes linger on the sinewy arms and bulging thighs of the male tumblers, he doesn't dwell on it.

Adam felt his pulse pounding in his temples as he stood at the entrance of the freak show caravan. Even though he was grown now and he knew that a lot of what they'd seen all those years ago was smoke and mirrors, he couldn't help but feel trepidation as he stepped inside the long trailer lined with cages. There were shrieks piercing the darkness up ahead. He walked on, passing the bearded lady who was sitting on a stool, knitting, and a man covered from head to toe in tattoos. He wore a loin cloth and had intricate patterns branching over every visible inch of skin. His earlobes were stretched out so they dangled down around his neck in fleshy pendulums, and he wore an animal bone stuck through his nose. There was a man with hair all over his face and hands and a bifurcated upper lip, who snarled as Adam approached the bars of his cage. The placard outside it claimed he'd been discovered living wild with tigers and elephants in the jungles of Borneo, and implied he'd actually been sired by a big cat which had forced itself on a human woman.

'It ain't possible,' Adam says. 'A tiger can't get a lady with child.'

'How d'you know?'

'I just do OK?'

'Yeah, but how?'

'I know about these things. I've done it with a woman and everything.'

Tobias stops dead and turns to face Adam. His eyes are huge in the dim light of the caravan.

'Liar.'

'It's true.'

Adam sort of regrets saying anything, because Toby will be like a dog with a bone now, but maybe it's for the best that he knows. Tobias has been coming out with the strangest things

recently and Adam's noticed the way he watches him sometimes with an odd look in his eye, sort of soft and cow-like.
It's been worse since Adam suggested they cut their thumbs
and press the slashes together, making them blood-brothers,
closer than close.

'You don't know any women.'

'Girl then. Whatever. And sure I do.'

'Who is it?'

'Leanne.'

The colour drains from Tobias' face.

'Leanne?' he repeats dumbly. 'My sister?'

Adam nods, biting down on his lip.

Tobias laughs then.

'Yeah, sure. Good one, Adam! You had me going there for
a minute.'

He claps Adam on the shoulder, but his laughter dies away
when he sees the confusion on Adam's face. His expression
changes in slow motion, and Adam is still trying to think of
something to say when his head snaps back and he tastes the
smell of pennies held tightly in a clammy fist.

Adam came to the cage of the Adult Baby, a dwarf wearing
a diaper and a bonnet. He drank milk from a bottle and
cooed and burped. These creatures that had terrified Adam
back then now filled him with a sense of pity. The Siamese
twins were not fused by flesh and bone, but rather sewn into
a special costume to make it seem that way. The woman who
lay motionless on a bed of nails could feel pain. The fat man
wheezed and struggled for breath as he gnawed on a turkey
leg, and the strong man winced and perspired, his muscles
flaccid and joints popping as he hoisted his assistant onto his
shoulder.

Everything was the same but different. The boy Adam had
thought these people monsters, but the truth was, it wasn't
deformities and strange abilities which made this place monstrous. No, something all too human had taken his friend
and swallowed him whole.

'Roll up, roll up! See Mooncalf, the world's only genuine

Katie Young

merman! Half human and half crustacean, this real life lobster boy is more at home in water that he is on land. Come and see the incredible Mooncalf!'

Adam made his way out of the trailer and down to where a large crowd was gathering around a huge water tank. The barker, a large, thuggish man, was poised halfway up a ladder beside it.

'I caught this beauty when it was just a child. Hauled it out of the White Sea with my own two hands!'

Adam pushed his way through the huddle until he could see the tank.

Inside the green-tinged water was a man, around his own age, with long, flowing hair fanned out all around him. He hung, suspended in the water, eyes closed as if in a trance or sleeping. Instead of fingers, his hands were comprised of two pink, crab-like claws. His legs were fused together from his thighs down to his ankles, and his toes were webbed, giving the impression of a fish tail and flippers.

Adam felt himself drawn forward, praying the merman would open his eyes. There was dark stubble on his pale cheeks. His skin looked puffy, a little bloated from the soaking. Adam flattened his palm against the cold glass and stared. It was hard to tell, refracted light distorting the man's features, his ruined hands and legs hovering there uselessly, but Adam couldn't shake the feeling that he knew the unfortunate creature.

The eyes fluttered open, and Adam gasped as he saw the bright blue irises. He'd know them anywhere.

'Toby?'

He slapped the glass with his hand. The cold blue eyes followed the sound but didn't look up to his face.

'Tobias?'

'Hey! No touching the glass!'

The barker was scrambling down the ladder.

'Get your greasy hands off the tank. No touching the exhibit!'

The merman showed no signs of recognition. He just continued to float tranquilly in his watery prison.

'How long's he been in there?' Adam asked a woman bystander.

'I can't be sure. At least ten…maybe fifteen minutes.'

Adam met the tout head on and grabbed him by the collar.

'You have to get him out of there. He'll drown. He ain't no merman!'

'Get your hands off me!' The barker snapped, shoving at Adam's chest. 'Get your filthy hands off me or you'll regret it, boy!'

Adam smiled – a twisted little thing – and found his knife. He tucked it up against the carny's ribs and flicked it open.

'I think we should take this somewhere away from prying eyes, don't you? Now send these good people on their way. Show's over for today.'

Adam finds Tobias watching Lobster Boy swimming around in his tank. He rubs his eyes furiously when he hears Adam approach but Adam can still see tears shining on his cheeks.

'Get lost, Adam.'

Adam goes to put his hand on Tobias' shoulder, but thinks better of it and lets it hang limply by his side.

Adam knows something is surfacing, something dark and dangerous which he doesn't want to unearth completely. He knows there's nothing he can do or say right now to make Tobias feel better without poking at it, so he tries to carry on like the last ten minutes never happened.

'Do you want to ride the Ferris wheel?'

Tobias shakes his head and Adam's suddenly furious with him for ruining their day. For ruining them.

'Well what DO you want to do then?' he yells.

Tobias sighs.

'You really wanna know?'

Adam hesitates, feeling like he just put his foot in a bear trap and the slightest wrong move is going to set it off.

Tobias laughs bitterly.

'I wish I could just… float. Like this guy.' He taps on the glass. 'I just wanna be left alone.'

Adam turns and runs for the Ferris wheel and pays his

three tokens. He's up at the very top looking out over the town when he sees Tobias standing a way off watching him. He almost waves before he remembers he's too angry. What the hell has gotten into him anyway? Adam turns his head pointedly away.

He regrets it for the next twenty years.

Madame Dvornikov was throwing the bones when Adam thrust the barker through the tent flap with the tip of his blade pressed to the small of the larger man's back.

'You again,' she said, lip curling. 'I told you, I know nothing of your friend.'

'He's here,' Adam said. 'One of your sideshow exhibits. Mooncalf. Tobias is Mooncalf. What did you do to him?'

'I don't know what you're talking about -'

Adam struck the old woman across the face with the back of his hand.

The barker sprang forward but Madame Dvornikov gestured for him to stay back.

'It's all right, Dmitry. The worm of his guilt has eaten away at his reason.'

She sat down and lit a cigarette, pushing the small bones around the table cloth with her index finger.

Tobias runs and runs, down to the shore of the lake. He's heard it's cold, so cold and deep that when people drown in there, you can find their bodies years later looking just the same as the day they died.

He wades out until the icy water comes up to his knees. His feet burn with how cold it is and he starts to cry. He wants to teach Adam a lesson. He wants everything to stop for a while, but he doesn't think he has the courage. He thinks hard about Adam and Leanne. He imagines them together, visualises them kissing, Adam's hand snaking under his sister's sweater and feeling up all the places where she's soft and pliant. All the places Tobias isn't. And then it gets easier. He doesn't feel the cold so much, and the water rushes in and fills the vacuum inside him, numbing him, soothing him. His heartbeat slows and he's really tired all of a sudden. He lets his eyes shut as the water closes over his head.

When he next wakes, there is a man standing over him, patting his face although he can't feel it, and moving his lips although Tobias can't understand anything he's saying. He thinks maybe he's in Hell because his body is on fire, and he's not surprised at all because he's been told over and over what happens to boys who have the kind of thoughts he has sometimes.

Adam. Where's Adam?

He drifts in and out. The burning stops, but it's replaced with a heavy, sleepy kind of sickness. Sometimes there's pain in his hands and in his legs, but it always slips away in the end along with his words and his memories and any sort of feeling at all. People come and go. He doesn't know their faces. He spends long minutes in warm baths, completely submerged, enjoying the silence and the dark. Sometimes he's on a pallet, sometimes he hears horses and other animals, and he knows they're on the move again, the gentle swaying of the wagon underneath him almost as soothing as waves. Disembodied hands feed him broth and water and brush out his hair. They shave him and wash him and let him slip into his tank where the blessed water envelopes him and soaks away the stains of his past life.

'Who knows how long he was in the water for. His heartbeat was so slow, I thought he was dead,' Dmitry said. 'I suppose in a way he was. Still is. His mind is still there I think – in the cold depths.'

Adam wiped at his eyes with his sleeve.

'You mutilated him. You hacked him up for your freak show!'

Madame Dvornikov poured three measures of liquor into cloudy tumblers and pushed one towards Adam. He sniffed it suspiciously, then decided to hell with it and tossed it down his throat.

'Did you know, young man, that contrary to popular belief, there are many species of butterfly that prefer dead flesh and animal blood to nectar?'

'What?'

'That's right. The males suck sustenance from putrid carrion, often fighting each other to the death in the process, and this they do to lure the female of the species. So often, beautiful things must undertake ugly acts for love.'

'I don't understand what that has to do with anything.'

'Our way of life is like the fragile butterfly. It cannot survive on beauty and sweetness alone. The grotesque act, the macabre spectacle is what brings the hordes. We may have used what remained of your friend, but we didn't kill him. He was already in his cocoon when we found him, ready to emerge as something else.'

'You're insane,' Adam said.

'No. I am merely a carnivorous butterfly, making good use of the thing you murdered with your callousness.' Madame Dvornikov sipped her drink and toyed with the bones on the table. The more Adam stared, the more they began to look like the small bones from a human hand. Finger bones. A butchered child's finger bones. His stomach heaved.

'He's coming with me.'

Madame Dvornikov laughed.

'Silly boy. He's not your friend. The boy you lost through lack of care is gone. He's been gone these twenty years. There's nothing left for you here.'

Adam thought of the limpid blue eyes, the skin which sloughed off as easily as wet tissue paper, the mouth which moved soundlessly. The livid red scars running down the lower half of Tobias's body. The old gypsy was right. There was nothing left. And it was all his fault. Better that Tobias had drowned in the lake as he intended. Maybe there was one thing Adam could still do for him. He stood and swiped the delicate jumble of bones from the table. Neither Madame Dvornikov nor Dmitry made any attempt to stop him. Adam put them in his pocket, alongside his knife. He fingered it lightly, tested the edge of the blade with the pad of his thumb, the place where he still felt the phantom cut and Tobias' touch, sticky with blood. He'd need to be quick. He ran out of the tent and towards Mooncalf's tank.

'I'm coming, Toby,' he whispered. 'I'm coming.'

The Teeth Behind the Beard

James Bennett

Another day in Sideshow City. Louis McCaw couldn't help but think this as his old Lincoln, a dented but elegant bug, crawled off Halsted and pulled up on 51st, just across from Luna Park. The headlights swept over a couple of kids playing in the street, their firecrackers sparkling off the kerb. The bangers fizzled out as the kids marked the copper, skedaddling back to ma and pa through the lavender dusk, back to whatever bad eggs rotted in this slum, obviously thinking that the copper was for them. McCaw grunted, took a swig of hooch from the crumpled brown bag on the seat beside him, holstered his iron under his raincoat, and climbed out onto the street. He put a hand to his head, Lake Michigan trying to snatch his fedora. February closed around him like a glove, the hand inside it made of ice. Yeah, this was the Windy City and no mistake, but to Louis McCaw, having spent a score of his forty-one years on the South Side beat, Chi-Town was an endless freakshow. Gangsters, bootleggers, swindlers and pimps had long rubbed off the romantic shine. When your daily business took you on a ride through clip joints, brothels, speakeasies and other assorted fleapits, you tended to lose your rose tinted glasses. McCaw had lost his along with his hair, hiding his baldness under the hat. All Chi-Town had given him were scars, headaches and an extra twenty pounds, courtesy of a bad diet, debts, bathtub gin and too many sleepless nights. He was a busted man, once handsome, now going to seed, his blue eyes dulled, his jaw pounded, his paunch visible under his shirt. Ambling across 51st, it came as no surprise to him that his routine of stick-ups, brawls, burglaries and murders, should lead him to the actual circus.

You couldn't make it up. Fuck it, maybe I'll join.

Luna Park was as rundown as he was. The place used to be an amusement park, built on an old picnic ground back in '07. The two decades since had seen half the plot sold off as a trolley station, with a food hall huddled on the edge. Somehow, Big Jim O'Leary, the notorious gambling boss and boxing promoter, had managed to hawk the dump to a real estate company, if McCaw trusted the records at the precinct. The Depression had crushed any dreams of development, just as it had crushed every other Joe's job, and the area languished now, a dilapidated blot on the landscape, stuck out here in the slums. The carny remained, or rather its bones, a vaudeville corpse sandwiched between the station and the food hall. He couldn't think of Waldo's as a funfair; clearly, no one had had any fun here for years. Fumes from the surrounding factories had long since exorcised the ghosts of candy apples and popcorn. As he drew near, McCaw didn't need to see the other three flyers parked across the potholed road to know he'd come to the right place. The skeletal hump of the rollercoaster and the litter-and-weed-choked midway served better than any map. Even if he'd been some kind of twit, the large, gaudy sign fronting the ballroom would have sparked the old light bulb dangling in his head.

THE WONDERFUL WALDO'S GRAND CARNIVAL HUMAN MUSEUM, HIPPODROME AND GREATEST SHOW ON EARTH!

A laughing broad, her breasts bulging out of her corset, rode a flaky-paint tiger above the rolling words. In the background, faded clowns cavorted through hoops, bordered by trapeze artists and fancy dress apes. Everyone's having a swell old time. Unimpressed, McCaw fumbled in his coat for his last snipe, lit it, and let the smoke curl up his nostrils and down his throat, hoping the tobacco would mask the smell of hooch. Three drags and he crushed the cigarette under his heel, shook his head at his luck and went inside.

He found the ballroom rigged out like a theatre. A nickel and dime one. The rows of seats edging the dance floor formed a threadbare audience of red velvet. There was a small stage at the end of the room, the curtain raised to reveal a mess of scenery, cardboard trees beneath a creased blue sky. McCaw looked up at a flutter of wings, startled by pigeons ruffling overhead, the birds clapping around a tangle of ropes that supported a risky looking walkway, the bones of the show. The wind played a harsh calliope through a hole in the roof, the dome arching like a desiccated grapefruit, seeded with garish frescos.

The Cadillac Palace, it ain't.

Apart from the cops, the place was empty. The uniforms stood in the middle of the dance floor, the dim electric orbs on the walls turning them into shadow puppets, caps and badges winking in the gloom. Tonight, the theatre had put on a tragedy. The men huddled around a sixth figure lying at their feet. Even from a distance, McCaw made out the sprawled arms, motionless on the scarred boards, and caught the gleam of pooled blood. He sniffed, smelling the familiar coppery scent, notes of lead wafting under it. The finale, he knew, had already happened. He was here for the aftershow party.

One of the cops, a rookie by the look of him, noticed McCaw and thrust out an arm.

'Hey, fella! You can't come in here.'

McCaw feigned a glance over his shoulder. 'Well, son. Looks like I already did.'

'This is a crime scene.' The rookie scowled and strode over, the other cops alert and rubbernecking. One of them already grinned. 'Unless you want to spend the night in the tank, I suggest -'

McCaw flashed his buzzer. 'Think I came late for the fucking matinee? Louis McCaw, 7th Precinct, Englewood.' Then louder, over the rookie's shoulder. 'You boys hit the blower for a detective?'

He ignored the rookie and walked over to the other cops, the young man waltzing in his wake. Some of these kids were truncheon happy and McCaw could feel the rookie's disappointment hot on his back as one of the cops, Ruby Byrne, pulled in his gut and hailed him. Despite Prohibition, the two men had shared drinks in one of Chi-Town's many underground saloons. A dive overlooked by the force. They'd met back when Byrne was a beat cop hunting Burbank for lost dogs, and though they'd not seen each other since Byrne's promotion to the First District months ago, time couldn't dilute a friendship that had so cheerfully flouted the law.

'Don't blow your wig, O'Malley.' Once Byrne had chided the rookie, he turned his grin up to ten for McCaw, his yarn spindle face too thin to contain it. 'Well, look what the cat dragged in. Half frozen and keen for the cream.'

'Wasn't my idea. What the hell you boys doing down here anyway? South Side ain't your beat.'

'On citywide patrol when the call came in. Looking for some hood or other.' Byrne, curt as ever, spat on the floor. 'Didn't find him. Checked in here half an hour ago.'

'Thought you were busy up in the Loop, mopping up after the bloodbath and all.'

'Damn straight. HQ's been a real shivaree since Valentine's Day. Ness has run the department ragged. Blood to fill a hundred breweries.' The two men shared a guilty look where once they had shared whiskey. Byrne coughed and cocked an eyebrow. 'So, you get any cards?'

The other cops laughed, but McCaw didn't take it personal. How could they know about Ruth? Another thing stolen by Sideshow City.

To change the subject, the detective looked down at the stiff on the floor.

'What we got here, Ruby?'

'Beats me.' Byrne shrugged. 'Looks like some whacko gave him the kiss off. A lady across the street heard the shots. At first, she thought they were firecrackers. Three bullets, one went wide. One to the chest and one in the brain. Blew him off the goddamn stage.' Byrne frowned; he was all police now. 'My guess is it happened about an hour ago. The blood ain't even dry. I'll tell you this, Lou: if this dive was running some racket, then this guy here was the ringleader. I mean, literally.'

The cops sniggered again. McCaw didn't blame them. Scenes like these couldn't dent their humour. Along with a hundred cups of coffee, it was how most of them made it through the day.

McCaw judged the stiff in his late forties, early fifties, the grey in his sideburns and curling moustache noticeable in spite of the lacquer and murk. The man stared at the dome overhead, seeing only angels. The burst veins on his nose and cheeks, congealing into purple, looked stark against the powder on his flesh, a pallor that rivalled his death. Evidence of heavy drinking made a strange contrast to the man's clothes. The gold buttons on his fancy jacket strained over his sizable girth. Grey matter clung to the epaulets at his shoulders, a thick, soupy braid. Tails splayed out from his fat derriere like a crow squashed by a steamroller. A few feet from the man's head, a black top hat rested on the floor, adrift on a sea of blood.

Toecaps at the edge of the spill, McCaw flashed on Byrne's meaning.

'This is Waldo?' He doesn't look so wonderful now. 'The carnival owner?'

'Call it a hunch,' Byrne said. 'But you tell me, Lou. We gotta split. Chief wants us back at HQ. Think we got another raid tonight. That's why O'Malley dialled in to 7th.' The officer patted McCaw on the back. 'Knock yourself out, old buddy.'

'Ah, nuts. You're gonna leave me on my lonesome?'

'Way of the world.' Byrne said, but paused to consider. 'OK, you can keep the rookie.'

'Hey, now -' O'Malley started, but Byrne held up a bony hand.

'Keep the rookie and keep him quiet. You know how these chicklings like to sing.'

O'Malley sank back into sulky silence. Byrne and his troops moved off across the floor. One even tipped his cap. Ness had them juiced all right. A small time murder in the South Side slums was obviously beneath them.

'Wait a minute,' McCaw called after them. 'That's it? No clues? No witnesses?'

'You got some frail waiting backstage,' Byrne didn't look around and now the officers did laugh, the echoes more cruel than amused. 'Belinda Honeybush. Saw the whole thing. No time to question her. Abyssinia, friend.'

Then the cops made tracks, leaving McCaw to the ballroom, a kid and a corpse for company.

Christ, I miss that cigarette.

He told O'Malley to stay with the body in case it went on the lam. He might have told the kid's expression that stranger things had happened. If Capone didn't smoke the rookie first, no doubt he would get to find out.

McCaw trudged up the steps to the stage and entered the cardboard forest. There were scuffmarks in the dust here, signs of a struggle, fanning out where Waldo took a stage dive. O'Malley looked up from the shadows below, his neat blond hair and fresh face serving as a marker for the distance. Must've been some up close shooting, the force of the bullets hurling the ringmaster several feet across the ballroom. McCaw guessed a Colt, a Peacemaker maybe, his suspicions confirmed when he bent and inspected the shells at his feet. Straightening, he put the caps in his pocket, patted the Walther strapped to his chest and walked into the wings.

Like a baby with a dummy, only you need a heater for comfort.

He found the dressing rooms down some more steps and along a short corridor, bare bulbs lighting the way. The freaks saved the razzle-dazzle for the audience; there was nothing fancy down here but the cobwebs. One door was open, a glittery star hanging lopsided on the chipped wood, and taking a gamble, he rapped softly on it. A softer voice answered, rising from the bottom of the sea. Pushing it open, McCaw found the dame.

She sat turned away from him, a smooth curve of skin in a backless red frock, her bare shoulders reflecting the bulbs that lined the dressing table mirror. Its call to vanity went unanswered. She wasn't looking at herself. The dame's head lay on her arms and her tawny locks, a spill of finger waves, shook in time with her sobs.

McCaw coughed. 'Miss Honeybush? Detective McCaw, CPD.'

'Go away.' A wet sounding, muffled rejection. 'You're about an hour too late.'

The wine bottle at her elbow told him that the wet sound wasn't just down to tears. In light of events, he was prepared to let the liquor slide. Next to the bottle, wilted flowers bristled in a vase and next to that, a pink valise, the clips locked. Uncomfortable, he looked around the room. It wasn't much to look at. More of a storeroom really. The wallpaper, some brocade Victorian affectation, was peeling bad, interrupted here and there by ratty posters. A few chintzy dresses hung on a rail, feather boas dangling from it like jungle vines. The feeble attempts at glamour gave way to stacked boxes and a floor lamp in the far corner, the bulb flickering, the tasselled shade covered in dust.

Clara Bow, eat your heart out.

Far more interesting was the frail. It had been a while and McCaw couldn't suppress a twitch in his pants at her shapely frame, her waist a wonder rising from the stool. When her shoulders shook, he shook a little too, and he coughed again, pressing his business.

'Look, I didn't come here to bump gums, lady. There's a stiff out there, in case you didn't notice.' He said all this and realised at the same time he was rusty with broads. 'This is a police matter. Anything you want to tell me...'

He left the idea hanging. Further sobs answered him.

'Unless, that is, you'd like a trip to the station.'

This got a response. She didn't look up, but the sobs faltered, her spine tensing a little.

'What good will it do?' The dame sounded as bitter as lemons. Her voice was deep, but not unpleasant, a rural Illinois drawl, kneaded towards a cultured twang by some stage school or other. Maybe just by pretension. 'Waldo is dead and Caleb took off. You gonna give me my paycheck?'

'According to Byrne, you're a witness to murder. Our only witness.' McCaw flipped out his notepad from his inside pocket. 'Afraid that comes with certain dues.'

'I don't want to talk about it!'

She was sobbing again, grief shaking like sand through her hourglass figure. A memory of Ruth wagged a finger in his mind and reluctantly shamed, he pocketed the notepad. He shuffled forward, stretched out a hand and patted her lightly on the shoulder.

'Bad break, Miss Honeybush. Guess Waldo was a friend, huh? Talking about it might help.'

'A friend?' Now she did look up, glaring at him in the mirror. 'Tell me, detective. Have you ever been in love?'

McCaw took a couple of steps back. The question nipped at his heart, but her face in the glass caused his retreat. Lines of mascara ran from her eyes, throwing smudges down her high cheeks. Her lips trembled, buds of pain. That rose was lost in a briar, and McCaw recalled the officers' laughter as they'd left the ballroom. He sent them a silent curse.

Thanks a bunch, fellas.

Miss Honeybush – what he now guessed was only a stage name – was wearing a goddamned beard. And not a fake one either. Not just a spectre of fuzz like some of the women he'd met, but a full-blown garibaldi. Her moustache drooped under her kewpie doll nose, joining with a thick, gingery brush that flowed down to cover her cleavage, a fact for which he was suddenly grateful. Faced with the stiff upon his arrival, McCaw had half forgotten he'd entered the freakshow. Belinda Honeybush, her gaze taking on the gleam of beaten hubcaps, served to remind him of it.

Nerves ruffled like the pigeons in the roof, McCaw replied more honestly than planned.

'Once. A long time ago. Somewhere around the Book of Genesis.' Well, if it didn't fucking feel like that. The dame didn't get the funny and McCaw rubbed his jaw to cover his blushes. 'I'm sorry. The other cops... they didn't tell me I'd be –'

'Shining the lamp on the Bearded Lady?'

McCaw glanced at the wine bottle, the pink valise, the floor lamp in the corner, anywhere but her.

'You're in Waldo's Grand Carnival, detective. What did you expect to find?'

There was no avoiding her eyes. He shrugged, a ten-year-old boy again.

'How the hell should I know?'

'So, there was a... girl?' The dame was already moving on, apparently used to his reaction. Of course she was. She put on an act. 'Whatever became of her?'

'My wife. The drink. She made like a tree.' He resented the fact that she was leading him round, taking advantage of his shock. 'Look, I'll ask the questions if that suits. Why don't you tell me about this Caleb? That the punk who squeezed the trigger?'

Her forehead, a polished crown, creased in recollection. Under all that hair, Miss Honeybush was still a looker. He'd never admit it in the precinct locker, but her angles and curves still wowed him. She gave a near imperceptible nod and pressed her fingers, bright with paste, to her swelling breast, stifling the sobs building there. With half a mind to sink what was left of the bottle on the dresser, McCaw flipped out his notepad again, giving his hands something to do. He tugged the pencil out of his hatband, licked the end and pretended to stare hard at the page.

'You mean you've never heard of Caleb Cole, the Human Chameleon?' She gave a humourless laugh. 'You flatter us, detective.'

'Lady, I think we both know that this show is over.'

'Yes. Such a shame. It began like a dream.'

'Well, how about you start there? I ain't got all night.'

Truth was, he did have all night, but the bag of hooch on the seat of his Lincoln had never seemed so sweet.

'It was three years ago now. I was just a farm girl, living in Utica, a hundred miles west of here, near Starved Rock. Heard of the place?'

'Can't say I have.'

'That doesn't surprise me. And starved is right. Papa barely managed a harvest that fall. What he did reap was mostly dust.' Her elocution had slipped a little, returning to the source of remembrance. She stared in the mirror, looking out on a different country. 'I was sixteen then. Sixteen and bored. Papa kept me locked up most of the time, on account of my... on account of this.' A hand fluttered around her chin. She didn't have to say. 'When I did sneak out, well, it was a real wingding for the farm boys. They threw stones, pushed me in the dirt. Their grubby hands...' She shook her head, wiped away a glob of mascara. 'You don't need the details, surely.'

McCaw looked up. 'Maybe it's best to stick to the facts.'

Honeybush nodded. She opened the drawer in the dresser and plucked out a handkerchief, dabbing at her eyes.

'Then Caleb came along. Caleb Cole and his Travelling Masquerade. Georgia, my tutor, couldn't shut up about him. Red rag to a bull and me the china shop. One night, I climbed down the apple tree in our backyard and took myself off to see him.' She sighed, her reflection swimming in nostalgia. 'Why, you shoulda seen him, McCaw. Caleb Cole was really something, with his animal impersonations and movie star mimicries. Even better was when you didn't see him. His camouflage act was so good; it was like he vanished right under your nose. He even did a Chaplin mime. You know, the scene from The Gold Rush, the Oceana Roll Dance?' McCaw grunted while she smiled at the memory, showing him the teeth behind the beard. 'Course, I'd only heard about it then. Who watches movies in Utica?'

She didn't seem to need him to answer.

'Anyhow, Caleb sees me up back in the audience. Throws me a bunch of flowers and bows low like a prince. The village

folks were horrified. They started yelling such names! There
I was, scared for my life lest Papa find out, but Caleb, he
just ups and hushes the crowd. Chides them, you know, for
being cruel. Then, quick as you like, he jumps down from the
stage – ha! Back of his cart, if I'm honest. Leads me up there
like a beauty queen. Shows me off, gets the folks all clapping
and cheering. In God's garden, he tells them, there are many
flavoured fruit. And you know what he whispers in my ear,
right up there in front of the village?'

'I'm on the edge of my seat.'

'He says you'll never have to go home again.'

She dabbed at her eyes. When the hankie fell, smeared
with black, her smile fell along with it, replaced by a savage
sneer.

'So you ran away with the circus?'

This ain't a new story, babe.

'Or it ran away with me. Oh, he promised me such things,
McCaw. The sun and the moon. Bright lights. Broadway. He
told me I was gonna be a star.'

'I bet he did.'

'Instead, you know what I got? This honky tonk. A hole
in the ground in the South Side slums. Six shows a day for
peanuts and a dream worth even less.' She looked about ready
to spit. Shaking off her reverie, she turned on the stool and
faced McCaw, knuckles throttling the handkerchief. 'We
were lovers, Caleb and me. Does that bother you?'

McCaw, who hadn't written a word in his pad, snapped it
closed and snorted.

'I've heard a lot.' And seen worse. 'Miss Honeybush -'

'It's Donohue, really. But please, call me Belinda.'

'All right. Belinda. Did it never occur to you to up and
leave? Go home to Utica?'

Or how about get a shave and a job, try to live a normal
life? But Ruth was wagging her finger again and McCaw discovered that he couldn't ask her that.

'Sure, I know what you're thinking.' The lemons had
returned too, squeezing juice all over her words. 'Some dizzy
dame togged to the bricks and taking a trip for biscuits. Boo

hoo. You've heard it a million times.' She fixed him with her smudged gaze. 'But you don't know what Caleb was like, especially when he got some booze in him. He didn't care about beating on a woman. You see, the show was doing OK back then. Oh, they all rolled up to see Miss Honeybush, the Famous Bearded Lady. What a hoot! I was Caleb's meal ticket. He wasn't gonna let me slip through his fingers. And somewhere in all the lickings, I guess a part of me died.' She clicked her tongue, a sharp regret. 'The curtains fell on Belinda.'

McCaw exhaled. The frail's story tugged at his strings, no matter how much he tried to ignore them. Chi-Town was far from a bed of roses and these days, most people got the thorns. Her beard, however, was like a wall, preventing him from patting her again. He'd offer her his linen, but she was too busy strangling her own. When all was said and done, Honeybush remained an outsider, a backwoods girl in the Big Bad City, pushed to its fringes by something as flimsy as facial hair.

Still, there was a dead man in the ballroom.

'So what changed? You say that the show was his bread and butter. How come your Human Chameleon filled Mister Waldo with daylight?'

She had already told him the answer to this. He wanted to hear her repeat it.

'Because I fell in love again, McCaw. I broke our special arrangement.' Bold as brass, the dame clutched the bottle on the dresser and tipped it up to her lips. She drank deeply, a red dribble weaving through her beard. Then she set the wine down and tears fell afresh. 'Waldo and me were gonna run away.'

McCaw let this sink in. It made perfect sense, the dragon and the knight, the damsel caught between. Just as he'd thought, it was the same sorry yarn, a nightly drama played out on the streets of Sideshow City. And as usual, something went wrong.

'We were never gonna tell him,' Honeybush breathed, a sinner making confession. 'Just slip away, shadows in the night. Two sweethearts hand in hand, running into the future...'

'Yeah. Doubtless with all the green.'

The oldest story in the book.

Honeybush glowered and shot to her feet, rocking on her high heels. She was a tall drink of water, taller than him, only prettier in sheer red silk. Like a flame, she came at him then, her face a mess, her beard and arm swinging. He caught her wrist before she could slap him, and Honeybush fell into him, grabbing the lapels of his coat.

'You bastard. How dare you? After what I've just said?'

'Save it for the judge, doll face. You got a corpse out there and they're gonna want to hear it.' Her perfume filled McCaw's nose, some cheap concoction aiming at bourgeois. The frock made her a fish in his arms, a distraction that he couldn't afford. 'Sure, you're a saint, but the Chameleon caught you, didn't he? Caught you and the Wonderful Waldo, acting out a scene from a Tijuana bible. No doubt Caleb applauded with three rounds of lead.'

'Bastard! Don't you ever get lonely?'

McCaw shook this off, jutting his chin at the pink valise on the dresser.

'Tell me, baby. What's in the bag? Don't tell me it's only knickers and makeup.'

She was kissing him before he knew it, his hat falling off and rolling on the floor. Her breath filled his mouth, passion warm and wine sweet, and for a second – a second he would never admit in the precinct locker – he found himself responding, his tongue tangling in time with hers.

Then he felt the bristles, rough against his cheeks, wire wool scrubbing out lust.

McCaw thrust her backwards, spitting out hair. Belinda tripped over her heels and tumbled to the floor, the split in her dress parting, revealing a spiteful length of stems.

'I -'

He raised an arm, ready to rebuke her, when he heard the shouting coming from outside. Footsteps pounding along the corridor. Ragged breaths at the door.

McCaw spun and saw O'Malley, the rookie red-faced, leaning on the frame. The kid took in the scene in a heart-beat. McCaw's head shining in the light from the corner floor lamp, the dame on the ground, sobbing in her hands. He didn't seem to have time to ask questions, garbling into McCaw's face.

'Detective, there's someone out there! Some Peeping Tom up in the roof!'

Ring-a-ding-ding. A blink and McCaw's gun was in his hand. Yeah, I'm forty-one but my wits ain't blunt.

'You stay here and watch the dame,' he snarled. 'The law ain't finished with her.'

Then he greased his heels, flying from the room to hunt for chameleons.

Out in the ballroom, the pigeons were cuckoo. Dust rained down, a fresh powder-puff for Waldo, still fancy and cold in his pool of blood. McCaw looked up and saw a figure moving above the stage, another furry face in the shadows. It only took him a second to realise he was looking at an ape, a monkey in some kind of costume, the polka dots on its baggy white suit and conical hat not much of a disguise in the gloom. Betrayed by the birds, the ape was shifting along the walkway, making a fast escape. Ropes whickered and slats creaked. Nothing up there looked safe.

McCaw would have let the ape go – what can you squeeze from a monkey? – but the glint of metal in the beast's hand, a rod that didn't look like a prop, convinced him otherwise. The ape was hinky as hell. Forget what he'd said to Honeybush: it seemed that the show wasn't over. He had walked in halfway through the act.

'Police!' McCaw hollered. 'Swing on down from there, bucko. Don't make me plug you.'

The ape half turned, but only swung the gun in his direc-tion, muzzle trembling. Apparently thinking better of it, the beast continued along the walkway, heading for the hole in the roof. McCaw wasn't fond of heights, about as much as he was fond of primates packing heat, but a recent mention of impersonations pushed him to the ladder at the side of the stage. Cursing Jesus and all the saints, he hauled himself up, paw over paw, wishing his wits would translate to his arms. His gut felt like a sack of lard, sliding over each rattling rung. He reached the walkway with cheeks like cherries and his smoke-stained lungs burning in his chest. Breaths ragged, he lurched along the walkway, seeing the ape vanish through the dome up ahead.

McCaw followed, a bald ballerina with arms spread, navigating the fallen beam that led up from the walkway and onto the roof. Levering himself on tendrils of rope, he emerged on one side of the dome, plaster dust giving way to rain. The weather lashed him, a chill whip coming right off the Lake, a bully wanting to dance. Mourning the loss of his hat, he slid down to where the roof was flat, jerked up his collar and took out his gun, and loped after the run-out.

'Stop or I'll shoot!'

The run-out didn't stop. It dropped like syrup over a ledge, down onto a row of stalls, and barrelled along above the midway, leaping the gaps between the Kissing Booth, Tin Pan Alley and Coconut Shy, an ad-lib acrobatic display for an audience of litter and weeds. And for McCaw, of course, who sucked in his belly and gave chase, his coat flapping, pistol waving. The rain slapped his face where Honeybush had missed, ice water sluicing down his neck. Splashing through puddles, McCaw almost slipped and broke that neck jumping after the ape. Thanks for the bath, buddy. When the ape reached the end of the row, it drew up short, arms wheeling, and looked around, its eyes all goofy and wild. The roller-coaster loomed over its head, the lift hill climbing to the sky like a stairway into the lap of Zeus.

'Be wise, greaseball. You'll never make -'

The ape didn't pipe it and leapt anyway, McCaw's cry swallowed by the sound of flesh hitting wood. A conical hat, pompoms fluttering, spun down between the stalls and landed in the mud. The gun went with it, thudding off the side of the Hoopla. Scrambling up the latticed supports, the ape hauled itself onto the track and started to climb, its hairy meat hooks using the sleepers as a makeshift ladder.

McCaw swore. He tucked his Walther into his belt, drew back to give himself ground, and launched himself off the top of the stalls, a clumsy blimp blown by the wind. He came down heavy, the stanchion beams socking into his stomach and earning him a little music. Fireworks burst behind his eyes, his own private Fourth of July. Aces. Hands slipping on wet timber, he watched the midway waltz beneath him, a waiting, derelict grave. Then, gut aching, muscles bawling, McCaw was up and over the rail, panting on the abandoned rollercoaster. Wrenching out his gun, he threw some lead after the ape, aiming inches above its head, a barked command where words had failed. The bullet sparked off a car at the edge of the drop, wheels stalled by splinters and rust. Dropping to its belly at the sound, the ape's cry didn't sound like it belonged to any zoo. Feeling like he was on the ropes in the ninth round, McCaw pushed his body up the slope and fell upon the ape, grabbing a rough handful of hair and turning the beast to face him, planting a bunch of fives in its mug.

'Start singing, chump.' Or should that be chimp? 'Bit late to take a bunk now.'

The ape was gabbling, jingle brained. In order to hear him, McCaw grabbed one of his lugs and pulled. The mask came away limp in his hand, a cheap thing of cloth and hair, a coffee and doughnuts joke that might work on a drunken crowd in a shady theatre, but seen up close missed the trick by miles. The way that the Joe had dusted out, his obvious panic, was all too human – as was the gun that had shaken in his hand, fingers unable to pull the trigger. A chimp with a conscience? McCaw didn't think so. In his grip was a little Chinaman, his slick Asian features frisky with jitters, rain joining the tears in his eyes. It didn't take a genius to see that this wasn't Cole, Chameleon or not. Whatever the run-out was saying, McCaw didn't speak the lingo. Disappointment was a balloon in his chest, deflating into annoyance.

'Speak English, damn you.' Most immigrants knew a little

and McCaw shook his iron to make his point. 'You saw the cat who bumped off Waldo? Where's Caleb? Speak up! You wanna sing it from the can?'

The Chinaman dug that all right. Last thing he'd want is the buttons putting the screws on him down at the club-house. The law wasn't kind to Asians; another of Chi-Town's many failings. The little man shook his head, his mush fran-tic. He put his hands up, flapping out a garbled confession. Keen to lay the blame.

'He killed him! He killed him!'

'You don't say. Where -?'

McCaw didn't get to finish the question. A sharp sound, faint on the wind, travelled to his ears and interrupted him. Gunshot. He'd heard it too often on the South Side streets, and more often in his dreams, to think it was anything else. He glanced over his shoulder, back at the ballroom's cracked dome, guessing at its source. The rookie was still in there and Caleb Cole could be anywhere. McCaw released his quarry and stood up, wobbly with bruises and the height, and squinted down the track.

When he turned back, the Chinaman was already off to read and write, clambering over the stalled car and scuttling on up to the drop, his apparent shock blinding him to the fact that McCaw could put a slug in his back.

McCaw let him go. The ape was clearly a dead end, a patsy or a distraction, another goddamned sideshow. Whatever the Chinaman had seen, there wasn't time to find out.

Yeah, he'd got it wrong all right. The show finale was yet to happen, and if he was any kind of cop, he reckoned it would feature its missing star attraction.

McCaw got back to the ballroom minutes later, soaked, muddy and far from laughing. Once, this place had dished out amusement along with the corn dogs, but both now were stale. Much like Ruth, the circus had rolled out of town, leaving only memories behind, painful in their brightness. The Great Depression took no prisoners and in its wake of dust and decay, a trail of haunted places. Places like Waldo's Carnival.

Death was the only player here, making puppets of desperate people.

The body in the ballroom was a pale punctuation mark to McCaw's line of thinking. The stench of rot was marked now, a creeping odour clogging up his nose. Dust and blood and burnt lead. With a weariness beyond his years, he knew he'd be the one to clean up the mess. Get O'Malley to call the precinct, have them send a meat wagon down here, maybe a couple more cops. Focusing on his lawful duties helped him keep panic in check, because he already sensed he was way too late. He hadn't heard another gunshot, the single report grim and final.

He hurried across the stage and through the wings, heading down to the dressing room. It didn't surprise him to find the rookie on the floor.

More powder hung in the air. More pooling blood.

Belinda Honeybush stood by the dresser, a bearded Aphrodite. Fresh petals marked her dress, red splashes staining the silk. From what McCaw could see of her face – most of it hidden behind the brush – shock had filled her skin with milk, soured by the makeup running down her cheeks, black, oily tears. The pink valise still rested on the table. So did the flowers and the wine. The floor lamp still shone in the corner. His hat was in the dust. The only thing new about the scene was the dropped rookie and the gun in the frail's hand. The muzzle wasn't smoking, but McCaw reckoned that it might as well have.

As he entered, Honeybush turned, pointing the gun. Another thing that didn't surprise him was to see it was a Colt. A Peacemaker.

'Aw, babe. You didn't have to pop him one. O'Malley was just a kid.'

When she spoke, her voice seemed to come from years ago, emotionless and cold.

'He shoulda let me leave. I got a train to catch.'

'A one-way ticket to Utica? Sure that's the place for a broad like you?'

'You got a better idea?'

'You might be safer under glass. Murder doesn't make you many friends.'

The naming of the crime got through to her. Now the gun and her voice shook.

'You don't know what it was like. What Waldo was gonna do to me.'

McCaw shrugged, more casual than he felt. 'Last I heard, you loved the guy.'

'Love can be a curse, detective. A chain around your neck.' He noticed her accent was even deeper now, her stage school lessons swamped by the rural Illinois drawl. 'They kept me caged like a dancing monkey, Caleb and the Not-So-Wonderful Waldo. And Waldo was fixed to ruin me. They never gave me a choice.'

'So you decided to blow them out of the picture.' McCaw jerked his head at the valise. 'Bag whatever was in the safe and light out for the sticks. Am I right?'

'Close enough. The Chameleon ran and hid. His belly turned yellow when Waldo bit the Big One. I was looking for him when the cops turned up.'

'Yeah. You put on your best performance. The damsel weeping into her beard.'

Honeybush winced at this. She swallowed, getting a grip, and raised the Colt a little.

'I'm sorry, detective. Really I am. But the night express won't wait.'

Her finger twitched on the trigger, ready to end McCaw's troubles. He was judging the time it'd take him to grab his piece, tucked again into his belt, when another voice spoke up and said,

'Break it up, honey. You know I can't let you do that.'

Like actors in a play, wooden with alarm, McCaw and Honeybush turned. The words seemed to float out of nowhere, the Voice of God in the wings. Then Honeybush gasped, glaring into the corner of the room.

McCaw followed her line of sight and took a slow step back. What crazy business is this?

'Why don't you tell him the truth?' the floor lamp said. 'If you're gonna cut the man down too, I guess that's the least you can do.'

The detective and the dame watched, frozen, as the floor lamp edged forward. A section of wallpaper shifted with it, the brocade design reshaped in the shadows. A glove came up, removing the lampshade like a sombrero and tossing it onto the floor. The bulb continued to blaze on the stand, brighter now, almost dazzling, as the figure put it to one side. He took another step forward and McCaw made out a man in a leotard, black silk stretched tight on his coat hanger frame, his arms tensed around a Chicago piano. The Tommy Gun swung between McCaw and the dame, and then quickly back again, the round drum and long muzzle taking on the guise of a devilish face, daring them to move.

Caleb Cole, the Human Chameleon, had lived up to his name.

'You shut the hell up,' Honeybush said, but she lowered the Colt regardless.

'Why don't you tell McCaw how I found you? A walking joke back in Utica. Why don't you tell him the real reason those farm boys pushed you in the dirt?'

'Shut up!' The force of her scream pushed Honeybush back, a hand flying to her face. The Colt clunked down on the dresser and the dame stood wobbling there, barely supporting herself. The vase fell to the floor and smashed, spilling flowers around O'Malley, a dead and tasteless wreath.

Fuck. McCaw tasted lemons at the thought. Cole was in the room the whole time.

'You see,' Cole said, as if reading his mind. 'Nothing at Waldo's is what is seems. I guess that's part of the attraction. When I found Belinda here, she was just some juvenile backwoods queen close to pulling the Dutch act. I took her away, offered her a fresh start. A little bit of glamour. And you ate it right out of my palm, didn't you, Billy? Chewed it up and spat it back out.'

Miss Honeybush didn't reply. The dame was sobbing again now – but dame wasn't right, and McCaw frowned at Cole.

'Billy?'

Cole snorted. 'You won't find anything under that dress that belongs on a broad, detective.'

McCaw's eyebrows pushed up the sky. He looked at Honeybush again – Billy Donohue – as though seeing him for the first time. The smeared face. The adolescent frame. The beard grown long enough to cover his breasts, what in all likelihood was a pair of stockings stuffed with flour or a bundle of rags. Maybe some grapefruit from South Water Market for all McCaw knew. He shook his head, huffing inside. Some detective. He shoulda guessed the truth from her voice...

'For a while, we were happy as clams,' The Chameleon went on. 'Then young Billy here started getting grabby. Suddenly it was all about the green. You were sick of me and sick of the slums. Thought you were too good for us. But you pulled the flimflam on the wrong Joe, didn't you, doll? And when Waldo was good and dizzy, he knocked on your door and you couldn't fight him off. That's how he found out your little secret. And Waldo didn't take it so sweet. Knocked you around a little, right? Said he'd see you on the streets before you swindled another dime.' Cole flashed a grin at McCaw. It was about as amused as the rides outside. 'I reckon you can guess the rest.'

McCaw grunted. In his head, he could hear the little Chinaman, gabbling on the track.

He killed him! He killed him!

Yeah, Donohue had killed him all right. He'd shown Waldo the teeth behind the beard.

McCaw wasn't sure what to feel. Donohue's shoulders, bare, smooth and delicately shaking, seemed to invite sympathy. This curdled with a vague discomfort at their earlier clinch. Sure, he'd heard a lot and seen worse, but this was a new gig. Well, he'd have to swill his mouth out later with the hooch on the seat of his car. There were a million souls like Billy in Chi-Town, blown here from the sticks by big city dreams, only to find sawdust and heartache. Still, Donohue's grift had wound up in murder and McCaw got the feeling that the only bracelets he'd be wearing from now on would be metal ones in the State Pen.

Depending on the judge's view of pansies – a tricky matter in these parts – it could even be the chair.

Once again, he put out a hand to Donohue's shoulder. To offer comfort, maybe. To end this matter, for sure.

Before he could do so, Donohue turned, spinning on his heel. What McCaw had taken for grief had soured into rage, the man's face a regular horror show, his beard split in a savage snarl, the fangs of a cornered wolf. The gun was back in his manicured grip and this time he didn't wait to squeeze the trigger – Blam! Blam! Blam!

The Chameleon flew back, the front of his leotard exploding in blood, a wild design painting the boxes and the wall behind him. McCaw hit the deck before Cole answered with his own fire, the Tommy Gun spraying the room. The mirror shattered, showering silver. The wine bottle went after it. The valise burst open, its skin torn apart, sawbucks taking to the air like strange green birds.

And the former Miss Honeybush – Billy Donahue – had time to chirp like a canary, his dress aflutter in a cordite wind. The silk erupted, his chest tossing out crimson fans. His high heels twisted and he fell to the floor, sprawling in the mess. He lay there staring upwards, only seeing into Hell. Blood pooled out around him like bouquets of roses, thrown at the stage as the curtain came down.

'Hell of a night.' McCaw had his foot up on the meat wagon bumper, looking at the crowd. He'd recovered his hat, and despite the red brim, he felt a little less rattled having covered his baldness. There were several Lincolns parked in the street and three ambulances, summoned here from the 7th Precinct by a payphone on 51st. The blowers in Luna Park had gone to the Great Exchange in the sky. As had Waldo, Donohue and Cole. The love story was over. Half the neighbourhood had come out to watch, braving the rain in their nightgowns and shorts for a lucky glimpse of a corpse. They made McCaw feel sick and he took another drag on his snipe, bummed from a passing friendly copper, and turned back to O'Malley, who lay on the bunk in the back of the wagon. 'Tell you one thing. Once this gets back to the chief, we won't be buffing any medals. He'll have us behind the eight ball on this one.'

O'Malley laughed. The kind of laugh you get when you're shot in the chest and live to tell the tale. The medics had wrapped him up like a mummy, the bandages as pale as his face, his blond hair no longer so neat.

'Win some, lose some, I guess.'

'Yeah? Lately kid, it's all lose.'

'Hell of a job.'

'Hell of a job.'

McCaw looked up at the sign across the street, the laughing broad, faded clowns and fancy dress apes, Waldo's name rolling between them. That was all that was left of the Joe now; he was just another ghost in a town full of them. Still, the circus played on, making them all jump through the hoops, on the way to the funeral.

McCaw fingered the caps in his pocket, evidence from the scene. There were a couple of dimes in there too, all that was left of his salary. He had it in mind to walk back to the corner, make another call. Times like these and a man got to thinking about what mattered, what might happen in the next act. Before the cops had arrived, and after doing what he could for O'Malley, McCaw had walked back to his car and sat there a minute, the brown bag clutched in his paw. He'd put the hooch to his lips, and then put it back down without taking a slug. He'd realised that the living could haunt you too. And who knew? Maybe Ruth would be glad to hear from him.

O'Malley, twitchy in the silence, pulled McCaw back to the present.

'You gonna be ok, detective?'

'Me? You'll learn, kid. This is all part of the grind.' And then, because he couldn't help but think it. 'Just another day in Sideshow City.'

McCaw tipped his hat and drifted away. Another actor in the Chi-Town night, taking an exit stage left.

Biographies

James Bennett escaped his cage at Waldo's some time ago. 'The Teeth Behind the Beard' is his first Crime story, based on the strange things he saw there. You can find more information about his stories on his blog: http://jamesbennett72.blogspot.co.uk/ and feel free to join him on Twitter: @JamesBennett72

Step right and up and see **Carol Borden** shamelessly bring the wrong in her writing and her art! Thrill as she abuses her education writing about pop culture for The Cultural Gutter (http://www.theculturalgutter.com)! Peruse, at your leisure, her articles gathered in The Cultural Gutter, available from Carnegie-Mellon University's ETC Press! Gasp as her hardboiled Godzilla detective fiction appears in Fox Spirit's Weird Noir! For the small price of one click, you can read her writing and see her art at http://www.monstrousindustry.wordpress.com.

Paul D. Brazill is the author of Gumshoe and Guns Of Brixton. He was born in England and lives in Poland. He is an International Thriller Writers Inc member whose writing has been translated into Italian, Polish and Slovene. He has had writing published in various magazines and anthologies, including The Mammoth Books of Best British Crime 8 and 10, alongside the likes of Ian Rankin, Neil Gaiman and Lee Child. He has edited a few anthologies, including the best-selling True Brit Grit – with Luca Veste. He blogs here <http://pauldbrazill.wordpress.com/blog-2/> .

Michael S. Chong was born a Scorpio in the Year of the Dog. He has lived in Toronto for most of his life but spent a few years in the Netherlands where he learned to love eating fries with mayonnaise. Now back in Canada, he enjoys the gravy and cheese curds of poutine but every once in awhile sentimentally slaps mayo on his frites. His story 'The Creep' is in the upcoming collection Masked Mosaic from Tyche Press.

Robin Wyatt Dunn lives in The Town of the Queen of the Angels, El Pueblo de la Reina de Los Angeles, in Echo Park. He is a Member of the Horror Writers Association, and is proud to have been born in the Carter Administration. You can find him at www.robindunn.com.

Richard Godwin is the author of critically acclaimed novels Apostle Rising, Mr. Glamour and One Lost Summer, a Noir story of fractured identity and ruined nostalgia. It is a psychological portrait of a man who blackmails his beautiful next door neighbour into playing a deadly game of identity, and is available at all good retailers and online here http://www.amazon.com/One-Lost-Summer-Richard-Godwin/dp/0956711340/ He is also a published poet and a produced playwright. His stories have been published in over 29 anthologies, among them his anthology of stories, Piquant: Tales Of The Mustard Man. You can find out more about Richard Godwin at www.richardgodwin.net

Joan De La Haye writes horror and some very twisted thrillers. She invariably wakes up in the middle of the night, because she's figured out yet another freaky way to mess with her already screwed up characters. Joan is interested in some seriously weird stuff. That's probably also one of the reasons she writes horror. Her novels, Shadows and Requiem in E Sharp, as well as her novella, Oasis, are published by Fox Spirit (http://www.foxspirit.co.uk/). You can find Joan on her website (http://joandelahaye.com/) and follow her on Twitter (http://twitter.com/JoanDeLaHaye)

Christopher L. Irvin has traded all hope of a good night's rest for the chance to spend his mornings writing dark and noir fiction. His stories have appeared in Thuglit, Shotgun Honey, Weird Noir, Action: Pulse Pounding Tales Volume

2, and The Rusty Nail Magazine, among others. He's one of the editors at Shotgun Honey and lives with his wife and son in Boston, Massachusetts. You can find him online at www. HouseLeagueFiction.com <http://www.houseleaguefiction. com/> and @chrislirvin.

S.L. Johnson is a well-known, if seldom seen, recluse living in the Windham area. It has been rumored that she was once a messenger for the French Resistance, going by the name of "Le Noir Pigeon." Or a rich Russian heiress, disowned by her family for falling in love with a poor Norwegian carpenter. Or a woman who took leave of her senses when she was jilted at the altar. It is known that S.L. Johnson works with local radio stations, bands, indie labels, authors, indie publishers, arts centers and individuals to create unique graphic images. She also crafts block prints, hand-pulling every print in each edition to create highly individual pieces. Visit her website at sljohnsonimages.com Feel free to ask her any questions about her artwork. But not about her past.

Hannah Kate is a Manchester-based poet, short story writer and editor. Her work has appeared in a number of magazines and anthologies, and her first full-length poetry collection, Variant Spelling, was published by Hic Dragones in 2011. Under the name Hannah Priest, she is an academic writer and lecturer. Hannah's two personas are meant to be separate but are currently locked in a battle for territory. Hannah's website http://hannahkate.net and she's on Twitter as @_Hannah_Kate_

Jan Kozlowski is a freelance writer, editor and researcher. Her first novel DIE, YOU BASTARD! DIE! was published in 2012 by John Skipp's Ravenous Shadows imprint. Her short horror stories have appeared in HUNGRY FOR YOUR LOVE: An Anthology of Zombie Romance and FANGBANGERS: An Erotic Anthology of Fangs, Claws, Sex and Love, both edited by Lori Perkins and in NECON EBOOKS FLASH FICTION ANTHOLOGY BEST OF

2011. Her websites are: www.jankozlowski.com and www.butshekeepsanicelawn.com

K. A. Laity chose the stories for this collection after she was foolish enough to agree to do a second anthology, drunk on the success of Weird Noir and due to the imprecations of 'the muse who punches you in the face' AKA Adele Wearing. She is grateful to Daz for doing the hard work of actually editing the stories and occasionally poking her with a stick. Cross her palm with silver if you stumble across her caravan. Her works include the Chastity Flame series of thrillers, Á la Mort Subite, The Claddagh Icon, Unquiet Dreams, Owl Stretching and many many more. All-purpose writer, Fulbrighter, uberskiver, medievalist, flâneuse, techno-shamanka, Broad Universe and Mavens of Mayhem social media wrangler, History Witch, and Pirate Pub Captain, she divides her time between Dundee & New York · http://www.kalaity.com will lead you to her many worlds.

Li Huijia is a former editor with a penchant for folklore and fairytales. Her writing has appeared in Singaporean magazines, and her short fiction has been published in the anthology Eastern Heathens. She lives in Singapore and blogs about life, books and ice-cream at www.jiawrites.com <http://www.jiawrites.com> .

Neal F. Litherland brings his own brand of chills and thrills from the exotic lands of Indiana, U.S.A., he puts on a show the likes of which folks won't soon forget. Witness the dark wonders of visceral horrors, and listen to tales of far away worlds. Featured in Sidekicks with his story "Relic of the Red Planet", and in the collection Big Damn Heroines with his spine-tingling tale "Terror on Saturn VI". Find out where he'll be and what he's doing at www.Facebook.com/NealFLitherland <http://www.facebook.com/NealFLitherland> .

AJ Sikes writes on the weird side of the aisle, down past the empty stalls and around back of the barkers' tent. His stories appear in Machina Mortis: Steampunk'd Tales of Terror and Mechanized Masterpieces: A Steampunk Anthology (co-authored with Belinda Sikes). Visit him at www.ajsikes.com <http://www.ajsikes.com> and on Twitter @SikesAaron.

Rebecca Snow would be a lion tamer if her cats preferred flaming hoops to sleeping. She spends her days spinning cotton candy threads and weaving them into stories. Her short fiction has been published in a number of small press anthologies and online. Her online merry-go-round can be found at cemeteryflowerblog.wordpress.com. Stalk her on Twitter @cemeteryflower. And find her bloody hand on Facebook. She plants her tent stakes in Virginia

Emma Teichmann loves cotton candy and the teacup ride, but can't hit coconuts for shit. She also loves writing, fighting, and music-making. On weekdays she can be found with her lawyer's cap on. She can also be found at https://www.facebook.com/#!/emma.teichmann.5. Emma's story 'Silvermelt' is published in the Fox Pockets Piracy anthology, and her story 'The Mimicians' will be in the forthcoming Shapeshifters edition.

Allan Watson is a writer whose work leans towards the horror and supernatural end of the spectrum. He is the author of four novels - 'Dreaming in the Snakepark', 'Carapace', 'The Garden of Remembrance', '1-2-3-4', and a motley collection of short stories called '.....And Other Stories'. His latest doomed venture has involved acting as ghost writer for the Reverend Strachan McQuade's opus of bad taste comedy 'Invergallus'. In between the books, Allan wrote extensively for BBC Radio Scotland, churning out hundreds of comedy sketches, in addition to being a regular contributor for the world famous 'Herald Diary'. He also masquerades as a composer/musician, collaborating with crime writer Phil Rickman in a band called Lol Robinson with Hazey Jane II whose albums have sold on four different continents

(Antarctica was a hard one to crack). Allan lives and works in Glasgow, Scotland, but has never worn the kilt or eaten a deep fried Mars Bar. He is currently pretending to work on something new.

Sheri White lives in Maryland with her family. She has been published in many small-press anthologies and magazines, and also has a collection to be published by Necon E-Books. In addition to writing horror, she reads and reviews for several horror publications, both online and in print. She is also an editor/proofreader for Morpheus Tales magazines, and submissions editor for SNM Magazines. When not immersed in horror, Sheri is usually on Facebook or listening to The Beatles. You can contact her at sheriw1965@yahoo.com, or on Facebook at https://www.facebook.com/sheriw1965.

Chloë Yates toured the world for many years with J.B. Lansbury's Travelling Circus Company as Scheherazade The Sibilant Snake Woman from Beneath the Hot Sands of Zanzibar (although no one is quite sure why as she is, in fact, from Kent). It proved an excellent cover for her real role as an operative for the Skulk, an elite band of ninja foxes. Forced into hiding after a routine job went bad, she embarked on establishing a new life. After extensive and excruciating epilation, Chloë turned to writing for comfort. In October 2012, under her new identity, she was one of the winners of Fox Spirit Books' International Talk Like a Pirate Day Flash Fiction contest with her story "Leave the Pistol Behind", which can be found in the first of the Fox Pocket series, Piracy, while her noirish chops previously slathered into this volume's predecessor, Weird Noir (2012). She's currently working on a big idea or two, and writing short stories. You can read her ranting at www.chloe-yates.blogpost.com <http://www.chloe-yates.blogpost.com/> and she sometimes wanders through twitter under the sobriquet @shloobee. She is suspicious of dolls.

When **Katie Young** isn't juggling projects in the high-flying world of kids' TV, she is mastering the beasts of her imagination and whipping words into shape. She has work published in various anthologies and with direct-to-mobile publisher, Ether Books. Her story, Atelic, was shortlisted for the 2010 Writers' & Artists' Year Book short fiction prize, and she is also a regular contributor to the Are You Sitting Comfortably? story-telling events in London, run by White Rabbit. Katie's first dark fantasy novel, The Other Lamb, will be published by the Erato imprint of Musa Publishing in September 2013. She lives in South East London with her lovely assistant and a ferocious second-hand cat.

Made in the USA
Lexington, KY
01 March 2014